P9-BIV-567

"Klaver dazzles with an adventure rooted in complex feelings about family loyalties, and magically full to the brim with faerie mystery."
— Tobias S. Buckell, World Fantasy Award Winner and *New York Times* Bestselling Author

"An enchanting and enthralling series opener."
— Kirkus Reviews

"Fantasy at its most fantastic. Monsters, mystery, and magic in a beautiful and frightening world all their own. Justice Kasric and her strange family are a delight from first to last."
— Steven Harper, author of The Books of Blood and Iron series

"This first title in a new series slowly builds into a magical adventure in a world that is dark and unique . . . the plot and world building are sure to enthrall readers."
— School Library Journal

"Klaver's rich, lyrical descriptions augment the fantastical source material in this engaging series starter."
— Publishers Weekly

JUSTICE AT SEA

KLAVER

JUSTICE AT SEA

CamCat Publishing, LLC
Brentwood, Tennessee 37027
camcatpublishing.com

This is a work of fiction. Names, characters, places, and incidents are either products of the author's imagination or are used fictitiously.

Hardcover ISBN 9780744304275
Paperback ISBN 9780744304299
Large-Print Paperback ISBN 9780744304305
eBook ISBN 9780744304329
Audiobook ISBN 9780744304343

Library of Congress Control Number: 2021947130

Book and cover design by Maryann Appel

5 3 1 2 4

To Katie, who started it all,
and Kim, who kept it all going.

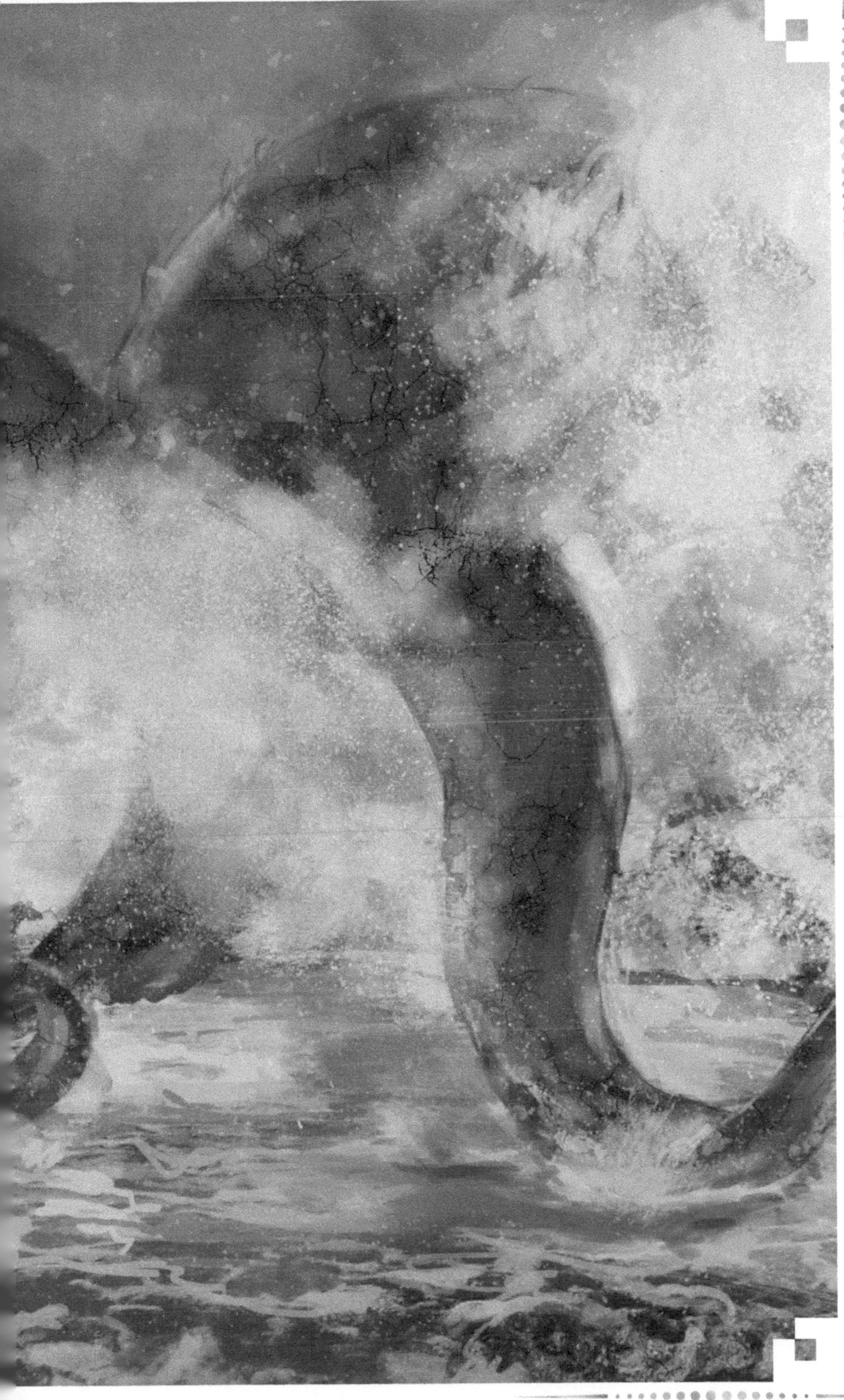

CHAPTER 1

Estuary Raid

The mist.

It pooled ankle-deep on the deck, moving in little eddies around our feet every time we moved. A slow, dank current of it flowed silently down the forecastle stairs in wispy trails, then down to the main deck where it pooled again before draining out the scuppers and down the hull to the ocean. But no matter how much fog drained out, there was always more. Made me itch to grab a broom or mop and get it all off the deck, only I knew it wouldn't do any good. There was plenty more where that came from. All around us, in fact.

I was at the front rail near the bowsprit, the very forefront of the ship. A lantern threw yellow light that clung to the deck behind me but didn't penetrate more than a dozen feet or so. All I could make out was more fog pooled on quiet, black, still water. The ship's prow barely made a ripple as we cut through the water without a sound. We'd been forced out into the Channel; coming back towards the English shore had a forbidden feel. We weren't welcome here in England anymore. You could feel it.

The mist had a way of dampening sounds, so that I kept looking back to make sure that everyone else was still there. I could see the rest of the quarterdeck that Faith, Sands, and Avonstoke shared with me, but the rest of the ship was lost in the haze.

Quiet should have been good. We were prowling in enemy territory. I'd given the orders for silence myself, but now the heavy feel of it was making my skin crawl. I thought the darkness was starting to show a little gray in it, at least, as if dawn might not be that far off.

"Justice," Faith hissed from behind me. "We're too far in!"

"Shh," I said, craning my neck to listen for signs of other ships, or possibly the English shore. England used to be home, before the Faerie took it and shrouded it in this bloody fog. Now it was enemy territory and there was no telling what changes the Faerie had wrought to it.

"Too far in!" she said again. I was supposed to be captain, but one of the problems with having my older sister on board was that she'd never taken orders from me and wasn't about to start now. Didn't matter if I was a captain, admiral, or a bag of rutabagas.

Faith looked unnatural in the eerie yellow light, with her white London dress and her long ash-white hair. No pants for her, despite being at sea. The Faerie might have conquered London, but they hadn't made much of a dent in Faith's sense of propriety or fashion. At least she'd forgone any hoops or a bustle.

She stepped closer, her dark eyes wild with panic. "You *know* the strain it takes for Sands to keep the shield up. He's going to collapse if we keep him at it."

I pushed my weather-beaten wide-brimmed black hat back on my head to peer up at her. She had to be prettier and older *and* taller. Life's not fair.

"What about *you*?" I snapped. "Do you feel anything? Anything at all?"

Faith's lips went tight. "No, same as the last time you asked. If I felt anything, don't you think I'd tell you? Everyone keeps calling me a magician, but that's all they can tell me. You don't learn magic as much as feel it, but I don't feel anything! I'm about as close to singing fish into a hat as raising a shield! You have to take us back!"

I shook my head. "You know we can't do that. They get one ship across the channel and it's all over." I turned my back on her. She made a smothered noise behind me and I could sense her frustration.

The worst part about Faith's warning was that she was probably right.

Sands looked an absolute and unmitigated shamble. The man's face, when I glanced back again, despite myself, was covered in sweat though he shivered in the cold damp. His black coat and tails were spattered with salt, and he'd lost his hat. His cheeks showed two day's growth around his blonde mustache and goatee and his blonde hair stuck out in all directions. His eyes, a startling emerald green under normal conditions, now shone like cat's eyes or undersea lanterns, washing the forecastle deck and our boots with lime, eldritch light. He stared out over the water, looking for dangers most of the us couldn't even see.

The Faerie invasion force had put up the mist to keep us out, of course. The Outcast Fleet stayed on the edge of the mist, where the rest of humanity couldn't reach us, but venturing further in, like we were doing now, was like taking out a rowboat into a monsoon.

My ghost eye, which helped me see through Faerie magic, allowed me to penetrate the first line of defense: the illusions, or glamours, as the Faerie called them. Dark flocks of predatory birds, specters gliding on top of the ocean's surface, that sort of thing. It was enough to scare the crew into a wailing froth and I was just barely holding that fear in check, constantly reminding them that the glamours weren't really there. The only person not showing any fear was Avonstoke and I had him to thank for bolstering the crew. Without him, I'd have a mutiny on my hands for sure. I looked back to where he stood, supporting Sands.

Avonstoke was tall, a Court Faerie like the stern and uncompromising Faerie marines. But Avonstoke wasn't stern, not by a long shot. The average Court Faerie was slender, with high cheekbones and angular features in a way that was disconcertingly inhuman. But Avonstoke wore it better somehow, more mysterious than inhuman, and with that kind of height and broad shoulders, he took the breath of every woman around him. I found him endearing, distracting, and exasperating in equal measures, but he'd become a sturdy support, my rock when things got dangerous, like now. His eyes, like the others of his kind, were pale gold, without any pupils. They were an echo of my ghost eye, a solid black marble in my left eye.

That ghost eye also allowed me to see the visions that really *were* out in the mist. Dark shapes cresting the water, ghost ships, an enormous bat-winged shape far overhead. But only Sands and I could see those, and neither of us mentioned it to the others.

"Ghosts," he muttered when another of the ships went by.

"Intangible?" I said, keeping my voice equally low. "So, they can't hurt us?" Avonstoke and Faith were close enough to hear, but I trusted them to keep their mouths shut.

Sands turned his glowing cats eyes to me and shook his head. "*Probably* not." There was the hint, like always, of France and other unfamiliar places in the lilt of his voice. "Ships, or other things, caught by a vortex and wrenched free of their place in time. If they are ghosts to us, or we are ghosts to them, I cannot say. Now they move through *when*, as well as through *where*. Let's hope they are not close enough in the fabric of time to reach us. Years spent in the mist would leave you quite mad. I should know."

I wanted to ask more, but now wasn't the time. He turned away, peering out into the fog with those luminous eyes.

What we were *really* worried about were the vortexes.

Dark twisters, like supernatural tornados, that threatened either to tear us to pieces or pull us entirely out of the world we knew. One false step and we could be ghosts ourselves. Or we could just be dead.

Even as I watched, another black tornado lurched out of the mist, moving far too quickly for us to avoid it, and battered itself against Sands' shield. The shield, which, through my ghost eye, I could see as a soft green shimmer around the ship, rippled under the impact. But it held. It was all eerily silent and unreal. I felt no sign of the impact under my feet, which was even more unnerving.

But Sands shook under the impact, as if he had been hit directly. Avonstoke's grip on him was the only thing that kept Sands from falling.

Faith wasn't wrong. The little blonde man couldn't take too much more of this.

I could see back to the rest of the ship, which was a far cry from a comfort. Every face that peered back was tight with sullen fear, watching me, or Faith, but mostly watching Sands, our only magician.

Except Sands wasn't a full-fledged magician anymore. Since passing his mantle to Faith, his powers had been slowly fading. To make matters worse, Faith, his replacement according to Father's plan, didn't seem close to taking his place.

I gnawed my lip.

The air was still, the rigging quiet, the splash of water soft, while we all struggled not to breathe too loudly. Everyone was listening hard enough to make their ears bleed. The ship itself made barely a creak under my feet. No scent of land came with the bare excuse for a breeze, even though I knew we had to be close. The chill off the water was like something off a grave.

A Prowler crew member ran up to report, knuckling his forehead. "Foretop lookout is seeing branches, Ma'am."

"Branches?" I said, raising an eyebrow. The man blanched, his greenish skin going visibly paler, but nodded. "Yes, Ma'am." Sometimes I forgot the reverence that the Faerie from Father's domain, most of our crew, felt for our family. If they only knew.

I opened my mouth to get a better explanation, but by then there was no need.

"There!" Faith said, pointing. "What's that?"

The mist parted to reveal a tree growing up out of the water, craggy and black and dripping with lichen and slim. The trunk was easily as wide around as the *Specter* was long, with branches angling up in all directions, long, jagged shapes that disappeared into the fog.

The tree was festooned with bodies.

There were dozens of them, all very dead, hanging from the branches on nooses. They'd been tall when alive, and not at all human, with great horns on their heads, white or black hair, gray skin, and talons on their hands and feet that immediately reminded me of the Soho Shark. The talons swayed, very gently, though there wasn't any breeze. Drops of moisture dripped down into the water with a morose and solitary dripping sound.

"Formori," Mr. Sands intoned, his green eyes still blazing. "Leaders of the Faerie once, but all wiped out by the Seelie Court."

"Much to everyone's relief, according to the stories," Avonstoke said softly behind him. "The atrocities they tell are enough to make even a hag's skin crawl." His handsome face looked thoughtful and a little curious.

"Formori," I repeated grimly. "Like the Soho Shark."

Sands looked confused and alarmed and I told him and the others, in as few words as possible, about our encounter with the Soho Shark and Victoria Rose. Just thinking about the two of them gave me shudders.

Mr. Sands whistled low. "The leader of the Formori was said to be missing one eye. A very dangerous individual, if this Soho Shark is the same person . . ." He frowned, lost in thought, while his hands plucked nervously at the brass buttons on his vest. He jerked with surprise when his fingers plucked one off completely.

"Damn," the little ex-magician said.

I had Mr. Starling ready a few crew members with long poles so they could push us off from the tree, if necessary, but we glided slowly and silently underneath the long line of hanged Formori.

Immediately after clearing that grisly obstacle, however, someone shouted up in the topmast. I heard a grinding sound, then the sound of breaking wood and the snapping of lines as a piece of the topgallant mast went splashing into the sea on the starboard side.

"What happened?" I shouted, breaking my own rule of silence.

"We hits a low branch, we did!" a gravely, squeaky voice shouted back.

"Was anyone up in the gallants?" I shouted back.

"Don't know, Captain!"

I leaned over the rail, calling to Avonstoke and Nellie down in the chains. "Have Wil check that wreckage and make sure no one is in it."

"Yes Captain," Nellie said. She called out in the soft and lilting Prowler language and Wil's head broke the surface of the water.

"What did you do that for?" Wil said after Nellie relayed my orders, but then he dove without waiting for an answer. Two minutes later he surfaced. I couldn't hear his words, but Nellie turned and shook her head up at me.

"Thank Heaven for that," Faith said.

I nodded in agreement, too overwhelmed with relief to speak. At least that much luck was with us.

There was a shadowy line of the riverbank on the port side now, with the gleam of white through the fog as the gentlest of surfs broke on the rocks.

"Shoaling on the far side!" Nellie called out softly.

I leaned over the rail, pointing so that there should be no confusion. "Port?"

Nellie nodded. "Yes, ma'am. Port."

"Pass along two points to starboard," I ordered. The waiting sailor nodded and turned to pass the message.

A flurry of breezes came, luffing the main foresail immediately above us with a snap like the crack of a whip.

"Hear that?" Faith said.

I stared at her. The entire ship had heard it.

"No," she said, shaking her head. "Not the sail. The *singing*."

"I don't hear anything," I said carefully.

She frowned. "It's gone now."

Then I spied what looked like not only a land mass, but a familiar one. The Girdler, a sandbank, which would put us in the Queen's Channel. I let out a long sigh. It was incredibly gratifying to know that this much, at least, of English geography remained.

Suddenly, the mist cleared. Well, not cleared exactly, but became more penetrable. More normal, like regular old English fog and not some supernatural abomination. There was even enough breeze to catch the sails and I felt the *Rachaela* make decent headway for the first time in hours.

"Well done, Sands," I said.

"Thank you, Captain," he said. His voice sounded normal, more human than when he'd spoken under the strain of his spell, but utterly exhausted, too. He looked more normal now, too. Still disheveled, but more like a man than a magical beacon. The eldritch light had faded from his eyes. He smoothed down his hair, then took a rueful look at his vest and trousers. He took a shaky step and Avonstoke steadied him.

"Through!" Faith breathed.

We'd thought it possible, but hadn't been sure. The Faerie could have had this stuff over the entire country for all we knew. But apparently not. That was worth knowing and information I had to get back to the rest of the fleet. Or what was left of it. Father had commissioned a dozen ships like the *H.M.S. Rachaela*, but they had been lost in the mist before I'd taken command. Now, all that was left was the enormous *Seahome* and a few schooners.

This was why it was folly to brave the mist, but also why it had been so necessary. It was worth all the risk I'd taken just to know we could navigate it. Now we could attack the invasion forces, rather than just wait for them to make a move. One bold move here could outweigh months of ineffectual engagements.

"Land on the port side!" came the hoarse whisper from the main deck. "Crow's nest reports land on the port side!" They were still relaying messages to avoid shouting. Good. We *were* in the Estuary proper, in the Queen's Channel just as I thought. I tilted my head, listening hard, suddenly sure I heard something.

"Take him below," I said to Faith, nodding at Sands. "Let him rest while he can." As soon as we'd done our business here, he was going to be needed for the trip back.

She opened her mouth to say something, then stopped, her eyes wide as saucers. She heard it now, too. Sands looked around as well.

Voices. Another ship? Then I could see them. Three dark silhouettes of sails and rigging slowly sliding across the still water. Yes. More than one ship, it seemed. The largest looked big enough to be second or third rate, maybe, comparable to our ship. Only they probably didn't know we were here because of the fog and our effort to remain silent. We might be out of the magical part of the Faerie mist, but fog was still fog. Also, the enemy ships, from what I could see, didn't look to have anything like a full complement of crew on board.

I passed the word for the spyglass and it came in short order. The nearest ship showed me silhouettes that were unmistakably men. Normal men, not Faerie. English men pressed into service by the Black Shuck. Probably not even sailors, since the Shuck had run out of those.

That didn't change what I had to do, because the ships' holds would be filled with all manner of Faerie infantry. Enough infantry to get and hold a landfall in France. Even just a few could be too much for mundane forces and the Faerie would spread over the continent. The only thing stopping the Faerie from crossing and taking over the rest of the globe was the remaining Outcast Fleet. For three months, we hadn't been able to penetrate the mist, but we'd easily thwarted an attempt at crossing the channel because the invading Faeries knew nothing of sailing. But we'd lost so many ships trying to raid the coast that our defense of the channel was stretched hopelessly thin. If the invaders realized that, we'd be in trouble.

Other figures, tall and angular, moved on the enemy deck. Court Faerie like many of my own crew, but in uniforms of dark leather and bone. The Unseelie Court. The Black Shuck's people.

The *Rachaela* might have been outnumbered, but that wouldn't matter as much if they were only partially manned and rigged. They barely had any sail up and all listed and wallowed uncertainly. They weren't using the wind like we were; they were being towed by rowboats. Foolish. In addition, something had gone wrong with the towing ropes of the lead ship and a knot of the enemy, Faerie and human, were huddled around the prow, arguing.

Good. The Faerie still hadn't learned any real seamanship. They'd never had the need before now, since all sailing in Faerie was done with magic. That was our only advantage and I was going to exploit it to the hilt.

"Oh God," Faith's voice came softly next to me. She and Sands were still here. She sounded like she was going to pass out. Or throw up. Maybe both. I had the same feelings when I'd been poring over maps and planning the engagements. I'd have them again, when I was looking over the lists of the wounded or seeing the damage wrought on my ship.

But now, all I felt was a sudden, thrilling rush. I could even feel a madcap grin crawl over my face.

"Oh God," Faith said again. "Whenever you get that look in your eye, I know we're going to be knee-deep in flying cannonballs right away. I *hate* cannonballs."

"That's why you're taking Sands below," I said cheerfully. "Go on."

Of course, cannonballs could penetrate below decks, but mentioning that to my sister wasn't going to make her feel any better. I could have had Avonstoke take Sands below, but I needed Avonstoke up here as much as I needed Sands and Faith out of the way.

Faith finally moved to go, and then stopped, glaring at me. "It's unnatural, you know."

"Of course it's unnatural." I turned and stepped past her to bring the spyglass to bear on the enemy ship again. "We're at war with the bloody Faerie. Where have you been?"

"Not them," she said stiffly. "You. You're not supposed to be happy on the brink of battle. It's unseemly."

I waved her away, keeping my eye to the glass, too busy to bandy words with her now. But I could feel a delicious thrill rising in me at the prospect of action, unmistakable now that she'd pointed it out.

"Unseemly," Faith said. "Especially for a *girl*." She finally took Sands below.

I turned and leaned down over the railing aft of us and called down softly to the main deck.

"Pass word to Starling. Bring us about on the port tack. Ready a turn to starboard and ready the starboard guns."

"Aye," a barely-visible crewman called back. They rushed off aft.

"Swayle," I hissed at the Faerie marine colonel, also on the main deck. "Have your people ready."

"Yes, Ma'am," Swayle said. She nodded at her people, who began nocking arrows to bows and readying themselves at the rails. All the marines were Court Faerie like Avonstoke, tall, slender, with those same blank, golden eyes. Most of them looked severe, but Swayle had an expression so stern you could crack walnuts on it.

She pointed twice, without speaking, and another detachment of marines started climbing lithely up the masts to elevated positions, silent as wraiths. For all that the Faerie weren't so great at seamanship, war was another matter altogether.

I looked back at the enemy ships. Amazingly, they showed no sign of having heard or seen us. The nearest of them were still arguing over the tangled tow rope. For once the mist was working in our favor, dampening sound.

Relieved of being Sands' caretaker, Avonstoke came and joined me at the front railing. He didn't say anything at first, merely stood there next to me, a comforting presence, tall and reliable.

The ships were still moving closer. Slowly, so slowly. I'd have to order the turn soon, but for now, we had everyone ready and our slow progress through the water only brought things into a better position for our maneuver. Better to milk our element of surprise for all it was worth. Only it sent my nerves jangling, knowing I could hear an outcry any minute, but holding, holding . . .

"Like an Avatar of Naval Warfare," Avonstoke murmured, very softly, "watching as battle draws nigh." He sighed solemnly and profoundly pained at the poetic sorrow of it all. "I wonder, perhaps," he went on, "if an Avatar should have, I don't know, a cleaner coat? Or a hat that isn't quite so lumpy?"

"Shut up," I said softly. "I love this hat. You, I barely tolerate." A captain had to keep a certain level of aloof decorum, but I let a whisper of a smile come out. Avonstoke had a way of bringing that out in me, even at times like this.

He grinned down at me, a wild light in his eyes. There never really was any way of telling what he'd do next, a creature of mercurial urges with so many apparently random emotions that it wasn't a matter of detecting them on his face so much as sorting them out. Did he think of that kiss we had shared as much as I did? Of course, that had been months ago and now things were different. I was his commanding officer. I couldn't look at him that way anymore, and yet, I couldn't quite forget.

If he was having any conflict with how he thought about me, I'd seen no sign.

The fog was breaking up even more, allowing me to see the full length of the *Rachaela* behind me. I made out Mr. Starling, my second-in-command, back on the quarterdeck. He was a burly Dwarf, completely bald except for a tall, startlingly-red topknot waving above him like a thin scarlet flag. His mustache and beard were equally red and his mouth, like always, twisted in a frown. He was also quivering with readiness.

The increased visibility meant that the enemy now had a clear view of us, too. Astonishingly, they still hadn't called out any alarm, though if it was because they didn't notice us, or simply didn't recognize the danger, I didn't know. It didn't matter. No point waiting any longer.

"Bring us about!" I shouted, no longer worried about anyone hearing us. "Ready cannon!"

"It's her!" someone from the other ship shrieked. "It's Bloody Justice Kasric!" A clamor went up, both from the enemy ships and the rowboats down in the water. That, at least, felt good. I could feel that grin on my face getting wider.

"Fire as you bear!" I shouted at Render, another Dwarf and captain of the gunnery crew.

"Aye, Captain!" Render said. He signaled one of his gunner's mates standing at the hatch, who would then signal the gundeck captains below. Then Render tapped both gun captains on the shoulder with his riding crop. Both the guns boomed, shaking the deck beneath my feet and throwing up two plumes of acrid smoke. The glyphs and sigils on the side of the brass cannon glowed a fiery yellow, then immediately started to fade. Extra enchantments to pierce Faerie protections, but also to keep the brass cannon from falling apart, since cold-forged iron couldn't be used by the Faerie at all.

I turned. "Swayle!" Hardly had the word left my mouth than the deadly twang and hiss of loosed arrows snapped all around the deck as our marines fired. Screams from the other ship floated across the water. Swayle's Court Faerie archers, unerringly deadly, would rack up as many casualties as the cannon by the end of this engagement.

Unfortunately, the enemy archers would be just as good, but we had a few moment's respite as they recovered from their surprise.

But the gundeck below was still silent.

"Render!" I snarled. "Why aren't they firing down there?"

"Aye, Captain!" He shouted and rushed to the hatch. Render was still new, having taken over as gunnery captain after the previous one had been killed. He was alert, but still trying to compensate for both not having enough Dwarves to man everything, and the bloody slow process of passing commands from deck to deck.

Finally, the gun captains down there must have gotten it together because more cannon banged and the ship shuddered with even greater fury. More smoke drifted up into view off the starboard side and more screams came from the opposing ships.

One of the Goblins on our side, a little fellow named Chuck-Chuck who had tufted bat's ears and a bulbous nose, cackled merrily and a ragged cheer went up from my crew.

"Back the topsails!" I shouted. I wanted to slow our progress now that we were in prime firing position.

"Aye," Starling shouted back.

Avonstoke, still next to me, clenched his hand.

I'd seen it before but hadn't gotten used to it. This was shadow magic, and part of why Father had assigned Avonstoke to protect me in the first place. One instant, his hand was empty, the next, a dull-black scimitar blossomed in his fist. It looked like three feet or so of heavy, curved metal, but I didn't think metal had anything to do with it. The material, whatever it was, trapped light rather than reflected it, a thing of shadow with an occasional glimmer of moonlight that hadn't come from any sky above us. The edges shifted slightly any time I tried to get a good look at them, making the exact dimensions disconcertingly fluid.

An arrow shot out of the cloud of gun smoke, coming right for me. I ducked, but Avonstoke batted the missile with a flick of his sword. Seemed the enemy archers had recovered.

"Glad you're here," I said.

Then the musket ball shattered part of the rail two inches from my right hand.

I looked at the broken part of the railing. Two inches. Two inches in the right direction and I'd never use that hand again, regardless of Avonstoke's protective intentions. I hadn't even caught any of the ragged splinters, which were deadly enough on their own.

But for now, I was fine.

The other ship was still a skeletal gray shape in the mist, with shadowy outlines on something flat a dozen yards ahead that might have been sailors on a deck. Some of them must have had rifles, because that's where the shots were coming from, but then a dozen more of Swayle's marines fired and more of our cannon banged away, shaking the deck underneath my feet, and then all opposition stopped. Men were fleeing the rowboats and already two of the three enemy ships were listing. We'd have them demasted and sunk in a few more minutes and the enemy could do little to resist us. More Faerie were pouring out of the holds and jumping overboard.

We'd won the day.

I could feel the grin return to my face. The Black Shuck wasn't going to get any ships across the channel today. If Sands was strong enough to get us back through the mist, we'd have dealt the invaders a bitter blow with relatively little cost to us.

Then the light wind tore the smoke barrier away and my grin died as I could better see what kind of damage we'd wrought. Just because we weren't the ones paying a cost didn't mean it wasn't being paid.

But I kept my mouth shut and let the firing continue, despite the taste of smoke and ash in my mouth.

The Faerie weren't going to carry their invasion forces across the English Channel. At least not soon.

We'd bought the rest of the world a few weeks' reprieve, at least. After that, it was still anyone's guess.

Faith came back out on the deck while the battle was continuing. If you could call it a battle. Mostly, it was our gun decks belching flame, smoke, and destruction and the other, smaller ships screaming. I could see in her face that it would be no use trying to send her below again. Her thoughts were as clear on her face as if she'd spoken them out loud. *I can't fire the cannon or shield us from vortexes in the mist, but I can stand with you here, now.*

She stood, very close, both our hands on the rails, which trembled under our white-knuckled grip as the topside guns and those on the deck below continued firing, over and over. There was little that needed done by way of sailing, so Avonstoke came and stood with us, too.

Having them next to me helped, some, but it was still horrible.

It was war.

We left the Faerie-controlled coast behind, moving through the mist to reach the relative safety of the center of the English Channel, where *Seahome* waited. It lay hove to in the No Man's Land between the world of Man and Faerie Lands.

The trip was a living, waking nightmare for Sands. Each time another vortex hit his shield, he collapsed and Faith and Avonstoke had to haul him back to his feet. And each time afterwards, I looked at Faith, the question unspoken in my eyes. *How about now? Can you see anything? Feel anything?*

Each time Faith shook her head no.

I was gambling in a few ways with these raids.

One hope was that I could do some serious damage to the invaders' efforts to get across the channel. Keep them bottled in England. We'd been successful so far. The invasion army was made of many factions from both the Seelie and Unseelie Courts. Factions that usually spent most of their time trying to murder each other, so we'd also hoped that stalling the invaders long enough would cause the invaders to start falling on each other.

Only, the Black Shuck had some hold on them we didn't understand, and that simply hadn't happened.

I'd also desperately watched to see if having Sands bring us through the mist would somehow kick off Faith's abilities as a magician so that *she* could do the crossing. But that, too, had spectacularly *not* happened. In the meantime, Sands' decline was near complete. His powers had been slipping and this last trip had just burned out whatever he'd had left. Without Faith or Sands, I had no way left to cross the mist. There were only a few magicians in the Outcast Fleet that could perform that kind of magic, and they weren't willing to work for me.

In fact, I was starting to worry about getting out of the mist this time when we finally cleared it. I felt an enormous sense of relief and pried my fingers off the railing.

"Ah," Sands said, and collapsed again. Avonstoke scooped the smaller man in his arms before he could hit the deck.

I put my hand on Sands' brow. He was burning up.

"Take Mr. Sands to the captain's cabin," I said to Avonstoke. "He'll be most comfortable there. There's brandy there, too."

"Aye," Avonstoke said softly.

"Thank you," I said. "I'm sorry." I spoke too softly for anyone else but Sands, Faith, and Avonstoke to hear. Or Faith and Avonstoke, anyway. Sands had already passed out.

At least I thought he had.

He roused himself suddenly and gripped my arm. His eyes shot open, luminous with green again.

"Llyr," Sands moaned. "Llyr is reaching for you!" Then his eyes rolled up into the back of his head and out he was again.

Faith sighed. She stepped closer and fixed Sands' hand, so it rested on his own chest, like someone arranging the dead. "The Faerie gods again," she said with utter exhaustion. Sands had been coaching both of us on the Faerie gods, which, along with dragons, were the sources of most magic. Magicians owed their craft to one or the other and so Sands had been heaping legends and stories about them on Faith incessantly.

Not that it had done Faith much good. Cernunnos. Llyr, the Morrigna, Arawn . . . a whole mess of them. All I could remember is that one of them had nearly killed me and my family with lightning. It didn't make for fond memories.

Avonstoke had clearly been reading my expression. He was developing an uncanny ability to know what I was thinking.

"Putting ourselves in the hands of the Faerie gods doesn't exactly fill me with hope and wonder," I said before he had a chance to offer some Faerie nugget of religious wisdom. His faith in the gods was a facet of him I didn't understand. "Besides," I went on, "I'd be a lot more impressed with Llyr, the God of the Sea, if you could find one Faerie, just *one*, that understood how to keep a ship afloat."

Avonstoke's eyebrows shot up, but he shrugged, with Sands still in his arms, and turned to take the small magician down the forecastle stairs to the main deck, towards my cabin.

I went back up to the quarterdeck and heaved grateful sigh when I could take our bearings and make sure we hadn't drifted too far north. Too far away from England and we'd be at the mercy of the modern ships patrolling outside the mist. The Faerie Mist was the reason that the rest of the world didn't even know that our world had *been* invaded. They knew *something* had happened to England, which had become shrouded, all of it, with a deep fog that thwarted all navigation. Any modern ships that went near it suffered complete engine failure and floundered. Visibility was nonexistent. Engines, compasses, even time pieces all failed. They'd finally stopped sending ships into that zone, which was all good. They stayed out of the channel completely.

A few brief and disastrous attempts had been made at approaching the governments of France, Spain, Denmark, and America to tell them the truth. No more. We'd lost too many people trying. There would be no help from the rest of the world.

Which left our little fleet sailing a tightrope while trying to keep the invaders from crossing to the mainland. That had been Father's entire plan. Let them take England—because there wasn't any way to stop it—but then keep the Faerie Army bottled up long enough for the factions to quarrel and fall apart. There was nothing in the world that could stop the Faerie if they ever managed to make landfall on the continent, which was why I'd been so anxious to destroy any naval power they had.

But this trip cost me more than just Sands. I could see that when I looked at the faces of my Faerie crewmen. Father's fall and my heritage had given me nominal command of the Outcast Fleet, as well as my own ship, but my authority was laughable. None of the schooner captains took orders from me, and *Seahome* was even further out of my reach. Which was why I was trying to do everything with just one ship. But I could feel my hold even on the *Rachaela* slipping. The Prowler deck hands, Dwarves gunners, Court Faerie marines, and Goblin sail crew all eyed each other with simmering hostility, and me with thinly veiled resentment. Faerie tradition and loyalty to the House of Thorns, Father's house, had driven them this far, but I didn't think it would go much farther.

What would Father have done if he were still commanding the *Rachaela*? I had no idea. The sunlight was making me rub my ghost eye and pinch my nose against the throbbing feeling.

In addition to leaving the mist behind, we left the flat, brown, estuary, moving into the heavy rollers of the English Channel. The sea was gray chop all around us, with white, foaming peaks that occasionally loomed up as the *Rachaela* slid down into the valley before each wave. We had about two hours of sunlight left, and I didn't have to look at the barometer glass to know that stormy weather was coming. You could feel it in the air.

I ordered the sails reefed to make better use of the prevailing wind and after that, we turned west into the channel and there wasn't much to do except ride it out.

When I drifted back to my habitual station on the quarter-deck, Avonstoke was lounging idly against the aft rail. In addition to the raven tattoo on his face, I'd caught an occasional glimpse of a serpent on his left wrist. He had a sword on his right wrist, too, and I'd seen the magical sword that he summoned with that. It made me wonder what the other tattoos did and how many more he had. Thinking about the nature and location of other tattoos on his long-limbed body made me blush.

Avonstoke didn't even seem to notice. For all the conflicting emotions that he kept stirring in me, he didn't show any similar tension himself. He nodded pleasantly at me, no salute, of course, but when had he ever? He balanced effortlessly with his hip against the rail and his arms crossed, his golden eyes gleaming as he stared at the back towards land. If I lived to a hundred, I was never going to get used to those eyes. Great pools of gold with no whites showing around the edges at all. Completely alien and maddeningly human all at once.

"Under normal circumstances," he said, "shouldn't we be able to see your beloved London from here? Gas candelabras and chandeliers and the like?"

"London is usually brightly lit," I said. "But we wouldn't see its light this far out. There should be plenty light coming from buildings on the shore, though. Lighthouses. Other ships. It shouldn't be dark like this. That's the mist." Reports were mixed as to how much of London was still intact after occupation from the Faerie, but if the darkened coast we'd seen was any indication, it wasn't much.

"I thought so," he said. "A shame. I've always wanted to see London. Seems unlikely I'll get the chance now." Some of his golden hair had come out of the warrior's braid, just a few loose stragglers that now hung over his forehead, but it made me want to reach out and brush them away from his eyes. Somehow I'd come to stand a bit closer to him than I'd intended. Not close exactly, but close enough to be physically aware of his presence. The kiss I'd given him before had been right here on this deck, but it might have been miles and miles away.

"Tell me," I said, desperate to create a distraction, "about Faerie. The place, I mean."

Avonstoke lifted his eyebrows and blew out his cheeks. "That," he said, "is a question easier asked then answered. What part of the Faerie, I wonder? I could tell you about the rivers and mountains and forests and castles I've seen, the masquerades and the hunts, which are not as dissimilar as they might at first appear. The Seelie Court, perhaps? What fowl we like best? Our favorite footwear?

Our cuisine and culture which has come in such a lovely fashion to visit your homeland?"

"Make fun all you want," I said. "I need to know more than I do. Sands keeps giving me history lessons, but I don't think he's seen much of Faerie. There's so much he doesn't know. Father's too ill and Prudence won't give me a straight answer to anything. When she's even around, which is never. It feels like no one knows much of anything. We're sending Father back to Faerie in the morning and I still don't know anything about the place. I don't even know what his home looks like, and I very much want to."

"Ah," Avonstoke said. "That would be a difficult question for me to answer, since I've never been to Gloaming Hall, your father's realm."

"Well, you've been to Faerie, haven't you?" I said testily.

He shook his head sadly, his handsome face troubled, his braid catching the light and swaying behind him as he looked out at the water. "It is not so easy with us, Captain." He turned to face me. "Let me ask you this: Can you tell me what songs are being sung in the court of the Mandarin Lords in China?"

"No," I said. "Of course not."

"Exactly," he said, turning back to me. "But you think of your world as a great round ball, do you not?"

"The planet?" I said. "It *is* a great ball."

"Very charming, I'm sure," he said brightly. "Not so with the Faerie. Best to think of Faerie as a great jumble of marbles, all different colors. Traveling from one part to the other is tricky, even for magicians, and yet, it happens accidentally all the time. There are parts of Faerie made of nothing but smoke, parts completely of water, places where the castles all hang in the sky. We have castles plagued by dragons and other castles where the occupants *are* all dragons, complete with trousers and waistcoats and taxes and all the rest. Each part of Faerie is very different from the next and I would not pretend to know even the smallest part. You think of China as far from you, but the distance is nothing compared to the distance between one realm in the Faerie and its closest neighbor."

He shrugged in eloquent helplessness. "Our realm is a mystery to most of us, you see."

I opened my mouth to object, but he cut me off with a pleading expression and a raised hand.

"However," he said, "since I am one of your few sources of information, inadequate as I am, I will do the best I can." He took a deep breath. I could see that he clearly meant what he said: Advising me on the world of Faerie made him feel uncertain and inadequate, but he didn't want to fail me.

I felt my heart go out to this brave and wonderful man who had made my problems his own.

"The realm I hail from," he went on, "is called Vasyil, rife with forests and woods, all of them well-peopled and quite tame. They are not the forests you know. They are like cities, nothing like the untamed wilderness that others talk about. You can walk from one edge to another and encounter nothing more dangerous than languid courtiers, sculptures, paintings, banquet tables and the like. Well, perhaps some of the court ladies were dangerous to one of my tender years."

I snorted at that.

He laughed out loud, a liquid sound, utterly unpracticed. "You have *no* idea. But, even so, Vasyil is quite a lovely place to grow up."

A light drizzle had started up. I pulled my hat down a bit to screen it. Avonstoke had no hat at all. He didn't seem to mind.

"And," he went on, "indescribably boring. Boring beyond comprehension to a young man. I left at the nearest opportunity, took up service with your father, and now I find myself here."

"You're right," I said. "That doesn't tell me anything about Father's home."

"He spoke of it only once," Avonstoke said. "When we were far out to sea. A conversation not unlike this one. He described Gloaming Hall as a large castle overlooking cold moors and a large, dark river. On the other side of the river sits another castle that once belonged to an enemy of your Father's, until they went to war."

"Father is said to have never lost a battle," I said, "until recently. I guess he must have won and thrown down his enemy?"

"He won," Avonstoke said, "but he did not destroy his enemy." He turned with a wild grin. His golden eyes danced in the middle of the raven tattoo. "My father, as it happens. Gloaming Hall and Avonstoke Keep are now like twin cities, though I've never been to either. Lady Avonstoke, my mother, does not like the cold. Or my father. Mother and Father didn't see each other much." His smile went very thin. He turned and put both hands on the railing as he looked out over the water.

"They're gone?" I asked.

"My father is," Avonstoke said. "But after the war, he was one of *your* father's staunchest supporters until his death."

"I'm sorry," I said. I reached without thought for his hand, which was still on the rail.

"A duel," he said. "With a lord of the Unseelie court. The Goblin Knight. Part of the Saltblood Tribe. A vile creature by all accounts. Rumor has it he now serves the Black Shuck. It was part of why I joined your father's cause in the first place."

I gave him a look, wanting to know more.

Avonstoke's mouth was a thin, tight, compressed line. "I'd thought to go to war, you see, because the Goblin Knight has a reputation for being at the front lines of battle. If I did the same, I'd have a chance to cross swords with him. He wears a skull mask. That should make him rather easy to find, wouldn't you say? If I can get to the right battle."

"Wait," I said, "you volunteered to go to war to try and kill *one* person? That's the most idiotic thing I've ever heard."

"Is it?" Avonstoke said, and now his smile turned into the high-wattage, sardonic one I'd come to enjoy. "War is a great idiocy itself. What could be more appropriate?"

I laughed ruefully. That made about as much sense to me as anything else lately.

We were silent for a few minutes, looking out at the water, our shoulders almost touching. His presence was a warm comfort next to me. I desperately wished right then that I wasn't his captain. I wished even more fervently that he wasn't one of the ageless Faerie. He'd lived for so long, he probably thought of me as a child. All this lay like a cavernous gulf between us. Between what I desperately wanted and what could never be.

"The Faerie don't go to church," he blurted out suddenly. "We don't even have churches."

"What?"

His brow was furrowed, thinking hard. "The English, and your other countries, build churches. We don't treat our gods like that. We have rituals, but it's different. My people treat them more like storms or hurricanes. Some of us love them, some hate them, blame them, dedicate our lives to them, but no one has ever *ignored* them. Or pretended to understand them. I'm not sure Sands understands that."

"So what is Faith supposed to do?" I said.

"Believe, I suspect."

"So, she dedicates her life to a Faerie god? Does she pick one out of a hat? It's not like anyone understands how this actually works, is it?"

"No," Avonstoke said slowly.

"Why doesn't anyone understand how this works?" I said with true anger.

Avonstoke sighed, clearly resigned to making me angrier with every word. "We don't," he said. "We don't even try." He turned to me and lifted his palms to the air helplessly. "We just . . . believe."

CHAPTER 2

Lady of Sorrows Takes Father

Fourteen hours later, we sat in the sun of the English Channel, riding easily on sea anchor, waiting for our rendezvous with the *Blood Oath*, the ship that was coming to take Father to Faerie. We basked in the sunlight, but the mist loomed uncomfortably close on our starboard side.

Three members of the *H.M.S. Rachaela*'s crew, two Prowlers and a Dwarf, were scrubbing the red stains out of the white deck planks behind me, near the forecastle. We'd barely had time for the funerals. Stanchion, Fulson, and Heller. When the stain was gone, gone would be the last physical trace of three good crew members.

There were other signs of our skirmish.

A perfectly circular hole in the fore staysail showed where a cannonball had passed only three feet above me during the battle, and the *whack whack whack* of an exhausted carpentry team coming from the aft told me that they'd at least finished the plug in the hull and had started on the shattered quarterdeck railing.

Another team of Dwarves were working on one of the cannon carriages that had been hit. The bronze cannon lay gleaming on the deck a short way away. Bronze cannon still looked odd to me, but an all-Faerie crew required alternate materials to avoid cold iron. The sigils and glyphs on the side were inert now, barely visible.

A Troll, an actual Troll whose name we didn't even know because no one knew its language, had been coerced out of the hold to help move the cannon. It was a lanky, rawboned thing, nearly twelve feet tall, wearing what looked suspiciously like several burlap sacks, with a long face and snout like a burly anteater. It stood, sullen and uncertain, waiting to move the cannon again when the Dwarves finished their work.

I strolled casually over to Mr. Starling, who was glaring at the working Dwarven crew. If it was a glare. It was hard to tell with Starling.

"Are we sure," I said, looking sidelong at the Troll, "that having him on board is . . . safe?"

"Absolutely no idea, Ma'am," Starling said bleakly. "Hidin' down in the 'old all this time." He shrugged. "Don't know what it's been doin' all this time. Don't know who let it on board. Didn't even know it were a Troll until one o' the woman folk told me." More of that appalling lack of knowledge the Faerie had about their own realm and people. Maybe I didn't know a lot about lions, say, but at least I'd recognize a lion when I saw one. We hadn't even known the Troll was on board for our first four weeks at sea. The Troll was frightened by sun, or the moon, or stars, or anything that smacked of open air, really. Rigging up a block and tackle would have been a far easier way to move the cannon.

"The women have it under control, don't they?" Starling assured me, but he sounded less than convinced himself.

Two female Dwarves, our self-appointed handlers, stood near the Troll, talking to it softly. It jerked at some sudden movement from the goblins in the rigging above, snarled, and reached for the nearest weapon, the railing.

"No!" I shouted, but it was no use.

The Troll tore free a twelve foot length of it with a horrific rending noise. Bits of wood and metal fell to the deck.

I lifted my hands at Starling in exasperation. "Under control?"

Starling had the grace to look embarrassed, smacking his palm to his head. "Oy!" he bellowed at the Troll, then gestured wildly at the handlers.

But the Dwarven women were already working on it, cajoling the section of railing out of the Troll's hand before it hurled it into the rigging and did even more damage. One of the women came and delivered the section of railing to Starling with a rueful shrug, both of them handling the fifty-or sixty-pound weight with minimal effort.

"Another job for the carpenter," the Dwarven woman said matter-of-factly.

Starling's sigh was deep and heartfelt. "I'll tell 'em."

That was another thing I hadn't known about. Women Dwarves! I guess I should have known they'd be around, somewhere, but they didn't look at all like I'd expected. Instead of stout, beardless counterparts of the men, these women were a trifle smaller, also stout, and surprisingly elegant if you didn't count their mounds of wild, curly hair.

"You sure they can control him?" I asked Starling yet again. A block and tackle wouldn't be that hard to set up, actually, but the Goblins and Prowlers kept getting them tangled up, while the Court Faerie wouldn't condescend anything so elegant as physical labor. The Dwarves were all occupied with other tasks, though if I pulled the women off Troll duty and put them onto fixing things, we might actually get caught up on repairs. Except then no one would be watching the Troll and there was no telling what damage it would do unattended. Maybe I could drop the Troll into a rowboat and . . .

"'Er actually," Starling said, breaking into my thoughts.

"What?" I said.

"It's a she-Troll. At least, that's what the women folk tell me."

I blinked at him, stunned. "Really?"

He shrugged again. "Who can tell?"

There were repairs happening on the mizzenmast, too. We'd lost Chuck-Chuck with that cannonball. Some of the blood they were scrubbing off the deck was his. Even an unmitigated success like we had last night had casualties. Telling myself that it was war didn't help much.

I watched the Goblins moving through the rigging, still working through the problems of getting my crew in shape. They were industrious and quick, but terrifyingly disorganized. Also, they didn't take orders well from either the Dwarves or the Court Faerie. All right, they didn't take orders at *all* from them.

No matter how much I needed them to work together, I still couldn't erase centuries of inter-Faerie hostility. Faith joined me at the rail, tall and poised in all the ways I wished I could be.

Today's dress was of the deepest blue, but far simpler and plainer than she'd used to wear. So that was something. She'd even conceded to wear leggings, too, so that she had some freedom of movement. She looked back at the crew members scrubbing the blood out of the deck and shuddered. She noticed that I'd seen and sighed.

"I can't help it," she said. "Sea battles scare me all to pieces. They'd scare you, too, if you had any sense. Or did Father transfer 'courage at sea' along with his admiral title?"

"Of course I'm scared," I said quietly. "I'm just too busy during battle to think about it."

"At least you have something to *do*," she said. "I keep waiting for all these magician duties Mr. Sands keeps telling me are coming, but so far he hasn't told me much of anything. Just history and tales of old magicians, but nothing about how to do actual magic at all!" She glared back at where Mr. Sands was talking to Avonstoke.

Sands had cleaned up after his ordeal in the mist, and Avonstoke looked, as always, like he was on his way to some kind of magical ball, so the two of them were a pair of dandies and no mistake.

Avonstoke was tall and lean in the dark and shadowy green uniform of the House of Thorns marine, complete with cloak and brilliant white gleaming piping all over. With the black, raven tattoo around his eyes like a domino mask, and with his eyes themselves all gold and inhuman, he looked a rakishly sinister avatar of naval warfare. His long hair, equally gold, was tied into a neat queue that hung down his back. Even the ties were that same green to match his uniform—a dark green in the full light, but faded to black in anything less. Just looking at him made my heart ache, but I was the captain, his commander. Also, I could not forget the gulf between his age and mine. So I kept that out of my face. I hope.

Mr. Sands was compact and dapper next to Avonstoke's towering height. He was equally blond, yellow instead of gold, with his neat mustache, pointed beard, and a wild explosion of short, yellow, spiky hair that fought its way out from underneath the brim of his black top hat. Yes, top hat. Sands' idea of practical seaweather gear today was a wildly inappropriate black dinner jacket, complete with tails and white gloves, and it wasn't even dinner time. He'd lost everything. His position as Father's magician, a role that had a great deal of magical power attached to it, now all gone. His violin, with which I'd once seen him conjure dragon fireflies. Acta Santorum, his steed and companion, which was the worst of all. I wasn't even sure if he even qualified as a magician anymore, and he wouldn't answer the question.

The door to the captain's cabin opened and an awkward stillness fell on the deck while two Dwarven crewmen brought out Father on a stretcher. Mounting the three short steps from the cabin floor to get up on deck, the Dwarves moving awkwardly because the steps were built at human height. But it was clear the stretcher was no real burden for them, wasted as Father was.

Here was someone else who had lost everything in the war, and he looked it, lying colorless and unconscious on the stretcher. He no longer led the Outcast Army, defending England and the world against a Faerie invasion. Now he was heading back into the arms of the Seelie Court, which would not take kindly to his betrayal. They'd as likely as not execute him the second he was back. Yet, if he didn't go, the spell compelling him to meet with the acting Lord of Thorns, a man Father had imprisoned in that role, would put such a strain on his poisoned, weakened body that it would accomplish what the poison hadn't—kill him. The compulsion, incidentally, was part of the spell that Father had cast himself. That same spell that had allowed Father to abandon his position as Lord of Thorns—leaving the real Rachek Kasric in his place—had also allowed Father to assume human form and take Rachek Kasric's home and position and family. That part had been the final, entirely-too-fitting act of accidental self-destruction, as existing for so many years in human form had drained Father of most of his magical powers.

The only saving grace had been that the Yellow Veil, a Faerie venom, would have killed any regular Faerie. It had been Father's humanity, his weakness by Faerie standards, that allowed him to survive the Yellow Veil. It had also been his humanity that made him our Father. From everything I'd heard, most of it from his own lips, he hadn't been a very honorable man as the Lord of Thorns. Now, he lay on the deck, weakened almost to death by the Yellow Veil and forced by his own mechanisms to travel back to Faerie, where it was as likely as not that they'd kill him for his betrayal.

His many sins had come back to roost and there wasn't a damned thing I could do about it. I'd known this moment would come and now it was here and I could feel my teeth grinding and tears threatening to well up on my eyes. I kept them back with pure force of will.

Lady Rue's ship and magician would be taking Father back into Faerie to the World Tree, because she thought that important. The same ship and magician that she refused to commit to any kind of real offensive against the forces occupying England.

Mr. Starling approached, his gaze thoughtful. "Winds backin' a little, I think, Captain?" His tone made the statement a question.

"It'll turn us a little," I said. "Can't be helped and no real worry with the sails furled and the sea anchor out." We were riding close the edge of the mist, though, and needed to keep an eye on it. It would be bad to drift inside while we were paying attention to something else.

He nodded, though clearly unhappy. "Still don't trust all this close-'auled, abeam to the wind nonsense. Tricky and unreliable. Relentless, too. Smacks of 'uman science. No good can come of it, I tell you."

"It'll keep us afloat," I said tartly. "Better than sinking."

Starling nodded reluctantly, but his expression suggested he wasn't sure he was getting the best of that bargain. He'd become a fair seaman, despite his distrust of the methods. I felt the same about controlling the winds through magic.

"Ship!" a muddled voice sang from the crow's nest. "Ship off the . . . er . . . that way!" I ground my teeth some more and looked up to try and make out which way our Goblin lookout was pointing. He still hadn't mastered fore, aft, port, and starboard.

There was the Lady Rue's ship, the *Blood Oath,* coming out of the mist and right on schedule. She was a lean, two-masted, fore-and-aft rigged schooner, black, with scarlet trim. Her sails were an even deeper scarlet that shimmered in the sunlight. It made the *Rachaela* look mundane and dreary by comparison. How did they even make sails like that?

Everything about the ship was foreign. Even the name, missing the H.M.S. dedication that prefixed all the ships Father had commissioned. Father's portion of the fleet had been dedicated to England, even if the Queen or the British admiralty didn't know it. Not so with the *Blood Oath.*

The ship was fast, too. You could tell watching it come across the water. It was clearly much faster than the *Rachaela,* just as Lady Rue had claimed. I had to force myself to stop grinding my teeth. God, I hated that woman.

The Lady herself was there in the *Blood Oath's* prow, a tall, stern woman that I'd been seeing entirely too much of, wearing long flowing robes and a mask of silver over her face. Her hair was long, black, and silky, with parts of it drawn up on either side of her face so that the ends stuck out like two black, spiny sea urchins grafted above her slanted ears. She wore a fancy red evening dress, lushly inappropriate for being at sea, but she seemed somehow past petty concerns like discomfort or snagging her clothes on hooks and pulleys.

"Are you sure we can trust Lady Rue's people?" I asked Mr. Sands as the other ship slid to within a few feet. There was a loud banging as the hulls bumped and shouting from sailors on both ships as lines were tossed across. Lady Rue had proven herself to be my main obstacle inside the Outcast Fleet. Every command I issued met barriers of haughtiness and disinterest, attitudes that rippled out to everyone around her.

Mr. Sands puffed out his cheeks. "Normally, I'd say trusting any of the Faerie was a risk. But *these* Faerie, with *this* task, most assuredly. They've vowed to get him there at any cost." A binding statement with the Faerie. "Besides, they're not Lady Rue's people."

"What does that mean?" I said, but the blond little magician didn't answer.

The *Blood Oath* was within shouting distance now. I knew what Lady Rue would see when looking at me. A wee slip of a girl, looking far younger than my sixteen years. Blonde hair, long but kept back out of the way by my wide-brimmed, battered, black hat. Not nearly as tall or as pretty as my sister, Faith, or the elegant Court Faerie like Avonstoke, and yet, not plain human, either. My half-Faerie heritage on freakish display in my eyes: one normal, glacial blue, like most of my family. The other an eerie black marble, a dark reflection and counterpoint of the many golden Faerie eyes in my crew all around. Father's worn, and too large, oiled boat coat flapping around me like a cloak. Nothing elegant to me at all. Faith had all the elegance in the family.

I pulled the hat lower to fight off the ache caused by the bright sun in my black ghost eye.

"If the people of that ship aren't retainers of the Lady Rue," I said to Sands, "who are they?"

Mr. Sands didn't say anything, but suddenly seemed to find something very interesting on the railing to occupy his attention.

I prodded him on the shoulder.

Sands sighed deeply. "They are part of the House of Thorns."

"House of Thorns?" I said. "Father's troops?" That didn't make any sense.

"House of Thorns, yes," Sands said. "Your Father's troops, *no*."

"They don't," I burst out, "even seem like good sailors. They nearly turned the wrong way and put their ship over twice just on the way over here, for all that speed." Actually, what I said wasn't true, but it *should* have been. The sails were improperly and dangerously set on the *Blood Oath,* but the ship rode easily in defiance of both tide and wind. Unnatural.

"They won't need to be sailors," Avonstoke said gravely. "They've got a storm serpent." He pointed at the foremast of the Faerie ship, where a long, black, white, and gray mottled serpent curled around the crow's nest. "I've never seen one before." His tone was filled with a grudging sense of wonder.

In addition to not possessing any seamanship, the Black Shuck's army was also missing any seafaring Faerie. A product of not having the right gods behind their venture, Sands said. All the

Prowlers, Water Fae and the like had either avoided the war altogether or become part of the Outcast Army.

I put my spyglass to my eye and found the serpent coiled on the *Blood Oath's* mizzenmast. It was looking right back at us, regarded us with a flat gaze. It ruffled one of the white, black-tipped feathered impossible-looking wings that marked it as a creature out of myth.

Even now, the gaze of the serpent, staring at nothing I could see, shifted, and the winds shifted slightly near the Faerie ship. I couldn't feel it over here, but the sails on the Faerie ship were luffing and filling in a direction completely at odds with ours. The Faerie counterpart to actual seamanship.

I shivered. "Unnatural."

Faith, who hadn't spoken for some time, looked at me incredulously. "We're on a ship crewed by Dwarves and Goblins and Mere-people," she said dryly.

"And Trolls," Avonstoke said helpfully. "Don't forget the Trolls. Or Troll, I guess. Just the one."

Faith ignored Avonstoke and went on. "We're sailing near a magical mist that leads both to England and to the land of Faerie. In fact, we're neck deep in spells and magical creatures and it's the way the *sails* work on that ship that bothers you?"

"Well," I said, my voice reaching a higher pitch. "Just *look* at it! It's unnatural, I tell you." I waved helplessly at the other ship.

Faith sighed and looked away.

There were only a dozen of the enigmatic storm serpents in the Outcast Fleet, one per schooner. That was because you couldn't trust the Faerie not to sink any ship that had to rely on regular sailing. The *Rachaela* was easily the best ship in the fleet, a fact which gave me enormous pride. Of course, *that* didn't help it keep up with the *Blood Oath*. It couldn't sail into Faerie, either, which is why we needed this ship and Lady Rue to take Father there.

Faith's gaze flickered to were Father lay on the deck. There was pity in her face, but also anger and revulsion and possibly much more. When she spoke, it was pitched low, for my ears alone. "Some would say that he's only getting what he deserves."

I winced, but she wasn't entirely wrong. Father had stolen everything the real Rachek Kasric had ever possessed. His wife, his son, his home, his career, his body . . . everything.

"You?" I said.

"Sometimes," she admitted, "but not all the time. He's still our father. Besides, he could have run when the invasion came, and he didn't. That's got to count for something."

"It does."

"He probably deserves some kind of punishment," Faith said. "Certainly Mother would say so, and she's got a right to say it. But this . . ." She shook her head. "Sands says the Faerie lack any sense of forgiveness or mercy. True for the Seelie Court, too, even more so, and he betrayed them. Now he has to go back or his own magic is going to kill him. Death might be kinder than what he's going to face."

"Lady Kasric du Thorns," the Lady Rue called out.

Probably some kind of slur from her point of view. Faith and I exchanged glances. If the title, good or bad, applied to one of us, it applied to both of us.

"It is time," she went on, her mask gleaming. "Your father's last duty calls." Her mouth, left uncovered, was red and full in a triumphant smile. No one knew exactly what she looked like underneath that mask, or where she'd come from, but she was clearly one of the Court Faerie, like Avonstoke and Colonel Swayle.

It was a safe bet she was from the Unseelie Court. The invasion had created some strange bedfellows by putting both Seelie and Unseelie, normally eternal enemies, together on both sides of the invasion.

With allies like these, enemies were almost redundant.

Then three other people came up from the hold and the skin on the back of my neck began to crawl with gooseflesh.

"Oh dear God," Avonstoke said.

"Who is that?" I asked.

"It's Lady Dierwyn du Epion," Sands said. "But she's known as the Lady of Thorns."

"That's not her only name," Avonstoke whispered. He looked at Sands, his expression challenging.

"No," Sands said softly. "Most of Faerie calls her the Lady of Sorrows."

"Of sorrows?" Faith said. "Why?"

Mr. Sands turned a ghastly, haunted look at us. "Can't you guess?"

Of course I could. Father had abandoned her, his wife, when he left Faerie and tried to dupe her by leaving a stranger disguised as him behind. Not just any stranger, but a human, which meant, to most Faerie, a bitter enemy. Now Father was trying to defend England against his own people. He must be viewed as a particularly loathsome traitor while his wife, the Lady of Thorns, would be left to deal with all the backlash his actions had caused. And we were the offspring of that betrayal. If ever there was a woman who had the right to hate us, it was her.

She was a tall woman, as tall as the Lady Rue, which was saying something. She was thinner, like a willow branch, hard and dark and angry. Where the Lady Rue was lush, this woman was lean, like a prominent rock that the sea would break upon. Her skin was unnaturally dark and shiny, like polished obsidian. Her hair was a streaming waterfall of ivory, long, and unbound and untamed and wild in the wind coming off the water. Her dress was black, so that it was disconcertingly difficult to tell where her skin began and the dress ended, except where it whipped in the wind. Her golden almond eyes were narrowed in suspicion.

When she took a step closer to the rail, there was a graceful, inhuman motion beneath her dress. Peering with my ghost eye—I'd developed an automatic habit of squinting so much when dealing with the Faerie that everyone around me must have thought I had a facial tick—didn't make her look any different, but using the spyglass, I could see that her legs under the black dress didn't move like human legs. Then the wind pressed the cloth harder against them and I could see they bent backwards at the knees, like a beast's.

Two young girls stood next to her.

The Lady of Sorrows held the hand of the youngest, a little girl with blonde curls, blue eyes, and white, cherub skin. Any other girl might have been alarmed at the splash of the waves or the rolling deck, but this little girl paid these things no attention at all. She wore a little red and white checkered dress, looking like an advertisement for a dairy farm. My ghost eye showed much the same girl, except for an aura of calm that her apparent eight or nine years didn't support and a gleam of nearly ancient, merciless wisdom in her blue eyes.

The other girl was plain, dark, and severe. She was older than her sister, our age. Or at least appeared that way. I was learning not to credit that with the Faerie. She wore her straight, dark hair short, just past her ears. Unlike the other women there, she didn't seem to have taken any effort with her appearance and looked plain and sullen. She wore a black quilted tunic with leather leggings that didn't look overly clean. Something about her shadow didn't look right to me, but I couldn't see it well enough from here to determine what.

She leaned on the railing of the other ship directly at us and pulled her lips back into a feral snarl.

"Who is that?" I asked, a nasty premonition tickling the back of my skull. I looked at Avonstoke. Right now, I trusted him far more than Sands.

"I have no idea," Avonstoke said.

We all looked at Sands again. The channel was turbulent around us, lifting and dropping both ships, but not quite in unison.

On the other ship, the severe girl spun on her heel and stormed off, presumably down into the lower deck. The little girl sneered at us and followed. The Lady Rue and the Lady of Sorrows, still on deck, didn't look any friendlier.

"They are the Lady of Sorrows' daughters," Sands finally said, even those words pulled reluctantly out from between his teeth.

"That makes them our Father's daughters, too," I said, "right?" A dark, cold feeling crept into me. The skin on the back of my neck and all down my back was crawling with gooseflesh.

"Our sisters?" Faith said.

"Half-sisters," Sands admitted. He opened his mouth and paused, unable, it seemed, to spit out the rest of it. But he didn't have to. He'd said enough. I stared across at the two girls. We shared a father, if not a mother.

"They don't look very old," Faith said.

"They are," Sands said, "far older than they appear." He was leaning heavily against the rail, refusing to look at us, twisting his black top hat in his hand. Now, he tried to put the mangled hat back on his head, but it didn't fit any more and the wind took it.

He barely noticed.

"The Lady of Sorrows," he said, "and the real Rachek Kasric, who is occupying the Lord of Thorns' place, have had no children."

"These sisters are part of the plan then," I demanded. "Aren't they? The one Father said isn't going to work?"

"Are you going to introduce us?" Faith said. "What are their names? Diligence? Courage? Etiquette?"

"Hope," Mr. Sands said. "And Charity."

"The dark, gloomy one is Hope?" Faith said, sneering.

Sands just nodded.

At a nod from the Lady of Sorrows, Lady Rue gestured at two of the Faerie behind her. A pair of gargoyles, stony, hunched over creatures with great gray batlike wings. They mounted the rail and then flapped heavily against the stiff breeze to launch themselves in our direction. Clumsy on their feet, they made surprisingly graceful figures in the air.

They were coming to take Father.

"You didn't say anything about giving him over to *them,*" I said, turning on Sands. "How can we trust them?"

"They're the only ones we *can* trust," Mr. Sands said.

I opened my mouth, the words on the tip of my tongue. *Order Mr. Starling to run out the guns. Prepare to repel boarding parties. Load the carronade with grapeshot.* That would show them.

"Justice," Faith said, grabbing my arm. "Don't fight this. Father *needs* to go back."

I ground my teeth again and said nothing. Just glared at the other ship. Which was how I saw, very clearly, what happened when the girl on the *Blood Oath's* deck, Hope, disappeared.

A spot appeared on the deck in front of me, a black stain as if someone had spilled a quart of pitch. The black liquid shimmered in the sun, then the blackness *twitched* and rose and growled, the upper part of it starting to take shape.

The black shadow of an enormous wolf.

The thing finished taking shape, standing over five feet high at the shoulder, black, with the texture of tufted furred and a wolf's face, but only half-seen. This was a thing made of darkness and shadow, nothing like a real wolf, not of this world. As if someone had cut a wolf-shaped hole out of our sunlit world.

The wolf thing snarled and Faith, Avonstoke and I all shied backwards.

Squinting with my ghost eye, I could see a girlish shape inside of the wolf. Hope. My half-sister was inside this thing.

The wolf lunged forward, snarling at us.

I danced backwards, out of the way, drawing my pistol as I did so. Avonstoke rolled backwards, then came up with his shadowy sword in hand. Moonlight shimmered on the shifting edges. Moonlight reflected off the wolf silhouette, too. That they were similar types of magic there could be no doubt.

A crash like a cannon shot thundered across the open space.

Again, the heavy thud of metal on wood, amplified, came from the other ship. The noise was unbelievably loud, like the gavel of a divine judge. The Lady of Sorrows was stamping her foot, or hoof, onto the deck of the *Bloody Rose*.

"Enough!" she called out. Her voice, laden with authority, carried far better than it should have across the water. It didn't sound as if coming from twenty feet away, but as if someone was shouting in my ear.

The shadow wolf snarled, but it backed away.

Now that I had a slight reprieve, I saw the crew all around me. They'd picked up ropes and boathooks and belaying pins, crowding around to come to my aid, for all the good it would have done. Still, their bravery emboldened me. Besides, I knew how the Faerie admired a good show and I was almost as worried about getting my crew to like me as I was of failing Father. Getting eaten by shadowy dogs, as terrifying as that was, still came in a distant third.

"Listen to Mother, now, Hope, dear," I sneered, trying to adopt a bravado I didn't feel at all. Any show I put on had to be for them, more than anyone. Best not to show any weakness.

Hope, the wolf, growled low. For a second, I thought she was going to attack anyway, then she melted away. A second later, Hope, in girl-shape, reappeared on the other ship.

"Justice," Faith said, her voice tight. "Are you all right?"

Christ, no, I wasn't all right. I was terrified. Why hadn't anyone told me I had sisters in Faerie, let alone sisters that could *do* that kind of thing? But I took a deep breath. "Fine," I said.

"Justice," said a husky voice said from the deck.

"Father!" He was awake!

I crouched next to him on the deck and took one of his thin, shivering hands in mine. Faith was next to me, her eyes glinting, and I realized she was crying.

"Don't cry," Father said. "It's *my* curse, remember? The one I laid on Rachek Kasric long ago, and on me. My curse will drag each of us to the yearly contest, the game. The stress of the compulsion could kill me under normal circumstances, if I resist. In my . . ." He swallowed and took a deep breath. "In my current condition, my own spell would kill me a surely as the Black Shuck."

There it was again, plain as houses.

If Father didn't get to the World Tree, he'd forfeit the game, revert to his Faerie shape, and be under the Court's dominion. This was the only chance he had.

"You can't win the game this time?" Faith said to Father. "Can you?"

Father shook his head, his wasted face covered in sorrow. "No."

"What will the Seelie Court do?"

"They have never forgiven my betrayal." Another spasm took him and he could only lie there and grit his teeth as it shuddered through him. "Imprisoned for eons is the best I can hope for. That is if Cernunnos does not get to me first. There is an old debt there and Cernunnos will not be denied. I do not think I will be coming back this time." He tried to keep a brave face, but I could see the fear and a deep, profound sorrow in his clear blue eyes.

The gargoyles landed on our deck with a heavy sound of claws scraping on wood.

Starling and the crew were all staring uncertainly, some with boat hooks and other improvised weapons. I hastily waved them off.

"Whatever you do," Father said, his voice near breaking. "Don't confront the Black Shuck. His power is too strong! This is all my fault. You shouldn't have to fight this way. Not against a thing like that."

I held his hand. I remembered it being so large and strong when I was little, and now it felt soft and feeble. "It's not your fault."

"There's more," Father said. "We lost . . ." His gaze clouded and he looked confused.

"The *Virtues*," Sands said with sorrow and pain deep in his voice. He looked smaller than I'd even seen him, defeated, as if this last admission was his complete undoing.

"Yes," Father said, remembering. "That was it. The Virtues. We lost one, or was it two?"

"Two," Sands said sadly. "Wandering in Faerie. Years ago."

I grimaced. Just hearing the term Virtues made me clench my teeth so much my jaw hurt. Faith and I were supposed to be two of those Virtues, but this part of Father's plan and the prophecy linked to it just sounded like hogwash to me. The prophecy, the one that Father half found and half made up, pitted the Seven Virtues against the Seven Sins, one a force for humankind, one a force against. Forget the fact that Father hadn't gotten the cardinal virtues correct when he borrowed them.

The gargoyles stepped forward and with none too gentle hands, each seized and lifted one end of Father's cot.

"I'm so sorry," Father said. "This shouldn't have fallen to you." His head sagged back to the rough cloth of the cot.

The gargoyles leapt, monster and cot jerking up and into the air in one awkward but powerful motion. They swayed, looking ungainly, but managed to right themselves without dropping Father, and started towards the *Blood Oath* with heavy, powerful beats of their wings.

"They'll drop him!" Faith said.

But, incredibly, the two gargoyles got Father over to the other ship without dropping him into the sea, bashing his head into the rail, or knocking each other out of the air.

"God, I hate that woman," I said, glaring at the Lady Rue, who made the smallest motion with her chin that might have been a nod, the spikes on either side of her face dipping slowly. I wanted to take a launch over there and brandish a cutlass in her face, but the laws of the Faerie were clear and Father had to obey. Besides, she'd probably stab me with her hair.

I took one last look, across the water, at Father's bundled and unconscious form on the other deck. He looked small, fragile, helpless.

And there was nothing I could do about it.

CHAPTER 3

Joshua's Letter

I gave orders for the *Rachaela* to resume patrols around the Thames Estuary at once. I was very eager to blast, burn, or sink something. Anything. There were other ships watching the other ports and coasts, but I thought the Estuary to be the most likely choice for a ripe target.

We found the lone sloop coming out of the Thames Estuary in the middle of the afternoon, with no effort to hide or evade capture.

Curious, too, was that it was just one ship. Hardly the large-scale attempt to carry troops across border that the Faerie had been attempting up until now. It was a small sloop, even smaller than the *Rachaela,* and apparently not armed. When I commanded the first warning shot, they did something the Faerie hadn't tried yet, and the last thing I expected.

They surrendered, hauling up a white flag and heaving to with the sea anchor so that they stood placidly waiting for our next actions.

I sent three boats over with boarding parties and the first of them came back with a British sea captain with a pale face and a scraggly black beard. His eyes nearly jumped out of his head looking around at the inhuman figures, particularly the two Faerie marines, with their uniforms of dark green and white cord trim, who led him each with a hand on his shoulder across the deck. He was dripping on the deck, as if he'd had some mishap with the water on the way over.

"Ship is empty, my Lady," one of the marines said. "Skeleton crew, all human. No Faerie at all." That hardly made any sense if their aim was to ferry over Faerie forces onto the mainland.

"Captain Justice Kasric?" the dripping captain asked.

The nearest marine, Swayle, pointed at me.

"I thought we were famous," Faith murmured next to me. "The fierce young girl admiral and her stunningly beautiful magician?" She was posing behind me on the quarterdeck stairs, trying to keep the properly intimidating picture for our captive. For some reason, that seemed to include not speaking, and she was talking to me in a low whisper out of the side of her mouth. "He doesn't even know enough about his enemy to recognize us."

"Stunningly beautiful magician?" I said lightly, not bothering to try and hide the fact that I was talking. "You think Mr. Sands is beautiful? Besides, he's not the magician anymore, you are."

"I *meant* me," Faith said, getting louder. "Of course I meant *me*."

I didn't bother answering, just grinned.

"You're impossible," she huffed.

The captain still didn't get it. As they brought him closer, he was looking past us at the collection of uniformed Faerie officers at the railing.

"Told you we should have gotten uniforms," Faith said.

"You might try this one," Avonstoke said from the top of the stairs behind me. He came down to the stairs to stand behind me and I looked back to see him pointing down at me. "The girl on the quarterdeck stairs," he said in a stage whisper, "with the scowl and the large floppy hat."

The man looked at me, shocked. "Justice Kasric is a *girl*?"

"The most remarkable sailor you'll ever see," Avonstoke said. "She moves among the ocean storms like a dance partner."

I waved off Avonstoke's comment, but Avonstoke took no notice.

"She sets the sails and brings down thunder," he went on. "With one spin of the tiller, she charms demons from the pit. And her clove hitch! She ties a clove hitch that could draw down unicorns and rainbows . . . oooffff . . ." I thumped him in the belly to cut him off.

"It's a work of art," Avonstoke finished with a grin.

I turned my glare from Avonstoke to the new man. "I'm *Captain* Justice Kasric," I told him. "If you're making a run for the mainland, it's the clumsiest I've seen yet."

"We're not," the man said. He fumbled a thickly padded envelope out of his vest pocket. He tried to step forward to give it to me, but the marines kept their hands implacably on his shoulders. The captain was probably average height, but looked small with the austere Faerie faces looming over him, their yellow eyes gleaming with suspicion.

"We didn't come to fight," the man said, "or carry Faerie to the mainland. We came to deliver this." He pushed the padded envelope at me.

"It's all right," I said, and they let him go. This poor soul didn't need to be controlled as much as he needed to be held up, so maybe letting him go wasn't the kindness I'd meant it to be. He looked near starvation. He also looked nearly ready to wet himself when some of the Goblin crew chattered at him from the rigging above us.

"Tell her," the marine said, "what you told me."

"The Black Shuck," the captain said in a quavering voice. "Has my Nora. My little girl. He has all our children. Wives and husbands, too." He had an accent that made me realize he wasn't English after all.

"Says he'll kill them all if their ship doesn't return to the shore," the marine added.

I took the letter with numb fingers. All this just to bring me a message? Victoria Rose had told us about the Black Shuck, their terrifying general of the Seelie Army, a demonic undead hound that drove them until the divided and fractious Faerie were like a pack of wild dogs.

The sea was gray and choppy, the sun overcast all day, but now, light broke from the clouds, and I grimaced as it flashed in my eyes.

"Dios Mio!" the captain said, looking at my face.

I knew what he saw. First, he saw a young girl, barely sixteen. And young girls were sea captains, not ever. Then he'd caught sight of my ghost eye and thought that I wasn't even human, which wasn't entirely wrong.

I pulled the hat lower to shield my eye from the sun and the captain's shocked gaze, then tore open the envelope. There were several photographs folded into a short letter. It was hard to make out the photographs with the sun's glare, but at the bottom of the letter was a clear signature.

Avonstoke, my sister, the rest of my crew . . . everyone was waiting.

"Take him back to his ship," I said to the marines. "Then let them go. No, wait. Feed him first. In fact, feed the entire crew before you let them go. A blanket or two wouldn't be out of line, either."

"Captain?" the marine said. "Feed the enemy? All of them?"

I'd turned to make my way up the stairs to the quarterdeck, but now I stopped and turned and regarded the marine, saying nothing.

The Court Faerie were usually a reserved, emotionless bunch, if you didn't count Avonstoke. But this one had a sudden twitch in his cheek and a spark of actual fear in his eye. It seemed the Kasric name and my ghost eye were good for something.

"Yes, Captain," he said quickly and just about fell over himself rushing off.

Swale, the marine captain, had drifted closer during the exchange. She spoke quietly once her marine was out of earshot. "Just as likely as not, these men are going to be loading cannon for the invasion forces. Cannon that will be aimed at *us*." Her tone was neutral, carefully unchallenging.

"They're the enemy now," I said gently, "and you're not wrong about the cannon, but these are the people we're here to protect. It would be nice if some of them *knew* it."

Swayle nodded, her careful, professional mask still in place.

"Mr. Starling?" I called out.

"Aye," the voice of my first mate said from behind me.

"As soon as the boats return from their errands, wear the ship around and take us back out into the channel."

"Aye-aye, Captain," Starling said.

"English terminology," Avonstoke said. "It is very confusing. Why would you *wear* a ship?"

I opened my mouth to retort, but saw a sudden curiosity revealed on Swayle's face. She didn't know what I was talking about, either.

Even Starling had stopped at Avonstoke's question, as if he suddenly wasn't completely confident of my meaning either, for all that he'd been about to execute the command.

"Not wear," I snapped. "*Wear!* You tack into the wind, you wear away from the wind."

"It *is* confusing," Swayle said, her face earnest and serious. Starling's face was carefully neutral.

"Perhaps a different word?" Avonstoke mused. "Could we not flugelstan into the wind, say?"

"I'll not be likely to mistake that word," Starling agreed.

I threw up my hands and left the quarterdeck, seeking refuge in my cabin.

I dumped my coat on the cot and lit a lantern, cursing as it took me three tries. The room's ceiling was terribly low, but the table, now covered with maps, a silver tea service, and navigational instruments, was of fine mahogany. A luxuriously thick carpet of rich brown covered the floor. The cot, padded and warm, was far better than the hammocks most of the crew used and I was grateful for it.

Light streamed in through the gallery windows that faced behind us. They were high up in the wall, with thick glass, but this too was a far cry from the little portholes most quarters had.

Two ember coals blinked open on the cot. Enemy, our ship's cat, wriggled her velvety gray body slightly and made a small chirping noise.

She was Sands' technically, but she'd attached herself to the ship and our cabin.

With Sands' connections to cats—and just thinking about the legion of cats he'd commanded at Stormholt made me shiver—I regarded Enemy as a potential spy in our midst. Sands' way of keeping track of my plans.

Which is how she came to her name, since Sands hadn't bothered to choose one. I scratched her belly once to shut her up and that was enough. She blinked sleepily and then went back to sleep.

In the other corner, on a small table, sat Father's chess set. This was somehow linked to the war, according to Father and Sands.

The idea was that changes in the war would be reflected on the board, if you knew how to read them, but the board hadn't changed in the past three months we'd been on blockade. The game was a tangled one, with a few pieces lost on each side but with much more bloodshed to come.

One of the missing pieces was the horse that I kept in my pocket, the one I'd stolen when the set was back in Father's study.

I turned my attention to the letter. I read it once and swore, then I read it again.

The cabin door came open again, letting in a little sunlight as Faith's shadow stood in the doorway.

"Justice?" she said. "What is it?"

"The letter isn't from the Black Shuck," I snarled. "It's from Joshua."

It read:

Dear Justice,

I have sent this letter out with the captain of the Porta Coeli, *assuming that you will fire on and board them just as you have with every ship to leave any English port for the last month. Reports from these encounters are few and far between, but they seem to indicate that the Eastern part of the channel and the Thames Estuary are part of your ship's patrol, and so I hope this letter finds you rather than one of the other Outcasts, since I do not trust them to deliver it to your hands.*

Give up this foolish mission of Father's. It's not fair that he should have laid this at your feet, especially since he knew it was doomed to fail. The world of men is nearing an end, and your small fleet cannot contain the Faerie invasion any more than short-sighted persons could contain the printing press, or the spread of the Catholic religion.

It is very difficult to get flash photography to work in the British Isles these days. (You cannot even begin to understand the changes that have been wrought here. If you did, you would know that the England you think you're fighting to save has already passed.) Even so, I was able to commission a series of photographs to try and convey just the smallest portion of the new world that exists here.

"How could Joshua . . ." Faith started, and then she turned and sagged against the table, clearly at a loss for words.

"This is the same loving brother," I said flatly, "who flung both of us around in Stormholt. Remember?" The massive scope of betrayal that Joshua and Mother were committing made me ashamed to call them blood.

"But that was just . . ." Faith started. "He was just doing what Mother . . ." She looked at me, desperate for some forgiveness or understanding in my face, but then her eye slid over to the pretty, acid-burned memento I had of Joshua's brotherly affection, my ghost eye, and she went silent.

Understanding when people need comfort in the way that cats do, Enemy had roused himself from the bed and now butted his head against my shin, demanding attention. Was it my comfort or his he was worried about? You could never tell with cats. But I reached down and rubbed at the base of his ears, and he purred loudly.

I turned back to the photographs. Here was the Tower Bridge, draped in bramble falling in a deep curtain on the far side so that the bridge now formed a massive portal into a dark bramble tunnel that led to the devil knew where. The north bank? Down into the Thames? The photograph had been taken near dusk, so that it was dark and ominous. There was no river traffic on the Thames, which would have been remarkable under any other circumstances.

We had some idea of the methods the Faerie had used to conquer London, gathered through reports from some of the refugees who'd made it across the channel, but there weren't enough details. The Seelie Army had crossed from Faerie to England, landing in Battersea Park, and met virtually no opposition.

England had fallen literally overnight.

Here was another photograph with the House of Parliament, or at least where the House of Parliament used to be. Now it was a burned-out pit. The Clock Tower with Big Ben was still there, sort of, with gaping holes that let beams of sunlight through. The rest of Westminster, however, the houses of parliament and the heart of British politics, now looked more like one of the ruins of the Roman Empire than a modern world power. In fact, it looked very much like Big Ben had only been left standing so that the rest of the ruin could still be recognized as the important structure it once had been. The photographer had gone to a great deal of trouble to time the picture correctly, just when the beams of light came through the clock tower at the most dramatic angle.

"What a pompous git," Faith said, echoing my thoughts. "How much trouble did he go to, sending a photographer out there just so he could send this to you?"

Another showed two pillars and a gate, but both sides of the fence had been cut off. This left it standing alone in an empty marsh, guarding nothing except weeds and cattails. The pillars, white with ornate decorations, but with broken lamp posts on them, looked naggingly familiar.

"Oh God," Faith said, clearly reading the confusion on my face. "You know where this is? It's Buckingham Palace! Or what's left of it."

"No," I breathed.

But she was right. Right there in the foreground where the two gate pillars and part of the gate came together, the royal crest was still visible. What had made it so difficult to recognize was that absence of the fence, to say nothing of the *palace* that should have been behind it. Nothing remained but a few remnants of the foundation, burned and charred down to almost nothing. The rest was a dismal, black marsh.

If Buckingham Palace was gone, where was Queen Victoria? Joshua hadn't chosen these landmarks casually. These were carefully arranged declarations of the devastation the Seelie Army had caused. The royalty, the government, the landmarks, the people—nothing had been spared.

A burning anger rose inside of me, looking at these pictures. If this is what had happened to Westminster Palace, to the Queen and all the nobles and important people there, what about the less important people that made London their home? What about Mr. Divers and Hercules plying their hansom trade in the streets? Driving a hansom was the only trade Mr. Divers knew and if anything happened to either of them, it would be the end for both. Our neighbors in Soho, the milk maid and the grocer and the four children that lived two houses down . . . all of them could be dead or enslaved or anything.

The Faerie had done this to London and to all of England and would spread, if we didn't stop them, to the rest of the British Isles, to France and Spain, and eventually, to the entire world.

Everything depended on stopping them here. If we failed, the rest of the world didn't have the slightest clue how to deal with the Faerie. Hell, they didn't even know the Faerie were here, only that England had been swallowed in a sudden mist, cut off entirely, and that no ship they sent into the mist ever came out again, and without the special provisions that allowed the *Rachaela* and other Faerie ships to navigate through, they never would.

I went back to the letter, chewing my lip hard as I got to the end.

> *Before extending my current recommendations, I also express my expectations that you will ignore these entirely. But at least this way I can say that I tried to warn you. There is no stopping the Seelie Court. They will have their way in this and in all things, as sure as the seasons.*
>
> *Better to fling yourself on the mercy of the Seelie Court now, when Mother and I might still be able to put in a good word for you.*

Best Regards,

Joshua of Scarsdon House,
General of the Seelie Vanguard,
Council to the Seelie Court of New London, esq.

I felt wetness in my mouth and realized I'd chewed my lip hard enough to draw blood. I wiped it away in an angry smear. We'd recently found out that our brother, long lost in the realm of Faerie, had returned, with our equally lost and estranged mother, and was now somehow part of the Faerie occupation. Collaborators, and high-ranking ones, from the sound of it. They must have given the Black Shuck some shiny pieces of silver to get that kind of reward.

"He's using Mother's maiden name?" Faith said angrily. "Can he do that?"

"That's the part that bothers you?" I said, staring at her.

"Oh certainly," she said bitterly. "You know what a stickler for names and titles I am. It doesn't bother me at all that Joshua helped tear down Westminster Palace!" She shrieked and swept her arm across my tiny desk, sending photos all over the tiny room.

I wanted to scream back, but I also knew exactly how she felt. So, I scraped my chair back and began to silently pick up the pictures from the slightly damp floor. Faith stamped her foot in frustration, but then she sighed and crouched to help me.

I carefully blotted away any moisture from the wet floor and lay them out on the desk again. One caught my eye while I was doing it, a long, long shot from across the riverbank, taken so that you could see what had become of the land for miles at a time. What had once been docks and fishing wharfs and, further in, market squares and roads and farmland, was now an expanse of dense forest. And not the kind of forest that was supposed to grow in England. This was thick, dark, and primeval, with trees larger than anything I'd ever seen before. Even in a picture, you could tell that the place would seem supernaturally still, but really was packed with hidden, dangerous life. It was the kind of place that would swallow whole regiments and not blink. A forbidden place. That's why he'd sent these pictures, to show me how hopeless it would be to return. This was the kind of place where beasts and trees all fought, in their own ways, for every single inch of breathing space.

This is what Faerie occupation was like. There was no more room for people in England.

"God," Faith said. "Can you even imagine what it was like for your average London citizen? One minute reading the newspaper and the next dragons and tree monsters are tearing down half of your drawing room. God knows I have enough bad dreams about it."

I looked up sharply.

"Ah," she said. "You have too, eh?"

I just nodded. Lots of bad dreams. Shadowy horses and crows on a battlefield. Not surprising, considering I'd had run-ins with battlefields and the Wild Hunt itself. It was a wonder I only had as many bad dreams as I did, and not far more. There was another where I remembered stuffing Lady Rue into the cannon and firing, but that was one of the good ones.

I was still flipping through the pictures. Something was odd about them, besides the obvious. Then I said it out loud. "There aren't any ships."

"You and your boat obsession," she said. "Honestly!"

"Not even at the docks," I said. "No fishing boats, nothing." What little information we had told us that the Black Shuck had been hording ships, parceling them carefully for small, covert attempts to get across the channel.

But this, this indicated something else entirely.

"Westminster Palace is a giant marsh!" Faith said. "Are a few missing boats really that surprising?"

"Oh yes," I said. "If he's moved them further down the pool, probably Graveshead, then he's getting ready to go for one massive, concerted effort, and soon."

"You can't know that," Faith said, but she sounded unsure.

I nodded. "It's the only thing that makes sense. You don't round up a hundred ships like this and then just let them sit there, do you?"

"They could all just be missing?" she said.

"I don't think so," I said. "Which makes it the height of poor planning on Joshua's part to taunt us with something that holds this kind of clue, doesn't it?"

"Perhaps," she said. "But that doesn't mean he's trying to help us. No, he's made his choice to stay by Mother."

I flipped through the pictures again. Looking at a broken dock here, a stretch of riverbank there. Almost all of these included some sign of the Thames.

"What if he just wants to goad us?" she said.

I shook my head. I wasn't sure what Joshua was thinking, but the ship movement meant something.

But what could I do about it? It wasn't as if the other ships listened to me the way they were supposed to, because of the Outcast Council's interference. With every command debated and heckled by the Faerie nobles, who also constantly debated and heckled *each other*, it was a wonder anything got done at all.

Father had used the prophecy to get the Faerie Outcasts to go along with him, but he'd had a military battle plan that he'd expected to do the real work. It was the part of this campaign that had given me hope, a carefully designed and detailed plan to cut England off from the rest of the world and hold the Faerie there, slowing them down until their internal politics tore the army apart. With the fractious army the Black Shuck had fielded, and Father's arrangements to hobble England, it should have worked. Especially since the Seelie Army, the Black Shuck's army, had no navy and no real sailors in it.

The problem now was, I had no idea how I was going to make Father's plan work under these conditions. Even worse, I was starting to become sure that Father's plan wasn't going to work at all, no matter how well-executed. He'd relied on the Faerie being disorganized and riddled with strife, the way they always were, only the Black Shuck had changed that. Father's plan just wasn't *enough*.

"You're thinking about trying to go there, aren't you?" Faith said.

"Maybe," I said. "I'm thinking about all of it, really. Not that my plans matter with the stupid Outcast Council standing in my way."

"Shame you can't shoot a cannon off at *them*, isn't it?" Faith said dryly. Even at sea, her hair was still perfect, practically glowing in the partial light. Her soft contralto grew more serious. "Sooner or later, our luck's going to run out. You can't keep exchanging cannon fire with those ships forever."

"It's not luck," I said gravely. "It's that none of the invaders can shoot worth a damn."

Faith snorted softly. "What happens when they learn?"

I didn't have an answer for that. Instead, I turned back to the photographs.

I picked up the Westminster photograph again, then let it fall back into the pile. Something was tickling at the back of my mind. I leafed through some of the other photos. Joshua's point was well made. Beside old, recognizable landmarks, there were all sorts of examples of enormous change. Rivers and lakes where there shouldn't be any, and forests where the water should be.

"I can't look at those again," Faith said. "It's just going to make me burst out into tears."

I picked another one randomly from the pile. This one had been taken from the top of Stormholt and showed, from a very high vantage point, a thick and formidable forest down in the valley below. There had been woods there before on one side of the road, but this was something else again. The road was gone, and the dense foliage looked impassible and forbidding.

"Besides," Faith said, "I wept my eyes out the first week and it didn't do a bloody thing."

I raised an eyebrow. Invasion or not, it was rare to hear Faith use that kind of language. It made me immediately think of Henry, who loved cursing and who was trapped in Faerie right now. If he was lucky. If he wasn't so lucky, he was already dead.

"I know," Faith said, divining my thoughts clearly yet again. "I miss the little hooligan, too."

I snorted. Henry wasn't exactly a hooligan, despite his language, except by Faith's pristine yardstick.

Of course, thoughts of Henry immediately brought thoughts of Benedict. Also trapped in England. Protected from the Faerie, but just as trapped. The Ghost Boys, too. And the Hussars.

We were going to have to get them all out of there.

"It's like what Father told us," I said. "Sometimes the hardest thing to do is exactly the thing you *need* to do. I think this is one of those. So, I don't know how yet, but we'll get them back, or burn all of England down to the water trying."

"How?" she said.

"That's what we need to figure out," I said, tapping the photographs again.

CHAPTER 4

The Council Meeting

"This," I started, "is the British Isles." I pointed to the map laid out on the table. "This is England, Wales, and Scotland, which are already lost to the Black Shuck's troops."

Well, that was a promising start. Unassailable facts. Problem was, the room was packed with Faerie. Even though every Faerie knew the story of their exile from England and the terrible ordeal of their forced exodus across the Bridge of Sorrows, there were few in the room who could even pick England out on a map, and they cared not at all for the rest of the world. I'd already had about a dozen meetings with the Outcast Council and every one of them had been as useful and enjoyable as flossing my teeth with a coping saw.

How did the Black Shuck do it? He wasn't having any problem keeping the Faerie troops together. Every expert agreed that the invaders should have fallen apart by now, only they hadn't. I cast a look at Sands, sitting next to Avonstoke in the corner. The council hadn't even wanted to let them in, but I'd insisted. The more Faith worked with Sands, the more I began to understand that what Father had said about Faerie magic was correct—no magician understood it all. That went double for the Black Shuck, Widdershins, and most of our other enemies. Sands, Prudence, and the others could only guess how their magic worked. We knew next to nothing about the enemy's most potent forces.

We were on the impossibly massive and impractical floating fortress of *Seahome,* in one of the more outrageous and grandiose rooms, which was saying something. Just being off the *Rachaela* made my scalp itch with tension. Being here only made it worse.

The expansive room was dominated by a massive battleship of a table, polished wood with whorls of lighter colors, gold and honey, all through it. There was room enough to seat the forty or fifty people here. Another colossal waste of space in any real ship. The walls were carved and painted in majestic frescos with Faerie religious icons adorning it. The images of the Morrigna behind me, with her triple aspect of the crow, horse, and hag, were unsettling. The hag had a mouth like an open wound, and they all had eyes that burned. The dark, brooding, bloodless countenance of Arawn presiding over the Underworld on the other side of the room wasn't any better. One of the more breathtaking paintings showed Cernunnos and the Wild Hunt, the horned god riding at the head of a marauding herd of dogs, horse and rider through the sky.

These paintings and sculptures were all lit by an artfully crafted skylight overhead that had no business being on a ship of war.

It would have been a magnificent room on land. Here, at sea, it was ludicrous. All of this might have been more tolerable if *Seahome* had been useful in a military sense, but it wasn't. It had few weapons and didn't weather well. It might have been a massive troop transport except it wasn't seaworthy enough to get that close to shore. There were some impressive spells attached to the thing, but all of them engaged in keeping the otherwise unseaworthy beast afloat or keeping the habitants comfortable. The best I'd been able to discern was that it held a *lot* of Faerie, but since only half of the Faerie themselves were at all useful—and since none of the competent ones seemed to be in charge—that, too, was a complete wash.

"What," said one of the Faerie officers in clipped tones that stank of a disdain, "is that . . . ugly little niblet there?" I think he might have been *Seahome's* captain.

I kept my face neutral, though it nearly killed me. "That would be *Ireland*." I needed help from these people, specifically a magician to get my ship through the mist, and I knew the Outcast Fleet, represented by the lords and ladies here, had at least three.

"That would be Ireland, *my lord*," the noble corrected icily. Incompetent *and* irritating.

"Yes, my lord," I said, ready to kick over the table and throttle every single bloody lord in the room. Which would be, of course, nearly everyone present. I took a deep breath. Get the magician, *then* murder everyone with bare hands.

The forty Court Faerie lords and ladies all looked the same: tall, beautiful, hard, and magnificently dressed. Coats, tunics, cloaks, capes, hatwear and slippers done up in swirling colors of cobalt, blood, silver, emerald, gold, and darkness. They clearly didn't care much for me, either. That might be partly because of my human heritage or the fact that I was one of the race that had kicked them out of England. Or it could be because I was trying to draw them into a battle tactic that none of them wanted. Plenty of reasons, take your pick.

I felt absurd now in the stiff broadcloth uniform that Sands had found for this occasion. The cobalt cloth, frogged with white, had seemed grand back on the deck of the *Rachaela,* echoing the many glorious uniforms I'd seen and lusted after in books, but it felt shockingly drab and austere compared to the Faerie finery. Also, it was damnably hot in this room and the uniform wasn't making that any better. I could have done without the hat, too. They look glorious in old paintings, those hats, but just try and wear one. All my vast reading in naval engagements had taught me how to weather out a storm and ride close-hauled to the wind, but none of those books had warned me about the hats.

"Could we get help from France?" Lady Druhagaren asked. "Or the Americas?"

Lady Druhagaren, short, dour, and durable-looking, was the leader of the Dwarves on *Seahome,* one of the dozen or so members of the Outcast Council that weren't Court Faerie. Most of them had been conspicuously silent and this was the first time the Dwarven woman had spoken.

"As if we'd want help from the French!" one of the Court Faerie nobles quipped and there was a smattering of strained laughter.

"It's a fair question," I said, "but I don't see how they'd be much help. Modern ships can't enter the mist at all. Engines break down. Normal gunpowder stops working. We know a few have tried anyway and were lost in the mist. Our own attempts to communicate with them haven't been successful. Every ship we've sent out of the mist has been fired upon."

"To the rest of the world," Faith added. "England has become lost behind the mist." Faith, sitting a little to my left, fit in with the Faerie nobility far better than I did.

"They can't tell the difference between us and the invaders," I said. If we'd been able to send ships peopled by human sailors, we might have been able to open a dialogue, but we'd had no luck at that so far.

"What good would they be, regardless?" said another of the non-Court Faerie delegates. She had a woman's face with a lion's body, and white eagle's wings, tucked carefully in these close quarters. A sphinx, though she didn't look Egyptian at all, being fair and golden-haired. Her accent marked her as French.

There was a murmur of general hostility. There was no love lost between the Faerie and the mortal governments. I tried not to sigh outwardly.

The door slammed open and Lady Rue appeared, her spiky hair plainly outlined in the golden sky behind her. I should have known she wouldn't miss the opportunity to harass any plan that might injure the enemy.

The Faerie didn't have a leader, exactly, but Lady Rue was the highest-ranked noble in the Outcast Fleet, and everyone fell silent. She strode into the room, damnably smug, and sauntered to the head of the table, where several other nobles hesitated, and then cleared out for her. I found myself biting my lip and made myself stop. All hope I had of getting a magician had died with her entrance.

Lady Rue looked askance at the most ornate of the chairs at the head of the table, so recently vacated, and looked from the chair to the nearest noble still sitting, then back at the chair.

The noble jumped up in a sudden fit of etiquette and hastily yanked the chair out so that Lady Rue could sit. She did, then looked back at the still open doorway as two more figures stepped through.

Figures I'd last seen on *the Blood Oath* next to the Lady of Sorrows: our half-sisters Hope and Charity.

Clearly, the Lady of Sorrows had taken Father to Faerie, as planned, but for some reason Hope and Charity had stayed.

This close, Hope looked even sterner, with flat, dark hair, pale skin, and a black haunting gaze that darted around the room. She was even less elegant than I usually was, in something that might have been a shift—or a burlap bag.

Then I looked at her feet and squinted. She threw a shadow not of a girl, but of a bristling wolf. It shouldn't have been surprising, considering what we'd seen before, but it made my hackles rise anyway.

Charity was in a navy-blue frock that set off her shiny, golden curls. Her eyes were a startling blue. She only looked about eight years old, but then she tipped her head to one side, clearly listening to the growl of Hope's shadow, and smiled. It was an ancient, timeless smile. No little girl had a smile like that.

"The bastard Kasric children," Charity said. Her voice was a little girl's, high and soft. Her tone was neutral, as if 'bastard' might be a nice thing to say, and I didn't know how to respond to that.

"Your lord and ladyships," Lady Rue said, "I present Hope and Charity du Thorns." There was a general clamor and buzz to the room and Lady Rue took her time waving it down. I heard the whisper, in the room: "The Virtues!"

This business again. The idea of seven daughters born of the Lord of Thorns banding together into a prophetic, mystical force sounded just as foolish to me now as it had before. Especially as most of us wanted nothing to do with it. Add the fact that Hope and Charity and Faith and I weren't exactly what you call *close*, and this just felt like another part of Father's plan that had already failed. Besides, Father had said that two of our sisters had died. But you couldn't tell Lady Rue that. I could see a lot of the other Faerie nobles nodding, too, so she wasn't the only one.

Lady Rue let the buzz and whispering go on for an interminable time, but finally she gestured, and the two girls took the seats next to her, all of them turning to look at me standing there like an imbecile with my pointer and map of England.

"You were saying, Admiral," Lady Rue said sweetly to me.

I mustered myself and pressed on. "The Lord of Thorns' plan . . ." I felt tripped up already. It felt too casual to call him Father, but Lord of Thorns felt strange too, and just the mention of him set the room abuzz again. Never mind. Keep going. "The plan was simple, but ruthless. While the Seelie Court can field a vastly superior force on land, they have almost no naval power at their disposal. So, since he couldn't stop them from getting to England, he opted for the only choice left. Cede England and Scotland entirely, but load it with booby traps, in this case black iron spikes laid out with the railroad tracks to hinder their movement, the hope being that if we could pen them up while making England and Scotland inhospitable, that the Seelie army would lose morale and leave."

"A plan, no doubt," the sphinx woman said, "relying on the Faerie invaders squabbling amongst themselves. There's never been a Faerie army of this size. They can't possibly remain united for any length of time." She was a brunette, wearing her hair in a tight bun and had spectacles on her face.

"There's never been an army composed of Seelie and Unseelie before, either," Lady Rue said. "Would any of you have thought that possible?"

"They'll be at each other's throats any minute!" a lumpy man in beggar's clothing said. He was the leader of the Jötnar—Trolls and Ogres and all manner of scary beasts. At least that's what Prudence had said. He looked like a short, wizened man with a missing arm and his ragged sleeve tied in a knot near the shoulder, but my ghost eye could see a hulking, tusked outline around him.

"They should have fallen apart already!" another of the Court Faerie said. "Months ago! But they haven't!"

There was a general murmur of denial around the room.

"Exactly," the Lady Rue said. "Unbelievable enough that the winter and summer courts can agree on a goal for any length of time, but the Black Shuck has actually found some way to keep their military forces working together, something that's been unheard of during my lifetime, which is extensive, I can assure you. That's why we can't take any chances. We bide our time. We wait."

"Wait for what?" Faith said.

"For the other two sisters, of course." She made a little shooing motion with her hand. "Then we send your little horde in. Couldn't be simpler."

"But how much longer?" one of the nobles burst out.

"What if they don't show up?" another said.

"We can't wait for mythical sisters that probably aren't even coming!" I blurted out. "We need to reconnoiter the coast. There's too much we don't know about what's happening there. The measures left behind, the black iron, our perimeter . . . it's all slowed them down, but how much longer?"

"Approaching the coast is too dangerous," another of the Faerie nobles said. A stuffy man with a purple and green waistcoat, an oversized raven brooch, and brilliant white hair cut into flattop bristles. "Expeditions might never come out again."

"I think," the Sphinx woman said, "that we all know that wars are not won by battle plans or strategies."

"What?" I said, disbelieving. What else was there? "Of course they are. The Lord of Thorns was your greatest general. He's never lost. That's the whole reason you follow the House of Thorns, isn't it?"

"He never lost a battle until now," the Faerie noble with bristly white hair said with a nasty sneer. I had nothing to say to that. The campaign this year had gone entirely to hell in a handbasket, and we all knew it. He'd lost battles by the bushel load now. Of course, with Father's slow progression towards humanity, you could make the very real argument that the Lord of Thorns, as the world of Faerie knew him, hadn't been leading the defense against the Faerie invasion. Father had. What little I knew of Father's machinations before assuming human form made my blood run cold, so I was grateful that he wasn't that man anymore, but it was clear that the amoral, cruel version of the Lord of Thorns was the better general. I wondered if those things *had* to go hand-in-hand. I hoped not.

"Strategy," Lady Rue said, "is a human tool. In Faerie, battles are won through *magic*. Through power. The Lord of Thorns must have bound his power up into the seven of you." She waved her hand at me, Faith, and our two hostile half-sisters next to her. "We just need to follow his plan. No sense for the rest of us to get ourselves killed to no purpose, is there?"

"That's nonsense!" Faith said. "You just kick us all into a boat and expect us to . . . what . . . just blast an entire *army* into submission?"

"No," Lady Rue said, speaking very slowly as if we were all very stupid. "The Seven Virtues will vanquish the Seven Sins. The Black Shuck, Widdershins, and all the rest. After that, I'm sure the Faerie army will simply . . ." She waved her hands. "Fall apart."

I looked over at Sands, still cowering in the corner. He looked so awed and intimidated by the two magicians as to be incapacitated. He'd become more and more nervous around magicians after having his own magical power stripped. It made my heart break to see him this way. It wasn't just magical ability he'd lost, that much was clear.

"You're off your rocker!" Faith snapped.

"The Lord of Thorns," the Sphinx said, "always emerged victorious because he had the favor of the Highest, the gods."

"Your gods?" I said, stunned. "You want to *pray* for help?"

"Of course the Gods," Lady Rue said. She swept the rest of the room with her gaze. "I ask you, which would you rather put your faith in? A hodgepodge of iron train tracks and ships and cannon and other human stratagems, or the real power of something like the Wild Hunt? The Lord of Thorns, through long years of planning, has harnessed the same powers that drove us out of England in the first place, human religion, and combined them with our own deities. A group of Virtues that has both the power of the human *and* the Faerie gods behind it."

"How do you know?" I said, with a sudden flash of insight. "Father didn't even tell his own magician the full details. What makes you so sure?"

The barest flicker of uncertainty went across Lady Rue's face, then was gone. "I can feel the surge of magical forces. The powers converge. Can't you feel it?"

"Oh," Faith burst out, "that is the purest load of tepid nonsense I've ever heard in my life." The room buzzed around us at Faith's words.

"Little fledgling magician," Lady Rue sneered. She had to raise her own voice as the clamor rose around us. "That is because you know nothing. You are nothing."

"Which is it?" I shot back. "Are we *powerful forces,*" and here I let all my formality drop. "Or are we nothing and no one? It can't be both!" I was more than willing to go sneer for sneer with this hateful woman. She was worse than the Black Shuck in my mind. I had to shout even louder now. "Next time you concoct a *lie*, Lady, try and make it at least a little believable!"

"I'll have your carcass on a platter!" the Lady Rue hissed.

Avonstoke was suddenly next to me, looking stern and *very* tall, but the Lady Rue didn't look at all fazed by his presence.

"Guards!" she shouted, and the door flew open.

But it wasn't guards at the door, only a single man, unarmed, not large.

"Oh *yes,*" a cadaverous voice said from the doorway, and such was the power of his voice that it cut effortlessly through the din. "Yes, let's bundle up our most powerful assets and put them in the brig. I'm sure *that* will solve all our problems. Then we can all go home, yes?"

The room went silent. Everyone turned to look, even the Lady Rue.

The man standing there looked positively ancient. Withered, and hobbled, but strong, like an old and dark tree root. He peered out with vulturous eyes over a huge, beaklike nose. He looked old the way mountains are old, strong rather than frail. He wasn't a court Faerie, or any of the other Faerie races, as far as I could tell, but human, although an unimaginably and inhumanly ancient one. Looking at him with my ghost eye didn't change his appearance at all. He wore a black robe that practically *screamed* wizard.

The old man took a few steps into the room and fixed Hope and Charity with a steely gaze. "Are you two ready to call yourselves Virtues and saviors of the war? Ready to take on armies on your own?"

Hope shook her head, looking angrily at Lady Rue. Charity had a thoughtful look on her face, which she turned from the old man to Faith and me, and then back to the old man.

"No," she said. "The first we heard of it was this morning. Us? Born and bred in Faerie? Carrying the burning spirit of some human religion? I hardly think so."

"What about you two?" he said, looking at Faith and me. "You want to take on that army single-handedly?"

"No," I said.

Faith shook her head.

"Did you really think," the old man said, turning to Lady Rue, "that five young girls were going to take this war off your hands?"

"Seven," the Lady Rue said stoutly. "There are seven Virtues, Drecovian, not five."

I knew the name, if not the man. Drecovian was one of the magicians for the Outcast Fleet, one I hadn't been allowed to meet until now.

"But we don't *have* seven," Drecovian said. "Do we? We don't even have *five*. Not really."

"They will come to understand," Lady Rue said. "And I know where the sixth is."

I stared at her. Father had said not to rely on that prophecy. Sands had said that they'd lost two of the Virtues anyway, years ago. Now it seemed that Lady Rue knew where at least one of them was. Unless she was lying?

"And the seventh?" Drecovian said.

Lady Rue waved a hand dismissively. "Not yet. She will be revealed to us soon. It has to be soon."

"Father told us," I said, "not to rely on that plan. He said the Black Shuck was too strong."

"Nonsense," the Lady Rue said.

"It was only *his* plan," I said. "What should he know about it?"

"His plan?" the Lady Rue said. "Is that what you think? He's merely a pawn in this, as are we all. These are movements of forces you can't possibly understand."

"You understand," Drecovian said mildly, "far less than you think. At least, that's what *she* tells me." He pointed up as he said this, but who he might mean, god or otherwise, I wasn't sure.

He stepped into the room, followed by Prudence, our half-sister. It was a family reunion now. I, Faith, Prudence and the two Faerie girls, Hope and Charity. Five Virtues, except that we were more likely to murder each other than fight the Black Shuck. I wasn't feeling terribly Virtuous right now.

"I, for one," Prudence said tartly, "am not planning on re-conquering an entire country by my lonesome, either. In case you were wondering." Prudence, as always, looked completely non-descript, with her drab clothes and ordinary face. She might have come from London, if you didn't notice how completely and uniformly gray she was—hair, skin, clothes, everything except for those clear, blue eyes. When she spoke, those eyes danced with a clever and caustic wit. She wasn't exactly a comforting presence to me, but Father trusted her, and she was clearly annoying Lady Rue, so that was something.

"We are done here," Lady Rue said, standing. "For now, we are content to follow this entertaining, if useless attempt at a naval blockade, but the *real* plan is in the hands of the gods." The room was still clearly hers, the other council members nodding at her every word.

"The House of Thorns," Drecovian said, "and their admiral, have my support. And *hers*. We'll continue the blockade, and the raids. I'll not see the entire war sink because of your blind foolishness."

I didn't know who he meant by 'hers,' but clearly everyone else did. His statement caused a stir and lots of silent looks among the council, but Lady's Rue flinty gaze brought them back around. They all stood, following the Lady Rue.

"You'll see, Drecovian," the Lady Rue said serenely as she swept from the room. "The gods will have their way."

Her departure triggered a glittering stampede as the rest of the Court Faerie nobles and other council members filed out after her. Most of them looked bored. They might have been following the Lady Rue and other capricious Court Faerie nobles around to innumerable inexplicable and unproductive meetings for centuries. Perhaps they had.

"Even *she,*" Prudence said, "won't keep Lady Rue at bay forever. Besides, if we can't keep the Black Shuck's army in England, the whole plan falls apart, gods or no gods. The minute any part of that army gets a foothold on the mainland, it's all over."

"I know," I said. "That's why we need to see what's going on behind the mist. If the Black Shuck is readying ships, we need to know what kind and how many."

"It probably won't be a surprise," Prudence said, "when I tell you that I'm not expecting a lot of help from *that* lot."

"I thought as much," I said. "I'm taking the *Rachaela* up the Thames. I want to see what Joshua is doing myself."

Prudence paced the length of the floor, then stopped and spun to face me. "Who knows what you might find there? What kind of magical defenses the Black Shuck has waiting for you. Who will deal with them?" She looked Faith in the eye. "You?"

Prudence turned on Sands, still frozen in the corner. He flinched as she stepped in his direction. "You?" she said with disdain. Sands bowed his head.

"Perhaps," Drecovian said in his grating voice, "an expedition is not such a bad idea."

Prudence spun on him now. "Idiocy."

"*She* thinks they should go," Drecovian said mildly. "*She* says that there are powers in the world of Faerie they need to confront. They need to go, and soon."

The magician hadn't raised his voice, but the words still stopped Prudence in her tracks. Mr. Sands, too, all but ignored in his corner, suddenly sat erect, his mustache quivering. Avonstoke, uncharacteristically silent this entire time, watched avidly.

Prudence stood, stunned, for the space of a heartbeat or so, and then she shrugged. "You didn't tell me that."

Drecovian shrugged.

"Does *she* say," Avonstoke said, "if *she* thinks that Justice and Faith will come out of England?"

Both Drecovian and Prudence looked back at him suddenly, clearly surprised.

Finally, Prudence looked at Drecovian.

Drecovian just shook his head. "She doesn't know. Or she won't say. I can never tell."

"Who is this *she* you keep talking about?" Faith said.

"It's funny that you should ask that," Drecovian said, standing up.

"Funny?" Faith said.

"She wants to meet you," Drecovian went on. "In order to begin your magician's training."

"Magician's training?" Faith said.

"This room is rather small," Prudence said, looking around, "to have such an echo." Drecovian grinned again. It wasn't a comforting sight.

"I thought," Faith said, "that Mr. Sands was going to help me with my training."

Drecovian snorted. "No."

"I'm not going anywhere," Faith said, "if you can't even answer a straight question. Who is *she* and why haven't I heard about *her* by now?"

"The most powerful living magician," Prudence said, "wants to train you. What else do you need to know?"

"Is *she* powerful enough have a name?" Faith snapped. She wasn't backing down for Prudence or Drecovian or anyone without some answers. I felt a strange premonition in my gut, like I was watching a terrible crash occur, very slowly, but I was powerless to stop it.

"Brocara is her name," Drecovian said, "and you've already met her, in a way. She saved your life. The lives of everyone on your ship, in fact."

Faith and I exchanged another look. I didn't have any idea who they were talking about. Sands' face was ashen. Obviously, he did, and just as obviously, it wasn't anyone he'd mentioned to us.

"Oh, sweet dears," Prudence said. "Brocara is the *dragon*."

"She's looking forward," Drecovian said, looking at Faith, "very much, to meeting you."

CHAPTER 5

The Dragon

"You want us," I said, "to meet a *dragon*?"

"No," Prudence said absently. "We want *Faith* to meet a dragon. Or rather, the dragon wants to meet Faith. But you might as well come, too. Just the two of you." She looked dismissively at Avonstoke and Sands. She seemed distracted, as if part of her was always listening to songs calling out to her, ballads from misty, rolling hills. Songs Faith and I, being raised in England, could never hear.

"That," Avonstoke said, "is a remarkably lax view of etiquette and invitation."

He flexed his hand and that black sword of his appeared out of nowhere, a slice of gleaming midnight in brightly lit room. He stepped forward so that the tip pressed into the front of Drecovian's neck. As always, looking right at the thing made me uneasy.

"You dare turn my own magic against me?" Drecovian hissed. He sounded stunned. I was a little stunned myself.

"I do, actually," Avonstoke said. His smile was dazzling. "Just consider it my whimsical nature." Avonstoke shot a glance my way, so fast I almost missed it, and yet I had no doubt whatsoever as to its meaning. In half an instant, he'd discarded his relationship with this magician and possibly betrayed an oath of loyalty with the Faerie.

There was gravity in the air. I could see it in Drecovian's expression. Avonstoke had done it for us, for *me*.

Avonstoke turned up the wattage on his smile and pushed at Drecovian's neck with his blade until the magician hissed and backed away, bumping into the table behind him. Avonstoke followed him unerringly, keeping the tip of his blade exactly in place on the other man's neck.

"You will promise them safe passage. Both of you." He flicked a sharp look at Prudence to make his meaning clear, but brought his attention sharply back to Drecovian.

"Just when you think," Prudence said, staring at Avonstoke, "that all the surprising things have gone out of the world. First, the platypus, now this."

"I can only promise so much," Drecovian said anxiously. "She is a *dragon*. She doesn't have to listen to me. She doesn't have to listen to anyone."

"At least," Avonstoke said cheerfully, "I'll have the solace of knowing that the dragon had to chew her way through two of Faerie's most powerful magicians to get to the people under my protection. Won't I?" Drecovian's neck was bleeding, a thin rivulet that ran down and stained the front of his robe. A thin curl of smoke floated up from the point of the sword's contact.

Drecovian sighed. "I promise. I'll protect her with my life." He seemed in pain and exasperated more than afraid.

Avonstoke grinned triumphantly, then, without moving the sword, cocked an eyebrow at Prudence.

She snorted. "Fine. I agree. Safe passage. On my honor."

"Delightful." Avonstoke pulled the sword back, then unsummoned it, sending it back to wherever the hell it came from.

Sands had called Drecovian a shadow magician. I remembered Avonstoke's tattoos and what he'd told me about them. He'd said a magician had cast them for his Father. Clearly, not just any magician.

"You made his Raven tattoo," I blurted out. "And his magical scimitar!"

"Yes," Drecovian snapped. "Clearly a mistake."

"You taught me about dragons, too," Avonstoke said. "About how dangerous they are. See how well I listened?"

"Bah!" Drecovian spat, but I thought I saw a grudging respect when he looked at Avonstoke.

"How much," I said, "will your promises matter if the dragon *does* get cranky?"

"Not much," Drecovian admitted. He glared at me. "So don't *make* her cranky, eh?" He gingerly touched a finger to his neck and then glared at the smear of blood on it.

"Of course," Avonstoke said, "if something happens to either of them, it won't be just *me* looking for revenge. The crew of the *Rachaela* are loyal to their captain and magician. Should they be harmed, the *Rachaela* could easily turn on *Seahome* and blow it out of the water."

I felt my eyebrows lift. Would they? Would they really? I'd been working hard to win them over, but I hadn't thought I'd been very successful. Maybe Avonstoke was overplaying things?

Prudence, who hadn't been even remotely upset by Avonstoke's threats, now suddenly got angry. "One Outcast ship firing on another? Might as well hand the Black Shuck the rest of the world!"

"Same could be said," Avonstoke said, "of losing one of our Virtues."

I groaned. "Don't tell me you believe in this Virtue nonsense!"

"Of course, my Captain," he said. He bowed deeply.

"Can't go," a voice in the corner croaked. It was Sands. He'd struggled to his feet and was trying to stay upright, swaying gently. "Dragons have their own agendas. Can't trust them. Could ruin everything."

"We're going," Faith said. Her mind was made up.

With those words, Sands seemed to lose his brief moment of strength, feeble as it was, and sagged. Faith had to jump forward and grab his arm to keep him from falling to the floor again.

"It'll be all right," she whispered, guiding him to a chair. "You'll see."

He just sobbed and put his face in his hands.

"You'll see," Faith said again, sounding less sure of herself. Then she stood up. "Let's go, before I lose my nerve."

"Yes," I said.

Faith left Sands with a last, helpless look. I hesitated.

"I'll make sure he gets safely back to the ship," Avonstoke said gently.

"Thank you," Faith said. She was about to turn towards the door, but then impulsively stepped forward and kissed Avonstoke briefly on the cheek. He looked as surprised by that as by anything else that had happened this visit.

"Thank you," Faith said again, and went out the door.

Avonstoke got an entirely different, more speculative, expression on his face as I stepped over to him.

"Thank you," I said, feeling awkward and stupid in my dress uniform. I didn't dare follow Faith's example, not even a kiss on the cheek. All I could think about were other kisses and I didn't dare. Only now, the brief, smoldering moments that Avonstoke and I had shared before felt incredibly distant.

I patted him on the arm, feeling a complete and total ass.

He grinned, as if enjoying my discomfort. Then he caught my hand, turned my hand palm up, and pressed his warm mouth to the soft part of my wrist.

"Oh, my Captain," he murmured.

"What are you doing?" I said, snatching my hand back. "That's not . . . oh!"

That smile of his flashed again, then he was suddenly serious. "Be careful of the dragon. Come back to us."

I nodded stiffly, my outrage washed away by remembering who it was we were going to see.

Faith was at the door, leaning back in. "Are you coming?"

Seahome was a bastardized hodgepodge of a place, a hundred or so different rafts tied together into a single big one. It felt more like a temporary city than a ship. But a city gone mad. The individual pieces of raft bobbed in a completely independent motion from each other, so each building swayed out of step with the next.

Looking at the place from one of the rickety, three-story wooden towers made me distinctly nauseous. The whole thing felt like a jigsaw puzzle that the sea was about to tear apart.

We made our way out of the council meeting chamber into a village square arrangement of primitive huts, then past buildings of livestock and several sections that formed an honest-to-God garden. Some idiot had shoveled about a ton of dirt onto a raft for the purpose of, not growing tomatoes or squash or something else you could eat, but a bunch of silvery little shrubs placed merely for decoration.

With my ghost eye, I could see glamours and minor Faerie illusions everywhere, as casual as tablecloths and lace, used in a variety of odd ways. Curtains glamoured to look blue instead of red. Doorways blocked with spells of darkness to spare someone the effort of installing an actual door. Laundry made invisible rather than washed. It was as chaotic as everything the Faerie did. None of it had any business being afloat.

The many multi-colored and differently shaped sails didn't make any sense, either. They were in contradictory positions all over, used to catch magical—and as far as I could fathom, *only* magical—winds. Even the breeze was a fickle thing on *Seahome,* on account of all the tampering, so that gusts and wisps came from all over like snatches of fifty different conversations I couldn't quite make out.

There were enough wide-open spaces to allow platoons to hold drills. From the center, you couldn't even see the water.

Prudence led us over a swaying catwalk above a stable. We could hear hooves moving restlessly in the building below and smell the comfy, homey scent of horses, which was nice, but the place was roofed in with a woven, latticed series of planks that looked far too pretty and delicate to stop any of us if we pitched off the wildly heaving plank bridge. That wasn't as comforting.

Faith was looking around, too. "Wasn't this a real bridge before?"

"I recognize that purple lateen sail," I said, pointing up. "We passed under it last time, but where did the row of tents go?"

"That's how you know you're in the Royal sector," Prudence said. "You're right to watch the sails. They're landmarks. It's easier if you pay attention to the sails rather than all the . . ." she waved her hands in a fluttering motion that took in everything around them. ". . . the things underneath. The various tribes, clans or families move the buildings around some, but never the sails. Your little boat is this way, in the Bittergourd sector."

"The sails never move?" I said. I knew the answer to my next question, but just couldn't help myself. "What if you need to change direction? They don't move *at all*?"

"Good lord, no," Prudence said. "I'd never find anything if they started moving the sails all over. You don't do that on the *Rachaela*, do you?"

"Occasionally," I said dryly.

"What an odd way to run a ship," Prudence said, looking honestly perplexed. She shrugged and led the way through an alley formed by two rickety buildings.

I took two steps into the narrow gap between two buildings and blanched. "What is that *smell*?"

Faith looked even worse than I felt. "Oh god," she said. She looked ready to vomit on the spot.

Prudence turned, fixed us with her blue gaze and shrugged again. "One is, I believe, a tannery run by the Jötnar. The other is a Goblin charcuterie. There's some relation between the two but

I've learned not to ask some questions. Honestly, I can't even tell you which is which. Come on." There wasn't much choice but to follow.

"How in the world do you live here?" I said. "With everything moving all the time?"

"I love the place," Prudence said. "Feels like home. Back in Faerie things were always moving around."

"Where was that?" I asked, curious despite myself. This strange woman was our half-sister, after all, and I knew next to nothing about her.

"At the Cragged Cliffs," she said. "Among the Jötnar. Things were always changing there, even the Jötnar themselves."

"Which Jötnar?" Faith asked. "You mean the Trolls?"

"The cities in the cliffs are mostly populated by Trolls," Prudence said, "but I lived in Wyck's Hall, which is a bit like a monastery, run mostly by Ogres. They're the best shapeshifters, you see. They work harder, I think, them being the smallest among the Jötnar. Father wanted me to learn from them."

"You learned magic from Ogres?" The only Jötnar I'd been around for more than a few minutes was the Troll in our cargo hold, and she hadn't impressed as a deep thinker.

"Oh yes," Prudence said. "I learned many things." There was a twinkle in her blue eyes, as if she could tell exactly how much curiosity burned inside of me.

The sky was grayish blue overhead, mostly clear, which was a blessing. This floating load of kindling was ticklish enough to handle or walk around on during calm weather.

Prudence led us around a short, square little building, little more than a glorified shed, though the Faerie had dressed it up with a few ragged tapestries.

We turned the corner and saw the dragon.

A hole the size of a house was cut into the raft, leaving only the green-gray water. The dragon lay on the far side, in a large stretch of raft left bare, it seemed, just for this purpose. It turned its enormous, black, scaled head and regarded us a moment. The tail swished restlessly on the deck. The movement was graceful, serpentine, and terrifying. There was that same sense of coiled power you get with a snake, only about a thousand times more so. The sense that, as unimaginably powerful as the thing looked, there was more strength and power hidden under the surface.

Then, moving quicker and more smoothly than anything that large had a right to, it shifted its bulk and slid into the water. The tail disappeared last in a flash of black spines.

The water lapped at the edge of the hole, showing no sign of the monster. A sail flapped somewhere in the breeze behind us.

"Where did it go?" Faith said. "I thought it wanted me to come . . ."

Then water exploded upwards in a giant fountain as the dragon flew out of the ocean right in front of us.

Someone screamed. I'm pretty sure it was me. I pawed for my pistol but then dropped it on the deck. I bent to grab it, but Faith grabbed my coat and kept me from it. She was probably right. No sense *making* the dragon kill us. Besides, what good would a revolver do? Six shots didn't seem near enough. Faith looked far calmer than I felt, which didn't make any sense to me.

Cannon and gunfire made her shriek, but dragons apparently didn't faze her.

But it fazed the bloody hell out of me. This was a *dragon.* A monstrous impossibility right in front of us. Unreasonable fear was the only reasonable response.

The dragon slithered up onto the raft within a dozen feet of us, so close that the water sheeting off the oilskin hide sprayed all over, leaving the salt taste of spray on my face. I realized I was about to pass out from holding my breath and forced myself to take a deep lungful of air. I noticed even Prudence, normally unflappable, had taken a step back. Drecovian and Faith weren't shaken the way we were, but even they were clearly affected.

No one said anything. The wind sighed and the mismatched rigging of the Faerie raft creaked all around us. The sea sloshed against the lip of the square opening and the deck groaned alarmingly beneath the weight of the dragon in front of us. The cascade of water coming off the dragon's back slowed from a rush to a drip, drip, drip. The dragon's breath was hot and heavy and carried an odor of steam and hot rocks basking in the desert sun. The twenty- or thirty-foot-long tail lashed the deck to our left with a restless whisper.

I squinted and looked at the dragon with my ghost eye, then immediately wished I hadn't. It wasn't that there was some horrible secret glamour over top of the dragon, but the fact that there *wasn't* was unnerving. On a ship reeking with magic and glamour and deceptions both large and small, the dragon was exactly what it appeared to be. And what it appeared to be was terrifying.

"Good," the dragon said. "You have come. I am Brocara." The dragon's voice was softer than I'd expected, but effortlessly powerful, like the most restrained and smallest of earthquakes. "Two of the Virtues, yes?" The massive head lowered until the mouth full of serrated sickles, burning yellow eyes, and crown of rough, jagged, black horns came down to our level. The dragon tilted its head with a sudden, terrifying, motion to fix me with one burning eye. Too fast, too fast, even with that small motion.

Nothing that big should be that fast.

"Name?" the dragon hissed, sending more of that hot, burnt air past me. "I have spoken *my* name. I require *yours*. Which virtue are you?"

"Justice," I squeaked. "Justice Kasric."

"Justice," the dragon repeated. "Justice." Tasting the name as if the sound and idea were both foreign, human concepts of which it had only a shallow understanding.

"Blessed of Llyr," the dragon rumbled. "I can smell the seawater. But I see the mark of the Morrigna on you, too. Curious." She turned her monstrous gaze on Faith. "You are the elder sister, yes. The magician?"

"Yes," Faith said. "At least I'm supposed to be." She looked tense, but not terrified, like I was. That angered and shamed me a bit, which helped me get my terror under control. Prudence and Drecovian, damn them, had retreated a short distance, which wasn't at all comforting.

"Hmm . . ." If mountains could purr, they might make the sound that now poured from the dragon's throat. "Which virtue are you?"

"Faith."

The dragon chuckled, a noise like giant hands crushing boulders. "Are you now?" The chuckle somehow made me feel as if the dragon understood the concept of faith as a virtue, unlike justice, and found it very amusing.

The massive head retreated to crow's nest height and regarded us solemnly. How did we not see this dragon before? Then it turned and slithered (the dragon had feet, fore and aft, in addition to wings, which acted like a third set, but its movement was so smooth and sinuous that a word like 'walked' just didn't seem to fit) a few steps to our right, which was about thirty yards to the rest of us, and prostrated herself bonelessly on the warm deck. She stretched in the sun.

"You will take," the dragon said, "*tea*." It wasn't a question.

Drecovian had acquired a staff somewhere when I wasn't looking, a heavy, dark, knobbed thing with a forked head that might have once been one of the dragon's spikes. Now he thumped it authoritatively against the deck.

One of the tiny little shacks we'd passed had its tapestry door pushed aside and half a dozen Goblins marched out, each of them carrying a bewildering array of wooden artifacts. They didn't seem in the same kind of hurry I'd probably be if a dragon had given me orders. More like business as usual, really, that organized flurry of activity that bespoke endless repetition. Brocara must order tea a lot.

Faith and I followed, somewhat in a daze.

Two of the wooden instruments fit together to form a low, avocado-colored table, carved with images, of all things, of turtles gamboling in the surf. A black tray embossed with silver dolphins appeared out of a box, as did a silver urn with steam trickling out of the spout, the rest of the tea service, also silver, and a white china tea set, all laid out with alacrity and precision enough to make me ponder the possibility of stealing any of these Goblins for my topsail crew. A small fire was laid out in a copper bowl and a kettle hung with a wooden bracket over the flame.

"You like," Faith said, "tea?" She still seemed supernaturally calm. I wasn't sure I could have spoken without stammering.

"No," Brocara rumbled. She lowered her head again so that she could regard us more closely, which wasn't a comforting thing. Not at all. Too many teeth and horns for that. She twisted her long, powerful neck so that she could look at us with first one yellow eye, and then the other. The huge, golden orbs were colossal versions of the Court Faeries' eyes, like Avonstoke's. In fact, it seemed like very little of the Faerie had anything like normal eyes and it made me wonder about the connection.

All magic stemmed from dragons, Avonstoke had said. The Faerie themselves were magical, I knew, which implied an interesting relationship. Avonstoke, despite being a Faerie, didn't seem to *know* a lot about dragons that he hadn't already told us. Or magic. Any more than I knew automatically about plumbing or sausage-making just because I was British, I suppose. Mr. Sands also had huge gaps, which meant that we didn't have anyone who really understood Faerie magic.

More and more, I was thinking that no one did. Maybe I should ask the dragon?

"If you don't like tea . . ." Faith said.

"It is too acrid for my taste," Brocara said. "But I adore the *ritual*. Rituals are your species' greatest contributions to magic and culture, don't you think?"

"I've never thought about it," Faith admitted.

"You *should,*" Brocara said. "How do you take it?" She fixed me with one eye.

"Um . . . extra sweet," I said. "No milk."

"Good," Brocara rumbled. "Common ground at last." She turned that great eye to Faith. "And you?"

"Just milk."

The dragon chuckled, as if Faith had committed a faux pas. "I have never cared for milk, myself. It seems like the wrong way to taste cow. The traces of it make me hunger for the rest. But there is no place for animal flesh in the ritual, is there?"

"Especially not the way you eat," Drecovian said mildly. The two magicians seemed to have relaxed a great deal. Perhaps we weren't going to be eaten after all.

The Goblins set out chairs before most of them disappeared back into the tapestry shack. The remaining Goblin set out the service, including a green ceramic pot, and then tended the small fire. When the water was at a rolling boil, he used a carefully measured amount to warm up the pot and then dumped that out. He then added a precise amount of black tea leaves from a cloth pouch and then added the rest of the boiling water. There was just enough remaining to fill the pot with not a drop wasted. I sniffed as the tea steeped. Despite all the care and ceremony, it didn't smell at *all* like good tea.

The goblin put a worn, lavender knit tea cozy on the pot while we waited. In addition to our smaller cups, there was a large, shallow bowl for the dragon.

Drecovian, sitting next to me, smiled ruefully. "I am not much for tea, either," he admitted. "But the cup warms the old bones in my hands, which is always welcome."

"Well," Prudence said. "I *love* it. One of the few things I get that reminds me of England, about which I know little." Her expression fell. "England as it was before the Faerie, that is. Not how it is now, of course." There was an awkward silence. No one wanted to talk about what England might be like now.

"That has steeped long enough, I think, Eegan," Brocara said.

The Goblin attendant, Eegan, presumably, serenely poured out the tea.

"Remember now," Brocara said. "Sugar for me and Admiral Kasric. Cream for Dra Faith, both for Drecovian and no sugar or cream for Prudence."

Eegan nodded.

"I am very curious," Brocara rumbled, "about the quality of tea, now that we have an actual Englishperson here to advise us." She gave Drecovian and Prudence a deep, blazing, one-eyed, sidelong glance of recrimination.

Drecovian shrugged. "Who knew that there was anything complicated about tea?"

Brocara sighed, a mountain range filled with steam pipes. "How can we possibly save a culture we don't understand?"

Faith was the first to put her cup to her lips, and when she did, her dark eyes bulged open and she gasped as if she'd just swallowed a hot poker.

"Mmm," Drecovian said, smacking his thin lips.

I took a careful sniff over my cup and then hastily put it down back in the saucer with shaking hands. If all the cats that once guarded Stormholt had found a festering, moldering corpse and decided, all together, to urinate on it, then the resulting smell might have been just . . . like . . . this.

"Oh God," Faith gasped. "That's . . . that's . . . *vile.*"

"Hmmm," Brocara rumbled. "Well, yes. That's not how it is supposed to be?"

"Heavens *no,*" Faith said.

"Well, I like it," Drecovian insisted.

"It was in storage," Prudence mused. "For an *awfully* long time before I found it. In that wet cave the Jötnar abbey used for a basement. A pod of Sea Salamanders *might* have used it for a breeding ground, but it seemed dry when I found it and . . ."

"You didn't notice the *smell*?" Faith asked.

"I thought that was the tea," Prudence said, surprised. "Father took me into Faerie the day I was born. What do I know about

England and tea? Oh, and there were all those Kellas Cats around it for just *ever*. You don't suppose . . ."

"Yes," I said firmly, pushing the cup away. "I think I do."

"Here," Faith said, pushing her cup and saucer half an inch in Eegan's direction. "We should have this buried, but since we're at sea, I supposed we'll have to settle for sealing it and dropping it into the ocean. For the love of all that's holy don't burn it. I have a stash of quite acceptable breakfast tea back at the ship. I'll send some over."

"You do?" I said, surprised.

"Yes," Faith said. "Most of it is in the cargo hold, but one of the packages has been sitting on our table for days."

"I don't remember seeing . . ."

"It's holding down the upper left corner of your map of the Baltic Sea."

"Oh, that," I said. "Is *that* what that was?"

I pushed my cup yet further away. There wasn't enough table to get the desired effect.

Eagan sniffed and started collecting the cups. He carefully poured the leftovers into the sea, ignoring Faith's instructions. He also missed one, leaving Faith's cup in front of her.

"Well," Brocara rumbled. "I asked Drecovian to bring you so I could get a sense of what kind of person you are. Now I believe I know. This has been informative."

"You called me Dra Faith before," Faith said. "What does Dra mean?"

"An ancient title for magician," Drecovian said. "It means, *of the dragon*, since all magic stems, literally, from them." He looked speculatively at the dragon's enormous head. "It means that Brocara is taking over your magical tutelage."

"What?" Faith said, stunned.

"Your magician is broken," Prudence said. I flinched, thinking of how I'd forced Sands to cross the mist and how rough he'd been looking since. "Surely you see that you need real instruction," Prudence went on. "Who better to learn from than Brocara?"

"It's a great honor," Drecovian said. "Which has not happened in millennia."

"Millennia?" Prudence said, turning to the older man. "Surely you're not . . ."

"Older than I look," Drecovian said mildly.

"I'm going to learn magic from . . ." Faith said.

"Yes," Brocara rumbled.

"Oh," Faith said, clearly stunned, her gaze moving back and forth from Brocara to Drecovian.

"Of course," Brocara went on, "you have to agree." The wooden deck creaked as the dragon turned her head to cock one golden eye at us.

I stared at the dragon, then slowly looked at Faith. This wasn't about me, but I couldn't shake a sudden, urgently virulent premonition of doom and disaster.

That feeling didn't get any better when Prudence opened a small bag at her waist. The bag was large enough to hold some coins, maybe, or a few handkerchiefs. But what Prudence pulled out was a long silver sword. It even looked slightly familiar, that sword, but I didn't have any time to figure out where I'd seen it before because the dragon had tilted her head slightly and Prudence was running the tip of that sword along the dragon's neck.

"What in bloody?" I snarled, jumping up. Now I had my pistol out, for all that it probably wouldn't do any good. Except I wasn't entirely sure who to shoot.

Prudence dragged the point a foot or so across the dragon's neck and I was shocked to the see the scales part and a long wound form. Blood pooled onto the table. Drecovian moved the one remaining cup, Faith's cup, so that some of the thick, almost black, blood fell inside. Plenty got onto the table, too, leaving a long black-red smear across the avocado table.

"Drink," the dragon said.

"Wait, Faith!" I said, but it was already too late. I should have known it would be. All the frustration and anger that Faith had been going through trying to be a magician without any real magic, she'd been dying for a chance to jump at something more and here it was. Maybe I would have done the same, but that didn't do anything to clear up the needle-sharp fear that jabbed into me.

Faith drank the cup down in one pull.

Her eyes rolled up into the back of her head. She dropped the cup and slumped out of her chair. It was hard to catch her with a pistol in one hand and I fell out of my own chair doing it. We both landed on the deck, my arms around her, her half in my lap. The cup hit the table, shattering.

Brocara reared her head back and hissed, as if Faith's collapse hurt her, too, and badly.

"I've got you," I said.

Faith's eyes were still open, but they were covered in milky white cataracts that put a chill in my blood.

Drecovian and Prudence were on their feet watching us. The anxiety in their faces just ratcheted my own fear up. Prudence's silver sword was still dripping dragon blood.

I put my head to Faith's chest and put my palm near her mouth. Her chest wasn't moving. I couldn't find a pulse at either her wrists or throat. My own pulse was pounding in my ears. It couldn't end this way! After all the danger we'd both been through to have this happen now, when we were supposed to be among allies? It was just too cruel.

"What did you do?" I screamed at the dragon. "Oh, God! *What did you do*?"

Brocara reared up, the wound still showing fresh on her neck. She was watching us. The dragon's motion caused a dip in this part of the raft and water flowed from the opening near us so that Faith and I both got drenched. The wind ruffled one of the sails a short distance away, the sound surprisingly loud. Nothing else made a sound, but very far away, I could hear people shouting.

"Did it work?" Prudence said.

"I don't think so," Drecovian said. "She's dead. Can't you feel it?" He pounded his fist on the table.

"No!" I looked down at her, with her head in my lap, and pulled her closer to me, willing her to breathe again. *Oh, please, God, I'll do anything if she can only breathe again!*

Prudence knelt beside us. "No!" she said. "That's not supposed to happen!" She sounded just as panicked as I was.

Then Faith drew in a ragged breath.

"Not dead, then?" Drecovian said.

Both Prudence and I shot a glare at Drecovian and he flinched.

"Shut up, Drecovian," Prudence snapped. "You're not helping." She took Faith's hand. "Come on now. You're all right."

Brocara made a brief rumble, like distant storms, and leaned a bit closer. She'd been worried, too, which surprised me. Brocara's, hunched-over posture blocked out the sun, throwing a shadow over everything.

"You're not helping, either!" Prudence yelled at her. "Move back! Give her some room."

The dragon shifted backwards, too, looking nonplussed and not very dragon-y at all.

Faith groaned. Then she blinked a few times and the white film over her eyes faded.

I thought my heart would burst.

"I'm out at sea?" Faith said dreamily, putting her hand on the section of wood bobbing gently underneath us. "I *hate* the sea. How did I get out here?"

"You're going to be all right," I said breathlessly. "I don't know what happened, but you're going to be all right." I had to brush the wet out of my eyes to see her clearly.

"Reese?" Faith said. "Is that you?"

"No," I said. "Who's Reese? It's me, Justice!"

Faith's eyes seemed to clear a little more, returning to their normally dark color. "Justice? God, where did you *come* from? I thought you were out in the Baltic or some such faraway place."

"The vision!" Prudence said. "She had the vision. It worked!"

Faith grabbed at my lapel, then she stopped, seeming stunned by the nature of her own hand.

"I'm young again," she said, turning her hand around in front of her face, her voice full of wonder. "Wait. I'm back. It's like I never left. I'm back with you and the dragon and everyone." She sagged in my arms, taken with utter exhaustion. "It's like nothing ever happened. It was all a dream. No, like two dreams."

"Tell us what you saw," Prudence said. "Before it fades."

"I got married," Faith said. "They rebuilt Whitehall so we could have it there. Oh, Justice, it was beautiful. Mother was there, too. She looked very happy."

"Who did you marry?" I asked, fascinated despite my still-racing pulse.

"I . . ." Faith frowned. "I don't remember that part. His face is all blurred."

"Was that Reese?" Prudence asked. "You asked for a Reese a second ago."

"Reese was my son. He was beautiful, too. And we had a girl, too. Flora. We lived in London and had everything we ever wanted. I'm the queen of London Society and there are grand balls and glorious dresses and we have servants and everything is so fine."

She frowned, her eyes distant, still remembering. "Then things were sad. Or maybe they'd always been sad, despite all the parties. I think Reese's father died in the war. The war, oh, it goes on forever, but it's far away. England is peaceful and beautiful again and we all live in Buckingham Palace because Mother is Queen. The Faerie have put her in charge and they run everything. Not just in England—everywhere. And the Black Shuck is behind everything. Runs everything. The Faerie gods are strong in the world again, but Arawn and the Morrigna, the Black Shuck's gods, are preeminent."

She sighed. "Then Reese is all grown and wants to go fight, too. Go fight you, Justice. You were still fighting, but running mostly, and Joshua and Mother were chasing you all over the Atlantic. A lot of people were dead, because of the war. Henry, Benedict, Father, all of you. You, too, Justice. Mother finally catches you and . . . oh, it's horrible."

"Was Brocara in that vision?" Prudence said.

Faith frowned. "No. I'd turned Brocara down. Never became a magician. But I had a dream where I said yes, too. I had that dream first and I don't remember it as well. But Brocara was there, and I do amazing things. I fly. I'm with the Wild Hunt. So are you, Justice, and Benedict. The Faerie gods are there, too. Cernunnos and Llyr and more. They want us to serve them. Represent them. Become their avatars."

"Hhurm," Brocara rumbled, a non-committal noise.

Faith struggled out of my arms, pushed back her disheveled hair, and stood up to face the dragon. Her dark eyes wet and filled with sorrow. Prudence and I scrambled to our feet, too.

"I can't shy away from becoming a magician," Faith said. "There's too much to lose if I do."

"You're already a magician," Brocara said. "We just need to teach you how to use that magic."

That seemed like an important distinction, but I kept my mouth shut.

"I won't worship the Faerie gods," Faith said.

"Dedicated to your Christian God?" Prudence murmured.

"No," Faith said, turning on her. "I don't know if I even believe in God after all that's happened, but it's not that. If I do this, *I* do it. Me. I'm not going to be the puppet of anything or anyone."

"That is well," Brocara said. "The Faerie gods are fickle and unreliable. Best not to rely on them. I do not know your Christian god, but I find all gods to be *distinctly* unreliable. Your pact is with me."

"Well . . . good," Faith said, clearly a little thrown by Brocara's capitulation. "Then I agree to your pact."

Drecovian, who had been watching silently, chuckled. "You already *did* that, child, when you drank blood of the dragon."

"Those visions," Faith said. "Are they true? Does it have to be one or the other?"

"No," Brocara said. She was still reared up to her full height and her basso profundo words fell, tumbled like stones through water. "It is two very likely futures. But nothing is set."

"Is that what you think of the Seven Virtues and Seven Sins business, too?" I asked.

"It's a prophecy," Drecovian said with distaste. "Unreliable by definition."

Brocara snorted, which shook the timbers underneath them. "Useless drivel."

"Utterly," Drecovian agreed, "but that doesn't mean it's not true."

"What?" Faith said.

"It's true or it's not," I said. "It can't be both." I didn't want to keep sitting here, but the rush of emotions in the last few minutes had exhausted me.

Drecovian moved closer, righting one of the chairs that had fallen over, and then sat down with a sigh. "When I was much younger, a child witch told me that I would one day be consumed by a dragon."

"There is still time," Brocara rumbled.

"Hmm," Drecovian agreed. "You can imagine my fear, girls, when I actually *met* a dragon. However, for all her bluster, Brocara did *not* consume me."

"I'd *just* eaten," Brocara said airily.

"But," Drecovian went on with a tight smile, "becoming bonded to a dragon has changed me in ways you cannot fathom. My entire sense of identity was consumed. Even my name, Recov, has become subsumed by the new dragonish person I have become."

"Ah," Faith said. "I *thought* someone called Drecovian who was bonded to a dragon was a little bit *too* on the nose." We were still sitting at Drecovian's feet, like children in front of a storyteller.

"Drecovian," Drecovian said with a smile. "Similar to Dra Faith only from a language much older." He leaned back and pursed his lips. "Prophecies are tricky businesses that often, but not invariably, come true. But when they do, they do so in a way that surprises no one and benefits few. It's a fine opportunity for lots of men in beards to stand around and say 'ahhhh that's what they meant!' afterwards. A great party trick, but that's all. It's no good to try and follow one. You'll just tangle yourself up in knots. It's either wrong, or it's useless. Best ignore it completely."

I was suddenly tired of sitting and managed to climb to my feet without falling over. Faith followed my example.

"So," I said, "you don't think we should go to England?"

Faith snorted. "As if that matters. Everyone knows you're going to go anyway. Just like I'm going with you."

"We still need a magician to take us across," I said. "Sands is spent and you're not ready."

"She is," the dragon rumbled.

"It will be very dangerous," Prudence murmured. "The mist..." She waved her hand dismissively. "That is nothing. It's what lies after the mist that worries me."

"What lies after?" I asked.

Prudence shrugged, then sighed. "We don't know."

"You see?" Drecovian said. "Prophecies are useless. We know that you will go. We know you *should* go, but it will be very dangerous. If you survive, Brocara can begin your real training when you return."

"Very dangerous," the dragon pondered. It scratched the deck idly and whuffed out hot air. "Hrrm. Just in case, could you possibly make arrangements to have the tea sent over before you go?"

"Well," Prudence said brightly, leading the way across a swaying rope bridge, "*that* went well."

"You mean how neither of us was actually eaten?" I said. "Or how we didn't get stepped on by Faith's new magical tutor."

"Or killed by tea," Faith said and shuddered.

"Both," Prudence said lightly. "Either." She seemed in fine spirits. "That reminds me, one of you had better take this." She stopped and handed Faith the silver sword she'd used to cut the dragon.

Faith took it warily. The sword looked delicate, but was, I knew, deadly sharp and strong. After all, I'd seen Victoria Rose cut wooden beams and a Hanged Dog's face with equal ease. The sun took that opportunity to appear behind the clouds a bit more and it shone on the brilliant, lethal metal. Faith turned the sword in her hand. A fine weapon, but I couldn't get the image of Victoria Rose's face out of my head, the expression she'd had when I'd shot and killed her. It gave me a shiver just to look at it.

"Where did you get this?" Faith asked.

"Where you left it," Prudence said, "on board your ship. Silver always leaves a certain delightfully deadly scent in the air." She grinned at us, shattering her incongruously pleasant and ordinary impression. It was a smile wicked with knowledge, with shapechangers and magical poisons and vampire flowers behind it.

I'd forgotten all about Victoria Rose's sword. Faith and I had hidden it after first bringing Victoria Rose through the now inoperable Faerie door into the captain's cabin on board the *Rachaela*. It was a stupid thing to forget, too. Silver had a special place in the Faerie world. This was a weapon made by the Faerie for war against other Faerie.

Faith held the sword out to me.

It seemed like a good idea to put it into someone's hands, but I wasn't sure how much use I'd get out of a sword. I was even less sure how much Faith would. I didn't think it would be good for either of us to get that close.

"Better you," I said to Faith anyway. "You don't have any weapon at all now." At least I had Avonstoke's pistol. The same pistol I'd used to kill Victoria Rose, in fact. Avonstoke had also given me a bag filled with cartridges specially made to injure and kill Faerie.

Faith's eyes were dubious, but she turned the blade over in her hands. She tested the tip and grimaced. She was starting to look a little green around the gills. The sword shone like angry starlight in the bright sun.

"The sharp part faces out," I said.

She rolled her eyes at me. "Thanks. But where does it go? There isn't any scabbard?"

"Not that I found," Prudence said.

Faith stuck the bundle awkwardly into her belt. "It feels like it's going to fall out and cut off my foot," she said. "Where did Victoria Rose *put* this? I don't remember even seeing it until she was fighting."

"Down one pants leg?" I said.

"She didn't wear pants," Faith said. "And you couldn't have hidden a salad fork in that dress of hers, much less this!"

"Faerie Glamour?"

"Wouldn't you have seen it?"

"I don't honestly know," I said. "There are levels. Some glamours are stronger than others. I don't see through all of them."

"That is just about the least comforting thing you could tell me right now."

The launch was waiting for us and Avonstoke and Sands both stood up in the thwarts as soon as they saw us. Sands had been drinking again and nearly fell over before Avonstoke grabbed him at the shoulder.

"Thank the gods!" Sands said, then nearly fell over the gunwale and into the ocean.

Avonstoke had to steady him. We stopped at the edge of the raft, looking down at the two men.

"The dragon," Faith said, "will help me learn magic. Or has, I guess. She says I'm ready to try the mist again."

"Blessed Tree," Avonstoke murmured.

"Ah." An awful, hopeless expression crossed Sands' face as he turned away. He sat aft and pulled a wine bottle up from the bottom of the boat and slowly, so slowly, uncorked the bottle and took a long pull. I had to look away. I couldn't forget all the man had lost. His magic, his title as magician, which was no small thing. Even worse, he'd given up Acta Santorum, his magical companion. Teaching Faith and helping us was the last scrap he had left, and now that was gone too.

I jumped easily into the boat, wanting to busy myself with getting the launch moving. Something to do with my hands. But when I turned back to help Faith get in, I stopped.

"When did you get that cut?"

"What cut?" Faith said.

"On your neck."

She put her hand on her neck and rubbed thoughtfully at the raised, red mark there. "I don't know." Faith didn't sound concerned. "Not careful enough with this new sword I guess." She nodded at the sword, which she'd laid in the stern. "I really need to get a scabbard for that."

"Allow me," Avonstoke said. He reached towards the sword, but stopped, waiting for Faith's approval. "If I may?"

Faith nodded and he gingerly took it up. Strange, that care, for someone who wielded a sword of flaming shadow. His expression looking at the sword was pensive.

I took another look at Faith's cut. Only it wasn't a cut at all, but a scar, months old, at the very least. Except she hadn't had it before we met the dragon. The other disconcerting part was that it was in exactly the same spot that Prudence had cut the dragon. On impulse, I squinted my right eye shut to check with the ghost eye. It looked the same.

I cast off the line from *Seahome.*

Everyone else was lost in their own thoughts on the way back, Faith fingering her new scar, Avonstoke with the sword, and Sands with his misery, so I shoved off from *Seahome* myself. I wasn't a powerhouse on the oars, and the wind was up, but I was eager for something I could understand: wind, keel, current and tide.

No one spoke as we headed back to the *Rachaela.*

CHAPTER 6

The H.M.S. Specter in the Mist

The *Rachaela* was a welcome sight, sitting as pretty as you could please on the rolling waves. No magic to it, just solid seamanship. The sails sparkled white in the sunlight and the crew had even touched up the paint, gold with heavy black trim, so that she gleamed. Perhaps the crew had come a fair way as sailors after all. I wondered again about what Avonstoke had said about the crew taking vengeance if something happened to Faith or me. Somehow, I doubted it.

The Faerie flutes sounded as the launch pulled up to the side of the ship and I flushed with pleasure. They were rendering captain's honors, using Faerie flutes in place of the boson's pipes. Some of the flutes were carved wood, and some worked copper, and they made an eerie hollow tune, like wind through an underground tunnel. I hadn't ordered that and there hadn't been any fanfare when we'd left, because, without the long-standing tradition of the Royal Navy, a few of the military protocols had felt too self-serving. But here they were.

"After you, oh captain, my captain," Avonstoke said.

I'd been about to jump off the side of the smaller launch and grab hold of the ladder rungs carved into the *Rachaela's* side, but something about Avonstoke's tone made me look at him again. I could feel one of my eyebrows go up.

"You're up to something," I said. "What is it?"

"Me?" his expression was as innocent as a child's.

I grunted in irritation and shook my head. There was no getting a straight answer out of him when he was in this kind of mood. I put my foot up on the gunwale and waited to time the leap when the water was at an upswell. Then I leapt.

The first time I'd done this, I'd been terrified of slipping and falling into the water. It wouldn't have been fatal, but it would have been an enormous embarrassment, which felt just as bad. I'd rather face a broadside again than be hauled up out of the ocean and dropped, dripping, onto the deck of my own ship. But after the first time I'd done it, I'd found that forgetting about my fears was as easy as feeling the ocean. It felt like home at sea and no more so than when I was on my own ship. I didn't think about it anymore and made the leap as neatly as if I'd been born to it. It was easy enough to go hand over hand on up. I went up eagerly, wanting to feel the already familiar deck slanting and swaying under my feet. Being back made me feel more at ease.

There were hands. Prowler hands, waiting to help me up onto deck. There was a clamor of people on deck as I got hauled up.

I climbed and straightened, looking around at all the people with a growing perplexity.

It was all hands on deck. The seaman that had assisted me stepped back and snapped to attention. Everyone else was already there.

The entire crew.

Swayle and the rest of her Crow Whisper Brigade were presented front and center, all of them at quivering attention, uniforms of emerald and ebony resplendent in the sun. Four of them were blowing on the eerie copper pipes that always sounded like cold winds through dark tunnels. They blew one final blast and went silent.

Mr. Starling, also in full uniform, stood at the head of the other officers. These were a mixed batch of Dwarf and Prowler. Starling snapped a flamboyant salute. Wonder of wonders, he'd foregone his towering topknot in order to manage the tricorn hat that went with his uniform. I must have gotten used to his topknot when I wasn't looking, because seeing him in the uniform hat seemed weird. Most of the other Dwarves in the crew were grouped close behind him, all of them decked out in their best finery. This included almost fifty Dwarves.

Standing prominently in the center were the Dwarven women, about twenty of them. I'd thought that they'd been kept out of the way by the over-protective Dwarven men, but now, looking at their proud, determined faces, I somehow couldn't see anyone keeping them somewhere they didn't want to be.

Because most of the women had kept to the hold, I'd had no idea there were so many on board. If fact, I'd only met a few, but those I did know had impressed me. They'd done a great deal of the minor repair, sails and nets and carpentry, that a ship needs constantly. They also maintained the gun powder room. Because the tasks had been done with a great deal of efficiency and competence, there had been no need for me to press the issue and question the women directly. They were diligent, hard-working, and imminently practical, to judge by their work.

Elegant and small.

Smaller and lighter than me, even, without the excessive and somewhat frightening bulkiness that characterized the Dwarven men. But I'd seen one of them drive a nail into wood with a careful thumb, needing no hammer at all. Even looking at them now, something in their frame spoke of a strength and toughness belying their small stature. They were wearing brightly patterned wraps the color of ruby, emerald, sapphire, and diamonds, and more than one wore a circlet or medallion with the actual stones. The display was spare, and tasteful, but I still suspected that they wore enough stones to buy my ship several times over if the London marketplace were still functioning.

The Goblin sail crew, the Prowler deck hands, even our few Solitary Faerie, like the Troll and a Gargoyle I didn't recognize, were standing near the back. Everyone was present and arranged like a crew, rather than in the hierarchal Faerie stratus I'd expect. The Court Faerie, top of the Faerie political food chain, were usually considered far above most of the other Faerie races like the Dwarves, Goblins, and Prowlers, who, in turn, considered themselves above Solitary Faerie. For all of them to present like this together was a stunning display of camaraderie. One I'd never seen from the Faerie.

"There is," Mr. Starling said, "some concern over our ship, Captain, and it's readiness for the raid that you 'ave planned into England."

Damn, damn, and double damn the Faerie penchant for gossip! I should have known that my planned raid on the shipyards would become common knowledge at *Seahome* the second I'd uttered it in a crowded room. I didn't know how it had spread over here, but it wasn't surprising considering the number of swimming or flying Faerie that could travel between the ships. I glared at Avonstoke, who was joining the others climbing up behind me.

Mutiny. It could ruin everything. Truth was, I couldn't blame them much, that's how dangerous this mission was. Just thinking about it made my stomach churn. But we had to! Or risk the Black Shuck getting an outfitted armada across the channel. Bad enough to face constant obstacles among the Outcast Council, but *here* too?

"We *have* to go," I said, trying as best I could to keep my tone level and commanding. Too weak or too tyrannical and my entire command could be over before I knew it. "The war could depend on it and there's no ship better suited to do it."

"Of course we must go," Avonstoke said smoothly and whatever was going on, my gut told me that he had some hand in it. But Avonstoke, mutiny? I couldn't believe it.

"Begging your captain's pardon," Starling said, "but it's not the mission. It's the *name*."

"The wha . . ." I said. I couldn't even get the word out. I had to clear my throat and try again. "The *name*?" I could feel my eyebrows shooting up so much it was a wonder they didn't fly off my face. Faith giggled softly, a sound out of sorts with her new magician status, and I realized that whatever was going on she was in on it, too.

"The ship's log shows," Starling said, "that the *Rachaela* was originally an English merchant ship that your Father purchased.

Named after the wife of some nobleman. As a merchant ship, 'er name was more than adequate. 'Owever, she 'as, under your command, risen in the few months to become the scourge of the English coast."

"Men and Faerie in England," Avonstoke said, "are whispering her name in dread. You've heard it yourself." He dropped his voice to a faraway whisper. "It's her! It's her! Bloody Justice Kasric! Oh, the port is near, the bells are here!"

"What are you nattering on about?" Faith snapped, though her tone was more fond than not.

"Whitfield," Avonstoke said proudly.

"Whitman," Sands corrected.

"Ah, yes," Avonstoke said. "That one. American, so probably godless, but no one is perfect."

"What *are* you talking about?" Faith said. I was still staring at the gathered crew and wondering what was going on and wishing to hell someone would get around to telling me.

"Beggin' your pardon again, Captain," Starling said, cutting through in his gravelly voice, bringing the conversation back around to what he was trying to say. "But in the Faerie tradition, a new role or new title rightfully comes with a new name. It's an insult not to get one."

"So we're giving it to you!" one of the Goblins shouted out gleefully.

"Yes," Starling said, glaring at the goblins behind him a moment before schooling his face and turning back to me. "A way of acknowledging and honoring momentous change." Render, the Dwarven gunnery captain standing next to Starling, had the barest trace of a grin on his face, then wiped it completely blank when Starling glanced his way.

"Your ship," Faith said, "needs a new name. You can't expect to keep striking fear into the hearts of the invaders using the name of a random someone's wife, can you?"

"Oh," I said, pretending that this all made sense. "Of course . . . the name."

Everyone was still staring at me.

"What is," Avonstoke said, "the proper ceremony for changing the name of a ship?"

"Ah . . ." I said, feeling absolutely brilliant about it. "Um." The truth was, it was an absolute abhorrence to the English Navy to change any ship's name. They were so against it that ships like the *H.M.S. Carcass, Great Burk,* or *Happy Entrance* continued to serve under these dubious titles rather than change them. As soon pray for bad luck and a severe loss of reputation as change a ship's name. The *Rachaela* had finally acquired a fearsome reputation. Why throw it all away now?

Because my Faerie crew clearly expected it. This wasn't an English crew and I had to allow for that. What's more, from the beaming smiles on the crew around me, I could see they felt they were doing me a fair honor and I appreciated their intent, if not the tradition. My crew had been surly before and now they were trying to honor me. I put what I was sure was a crooked and bent smile on my face. Best to swallow the affront to English tradition.

"Have you chosen it yet?" Starling asked.

"What?" I said, feeling my smile crack already. "Chose one *now*?"

"Well," Starling said sheepishly. "We did gather the crew together and all. They're kind of expecting it now."

"Perhaps the list?" Faith said.

"Ah yes!" Avonstoke said. "The list!"

"I have it here," said Sands, who had been standing behind us at the railing silently until now. "Ahem." He pulled a pair of spectacles out of his coat pocket, fumbled with spectacles and bottle before finally handing the bottle over to Avonstoke to hold. He seemed a little more himself with having a purpose, however slight.

"I thought," Sands went on, "that some historical perspective was in order when considering something like this." He drew himself up to his full height, which wasn't much, but managed to summon some of his former dignity. He pulled a thin, cream page of foolscap, folded longways, out of his jacket pocket.

He adjusted his glasses and began to read. "Yes, let's see. We've been accepting suggestions from the crew for a few days now, a much larger list, which I've trimmed and cultivated extensively. This is what I have so far." He cleared his throat. "The Spectral Blade. The Ghost. The Phantom War Machine. Hmm . . . sensing a trend there."

"Hmm . . ." I said, trying to derail my brain from the serious details of the actual mission and consider, however briefly, this nonsensical request. Ghost, Phantom . . . I did like the idea of striking unseen.

"The Clandestine," Mr. Sands said. "Wargan's suggestion, I believe."

"Wargan?" I said, still completely trying to keep up. I knew all the crew's names, but not that one.

"The Troll, Ma'am," Mr. Starling said. "Discovered the name while you were out, Ma'am."

"Discovered how?"

"The Gargoyle told us, Ma'am," Starling said.

"Discovered the Gargoyle while you were out, too," Render added helpfully.

He nodded at the Gargoyle I'd noticed earlier. It's hard to have stone skin, fangs, horns, wings and claws and still look sheepish, but somehow the Gargoyle managed.

I glared at Starling to see if I was the butt of some kind of obscure Dwarven humor, but he looked as stern and serious as always. Render, too.

"We didn't *have*," I said, "a Gargoyle on the ship when I left."

"Begging your pardon, Ma'am," Starling said, "but we *did*. Just didn't know it. He's been hiding down in the hold, as well, Ma'am. Seems he and the Troll, that is, Wargan, Ma'am, have become mates of a sort."

"But we digress, my Captain," Avonstoke said with just the barest trace of laughter in his voice. "Should I repeat the list of names so far? Of course, these are just suggestions."

"Oh, obviously," I said.

"There's more," Sands said. "The Crooked Knife. The Fighting Fish. The Scourge of the Seven Seas . . ."

"I think that last one's been used," I said.

"Ah, yes, of course," Sands said. "The Bonesmusher . . ."

"Smusher?" Avonstoke said. "Really?"

"Yes," Sands said, sounding irritated now. "That's what is says here."

"And you didn't," Avonstoke said, "weed that one out during your cultivating?"

"Apparently not," Sands said.

"What *did* you weed out, I wonder?"

"Gentlemen!" I said.

"Yes," Sands said, glaring up at Avonstoke. "The Fighting Filly. The Salty Specter. The Gray Ghost. The Ungaungacruchcrunch."

"That made the cut?" Avonstoke said. "Ungaunga?"

"There are a number," Sands said, getting even more agitated, "of languages spoken on this ship. Not all of the names were presented in English, you know. Some of them do not lend themselves to translation."

"Specters in the Mist!" I said, desperate to get this foolishness over with. "That's us," I said. "The *H.M.S. Specter in the Mist.*"

"Hmm . . ." Sands said. "That wasn't on the list."

"Doesn't matter," Faith said. "She's the admiral. She can pick whatever name she wants."

There was a quiet, but appreciative murmur among the crew. Somehow, I'd picked one they liked. So, perhaps, no mutiny today.

"The *Specter in the Mist,*" I said firmly. Somehow it just felt right. "Because," I raised my voice, "we shall *be* ghosts in the mist, appearing out of nowhere, and disappearing just as quickly. The Black Shuck created this mist to be their weapon, but we shall make it ours!"

"A year from now," Avonstoke called out, "the invaders won't be telling each other the same scary stories in the telling circles that they do now. Instead of haunted hounds out on the moors or the dead returning from the graves, they'll be telling stories about the ship they never beat. They'll be telling stories about us! They will know fear."

There was an enormous cheer at this, and Avonstoke and Faith looked at each other and then at me and grinned. Even Starling had a sickly expression on his bearded faced that I realized was supposed to be a smile.

"Mr. Starling," I said, my voice pitched to carry. "Make sail for the Thames Estuary."

"Aye aye, Captain," Starling said, and for once he didn't sound reluctant to say it.

"There is," Starling said, "more. War leader, admiral or general, needs 'er magician, don't she?"

"What?" Faith said. She clearly hadn't been expecting this part.

"Beggin' your pardon, captain, and I 'ope we 'aven't overstepped, but the other magician sent word over and blast me for a beardless git if I can tell you 'ow 'e knew, but 'e did."

"Knew what?" Faith said.

"Which other magician?" I said "Prudence? Drecovian? Or one of the others?"

"Drecovian, Captain," Starling said. "The one with the dragon, Ma'am, so we 'ad to do it."

"Do what?" Faith said. Her voice had reached a higher pitch, showing she was more than a little unnerved.

Starling waved one of the Dwarves in from the back row. He was one of the carpenters, with a black bushy beard and a bald head, but I couldn't remember his name for a second until Starling said it.

"Drerth 'ad them," Starling said. "Didn't even know they weren't all burnt up."

Drerth was carrying a long staff, heavier at the top and charred. No, not charred, but with bits of charred wood worked into the top, so that it was spiked and dangerous looking.

"Don't even know why I did it," Drerth muttered in a dazed voice. "Just seemed proper, somehow. "Pieces should a been all burned up, anyway, with that blue flame and all, but they weren't."

He was standing in front of the group of us now and I got a better look at the staff. Ash, gray with runes and images worked carefully into the length of it. Now I knew where the charred wood had come from. Sands had broken his violin, months ago, which had shattered both his link to Acta Santorum and his power in one fell stroke. They'd burned that day, with a blue flame.

"'Im," Starling said to Drerth, nodding his head at Sands.

The burly Dwarf handed it to blond, little magician. Sands took it gravely, carefully.

"You're supposed to give it to 'er," Starling said, nodding now at Faith. "Somethin' about completin' the ritual."

"I didn't know," Sands said, cradling the staff carefully. "We must not have done enough before. I didn't know the pieces had survived. I should have known there was more. It makes sense now."

He went to stand before Faith and held up the staff parallel to the deck, in both hands. "When the world was young," he intoned, "Cernunnos, Leader of the Wild Hunt, cut for him a piece of the World Tree and used it to carve himself the horn he would use to call the Hunt. Doing so, he left fragments and chips of wood behind, in a hidden grove near the World Tree. Later, a powerful magician, Lessard, the Lord of Thorns, found that grove, and the fragments, and knew them for what they were, touched by Cernunnos. Lessard crafted them into several useful and powerful objects." His French accent had grown stronger while saying all of this, but now it dropped back down into his more normal, slightly whispery voice. "One of these is the chess piece that you carry, Justice. The other is the violin that he made and then passed to me." His voice became a chant again. "Here now, are the fragments of that masterwork, crafted again. I now pass them to you."

He ceremoniously handed the staff to Faith.

She nodded and took it, staring at it with wonder.

The wind was strong but temperamental, but I'd had Mr. Starling reef the topgallants, so the ship rode under power of the lower sails, the mains and courses, which made for a jerky ride. The sails flapped and the wind whistled through the rigging as the *Rachaela*—no, the *Specter*—lifted up on the next wave and then paused as the ship tipped down into the wet trough with a new burst of cold spray and a fresh clattering of the wooden blocks and tackles. This was the smoothest that could be hoped for on this point of sail in a lively sea.

Following Joshua's clues was certainly dangerous and might even mean stepping into a bear trap, but all I could feel was a deep exhilaration as the *Specter* heaved and pitched around the cliffs of Dover and headed towards the opening into the Thames Estuary. It was a brightly lit, fine English afternoon in the channel. An auspicious beginning to our raid.

I ordered the sails lowered, then noticed one of the deck crews was several people short because of preparations I'd ordered on the gun deck. The Prowlers hauling on the rope looked at me bug-eyed when I stepped in to help, which was as much of a reward as I could have asked. I had some ideas for changes, and this was as good a way as any to break the ice.

"Heave!" I called, and we heaved. It took a dozen more pulls to get the sail up, and I was feeling the burn in my arms, shoulders, and lungs by the time we got there.

"That's it!" I shouted and braced myself while Avonstoke tied off the line. My efforts didn't add much to the total, but I was pleased nonetheless. It was a slight break in military discipline, but if I admitted the truth to myself, we were more like a pirate vessel than a military ship and anyway, we needed all the hands we could get. The slightest wrinkle in protocol would have had me screaming months ago, but not every English tradition held the same weight here, because it wasn't an English crew. The Faerie hierarchy was even more stilted and useless than our version and had a way of throwing the society I'd always grown up with into stark, uncomplimentary relief. Now that I'd gotten a feel for some actual good will from the crew, I felt I could make a few changes without sparking a mutiny.

A half an hour later, we were nearing the turn we'd need to make.

"Heave to, Mr. Starling," I said.

"Ma'am?" Starling's leathery scalp, with its red topknot, and his reddish beard were all brilliant in the sun.

"We've got a bit more to learn before we begin," I said.

I cocked an eyebrow at him, and he bit his lip and then turned to start bellowing out orders to throw out the sea anchor and heave to.

"Oh God," Faith murmured from behind me. "More drills." I hadn't even heard her come up behind me.

I turned to make a firm comment, but the words died on my lips.

Faith wasn't Faith at all. At least, she didn't look like the glamorous Faith I'd known my entire life.

She'd cut her hair.

Her glorious, ash-blond hair, so pure it was almost white in the sun. And not just a trim, either. She'd hacked it all off. All of it. And then shaved the rest down to her scalp. I felt a sudden surety that she'd used the supernaturally sharp edge of Victoria Rose's silver sword to do the deed. Her new scar, clear as anything without all that hair, stood out against the fair skin of her neck.

"What in the world?" I said, stunned.

"Being a magician," she said levelly. "Your magician, in fact. This war means giving things up. Some of our dreams. To become someone, something else. The dragon showed me that, but probably I already knew it. I felt I should look the part. Especially if you're determined to try going through the mist again." She did look the part, at that. She still wore a frock, but of faded green with leather lacings, rather than the sapphire, ruby, or emerald dresses she usually favored, even at sea. Her dress had been shortened and gathered so that it would have been scandalous if not for the leggings she wore underneath, so that now the whole thing was practical to a fault and wouldn't hinder her actions at all. Avonstoke had clearly been as good as his word and found, or had someone make, a scabbard for her silver sword, which was buckled around her waist. Even her boots looked sensible. She also held the staff made from fragments of the world tree.

"Go on," she said, still speaking low enough so that only I could hear. "You were in the middle of something."

There was just one thing missing.

"Someone," I said, pitching my voice to carry, "get my sister a hat. She's going to fry her scalp out here in the sun."

Faith gingerly touched the skin on top of her head. I nodded in the direction of Starling, who also had most of his head bare. Only his skin was a deep and ruddy brown, while Faith's (and mine, to my chagrin) was pale.

One of the Dwarven gunners dragged a piece of dark brown cloth off the top of his head and threw it at Mr. Starling, who brought it over to us diffidently.

I opened my mouth, sure that Faith would want something of her own choosing, but she surprised me again by taking the dark cloth from Starling, shaking it out once, and settling it onto her own head. It was a sort of hood, without the cloak attached, but with two long braided leather thongs that hung down the front to help keep it in place. It fit her new look. Of course, being Faith, she still managed to look both glamorous and entirely feminine, even with all the changes. Otherworldly, almost.

I tore my gaze away. I needed to get something else done. Something I'd been putting off for a while now.

"Swayle," I called out.

"Yes, Lady," Swayle responded.

"If we do find the enemy shipyard," I said, "we're going to need to fire repeatedly on both sides. We don't have enough gunners for that now, so I'll need your help."

"My help?" Swayle said, the amusement fading from her face. She shifted her bow, a long, elegant weapon nearly as tall as she was, from one hand to the next. This was her weapon of choice, but it wasn't going to sink ships no matter how well she used it.

"Yes," I said. "I'll need your people to take up station with the gunners, two marines to a gun, to help them run the guns out after loading."

"My brigade doesn't know anything about handling cannon," Swayle said instantly. "Those are Dwarven contraptions."

"Which is why the Dwarves will load and fire, I'll just want you to help them push the guns out before firing. The gunners will direct you."

Her eyes narrowed to dangerous slits. "That's hardly . . ."

"That's an order, Swayle."

I held my breath, waiting while Swayle's face went through a visible struggle. The truth was, the Court Faerie marines scared the hell out of me. Her more than most.

But Swayle, after a long pause, nodded. "As you wish, my lady."

"Good," I said. I turned to where a Prowler deckhand stood, staring. They couldn't believe it, either.

"Get down to the gundeck and bring Starling and Render up here so they can hear this." The two Dwarves were going over the gun dispositions now.

Starling's answer, after he'd come up to the main deck, was entirely predictable.

"But," he sputtered, "those are Dwarven cannon!"

"So Swayle informed me." Their obstinacy was really starting to burn my britches. A captain should have a more enigmatic face, perhaps, but I couldn't summon it right now. I took two steps and pointed to the lines around the nearest cannon, where the ropes were lashed to the cannon carriage so that hauling them pulled the carriage forward.

I looked back at Swayle. "Do you think your marines can learn how to haul on a rope? It's not complicated."

"Of course," Swayle said, indignant now.

"Do you think," I said, twisting the knife by letting an edge of solicitous concern edge into my voice, "that only two marines will be enough to move the cannon?"

"They *will*," Swayle said, angry now, which was exactly what I wanted. The entire ship had seen two Dwarven gunners do the same work innumerable times and knew that Swayle would see her marines perform the same feat or rip their arms from their sockets trying. It was petty on my part, but effective.

"Your gunners," I said to Starling, "will need to tell them when."

"Aye aye," Starling said, clearly warming to the idea of Dwarves giving directions to the Elvish Court Faerie. Render's eyes, behind Starling, were as wide as saucers.

Swayle looked like she'd swallowed a bag full of carp heads, but she nodded her assent.

"See to it," I said, and the three of them, Swayle towering over the burly Dwarves, moved slowly over to the group of marines who, having heard everything, were stunned. Four of our cannon were on the main deck, so Swayle posted eight marines here before leading the rest down into the gundeck.

"Oh, my captain," Avonstoke said. He wore that kind of grin that spoke of clear enjoyment at others' misfortune. "I wonder if the Lord of Thorns had any idea what a tumultuous storm he has sent upon the Faerie. You'll have dogs and cats working the pumps together next."

"Well done," Faith murmured.

"I'm just getting started," I said.

I was waiting for Starling when he returned from the gun deck.

"We'll be trying uncertain waters, Mr. Starling, who're your best two hands with the leads? We'll need them in the chains."

This was still a new procedure to the Faerie as we'd not gone often into shallow water to need it. The 'chains' were shelves on the outside of the ship's hull where someone could stand and toss a weighted line into the water to try and measure how deep the water was. A handy bit of information if you wanted to make sure you didn't run the ship aground in shallow water.

Starling fingered his naked scalp for a moment, considering. "You'll want a Prowler, then," he said finally, his bright red topknot bobbing as he nodded.

"That would mean us," a young Prowler girl said from the other side of the deck. "Me and Wil. We're the best, ain't we?" She nodded at a small boy next to her. The two of them had been coiling rope, but now the young boy dropped his.

Mr. Sands had spent a good deal of time teaching us more about the Faerie, and I now knew that the Court Faerie and the

Prowler Folk were both descended from the same Elvish stock, but had long ago segmented into different peoples. No one could say how. There were even two kinds of Merfolk, but the Prowler Merfolk were the more human kind, and the only kind we had on the ship.

With seafoam green skin, angular Elvish faces, and the same all-yellow orbs as Avonstoke and the other Court Faeries, they showed elegant grace. But Prowlers also had mouths full of barracuda teeth and webbed-talons for both hands and feet, making them fearsome and strange. Brightly-colored fins ran along their arms and calves, as well as long, spiky hair that reminded me of nothing so much as the barbs of a lionfish. The fins ran a gamut of colors among the crew, but the fins on these two were a bright, pinkish red, like something's gullet.

"Is that true?" I asked Starling. "These two?" I didn't want to say it out loud, but Wil, at least, seemed too young, too small for the job. The girl was tall, a head taller than me, anyway, but without a lot of meat on her. Underneath all the fins and fangs, I thought she couldn't have been any older than I was. I thought Wil younger still.

"It is," Starling said. Something was bothering him, though, because he was chewing the ends of his red mustache.

Nellie's pale eyes regarded me with triumph, but also a surprising and barely suppressed hostility. Wil's gaze was no better. Like the rest of the crew, she'd sworn to follow Father's house into battle, but it didn't mean she had to like it.

"Perhaps you don't know these two, my captain," Avonstoke murmured.

It was my turn to glare. This was a sore spot. I'd memorized the crew's names during my first week of command, only to find that most the ledger was old and incomplete. I'd been trying to learn the names of everyone, but the Faerie had a maddening habit of using multiple names and a shocking aversion to giving a straight answer when asked about them.

"They are," Avonstoke said, "Nellie and Wil *Lacon.*"

Bloody hell. Lacon. *That* name I knew. Patrick Lacon had been the helmsman when I'd come aboard. Now, he was dead, killed during the dragon attack. He'd also been close to Caine, who I'd wrested command from. I shuddered when I remembered the man's wild and terrified howl. War had been bad enough, with the fire and death and men screaming, but the dragons had tipped some Faerie over the edge, Lacon included. He'd abandoned his post, flung himself in the water, and never come out again.

Nellie and Wil probably blamed me for that. Or at least my house, which was fair enough, really. The House of Thorns had gotten them into this mess, no doubt. Nellie and Wil glared at me as I processed all of this.

I hardened my face and turned to where we had the newly-made lead lines coiled. I grabbed an end and showed them.

"I need two people to stand in the chains," I said. "Throw these lead lines out, use the markers to see how deep the water is and call it out. These are the fathom markers here. You see?"

Nellie took the line I handed her and looked at it dubiously. She held it to Wil to look, but he shook his head.

"I could do all that English nonsense," he sneered. "Or maybe I could get in the water and just *tell* you 'ow deep it is. That other way is just idiocy, ain't it?"

"And what happens when the moving ship leaves you behind?"

"This lumbering thing?" he said, surprised. "I can swim as fast as any bloody ship. I'm Prowler, ain't I?"

"We can take turns swimmin', Ma'am," Nellie said placatingly to me. "So's we don't get too tired."

I looked at Avonstoke who shrugged. "They *are* very fast swimmers," he said. "It's the fins, I expect. Always wanted some myself." He leaned a bit closer to the sullen boy and waved his hands around the boy's head. "How do the head fins work? I've always wondered."

"Get away from me you bloody idjit!" the boy snarled.

"Perhaps not, then," Avonstoke said.

I rubbed my jaw thoughtfully trying to hide the rising flood of anxiety and questions. Everyone was looking for me to know how to guide the ship, but none of Father's books offered details about shipping with a Faerie crew! If the Prowlers screwed up, it was going to be *my* ship that sank and *my* bogus admiralty and captaincy that became exposed. Those fates were all grim enough, but what was even more horrifying was the fact that everyone would blame *me* for that, too.

"We'll still need to throw the lead," I said adamantly. I wasn't going to risk the whole ship on the judgment of a surly Faerie boy until I knew I could trust it.

"Perhaps I could throw your lead?" Avonstoke offered. "In order to compare? Then we'll have two methods of measurement?"

I raised an eyebrow at Avonstoke, surprised, but imminently grateful for a way to test the Prowlers abilities without risking the ship. But the reaction he got from Starling and the two Prowler children was even more extreme. They goggled at him as if he'd just promised to set his own hair on fire. To their way of thinking, a Court Faerie like Avonstoke offering to do sailor's duty was a bit like a duchess offering to do the dishes. I'd already shocked several Faerie with my own willingness to break with their perceived station, but they'd clearly written it off as evidence of a human lack of understanding. Avonstoke's gesture meant a lot more to them than anything I could have done. For all that I and most of my siblings were Faerie, too, the gulf between them and us felt mammoth.

Both Prowlers went easily over the side without a splash.

"Don't be too hard on them," Avonstoke murmured as he coiled line over his shoulder. "The Prowlers have not been treated well by many of the other Faerie races. As a result, they are, perhaps, prouder than most. Lacon's actions shamed the other Prowlers on this vessel. Deeply. There are some that blame you for that."

"Because it's the House of Thorns that brought them here," I said, sighing.

"Goodness no," Avonstoke said, shocked. "They honor you for that. But you took command that day, the day their kinsman dishonored himself. You began a new history on board this ship. Yours is the face of change and they resent it."

"How does that make any sense?"

Avonstoke just shrugged. "It is a very Faerie way to view things." He patted the rope coiled on his shoulder. "Best I man my post, yes?" He snapped a salute so precise it became nearly a farce.

I was never going to understand the Faerie. Hell, I was never going to understand this one Faerie, Raythe Avonstoke. His handsome and mercurial face was as expressive and impossible to read as ever. He seemed alternately amused, sorrowful, and delighted at our current situation. Probably a dozen other emotions besides, to judge from the expressions moving one after the other across his face.

"Yes," I said. "Thank you."

"We're ready, Mr. Starling," I shouted. "Bring the ship around on the starboard tack and make for the estuary."

"Aye, captain," Starling said.

I turned my attention to watching Starling issuing the orders.

He still wasn't as comfortable as he needed to be with the details of sailing a ship without magic, but he had the tillerman prepare to turn, then got the sail crew to man the braces, ready to haul the sails from their positions with the starboard ends pulled as far forward as possible to the opposite position. I waited, feeling the ship still moving forward on momentum only. Finally, Starling gave the order to the tillerman, and the ship came around. There was a slight hesitation as the ship swayed and threatened to falter because Mr. Starling hadn't got the timing right.

"Too slow," I murmured. "Too slow."

Then the sails caught on the other tack and the ship was gaining momentum so that the keep and rudder were biting in the water better and the hesitation passed as we entered fully on the new tack.

"I'll give you this," Faith said next to me. "The ship moves better when you give the orders. I'd swear it likes you better. How did you get such a feel for this? And don't tell me Father's books. There's more to it than that."

Captain Caine had asked me the same question a few months ago, just before Father was shot. I hadn't given him a satisfactory answer then. I'd read every manual of seamanship Father had owned many times over, but that didn't account for the feel I had for the sea and the ship. I could sense the pressures of wave and wind as if her fore and aft were my outstretched fingers.

"I don't know, exactly," I admitted. It hurt my brain to think about it, like a dark hole in my mind that didn't want to be examined. "I can't explain it."

"Do you have dreams about the sea?" she asked suddenly.

I stared at her, flooded suddenly with the memory, submerged and inchoate, of violent and deeply disturbing dreams last night. But then, I'd met a dragon yesterday. *Not* having disturbing dreams would be surprising, wouldn't it? But yes, yes, the sea had figured prominently in them, too, and something told me, suddenly, that this part of the dream was not new to me.

Not new at all.

Still, I didn't say anything. Talking about them would make them too real, give them more power during the daylight hours than I wanted them to have.

Faith nodded as if I'd answered her out loud. "It's the Faerie gods' way of reaching out to us," Faith said, and her face looked strange, older, as she said it. "They want champions for their cause and they reach out to beings they think can help them." Her expression suddenly changed into one I recognized. "Of course, how we answer them, if at all, is entirely up to you."

I stared at her, still not able to voice these thoughts out loud. Instead, I said, "Do you have dreams?"

She nodded. "For some time now. But they've changed. Before, it was winds, thunderstorms, the call of a horn."

The call of a horn in a stormy sky. No question which god was reaching out to *her*, was there? That seemed infinitely worse than dreams of the sea.

"Now, of course," Faith said, "she dominates everything."

"She? Brocara? The dragon?"

"Who else?" she said. She gave me a tight, exhausted smile that didn't reach her eyes. "My training continues, even when I'm not with her. Because she's with *me* at night, every night, in my dreams, telling me stories of the first magicians, what they've done and how they did it. It's *exhausting.*" She closed her eyes and took a firmer grip on her staff.

She was carrying it everywhere now.

That sounded terrifying, having dragons wait for you in your dreams, no matter if you knew them or not.

"I wonder," Faith said, "where Father is now."

"Lady Rue wouldn't tell me where he is," I said. "She came back, so he's holed up somewhere waiting for the game."

"I know," she said. "I wonder if it's somewhere nice or somewhere horrible."

I realized that I had no idea and that idea dug into my heart. I should at least know where he was, but I didn't. It wasn't that long before the game, either, a match that would decide so much more than just his fate.

"This feeling you have," she said, shifting topic suddenly. "About this shipyard, are you sure?"

"Absolutely," I said automatically. Then, seeing a glitter of amusement in her eye, I thought again. Did I see that in a dream too? Maybe she hadn't shifted topics as much as I'd thought she had. The truth was, there were forces working here, working inside of her, inside of me, that I didn't understand.

I closed my eyes, trying to block out everything so that I could think about how I could be so certain about the shipyard. But it had the opposite effect because, with my eyes closed this way, the feelings of wind, sail and sea dominated my attention. Were my love and feel for the sea something passed to me *just* from Father? Something I'd cultivated myself with long hours of staring at maps and dreaming about joining Father at sea? Or was it something passed through his Faerie blood, from the god of the sea, down to me?

It was all these things, I realized. Mine, and Father's, and something passed down to me from the Faerie, through our inhuman blood and dreams. But what I did with it was *mine* and mine alone.

I dragged my concentration back to Faith's question. How sure was I that this shipyard was there?

"Pretty sure," I finally said out loud. It wasn't some vision or gift from a Faerie god, but it just made sound tactical sense, which I trusted a lot more because that was something I'd developed all on my own.

"Good," was all Faith said, but her eyes had an amused glitter about them, hints of knowledge more than human in their depths, as she looked out across the water.

CHAPTER 7

Faerie England

We were nearing the edges of the mist now, the dividing point. Dense and thick near the shore, roiling like soup in a cauldron out onto the choppy gray water. Questing tendrils stole out across the water as if it meant to seize the *Specter*, or any other ship, and drag it in, which was probably true enough. Occasional patches of fog near the shore lit up, flashes from a storm further inland that I couldn't even see. Sometimes, low rumbles made it out this far, strangely disconnected from the flashes, but mostly there was only the sounds of the sea around us, and from the shore, only oppressive silence.

We completed the turn with clocklike precision, and then, our goal was directly forward.

The mist roiled, waiting for us with smoky, serpentine patience. I gripped the railing and eyed Faith, feeling ready to chew through the mizzenmast if she didn't say anything. All around, everyone else looked jittery. No one had forgotten our last trip into the mist. Sands was there, too, watching with all the rest. Just one look at his shaking hands told me he wouldn't be helping any.

"Justice," Faith said. "I *feel* it." She was leaning on her staff, which was pulsing with a dull, orange light.

I let out a deep breath. "You do?"

She nodded. "Yes. Yes, I do."

It was my turn to nod. "Well . . . good. Is it the staff that makes the difference?"

"No," Faith said. "The staff helps, but the difference is in me."

We'd reached the first wavery trails of gray now, and started in.

Faith lifted her voice in sudden song. It was an unreal sound, like sunlight splashing off the water's surface. It wasn't just one voice, either, like it should have been, like it usually was, but it was a trio of Faiths. She'd done that once before, I remembered, when Widdershins had attacked us, and it had saved us all. Brocara had been right. Faith had been a magician all this time.

A sudden gale whipped the water in all directions, churning it into foam. The order to reef sail sprang to my lips. Wind like that would tear the sails right off! Snap spars, perhaps even capsize the ship.

But when I turned to make the order, I saw that the sails were still hanging limply, barely filled. When I turned back to the wind, I could make out the line of it on the water, a line about a foot wide that lay around the ship about three feet out. The scent of a storm on water came with it, and a loud whispering like silk on silk.

"Ah," I said, still trying to absorb what was happening. This was Faith's shield. Of course her magic wasn't going to be anything like Sands' magic. No wonder no one magician understood how it all worked.

Faith herself stood with her hands up and outstretched, her staff raised high and pulsing wildly. A wind that didn't touch the rest of us whipped at her clothes. A look of pure exaltation graced her face. Her brow furrowed as she sang, and reflections of dark storms danced in her eyes. I was suddenly more than a little afraid of my older sister. With her shaven scalp and fierce expression, she seemed a different, more terrifying person than she had moments before. Perhaps to be a magician meant to engender fear in others.

She stopped singing, but the wall of wind remained. Her staff still pulsed, but softly now.

"I'm going to need your help," Faith said in her usual voice. "I have the shield and I can feel where the vortexes are the mist, but not as clearly or as far away as I'd like."

"What can I do?" I never had any feel for this business at all.

"Watch out for them," Faith said, all confidence now. "Warn me, so I can brace myself. I'll do the rest. You can see them clearly with your ghost eye, can't you?"

"Yes. But only a few seconds before they hit."

"How many seconds, exactly?"

"Perhaps twelve to fifteen, I guess. It varies."

"That's more time than I'd have without you. Just give me a warning when you feel the largest vortexes coming at us and tell me from which direction."

"Yes," I said, squinting so that I was peering through my ghost eye. Dark vortexes moved in the pearled soup all around us. "I can do that."

"Good," she said. "Then we'll do it together."

Less than a minute later, I called out: "Here's one, coming fast. Directly ahead!" I knew that terms like fore, port, starboard, and aft weren't second nature with Faith. I'd have to avoid those. "Three, two, one . . . now!" I saw Faith clench her jaw and a then a shudder went through the ship. Then nothing. I could see the vortex, a black wall of volatile space, go sliding by on the port side, deflected by Faith's protection.

"Not too shabby," I said with a grin.

"No," Faith said. "It wasn't, was it?" She grinned at me.

This trip through the mist was nothing like our last one. With Faith's wind shield and my ghost eye, we weathered the vortexes with surprising ease.

Then the first of the visions came, burning, crimson wings the size of our mainsail unfurling a dozen feet over the crow's nest.

I peered with my ghost eye as screams broke out over the deck and Swayle's marines fumbled with their bows. Fire was a terrible and fearsome thing to a ship. But right now, I feared we'd capsize the ship ourselves if we panicked.

"Nothing!" I roared, surprising myself with the power of my own voice. "Do nothing! It's not real!"

I'd shocked them into silence, but I could still see half the crew praying or shuffling closer to the rail.

"Wait," Faith said. "I have it." She raised her triple-throated voice again and her staff glowed. The phoenix, or whatever it was, simply faded away.

"Not real," Starling murmured gratefully.

"Not real to us, anyway," Sands murmured next to me.

I nodded, Sands' explanation coming back to me. Other things trapped in the mist, moving in other times, but occasionally coming close enough to graze ours. We would be the ghosts to them. Point of view mattered a lot.

The *Specter* moved quietly along, the only sounds being Avonstoke calling out depths from his station down in the chains and the occasional echo of Nellie doing the same. So far they agreed—plenty of clearance for the *Specter's* hull. I was crouching near the railing on the main deck so that I'd be close enough to hear them. We didn't want to announce our presence with shouting.

Then we were through, just like that, suddenly clear of the mist and looking around at the wide, flat, brown, watery terrain of the Thames Estuary. The prow of the *Specter* broke through the few remaining tendrils of fog, dispersing them across the flat water's surface. We were in the Estuary proper, and the ship had none of the sea's rolling motion to her. But this wasn't some property of the mist. This was normal for the Estuary. Familiar terrain, at last.

"Seven bells into the morning watch, Ma'am," whispered the Prowler sailor, passing the word along from the quarterdeck at the rear of the ship, where the bell and the sand glass were by the binnacles.

I moved to the railing, leaned over and peered down at Avonstoke, who was dutifully casting out the lead. It was a difficult, grueling task, but he made it look effortless, strong shoulders moving as he swung and cast the rope. Wil was crouched near him, waiting his turn while Nellie swam. Wil pressed himself close to the hull to stay out of Avonstoke's way.

Under normal conditions, the tide should be going in, which would make our passage a little easier even if the wind failed, and that still seemed to be holding true. There was something comforting in that fact. Even if the Faerie could wreak havoc and change on the land of England, perhaps not everything had been altered.

"I'm touching bottom with the lead," Avonstoke called out softly. "Eighteen feet!"

There was a splash in the water and Nellie's head poked up through the surface. She whispered something up to Wil, who turned and said, "Sixteen feet."

Avonstoke's lead was twenty-four feet long, but even with the ship's gentle movement the line was bound to trail behind, causing the extra two feet to his reading. Sixteen feet was probably correct. I nodded at them both. The *Specter* drew eleven feet of water. Five feet to spare only, which was far less than the Thames should have had. I would have to be very careful.

"Have Mr. Starling pull in the courses," I said to the sailor behind me. "Less sail, reduce our speed."

"Aye aye."

The sailor had turned to pass my order back along the deck. There was a flurry of whispering and hushed activity as orders that would normally be bellowed across the deck were passed quietly, followed by the patter of bare goblin feet on the spars and the creaking as sailors moved up the shrouds.

"Mr. Render," I said to the Dwarven gunner. "Run out the guns on both sides and wedge them up so we're aiming as low as possible. If we find that shipyard, I want to be ready to sink as many as possible and it'll be at close range." Render nodded and another messenger sailor ran to repeat my orders for Render to Starling.

Time crawled.

I could see a faint whiteness on the port side now, a wild tangle of rocks and brackish weeds. This wasn't the Thames I knew. The shoals might be narrower and shallower than I remembered. Wil, now taking his turn in the water, was reporting far more dangerous shallows than should be here, so it was tricky work to keep the ship moving forward. But the Prowler team continued to echo, only more accurately, Avonstoke's readings. I'd let the current system ride out this mission, but probably I didn't need anyone in the chains after all.

Nellie and Wil had been right.

The banks on either side were narrowing, but more familiar nonetheless. Judging by that, and by my estimate of our speed and the distance, I thought we might be near Graveshead, the location I'd expected Joshua to use for his shipyard. But all I saw were bleak riverbanks. Once full of fisherman's houses and small docks and piers, they were deserted now.

"Look," Faith said.

Yes. A shadowy shape, darker even than the black surface of the river around us. My eye could just pick out the tall lines of masts. These were ships. We glided in closer, and I could see more silhouettes of ships. I could see armaments, too, but only a few, and no crew. These ships were still being readied for war. There were no sentries, but I had a hunch they had crew down below that would make themselves known once we started shooting.

"Pass the word to Starling," I said. "Bring the tiller three points to port. Have the starboard guns made ready. Not a whisper until I give the order to fire."

"Aye aye, Ma'am," the crewman said and passed the word.

I took a sly look at Faith, standing next to me, thinking about the artillery going off. It wasn't going to be one-sided, this fight, for all that we'd caught them by surprise. I still didn't have a complete guess for how many ships were here, but a dozen was the lowest possible estimate, all of them with some cannon and crew to man them. We were ready, but also just one ship. It was guaranteed we'd be taking fire soon.

"Not a chance," Faith said, clearly guessing my thoughts. "I'm staying on deck."

I could tell from her expression that ordering her below was going to have as much effect as ordering cannon to fire quietly.

"Fine," I said.

"Fine," Faith agreed.

I crossed the deck far enough to catch Swayle's eye, pointing at her and the cannon. To her credit, she got the message immediately and issued marines to assist in the cannon at once. They rushed to their stations with no sign of the reluctance or distaste they'd shown for the task before.

A cry of alarm came from the nearest ship. Someone, at least, was manned there.

"Too late," I said with a grin. The *Specter* was just turning to bring her guns to bear on the nearest of the anchored ships.

"Fire!" I shouted.

Starling bellowed to the Dwarven gunner captain, and the gunner captain bellowed at the gunner teams, and the starboard broadside exploded with a deafening crash that I could feel in my feet through deck planks. Several crashes on the anchored ship spoke to at least some of the cannon hitting their targets. Smoke billowed out in a screen that momentarily blocked our view and filled my nostrils with the smell of powder smoke. The wind took the smoke screen away in thin strips to reveal the anchored ship listing to one side with the nearest rails sagging down to the waterline. She was taking on water, and it wouldn't be more than a few minutes before she was at the bottom of the Thames.

"Ha!" Faith said with a grin. "Let's see Joshua ferry troops across the channel with *that*!"

I grinned back at her.

More shapes were becoming apparent in the gloom, a row of ships lined up after this one, all waiting for our attention.

Turned out, I'd overestimated the chances of taking fire. The docked ships barely put up a fight. The *Specter* slid slowly up the Thames, hammering out broadside after broadside until my ears rang and I thought I'd never be free of the smell and taste of smoke.

One of the anchored ships finally managed to return fire, using a bow chaser or some other cannon already pointed in our direction from the ship's aft. The angle wasn't right, and I thought they'd missed until I looked up to see a round hole in the mizzen course sail above me.

"Again!" I shouted. "Fire again!"

Two more broadsides crashed into the enemy ship and their cannon fell silent. I tried not to think about who the enemy gunner might have been. A Faerie related to Avonstoke or an innocent British seaman who had the bad luck to be on the other side.

We fired again and again, using the guns on both starboard and port sides without any need to tack back and forth, as there were targets aplenty on both riverbanks. It was well that I'd made provisions for the Court Faerie marines to help, for every one of them was needed. More Prowler children, similar in age to Nellie and Wil, were sent scurrying down into the hold for more gunpowder cartridges.

The coordination between Court Faerie and the Dwarven gunners was shaky at first, with the marines not having the rhythm of running out the guns in coordination with the others. The gunners did not communicate their needs except in grunts and muttered insults, often heaving the cannon into the proper place themselves in a blatant demonstration of how better suited their burly limbs were to the task. The Court Faerie were tall and certainly as strong as men, but it taxed them to be put to such a strenuous, repetitive task. I was on the verge of interfering and repairing some of the sloppy teamwork when Swayle, having conferred with Render, the Dwarven gunner captain, took on the task for me. Between the two of them, bellowing admirably in perfect tenor and baritone counterpoint, they got the operation running smoothly on both decks. After that, the deck was a veritable storm of cannon thunder and gunpowder smoke as the guns banged out shot after shot. In close engagements with other ships, the victory could often be decided by rate of fire alone, and I was pleased at our progress.

Swayle and Render disappeared below to the gun deck to perform the same feat there and I was able to focus my attention on making certain Starling didn't let the *Specter* run aground.

I scanned with the glass, using my ghost eye, which saw things better in the half-light. Every ship I could find now lay broken and askew. One was burning. Scanning the docks on both sides of the water, I was ecstatic. Our job had been done and done well. Joshua wouldn't be making any kind of ferrying initiative with this fleet.

"Excellent, Mr. Starling," I said, loud enough for the entire crew to hear. "Bring us around and take us back out to sea."

"Aye aye, captain," Starling said. "Out to sea." The deckhands and gunners gave a mighty cheer, followed by a chattering and gibbering from the Goblins above. Everywhere I looked, faces were grimy with power and exhaustion, but also elated.

I turned, well pleased with the day's work. Let the Faerie try and cross now!

"Seven feet, captain!" Nellie, down in the water. That was as shallow as I dared.

"Time to turn back, Mr. Starling," I said. "We've done all we can here. Wear the ship and bring us around. Time to go home."

Starling looked at me uncertainly.

"Blast it!" I said. "Flugelstan the bloody ship, then. Away from the wind!"

"Aye Captain," Starling said.

"Not bad," Faith murmured next to me. "But what happens when we meet someone who's ready? Someone who can fire back? We can't hit all their shipyards, can we?"

"We can try. We sink enough ships in dock, we won't have to worry about fighting them at sea."

Starling called the hands to braces so they could haul the main sails to better catch the wind. He ordered the helm over and we began the touchy business of threading the *Specter* back out to sea. A few members of the Dwarven gunner crew were shouting in merriment, now that the shooting was all done and everything had gone our way with no casualties. I felt a grin of my own come out.

The ship, coming around, was now facing one of the few remaining buildings. It looked strange and out of place to me, especially after I recognized the reddish-brown bricks with their yellow trim: St. George's Church. I remembered a day the family had spent in Graveshead during one of the periods Father was home. It had been near Christmas, so everyone was together: Father, Mother, Joshua, Benedict, Faith, Henry and I, all eating croissants and drinking hot coffee or cocoa at a little café next door. It had been a happy time and I'd been very young, but it stuck in my memory like a sunlit spot in a dark place.

There was an odd split in the land to the right of the church that didn't match my memory, as if two very different paintings were set side by side. My grin fell away, replaced by confusion and wariness. Manicured smooth lawn and the church on one side, ragged hillocks, black craggy trees, and dark, swampy pools of water on the other. Fog lay on the swamp, though the light by the church was bright and clear.

Then the tree monsters came over the rise, out of the swamp, and the whole scene became more disturbing.

The first arboreal monster had a catlike face, with small horns and a long serpentine body. Barklike scales shaped like kite shields covered its back, and talons the size of carriage wheels showed as it lifted them from the marsh. A lizard-like tail with spikes at the tip lashed the air behind it. The whole thing was easily the size of the *Specter*. It turned to look at the ship, facing into the wind, and the feline countenance *rippled,* breaking apart. It reassembled itself immediately, still staring at us. The creature had a solid skeleton of dark tree limbs, with a body of leaves that shifted and quivered in the wind. The fake semblance of a cat-faced dragon broke apart constantly. It was nauseating to watch.

Another tree monster came behind the first. This one walked like a heavy, two-headed giant with a colossal cudgel. The two faces—one man, one woman—wore expressions of ancient guile and anger. This one, too, shifted in that same, disconcerting manner.

Behind them came yet another, this one a squinty-eyed green bear that regarded us with suspicion, snuffling the air while the head and body shifted, revealing that same black skeleton. Further back in the distance, more enormous and ill-defined shapes loomed in the mist.

"Wealdarin!" Sands whispered.

"Wheel what?" I hastily checked with my ghost eye, but nothing changed. They were there, all right.

Then I my gaze fell to the ground, and the nauseating, unsettled feeling climbed to full-on horror. They moved through the green grass the way a bather wades through water and the ground around them *changed,* sloshing and throwing droplets of dark loam, rippling as the monsters walked. Grassy green waves lapped at the church and the English countryside like water on the shore, washing the manicured lawn away. The swamp was growing, the lawn shrinking. The upper half of the tower remained, but only for a second, and the tower crumbled in a cloud of brick dust. Another few steps by the Wealdarin and even the rubble was wiped out of existence.

"This is how the Black Shuck remade England so quickly," Sands said. "The Wealdarin are *creating* the Faerie realm out of thin air, thus wiping out England with every step. Rooted as they were, they carry bits of the Faerie Realms with them. The mist, too. It's all their doing."

"This is how the Faerie make war," Faith said.

"But he shouldn't have the strength to control them," Sands went on. "Any more than he should be able to control dragons. Or keep his forces together the way he does. How? *How* does he do it?"

"I'm getting awfully tired of wondering that," I said bitterly. A fury was rising inside of me watching the awful, majestic Wealdarin stomp around on the banks of the Thames.

"I'm getting tired of saying it," Mr. Sands said.

"Ready the guns, Mr. Starling," I bellowed.

"I'm not sure that's wise, captain," Sands said. "They shouldn't bother us if we don't molest them. I suspect engaging them would be . . . unfortunate."

Lord knew I didn't want to get close enough to that shore to get within reach of those things. Could they swim? I held the guns at ready, but the creatures made no move in our directions. They merely watched as we glided slowly away.

Shortly, they were out of sight.

"Very well," I said. "Starling, belay that order."

"Aye, Captain," he said. The relief in his voice was palpable.

CHAPTER 8

Shore Party at Graveshead

"You're still set on doing this?" Faith asked.

"You don't want to try and get Henry and Benedict back?" I asked.

"Of course I do."

We were in our cabin, getting our things together for our landing at Graveshead, where we'd try and make our way to Stormholt. I pulled my pistol out of my chest. It was a dangerous-looking thing, that pistol, made of black iron and chased in silver. Avonstoke had given it to me, but it didn't seem like an object he'd ever own.

It would be painful to touch for him, with those metals, like handling the wrong end of a hot poker. When I'd asked, he'd admitted that it had been given to him, for unspecified reasons, by Father. Just as I'd suspected.

It came with a large bag of ammunition, too, also silver and black iron. I checked the weapon and then made sure my inside vest pocket had plenty of spare cartridges. I was just putting the ammunition bag back under my bunk when Faith came in.

She shut the door behind her, leaning on it and giving me a pensive look. I still wasn't used to her with that scar and hood and short hair. This Faith, the magician, looked like a whole new person to me. I thought she might be beginning to think differently, too. I was also struck by the sudden realization that my sister, with her tall grace and beauty, looked very much cut from the same cloth as Avonstoke or Swayle, the Court Faerie. Sometimes it was hard to remember that Father being a Faerie obviously meant that some Faerie blood was coursing through our veins, too. I shuddered as that thought brought back the memory of the monstrous form of the Faerie King I'd seen so many years ago out in the woods. Hard to remember that *that* had been Rachek Kasric, British sea captain, trapped in Faerie form by Father's spell, and not an actual Faerie at all. Made my head hurt.

"Has it occurred to you this raid of yours isn't at all part of Father's plan?" Faith said, bringing me back to the task at hand.

"Of course it is," I said. "Our family is at the center of all of this. Father knows that better than anyone. That's why he's been preparing us for so long." I'd finished loading the pistol and snapped the cylinder shut with an angry jerk.

"Which Father, Justice? Father, the merciless Faerie lord, or the human Father that's been outmaneuvered at every turn?" She was talking faster and faster now. "Because the first one viewed all his sons and England as expendable, didn't he? Now, Faith,

Justice, Prudence, Hope and Charity and whatever he named the other two we can't find, because leave it to a Faerie to get the seven Cardinal Virtues wrong . . ."

"Father always said family was important!"

"Ah!" Faith said, holding up a finger. "He says that now, but the Faerie lord that came to England, leaving his own family behind and tearing apart the Kasrics, not much of a family man, that one. You think the original Lord of Thorns would risk a ship and crew, let alone his admiral, for either Benedict or Henry, because I sure don't!"

"What do you want from me!" I said, standing up. "You think it's a mistake to try and rescue them?"

"No," she said. She took a deep breath. "No, I don't." She reached out her hand and put it on my shoulder. "It's not what Father would do. But it's the right thing to do."

I frowned to myself. "That was something Father said to us once, wasn't it? Sometimes the hardest thing to do is also the right thing to do."

"Exactly," Faith said. "We've got all these things tugging us this way and that. Father's plan. This weird prophecy the Outcast Council is so bent on. Faerie protocol and tradition. But you've gotten more done than all the rest of the Faerie put together. Only it's not a continuation of Father's plan. It's *your* plan. I think it's important that you realize that."

"That's what you're arguing about? Who's plan it is?" That hardly seemed important at a time like this.

"It's just," Faith said, "I've been thinking a lot about this and I believe there was more to the Lord of Thorns' plan than we know. What's more, I have a feeling we wouldn't have liked the rest. I just wanted you to think about that. Remember that it's your actions and planning that have held the Faerie at bay for the past few months, not his."

"All right."

"Good," she said. "We're going into England on a rescue mission. On our terms. Not Father's."

I thought about that and nodded. "Right." This would take some time to digest properly.

"That's all I wanted to say," she said. "I'm ready."

I nodded. "Me too."

The sun was out and the deck was already warm despite the breeze.

"Mr. Starling," I said. "Lower the launch, if you please."

"Aye, Captain," Starling said.

"You still mean," Swayle said, "to attempt this rash endeavor?"

"I do," I said.

"It is unwise," Swayle said sternly. "Did not your father say you should *not* go to England?"

I caught Faith's eye. She nodded.

"He said not to engage the Black Shuck," I said, "and I'm not. At least that's not the plan."

Swayle's sour expression made it all too clear what she thought of that distinction. "If you were rescuing your sisters, I could understand. There is the prophecy to consider. But brothers? They wouldn't seem to be worth the risk." She looked honestly baffled.

"The Black Shuck gave positions of enormous power to Joshua and Mother." I lifted my voice. If Swayle thought this, probably others did too, and I wanted them to understand enough to be behind this decision of mine. "He also went to a lot of trouble to try and eliminate Father. My entire family is involved, not just my sisters. I think Father, a few years ago, would have understood this better than he did in his last days. His mind wasn't what it used to be." I cringed a little at this last comment, which felt like a deception, for all that it might be true. But it was a story I knew the Faerie would buy. Their infallible general couldn't be wrong, not him, unless he was tainted with the spell making him more and more human. In my mind, human morality, compared to the calculated ruthlessness of the older Faerie, more than made up for any downfalls.

"The Shuck," I went on, "and the Seelie Courts clearly think my brothers are important, too. It's what makes their strategy worthwhile. So I'm going to rescue Henry, Benedict, and the ghost boys, if I can, not just because it's important to me, but because the opposition clearly values them."

"Mmm . . ." Mr. Starling had drifted closer during this conversation. He stroked his beard thoughtfully and nodded. "Makes sense."

Swayle looked less convinced, but she nodded reluctantly.

"But that's not the only reason," I said, raising my voice yet again. "Perhaps it's not even the main reason."

Swayle and Starling looked at me. So did the rest of the crew. I had their attention now.

"What's the other reason?" Avonstoke said.

"I promised," I said simply. "It's the right thing to do."

I could see the ripple that made in the crew. They liked that answer.

Also, it was emphatically true and the sooner they understood that about me, the better. The promise, rather than the rightness of it, would appeal to the average Faerie. Avonstoke beamed and Swayle, Starling, and the rest of the crew were bobbing their heads in agreement. Faith nodded approvingly.

"Call Nellie and Wil up," I said, but there was no need. The two Prowlers were hanging onto the railing behind me. I thought, perhaps, even Wil looked a bit less surly.

"You did well during the raid," I said to them both. "I was going to ask Mr. Starling to hand pick me a few expert swimmers to send ashore with me, but now I think I've got two of those to hand already."

"I'm game," Wil said at once. "That little lark there weren't nothin' to tire a body out."

Nellie nodded too. "You'd be a fool to take anyone else."

"I'm beginning to think you're right," I said.

That grim forest had bothered me, so I'd asked Avonstoke for a recommendation earlier. He'd spoken to the Goblins and learned that the leader of the Sail Crew, Mog, was from Sazurwood, one of the largest forests in Faerie.

I had Starling call him down and the largest Goblin in the crew dropped easily to the deck, driving some crewmembers to scramble out of the way of his enormous bulk.

Goblins varied a lot more from one to the other than humans did, and this one was the proof. While most of the Goblins were half my size, Mog had to outweigh me by a hundred pounds or so. He wasn't any taller than I was, but his wide leathery shoulders stuck out to either side and his huge arms hung to the floor. His eyes were small, with bristled eyebrows over a large, hooked snout. He had whiskers around his mouth like a cat. Large, batlike ears flopped down on either side of his wide, bald head all the way down to his shoulders.

"Mog," I said. "We need your help."

"Mog best forester," he said, already knowing what we were going to ask him. "Lady need Mog. Mog come."

"Good." I nodded and was about to turn away to ask Avonstoke about the next one when Mog grabbed my sleeve in his leathery grip. It was meant to be a deferential tug, I think, like a youngster getting a mother's attention, but the squat Goblin had such enormous strength he nearly tugged me off my feet.

"Is good, Lady," Mog said. "Interregnum over." His face was split with a fanged smile.

Avonstoke, looking suddenly alarmed, summoned his shadowy, shifting scimitar. I hurriedly waved him down with my free hand. Mog wasn't hurting me, though his grip on my wrist could clearly have pulverized bone.

"Interwhat?" I said.

"Interregnum," Mog said. "Is right word? English is slow and clumsy language." He followed this with a babble of harsh, graceless, monosyllabic Goblin speech.

"Yes," Swayle said. She too had brandished a weapon when Mog had grabbed me, her spear. Now she lowered it slightly. "That's the right word."

"First Father o' Thorns in charge," Mog said, seemingly oblivious to the weapons around him. "Now 'e gone. Lady o' Thorns in charge now, but there is a . . ." He waved his taloned hands. "A nothin' that 'appens. Now . . . no nothin'. Now it is 'appinin' again. Lady captain. Is good."

Mog released my wrist and finished with a bow that suddenly didn't look so clumsy. I was going to have to modify my thinking drastically about the Goblins, it seemed. With their unpretty faces and halting English it was easy to forget and reckon them stupid. Mog, at least, seemed anything but.

"Fightin'," Mog said, and barked something in Goblin. Two other smaller Goblins scrambled off and came back less than a minute later with an enormous chunk of wood, stout and fat, that easily weighed more than I did. Mog gripped it and hefted it easily.

"Mog ready now," he said. "Will join fish prowlers in the boat."

"Yes," I said. "Um . . . good."

"I am going," a tiny voice said, "with a boatload of children."

I turned to where Sands was climbing out of the hatch from down below. At first, I thought Mr. Sands had spoken in a falsetto, but the voice was coming from a tiny figure on his shoulder. Mog, paying no attention, clambered over the scuppers down towards the boat.

Sands carefully put his hand up to his shoulder and the tiny figure moved onto it. Sands then held out his hand.

"May I present," Sands said, "Dream of the Leaf Riders."

"Charmed, your ladyship," the tiny figure said. "Beggin' your ladyship's pardon."

It wasn't one tiny figure, but two, rider and steed. The rider was a small, cornflower-blue, mushroom-shaped person an inch high with yellow hair. She—at least I *thought* it was a she—rode an elm leaf, wide, with serrated edges and flecked with small red dots. The leaf bucked and pawed restlessly like an eager, unruly stallion, in Sands' palm. Dream rode easily, keeping her seat with the ease of long practice. She twitched her reigns, and the leaf came to parade rest, then they both bowed low.

"You asked for a scout," Sands said. "The Leaf Riders are the best there is."

I thought about when I'd first come onto the *Rachaela,* when I'd seen Caine order the Leaf Riders out. I'd forgotten entirely about them and hadn't seen them since. Another omission in the ledger.

"Pleased to meet you, Dream," I said.

"You'll need me, dearie," the tiny woman said, sounding for all the world like an indulgent grandmother. "Need some experience to season you younglings. Begging your ladyship's pardon, again." She didn't sound all that contrite, but I nodded, and she tapped her leaf on the rear with a brown riding crop the size of an eyelash and the leaf took to the air, moving like an airborne sting ray, ripples running along it's serrated edges with hypnotic grace. Dream used the reins to guide her mount down to the boat with lazy bumble bee speed.

Avonstoke and Faith were going, too, of course, as if I could keep either of them away.

"Don't worry," Avonstoke said. "She talks to all of us that way."

"She's older than you, too?" I asked.

"Oh yes," Avonstoke said. "I'm only a year older than you are, my captain."

"Oh?" I could feel my eyebrows raise.

"Certainly," Avonstoke said, his hand on the railing. "I'll need at least another eighty years or so before I'd be considered an adult among my people. Surely you'd noticed?"

"That," I said primly, "explains so much."

And it did. Knowing that the Court Faerie lived for hundreds of years, I'd assumed that he was some unfathomable number of years in age. The sudden knowledge that he was only a year older than my sixteen years rocked my perception of him. Far closer than I'd suspected. That gulf I'd always perceived between us, between what I wanted and how things were . . . it had never really been there. Of course, I was still his captain, but I knew for certain that this was something that didn't matter to him at all. It mattered to me, but . . . did it have to be everything? Perhaps . . . I suddenly felt cold and clammy, my hands sweating.

He gave me a wicked look with those golden eyes of his, and a grin that seemed to understand all my thoughts. The combination sent a hot shiver through me that wasn't at all blunted by the slight breeze coming off the water. He climbed easily down to the waiting boat.

I was surprised to see Sands waiting, his silver sword in his hand.

I shook my head at him. "You're in no condition," I said. The little magician was still looking unsteady on his feet.

"I have to come," he said simply. "I have things to show you that I can't show on a boat."

"Ship," I said automatically.

"Yes," Sands said, his neat yellow beard twitching. "Ship, then. Be that as it may. I still have resources in England to help us collect information and you may need my help to find all the ghost boys. Besides, my condition is the result of trying magic as my powers slip away. Without that drain, I should recover quickly. The physical activity may even do me good."

I wasn't convinced. It had been days since his last magical endeavor with the mist and he still looked worn out.

"We're going into danger," I said. "I don't want to put you in a position where you might have to use magic again."

"Little danger of that," he said simply. "My magician's power is gone completely now."

His green eyes flared with so much pain it made me wince.

"Please," he said, gripping my arm and dropping his voice low. "I'm no sailor. I'll be of no use here. But there," he nodded inland, "there are things that I know, skills I have . . . I can help. Please, I need to help."

I took a deep breath. "All right," I said. "Don't get killed."

He took his own deep breath. He'd been terrified that I'd turn him down. "Don't worry," he said. "I won't."

I hoped he was right. I turned and gripped the rail, preparatory to climbing down, and Starling, obviously waiting, bellowed an order.

A trio of Goblins stepped forward, small copper tubes in their hands. They lifted the tubes to their mouths. Musical instruments. Something a bit like curved copper oboes. They made an eerie, haunted noise, like wind moving through a small coastal cave.

Swayle barked a command and her tall marines jumped to attention. They were rendering honors as the captain left the ship.

Starling and Swayle, standing on deck, saluted, two unreal, inhuman figures in their naval uniforms. Starling, with his flaming red topknot, otherwise bald head, and long red Confucius beard and mustache, cut a solid, barbaric figure in the misty morning with his blue officer's uniform. Swayle, tall and slender in her dark green marine uniform, a good foot and a half taller than the stocky Starling, looked as tough and dedicated a ship's marine as any captain could ask for.

I must have had something in my eye, but I'd be damned if I was going to rub at it. All I'd ever wanted was to be captain of a ship and here I was leaving mine.

But if there was a chance to rescue Henry, Benedict, and the others, I had to take it.

CHAPTER 9

Henry—Newgate

Days passed for Henry in total solitude. Mother had said that he'd be executed in a few days, but days stretched into weeks and weeks stretched into . . . Henry couldn't be sure. Time had a surreal quality here. Months? Perhaps longer. Henry couldn't have said how long, but it seemed an interminably long time and he was surprised that he hadn't grown a long white beard.

Then two human guards opened his door one morning. Henry stared at them in shock, waiting for them to reveal corpse eyes or transform into huge, cadaverous dogs or something equally horrible.

But none of that happened; they simply waved him out. They looked extremely normal and supremely bored. Henry had been prepared to see any sort of Faerie madness on the other side of his cell door, but not this.

He thought the guards would notice the indentations in the bars. The ones that matched Henry's hands precisely. He'd done that. Bent iron the way someone else might have made an impression in clay, even if Henry had been too afraid of the Hanged Dog guards to try an escape.

But the Hanged Dogs weren't there and the human guards didn't so much as glance at the bent bars.

They let him out of the cell and led him down the hallway, holding onto his arms from either side as if someone who could bend iron couldn't possibly break their casual grip. They were grown men, so much bigger than Henry, but he thought he could have broken free if he wanted to. But then what? He didn't know. The Black Shuck, Widdershins, and all the Hanged Dogs had to be around somewhere.

The guards led Henry to another gate and opened it. It led into a long wardroom with a number of benches and tables. Two dozen men, inmates, were gathered loosely around the modest fireplace at the far end. Several wore shackles, but most didn't. Four of them, closest to the fire, had been playing whist and talking loudly, while the others kept a sullen silence. But now they all turned and looked at him.

"'Ere now," said one of the inmates who'd been playing cards. He stood up and dropped his cards to the table with a snort of disgust. He was a tall man, with a military bearing, and a heavy, black handlebar mustache. "Shouldn't 'e be in the boy's ward?" He wore a prisoner's gray uniform and a blue workman's cap that had seen better days.

"I don't know," Henry said. "They put me in here."

The man spoke to his fellows, rather than to Henry. "They *did*, didn't they? 'E must've done somethin' right terrible, eh? Not a debtor, I think. Not a common sneakthief, neither, I'll warrant. Common trash, then? Mmm . . ." He stroked the mustache and walked over to stare disdainfully down at Henry. "Murder then? 'E's got the look for it, I'd say."

"Leave him alone, Jenkens," an older man said from one of the tables. "He ain't done nothing." The older man didn't have the clipped tone Jenkens had, but the sing-song cadence that came out of the southern part of Wales.

"Shut up, you," Jenkens said without looking back. "Of course 'e's done somethin'."

Henry wanted to turn back and leave, or better yet, melt into the floor, but of course the turnkeys had closed the gate behind him, and floor melting wasn't something he could pull off, was it? Henry knew he didn't belong here, being only fourteen. Surely there must be a ward for children? Was this another trick of the Faerie? It had to be, but why the charade?

Newgate had to still be in Faerie hands. To pretend otherwise seemed foolish, but the undeniable, concrete reality of the situation was right in his face and there was no ignoring it. Probably some of these normal, British men were actually some kind of Faerie, but clearly he had to deal with the problem in front of him now and keep an eye for Faerie tricks later.

Jenkens must have seen the despair on Henry's face even if he didn't know the cause. "What then," he said. "What did you do, boy?"

"I didn't do anything," Henry said.

"Must have done somethin'," Jenkens said. "Nobody gets put in 'ere for nothin'."

Henry wasn't about to talk about Widdershins, Mother, the Black Shuck, or his fight with the Hanged Dogs in an alley with this stranger. Maybe that was what the Faerie wanted out of him, answers? That didn't make much sense after Widdershins' mental assault, but Henry couldn't figure out any other motive. Of course, maybe he was looking at this wrong. Who knew why the Faerie did anything? Maybe they'd made some kind of bargain to maintain the prison, complete with prisoners that knew nothing about what was going on outside. Hell, probably most of London didn't know either.

"Not too bright," Jenkens said. "Are you?" He shot out a big, meaty hand that hit Henry a cuff on the side of his head, bringing red flashes and a ringing in his ears with it. Henry staggered back and hit the gate behind him before falling awkwardly to the stone floor.

"Just stay out of me way, then," Jenkens snarled. He turned heavily and went back to his place by the fire. It was cold enough in this place that his seat must have been prime real estate, but clearly he was top dog in here. No one said anything, or even looked at Henry much, while he got the pain under control and climbed to his feet.

The others didn't look like hardened offenders to Henry. Even Jenkens, for all his rough actions, didn't really look like Henry's idea of a criminal. The same group of men, in average work-a-day clothes, might have gathered just as easily in a pub or around a card table. Most of them had coats on against the cold, even inside near the fire.

Henry, glad to be ignored, managed to get to one of the far tables, close to the older man who had tried to call Jenkens off, that being the closest thing here to a friendly face. But the older man wouldn't meet his eye. Not at first. Henry let his head fall to the table. It was cold on this side of the room. He could already feel his hands and feet going numb, but at least for now the cool wood of the table felt good against his throbbing temple.

A roar went up from the card game and Jenkens started hollering at one of his fellow players. The old man used this distraction to approach Henry.

"Here," he murmured, pouring water from a pitcher into a tin cup. "Don't mind Jenkens." He offered the cup to Henry.

"What?" Henry said. He shook his head at the cup.

The man was small and thin and looked like the oldest man in the room. But he had a lively face, with bright eyes like a bird. White wisps of hair stuck out from underneath a cap, and a tweed suit peeked out underneath a dirty grey overcoat. He set the cup down.

"I said, don't mind Jenkens," he said, speaking low. "He thinks because they made him wardsman that he's not guilty like the rest of us."

"Is he?" Henry said. Perhaps that was a rude question, but the other man just shrugged.

"Most of us are," the man said. "Guilty of not paying our creditors, at least." He stuck out his hand. "Daffyd Wyn." Henry found this reference to a normal, if uncaring, world outside so disconcerting that he stared at the older man for a stretch of seconds before he remembered to extend his own hand.

"Henry Kasric," he finally said and shook hands. The older man had surprisingly large hands, much larger than Henry's, even though Daffyd wasn't much taller. Probably Henry would be taller than the old man in a few years.

"You look a bit shaken," Daffyd said, "Understandable, in a place like this. Easy to lose your hold on civilization."

"Yeah," Henry said, not sure what the old man was talking about.

"Here," Daffyd said. "Sometimes, I find that music helps." He picked up a bundle of oily rags on the bench next to him, tied together with twine. He set it on the table and carefully unwrapped the rags, revealing a long copper flute.

The chatter of men near the fire died down suddenly. Even Jenkens put the cards down and leaned back to watch. Daffyd held the flute up, making a little show of limbering his fingers. Finally, he put the instrument to his lips. The men around them had fallen to absolute and total silence.

Daffyd blew, playing softly at first. The tone was haunting, deep, and breathy, like the wind through a tunnel at sea. Daffyd swayed gently as he played, his eyes closed, absorbed. The near lullaby soared, then, getting louder and livelier. It brought the hairs up on the back of Henry's neck. The song fell into a low, heavy rhythm, like hooves on frost-bitten snow, broken only occasionally by one trilling note, high and clear, like a hunting horn.

Henry started at the old man. This was it, then, the trap that Henry had been put in here to fall into. This was the reason the Faerie had put him in here. He could hear the creaking as the wood splintered and gave under the pressure of his fingers and realized he'd been gripping the table impossibly hard. Henry expected pressure, like Widdershins, to start pummeling at his brain, but he felt nothing. It was haunting music, but nothing more. Just music.

Still, no one paid any attention to Henry and no one else made any sound until the old man stopped and the last lingering note had drifted completely away. Then the men picked up their conversation again without applauding or saying anything by way of thanks to the old man. It was as if the man had never even played.

Seconds later, no one was paying either Daffyd or Henry any attention.

"An old Faerie song," Daffyd said quietly when he finished. "Used to be my wife's favorite—when she was still with us. I guess it's got a little magic left in it yet, but not enough to keep me out. You know something about the Faerie, don't you boy?"

"Yes," Henry said, his voice rough. "I know something about the Faerie."

The man picked up the cup of water and splashed a little onto the table as if by accident. Then he lay his arm on the table to screen the small puddle from the rest of the room and fixed Henry with a curious stare. His other hand made a curious gesture over the water, as if dropping some pinched salt.

The small puddle quivered, and suddenly part of it *jumped* up, two small droplets in the shape of fish that arced up and down before splashing back into the puddle they'd come from. A third large, transparent shape with the long, projecting nose and sailfin of a sword fish followed, chasing the smaller fish back down into the depths of the tiny puddle. Then the water went flat again as if nothing had happened.

"Aye," Daffyd said. "I thought you might. I've some experience with them, too, you see, and you can always tell when another Faerie-touched person crosses your path."

"You!" Henry hissed, jumping to his feet. "You're the reason I'm in here!" The others in the room looked idly over at Henry's outburst, but without any real interest.

"Don't be daft!" Daffyd said, waving Henry down urgently, but still trying to keep his hand motions contained, so as not draw further attention. He looked anxiously over at Jenkens and the others. "Do you think I'd be in here if I was important or powerful!

The likes of the folk that run this place don't have any use for me, so here's where I go. I'm just as much a prisoner as you are!"

"You're a Faerie!" Henry said.

"A bit," Daffyd admitted. "Faerie touched, some call it. But so are you! Think that all Faerie are on the same side, do you? Why do you think they put me in here?"

That made some sense. Henry's interrogation with the Black Shuck and Widdershins, and then later with Mother, was proof enough that not all the Faerie were on the same side. Proof that Henry had some Faerie in him, too, but that still didn't cure him of his knee-jerk aversion to tripping over one. Still, he sat down, and the rest of the room turned back to the card game, having lost interest in them.

"You can see it in others," Daffyd said, "once you seen enough of them. The way I can see it in you. You're more touched than I am, I think."

"My father," Henry said curtly. He still found the idea terrifying, the same way he found his newfound strength terrifying, but he couldn't deny it any longer.

"Ah," Daffyd said. He was still speaking low, so the others couldn't hear. "Both my parents were human, but stolen from my crib I was, when I wasn't yet off the teat. Raised in a place called the Gloaming, somewhere in Faerie. I learned much later, around ten or so, that they'd left something in my place that died right off so that me Ma and Da wouldn't even know I was alive. That part hurts a bit."

"Who took you?" Henry asked, terrified that the villain would turn out to be Father.

"Some woman noble," Daffyd said. "Don't even know which one and it don't matter none. She lost interest a few years later.

That's how the Faerie are. Weren't such a bad life, though, in the Gloaming Court, but when I heard they was looking for troops to go to England, I signed right up. Soon as our feet hit Battersea Park, I went lookin' for a chance to desert and it weren't long in comin'. Only problem was I got caught a few days later by the Hanged Dogs and they put me here. Guess my only act as a Welshman will be to die hanging from a noose in an English court. There's a fine tradition o' that, I hear."

Henry stared, stunned beyond belief both by the man's astounding story as well as the nonchalant way he referred to his own imminent death.

He put Henry's own fear to shame.

"Unless we escape!" Henry said.

"Well," Daffyd said, "can't say as I'd mind that. Not a bit, and stranger things have happened." He sighed and leaned back, visibly putting off the macabre topic of their own impending executions. He tapped the flute. "I like to play. Reminds me of my Ava, who taught me."

"How did you get that in here?" Henry asked.

Daffyd winked at him, but kept on talking as if Henry hadn't spoken.

"We met in the Pavilion, Ava and me. In a sort of theater. But then she fell sick. I used to work at the theater, writing music during the day and playing all night. I'd come home very late, and she'd always make me play that tune in our dark little bedroom before I came to bed. She said it made her dreams restful. She passed a month before I heard about the war, or I would never have left."

"I'm sorry," Henry said.

Daffyd nodded. "Me too. That's why I keep the flute. Last thing of hers I have left."

Henry looked at the flute curiously. "I've never heard anything like that music you just played. I've never seen or heard a copper flute before, either."

"Ah," Daffyd said, waving a hand. The twinkle in his bright little eyes showed he'd felt the praise. "It was nothing. My wife's Da made the flute and she taught me to play the song. They deserve the credit. I just play it."

The card game had started up again. There wasn't much else to do here, it seemed, besides play cards and wait.

"Here," Daffyd said, handing the flute to Henry. "You try it."

"Me?" Henry said.

"Why not?"

"I'm not the musical one of the family," Henry said. "That's Faith. She can sing and play the piano, but I never learned."

"Try it," Daffyd insisted. "What else have you got to do to keep you busy? Teaching you to play flute will help me pass the time. If you're bad at it, so much the better. Kills more time that way."

The man had a point. The only reading material available was a neglected book of Testament on the table and Henry didn't feel like that right now.

"All right," Henry said, and took the flute. It was heavier than it looked.

"Good. You blow across the hole at the top here. And put your hands like this."

Daffyd talked Henry through the preliminaries, not playing much, but moving again and again through the finger positions. He kept Henry at it, gently coaching him, and slowly Henry found himself catching on.

Later in the day, another of the turnkeys called out: "Time to stretch your legs, you wretches!"

Daffyd grabbed Henry's arm when he got up and gave Henry a warning look.

"We'll stay inside, sir," Daffyd said to the turnkey. Henry sat back down.

The guard shrugged. "Suit yourself." He led the other inmates out of the room and presumably out into the yard.

"It's a bad business," Daffyd whispered, "out in the yard. More of the really bad ones out there. You don't want any of that." He peered suspiciously at Henry. "How much do you understand of what's happening?"

"The Faerie have come back to England," Henry said.

"Aye," Daffyd said. "I know that part. But why now? After all this time?"

"It's war," Henry said. "What's to understand?"

Daffyd sighed. "From the mouths of babes. You have that right."

"They own this entire prison, don't they?"

"Aye," Daffyd said. "But not so much of London as you might suppose. Not yet. Now, let's see if you can make some actual notes on that flute. Better to practice this part when the others are out. You don't want to irritate Jenkens."

It was bizarre, working at something so mundane as music when the entire world was falling apart, but to Henry's surprise, he found himself going along with the lessons. The old man showed Henry how to place the flute against his mouth and Henry blew hesitantly. It didn't come out right the first time, but in less than an hour Henry was making actual notes. He didn't produce anything like the ghostly melodies that Daffyd played. In fact, Henry's efforts didn't even string together enough notes in a row to be called music. But Daffyd seemed pleased with his progress and Henry found that it was a much needed distraction from wondering what was going on outside these walls. He could go mad with worry trying to figure out a way to escape the inescapable, or trying to guess what the Faerie were going to do next. The Faerie didn't seem to need reasons for doing *anything* the way men did. Staying here and working the flute inside the pocket of normalcy was far better.

By the time a gristly and meager dinner had come and gone, Henry was able to string enough notes together to realize that Daffyd was, of course, teaching him the Faerie melody the old man had played earlier.

The turnkeys came for Henry shortly after that. The rest of the inmates would bed down in the same room they occupied during the day. But the turnkeys each took one of Henry's arms in preparation of marching him back to his own private cell.

"See you, boy," Jenkens called out nastily as the turnkeys walked Henry out. "See how much you can learn at that flute. Better learn fast. Only one more day until your trial, then the next day, your hanging."

"How do you know that?" Henry said, turning as much as he could in the doorway with the turnkeys' hands on his arms. He hated how small and frightened his voice sounded.

Jenkens' laughter followed Henry down the wide darkening corridor as he was ushered back to his cell.

After it got dark, he stood gripping the bars of his cell, looking down the long, wide hall to watch for any sign of the Black Shuck or Widdershins. The lurid orange light of a coal stove spilled out in the far end of the hall, but that was all. This late in the night, it seemed the only light in Newgate.

CHAPTER 10

On Shore

We left the Thames and made our way up a river that I'd seen in one of Joshua's photographs, a river I was sure hadn't been here before the Faerie had come. Even so, I'd gotten a pretty good idea of how far it went and when we would have to leave it behind and make our way through the thick forest to get to Stormholt.

The forest we'd seen was all around us, thick and dark and silent, as if the massive black trees and hanging lichen and vines had left everything too cramped for anything other than insects. Perhaps more jungle than forest, though I couldn't remember the difference right now. Memories came back to me of another forest in Faerie, the forest I'd followed Father through when I was a child, where I'd seen the Faerie King. But that forest had had space for moonlight to slant through and reach the ground in places. This one was far too cramped, with an undergrowth every bit as crowded as the branches above. Some light trickled down, to be scattered on the undergrowth leaves like gold coins, but no light ever made it all the way. Pockets of leafy darkness containing who knew what waited to swallow anyone foolish enough to venture in. There was a weighty presence to the place. A small bird, or serpent, or stoat would have to fight every second of every night and day just to have enough space to live and breathe, the presence said. There would be no room for anything larger and no room for anything civilized. Certainly *people* could not survive in there.

Nellie had scouted ahead, swimming ahead without sound and effort, and was now manning the tiller while Wil took his turn scouting. (Womaning the tiller? Girling? English was a bloody awful language sometimes.) Dream was doing her own scouting by air and between her and the Prowlers, we had a pretty good idea what was up ahead. So far we'd avoided two armed patrols on the shore and drifted silently past a massive sea turtle sleeping down in the soft mud, so our luck was holding. Avonstoke had taken one of Mog's oars and the two of them were still going strong.

Avonstoke had taken off his cloak and uniform coat and there was something entirely too distracting about watching his pale shoulders bunch and release, bunch and release.

"There," Nellie said. "That's where we want to land the boat."

"Dream," I said. "Check it out."

We rounded a willow the size of a barge covered with creeper vine and saw part of the bank that had a little clearing of sorts, about fifteen or twenty feet that wasn't packed with foliage.

"Wait," Dream said from above. "There's something there, waiting for us."

"Hanged Dogs?" I asked. That was what we'd run into in London. But Dream was already riding silently into the foliage near us, clearly planning on circling behind whatever it was that was waiting for us.

"Anchor," I said. "Drop the anchor." I didn't want to float into a trap. I yanked my pistol out. Everyone else was pulling out weapons, too, Faith next to me transferring her staff to her other hand so she could pull the silver blade free of its leather sheath, Sands his rapier, Avonstoke his magical blade. Mog, for his part, hefted that enormous club.

But no sooner had Mog dropped the anchor over the side with a heavy plop, than a small form slunk out from behind an enormous willow tree.

"It's all right," Mr. Sands said, pushing my hand that raised the pistol down, and walked past. I hadn't even realized I'd drawn it, but there it was. I kept it out as Mr. Sands approached the sets of glowing eyes.

"It's a cat?" Faith said.

"Cats, plural," I said.

We clambered out into the water and hauled the launch up onto the grassy bank. I turned, feeling the sudden nervous prickle of being watched. I turned to see four pairs of eyes glowing in the foggy gloom. Avonstoke must have become aware of it at the same time because he turned to face them.

Avonstoke sidled over to me. He'd lowered the point of his sword, but still had it pointed at the trees where the glowing eyes were. "Are you sure we can trust them? I mean, cats?"

"It's all right," Faith said. "Mr. Sands has a way with cats. Remember, Justice, at Stormholt?"

I flashed her a look of incredulity.

As if I could ever forget that writhing sea of yellow eyes. One cat could be a lovely thing. When I thought about more than one, that's when the nightmares came.

"Unsettling things," Avonstoke said with a shiver. "The way they *look* at you." Maybe he'd had his own run-in with cats.

"You're both just being stupid," Faith said. I couldn't tell if she was kidding or not.

Four cats slid silently out of the shadows and Mr. Sands knelt, rubbing the lead cat's head, around the base of the ears, and down its sleek back. It was a large black female, and something about her bearing suggested she might be the mother of the three tortoise-shell kittens that trailed behind.

"Oh look!" Faith said, moving forward. "Kittens!"

"Oh," I said warily. "It starts with just a few . . ." I followed slowly.

"Food?" Mog grunted, taking a step forward.

Avonstoke put a hand on Mog's shoulder, restraining him. "Best not. I believe they're friends. Sort of."

"Mm," Mog said. "Very sad." The Prowler children were nodding in agreement.

Mr. Sands, still on his knees, murmured something to the mother. She responded with something between a meow and a coo. Sounded like 'mrrrr.' Mr. Sands spoke again, quietly and the mother mrrrrred another response.

"Is he," Avonstoke asked, "*talking* to them?"

I shook my head, having no idea. "*I* was just going to ask *you* that."

"That's not natural," Nellie said judiciously. "Can't trust no cat."

"Too true," Dream said, landing on Mog's shoulder. "Too true." She shuddered. Not big cat people, the Faerie, it seemed.

"I thought," Avonstoke said, "that all his magic was gone."

"Must be more of a skill, I guess," I said, thinking of Sands' claims back on the *Specter*. He hadn't been blowing smoke, at least.

The three kittens, deciding that Mr. Sands must have their mother's seal of approval, came friskily after mom, but still carefully watched us, especially Mog, with cautious eyes.

After another minute of this conversation, Mr. Sands stood up.

"Thank you, Minerva," he said. "Good luck to you."

Minerva turned and ran towards the bushes and trees a few feet away. The kittens dawdled, the three of them looking at us with their heads canted to one side and their ears up. Mother Minerva turned once and chirped at her kittens to follow. They did. The last kitten to disappear turned one last time to look at us, her white-tipped tail quivering with excitement, before she followed the others and disappeared.

"You can't just let them go off," Faith said, "into the woods while all this is going on? Faerie monsters might get the kittens!"

"Like Mog," Mog suggested.

"Like Mog!" Faith said, getting louder and pointing at Mog, who seemed extremely pleased with himself.

Mr. Sands gave a rueful smile. "Minerva has experience in places like this and she'll watch her kittens. It's a perfect wilderness. They're as safe now as they were before the Faerie came. Probably safer. I'm far more worried about the news they just gave me."

"Scouts!" Avonstoke said, delighted. "You're using them as scouts."

"Of course," Mr. Sands agreed. He turned back to me. "The Faerie may have compromised Stormholt."

"I thought you said that wasn't possible?" Faith said.

"It shouldn't have been," Mr. Sands said angrily. "It's protected against that very eventuality. The reports are second-hand.

Minerva hasn't seen for herself. So it's not certain. But there's more." His face grew even more grave, if that were possible. "It's Henry. He's in Newgate Prison."

"The prison?" I said. "It's still there? All the buildings they wiped out and they left *that* one?"

"I doubt," Mr. Sands said, "that most of their decisions were that calculated. But yes, Newgate Prison is still intact. In fact, a great deal of London is still intact, if overrun. The Faerie seem to be quite partial to it. The prison, it seems, is still being used in precisely the same capacity. I understand it was one of the first places the Faerie took over."

"How do the cats know Henry's inside?" I asked. "Can they get to him?"

"No," Mr. Sands said. "There's more than just stone and bars protecting that place. They don't dare go near it. But Minerva herself saw Henry being taken in days ago and no one's seen him come out."

"Days ago!" Faith burst out. "Oh, Henry. We must get him out. He's sensitive and sweet. He can't take a place like that!"

"I'm afraid," Mr. Sands said, "that captivity under the Black Shuck's care is almost certainly horrible and dangerous. I won't lie to you. I fear for his life."

"We'll have to get him out of there," I said. "As soon as possible."

I could see Sands clamp his mouth shut behind the obvious statement that it might be too late.

"What about Benedict?" Faith asked.

"They've not seen him at all," Sands said. "We have no recent eyes on Stormholt. He may be there. But . . ." he said, raising his hand as I was opening my mouth to ask a question, "they have *not* seen the Wild Hunt, so that is something."

"What about Étienne and Percy and the other Ghost Boys?" I asked. I'd been hoping that they'd found out somehow about our coming, that one of Mr. Sands' messages had gotten through even though we'd gotten no reply.

Mr. Sands shook his head. "Nothing. I'd expected them and the cats to coordinate, but there's been no sign of the Ghost Boys at all."

"These poor boys," Faith murmured. "And Emily." The Ghost Boys, despite their name, also included one girl. I didn't want to imagine what any of them might be going through.

Faith's face looked pinched, too, obviously thinking the same thing.

"If they're ghosts," Avonstoke asked, "can cats see them?"

Sands sniffed. "Cats see far more than anyone gives them credit for."

"Well, that's just disturbing," Avonstoke said.

"Really?" Faith said. "Magic swords out of the air and dragons and towering tree creatures and that's the part that bothers you. Talking to cats is like biscuits and tea on a trolley compared to all this!" She waved her hand around.

"Well, it's not like everyone can talk to cats, you know," Sands said peevishly. "It took a rather long time to learn."

"Oh," Faith said, "I'm sure."

"The hard part," Mr. Sands went on, "is learning to weed out the details *we* care about from the constant and, I don't mind telling you, somewhat tedious tirades about the best places to sleep, for instance."

"What about . . ." I started.

"It's more a feat," Mr. Sands went on, "of mental endurance. You have no idea. Minerva, at least, I've trained from a kitten, but most cats! Good Lord! I once spoke to a ginger tabby for a good sixteen hours just trying to find out if . . ."

"Sands!" I snapped. "What about Father's troops still stationed here? Could they be any help?"

"Oh, right," Mr. Sands said. "Sorry. The Hussars, you mean. Well, there's been no sign of them, either in what's left of the city or in the countryside, though our coverage there, with all the changes, is very sketchy. My guess is they'd be holed up in Stormholt. But I don't know what's going on there."

"Would the Hussars help us get Henry out of Newgate?"

"They followed your father," Mr. Sands said promptly.

"Will they follow me?"

"I don't know," Sands admitted. "But leadership isn't really the issue. They're an aggressive bunch and they hate the Faerie. It shouldn't be that hard to point them in the right direction."

"Good," I said. "That will give us a chance to collect Benedict, as well. Stormholt should still be a safe haven from which to launch our rescue, yes?"

"If there is any place in England that is safe," Mr. Sands said, "it would be Stormholt."

"Now," Mr. Sands said, "it is time to teach you how to summon Pavor Nocturnus, the creature that resides in the token of your father's."

I pulled out the chess piece.

"Get me some wood," Mr. Sands asked Avonstoke. "Enough for a small fire."

Avonstoke summoned his sword immediately. "I shall cut you enough to build a bonfire the gods could look down and see!"

"We don't need that," Mr. Sands said. "And we don't want anything that large. Enough for a small fire, I said."

Avonstoke sighed, but quickly lopped off some of the brush, which Mog and Nellie brought over.

"Good," Mr. Sands said.

I guess I'd hoped for some sort of magical display, because I was slightly disappointed when Mr. Sands pulled out a box of matches. The wood, though encrusted with mud, was dead and dry, and he got it ablaze easily enough. An oily black smoke curled up at once like a smoky tendril.

Mr. Sands pulled out a small knife. "Give me your hand," he said to me.

I hadn't even seen Dream leave, but she flew back now, weaving in and around the leaves with the speed and ease of a dragonfly.

"Hanged Dogs!" she shouted out. "I saw them less than three miles away, heading this way. It looked they knew exactly where they were going, straight here!"

A long, drawn-out howl ghosted through the forest from behind her, just in case I'd had any doubts.

"Hurry," Mr. Sands said, shaking his open hand at me. "We don't have a lot of time."

As soon as I laid my hand in his, he flicked the tip of his knife across my palm, cutting a thin slit in the center of my hand. It happened so fast I barely had time to flinch.

Faith, Nellie, and Wil crowded closer to the river, away from the forest.

I looked back at the launch. Damn. My mission was damned from the very beginning.

I looked down at Sands. "Can we escape?"

"Doubtful," he said. "But we may be able to fight them off."

The Prowler children could probably escape in the water, if it came to that, and Dream could fly away at any time, but the rest of us didn't have any such recourse. It was unlikely that we could move very quickly in the launch, or through the woods. So flight wasn't an option.

"We fight, then," I said.

"Then this will help," Mr. Sands said. "Hold the chess piece out over the fire, in the smoke, and repeat 'Pavor Nocturnus' three times."

I moved to do as he said, but he caught my hand in his.

"Wait," he said, and his voice throbbed with intensity. "This holds the spirit of a demon, Justice. Pavor Nocturnus."

I furrowed my brow, trying to remember my Latin.

"Nightmare?" Faith said.

He nodded. "A closer translation might be 'night terrors,' but yes, you have it right. Be careful with the name. Do not lose the totem. It is crafted using wood from the World Tree, as was my totem that summoned Acta Santorum. They are paired, you see, angel and demon. The angel is lost to us, but you can still control the demon."

He took a deep breath and went on. "But there are dangers. The binding won't hold if the demon gets submerged. Do not take it into any body of water. Above all, do *not* take Pavor Nocturnus into the sea."

"Isn't she," Avonstoke said, "an admiral? With all the ships and such?"

Sands just glared.

"We're running out of time!" Faith said. The noises were getting closer.

"Just say the name three times?" I said.

Sands nodded. "And hold the token in the smoke."

The carved wooden horse throbbed warmly in my hand.

A hum ran through the woods, shaking the leaves and branches around us. It was regular, even, a heartbeat.

I held the chess piece out over the fire. "Pavor Nocturnus," I said. "Pavor Nocturnus. Pavor Nocturnus."

The heartbeat increased until the woods rattled with every pulse. A warm and sulfurous wind enveloped me, whipping my coat and hair all around. I had to grip my hat with my other hand to keep it from flying off. Faith was standing behind me, gripping her staff. Avonstoke had his sword out while Mog had his club. The two of them took positions near the forest.

Another howl cut through the air. The Hanged Dogs were close now.

Then I forgot all about the Hanged Dogs, for just an instant, because the smoke coming from the fire wasn't acting right.

It swirled in place underneath my hand instead of flowing up like smoke was supposed to, as if it were caught in a great, upside-down glass bowl. It spread out, a growing stain in midair, gradually taking shape.

A long, hunched back appeared, clearly part of something enormous. Then the top *unfurled*, and a dozen tentacles burst out, reaching towards us. A bestial bellow reverberated around the small open space, horribly loud in the near silence. Faith made a vague sound behind me and I thought I heard the Prowler children gasp. Mog growled, and so, surprisingly, did Avonstoke, and the two of them started towards us.

"Stay back!" Mr. Sands snapped.

They stopped. I could see Avonstoke watching me for a signal. I shook my head at him. *Stay back.*

My hand, holding the chess piece, was shaking now. This was the creature bound to the chess piece that Father gave me? The one I'd lost? Or was it another one? I'd stolen the chess piece years later, in part, because I was sure it was the one that Father had given to me. But what if there was a mistake? I shot a glance at Mr. Sands, but that was no help. His face was quivering with delight. I looked back and forth from him to the monster coalescing underneath my hand.

Another howl came from the Hanged Dogs, this time much, much closer.

The creature in front of us twitched and moved and the tentacles seemed to realize I was standing right in front of it. They reached out . . .

. . . and the shape fell suddenly apart.

It broke into smoke again, falling, and then suddenly reforming . . . into an entirely different shape. It happened so quickly that it was like the demonic shape had never been.

Now, a beautiful mare stood in front of us, silky black. She stamped the wet earth in a sudden burst of joy and happiness. She didn't seem dangerous, only excited. The eyes were a soft and gentle brown with no kinship whatsoever to the baleful yellow demon eyes from moments before.

"Pavor Nocturnus," I said, suddenly understanding. Mr. Sands had had Acta Santorum. She'd been his, and when he'd broken his magical token, he'd lost her. Now I had Pavor Nocturnus. And I didn't want to lose her, ever.

More howls came through the woods, this time very close.

Nocturnus snorted, blew air out of her nostrils, and pranced to face the growing noises from the brush. Nocturnus' movement was such a typical reaction for a horse that my heart swelled with relief. Her solid, glossy flank, hooves thudding lightly on the ground—these things seemed so much a part of our world, flesh and mud and warm breath, nothing like the flaming eyes of the demon before her. I remembered what Father and Sands said about taking on the attributes of something when you took its shape.

"Up you go," Mr. Sands said, giving me a boost. Not only had Pavor Nocturnus materialized with a fine saddle, but it appeared to be the right length, and I got my toes in the stirrups without trouble.

"Faith," Mr. Sands said. "Get up behind her. She'll carry you both." He stopped, reaching up and touching Nocturnus' black glossy neck with a haunted reverence.

Then he shook his head and seemed to remember where he was. "Go on," he said. "The Hanged Dogs will be after the two of you and may ignore the rest of us. She can carry you to safety."

"No!" I snapped, drawing the pistol that Avonstoke had given me. "We fight!" I didn't bring the rest of them along to abandon them in a Faerie woods now.

Mr. Sands opened his mouth to argue, but I was saved the trouble of ignoring him, because it was too late. The nearest scrubby bush burst and a brown, furry shape burst out of it. Two more followed. A rotten and sickly-sweet stench came with them. The Hanged Dogs were here.

Sands had told us about the Hanged Dogs. The spirits of men hanged that were too foul, too cruel, too hateful to die. The spirits lingered in the shape of huge black dogs the size of ponies, no longer living, but still animated. Part man, part feral mastiff, and all of them dead flesh.

Avonstoke and Mog met them with magical sword and stout club, but there were too many and they came too quickly. Four of five of the beasts rushed Avonstoke and Mog, and I saw

Avonstoke go down under two of them at once. Mog clubbed another down, but a fourth was on him almost instantly.

Mr. Sands had a sword out, trying to protect Faith and I, but the thin rapier looked ludicrous next to the hulking dog beasts swarming past the others. I could still see where other dogs were trying to get their teeth into the throats of the struggling Avonstoke and Mog. Mog had lost his weapon entirely and was trying to hold off a pair of slavering jaws with his clawed hands. Avonstoke still had his, but one of the dogs on him had its jaws around his forearm, pinning the weapon and making it useless. It was trying to drag him to one side while another was trying to get past his kicking feet and bury its muzzle into Avonstoke's innards.

I gave a wordless, inarticulate cry, but Nocturnus clearly knew what I wanted, because she surged forward and charged into the Hanged Dogs in front of us like a freight train. Two well-placed hooves struck down the Hanged Dogs trying to finish off Avonstoke like thunderstrokes.

Another Hanged Dog was trying to drag me and Faith off Nocturnus' back, but Faith lashed out with her sword. What she didn't possess in accuracy she made up for with determination. It took her four or five strokes to finish the dog, but she swung gamely, shrieking like a banshee with every swing.

I was guiding Nocturnus with my left hand on the reins, while my right held the pistol. There was no tremor in my hands now. At first, it was all I could do to cling to the saddle, while Nocturnus surged underneath me and Faith nearly throttled me from behind.

"Stop choking me!" I snarled and her grip loosened a tiny fraction.

I drew a bead on the dog on top of Mog and with a prayer, squeezed the trigger.

I'd been as worried about hitting Mog as hitting our enemy, but the bullet put a neat, tidy hole in the back of the Hanged Dog's head.

Mog got to his feet, flashed me a toothy grin, and recovered his huge club in time to ready himself for the next rush.

Avonstoke was up, sword in hand, with his back to us. "I am suddenly," he called out over his shoulder, "very glad that you brought the horse! I am far less perforated for it!"

More Hanged Dogs loped out of the woods. They were everywhere now, snarling and stinking to high heaven.

Mr. Sands was right about one thing, too, they came straight at me and Faith.

Avonstoke and Mog intercepted two of them. Two more raced past them, coming at Nocturnus to try and slash her from underneath. I tried to bring the gun to bear, but things were happening too quickly.

Not too quickly for Nocturnus, though. She danced back just out of reach, far nimbler than any horse that large had any right to be. She wasn't waiting for me to tell her, either. The dog rushed again, and two hooves struck out like machine pistons. The dog went down, twitching like an electrocuted spider.

Another Hanged Dog crouched for a leap, clearly looking to jump over Nocturnus and right into our laps.

"Oh, God!" Faith said. She had the silver sword out in her right hand, but her left was empty. She'd dropped her staff, as ungainly as it was on a horse.

The dog sprang, fur bristling, and I shot it full in the face. Nocturnus danced aside and the dog, very dead, sailed harmlessly past, crashed to the ground, and did not move again. It was a woman, long dead, with a decayed noose around her neck. I grimaced and looked away. I couldn't afford to think of them as people just now. Even dead people.

Sands had said they were invulnerable to normal weapons, but both Faith's sword and my bullets were made especially to war on the Faerie.

That thought made me spin to look at the others, many of which didn't have such weapons. I hadn't planned on fighting our way through in any case and certainly hadn't reckoned on meeting anything as fearsome as the Hanged Dogs the second we set foot on land.

Avonstoke leapt and cut like a man possessed, perhaps spurred on by his near-death moments ago. His curved, black blade took the head, arm, and shoulder of the nearest beast as neatly as gardening shears took an offending weed. He spun to face another and this time, the dog backpedaled as he advanced.

Mog was standing between the Prowlers and another dog, battering it with his club. It might not have been a weapon especially enchanted to fight the Faerie, but it was a good forty or fifty pounds and it sufficed to knock the beast down again and again. Then the Prowler children proved they weren't exactly easy prey by pinning the downed dog to the earth with surprising strength. Even Dream was contributing as best she could, weaving a path around the Hanged Dogs' heads. She used a blowdart to fire darts into unguarded ears and eyes, making the dogs howl in fury and pain.

Then Mog settled the matter of effective weapons by taking the opening the Prowler children gave him and burying his fanged snout into the dog's neck and tearing out great chunks of dead flesh until the dog quivered and lay still.

"Bah," Mog spat. "Dog taste stink!"

Mr. Sands had his own silver sword, a thin rapier. I was surprised, and yet somehow not, to see that he was no slouch with a blade. But the thin weapon didn't look very deadly with two of the dogs backing him towards the riverbank.

I'd already lost track of how many dogs there were, everything was a blur of fur and stink and fury. At least seven or eight still alive, or was it nine? Ten? They moved too fast to be sure.

Avonstoke rushed forward and peeled something off his left wrist. I could see it writhing between his pinched thumb and finger like a living and angry viper. When he flung it at the two dogs that had cornered Sands, it was with a quick flip, as if he was afraid to get bitten.

The black strip of darkness unfolded and unfolded again, writhing angrily as it flew, growing a dozen feet long and landing on the nearest dog. A black serpent, with a pike's mouth, long and filled with dozens of needle teeth. The thing hissed and bit the dog's face, popping the entire decayed face like huge scissors through a melon. The serpent was still forming, even as it killed, and now it had two long, greenish-black sets of fins, and a wicked-looking forked tail. The whole thing looked to have crawled from the primordial depths at Avonstoke's command.

The serpent turned on the second dog, grappling with it long enough for Sands to run it through with his silver blade. The dog shuddered and life left it, but that didn't stop the sea serpent from savaging the body. Sands was careful to back quickly out of the serpent's reach. It didn't look like the kind of creature that cared about friend or foe.

I shot twice more, dropping two of the dogs, and then my pistol clicked empty. Nocturnus spun and lashed out with her hind hooves to crush the chest of a dog behind us. I whirled, looking for more opponents, but saw none . . . perhaps it was over? More beasts crashed from the brush.

My gut twisted in a sickening lurch. There were easily twice as many as we'd handled before, snapping their teeth and hemming us in from three sides. Behind us was the river, but I didn't think we'd be able to launch the boat before we had the dogs all over us. I was fumbling in my pocket for more cartridges, but had no time to load them.

Faith, still behind me on Nocturnus, suddenly raised her voice.

She sang with a trio of voices, all sounding like her, combined in a diminished chord that rang out around us. Thunder rolled in her voice and lightning flashed overhead. Avonstoke, near me, looked up at the sudden storm and hesitated long enough to drop his guard. I gasped, sure the dog would slash open his throat.

But instead, the dog attacking Avonstoke staggered and fell like a puppet with its strings cut. All the dogs were falling now. They quivered on the ground, but that was all.

Mog took the opportunity to bash one's brains out with his club. It didn't even try and avoid the blow.

Faith slid off Nocturnus' back and I followed. She snatched up her staff. It blazed. My gun was out of bullets and I fumbled to reload, but, as it turned out, I didn't need them.

Faith took three steps and put her hands on the nearest writhing Hanged Dog. Her staff flashed and the dog sighed out a breathy death rattle and went still.

The others didn't need a better invitation. Avonstoke, Mr. Sands, and Mog clove and bashed the remaining dogs as easily as farmers reaping wheat. Faith dispatched the rest with a touch.

Faith kept up her song until Avonstoke had beheaded the last one with a negligent, backhanded sweep of his black, curved sword. Then she stopped and her staff went dark. Suddenly everything was silent except for Avonstoke's serpent, which was making a lot of gurgling sounds trying to swallow one of the Hanged Dog bodies whole.

"How on Earth did you do that?" Mr. Sands asked, looking at Faith.

"Same as the mist," Faith said, talking slowly, sounding as if she was just working it out for herself. "I could feel their magic, like candles of blackness, and it was as if I could suddenly reach out and snuff them. So, I did."

"Astonishing," Mr. Sands said, shaking his head. "That far surpasses anything I did as your father's magician. But it doesn't seem to conform to normal magic. At least none that I know."

Faith shrugged helplessly.

"Glad we brought you along," I murmured to my sister. She nodded and returned a hesitant smile.

"What about you?" I said, smacking Avonstoke with a backhanded blow on his arm. "You didn't tell us you could do that!"

"Drecovian's magic?" Faith asked.

"Yes," Avonstoke said, cradling his arm with mock injury. Then he laughed and grinned that wicked grin of his.

Behind him, Mog took another step away from the serpent that was trying to swallow one of its prey. It was getting along nicely.

"Drecovian do that one, too?" I asked, pointing at the huge raven tattoo around his eyes.

"Guilty as charged," Avonstoke said.

"Can we *please* move away from that thing?" Faith was pointing at the serpent, which was almost done devouring corpses.

I ignored her and grabbed Avonstoke's wrist. There'd been a coiled pattern there before, but now it was gone.

"How many of those do you have?" I asked the question I should have asked long ago. "What can they do?"

"A few," Avonstoke admitted. "Though part of their magic works best when kept secret. Besides, some of them are in . . . hidden places that I'd prefer not to reveal now."

I was going to press him, but he waggled his eyebrows in a mock challenge with the word 'hidden' and I blushed. Try as I might, I couldn't seem to think of Avonstoke as simply one more person under my command. If he could be said to be under anybody's command.

"But," Avonstoke said, his voice suddenly serious, "I forget myself. I still have someone to thank." He stepped around me to Nocturnus, who was still stamping the ground, ready, it seemed, for more dogs. She calmed immediately at Avonstoke's approach.

He stopped and put a hand affectionately on the side of the horse's neck. "Thank you, my friend. I owe you my life. I shall not forget." His voice was soft, and far more serious than it usually was.

"That was," Mr. Sands said seriously, "an amazing display you just put on, Faith. Your powers are already growing tremendously."

"Yes," Faith said, her face first displaying pleasure and then worry. I could see that this new and terrifying power gave her pause. The world had changed, and now she was discovering the depths to which she was changing with it.

She didn't like it. These gifts were unsettling and uncontrollable and yet we'd been thrust into situations where we needed to rely on them daily, without completely understanding their connection to us or what might be connected to the other end. And yet, if we *were* going to be at war with the Faerie, better to be armed with new, unreliable, unsettling powers than not to be armed at all, if only barely. At least I got compensated with a horse and a ship, both of which I'd wanted since childhood. Near as I could tell, Faith wasn't getting much of anything *she* wanted.

"Well," Faith said softly, but with forced brightness, "I guess I'm a magician after all."

"You are," Mr. Sands said. His voice too, was hushed. "I'm sorry, for what that's worth."

Faith nodded. "Come on," she said. "We have to get going, don't we?"

I nodded. We certainly did.

CHAPTER 11

Journey to Stormholt

Mog held out a clawed hand, stopping the rest of us from passing him. We were in a thick part of the forest. There was nothing as formal as a path in front of us, and there hadn't been for miles. Trees were crowded all around us, very tall, with their leaves all at the top so that the forest seemed stark and bare, as if looking through a gallery of pillars. We could see a fair distance and leaves crunched loudly underfoot as we moved.

The forest floor in front of us, covered with more leaves, looked the same as all the rest to me, but Mog didn't like it.

"Smells funny. Look again." He pointed at my ghost eye.

I squinted my right eye shut, looking with the left, and then sucked in a short breath in surprise.

"Something there," I whispered back. "In the leaves. Can't tell what."

Mog fished through the leaves at our feet and came up with a stone, which he flipped out ahead of us.

I jumped, we all jumped, as part of the forest floor twenty or so feet across heaved itself up in a sudden flurry of agitated motion, scattering leaves in all directions. It shook itself, like something just waking, and glided slowly away from us with the slow, silent motion usually reserved for the ocean floor. Wide wings rippled as it went and a long, thirty-feet whip-cord tail lashed the leaves behind it. And then it was gone.

Mog nodded. "Safe now."

"Well done, Mog," I said. "Again." I patted the Goblin on the shoulder as I walked past.

We'd had to unsummon Nocturnus, which had given me some pause, now that I knew the demonic shape she normally wore, and the hellish place she'd come from.

"She was born in a world of brimstone and fire," Sands had said. "But now, she is bound to the chess piece. She'll simply sleep until you bring her back."

"We'll bring you back as soon as we can," I'd murmured to Nocturnus' gentle face. She'd nickered back at me softly, her breath warm on my face and hands.

"Ha ha," Mog had said. "Nightmare will sleep. Perhaps to dream? Perhaps even like *Mog's* dream. Little magician is very funny."

"Does she dream?" I'd asked.

"I . . ." Mr. Sands had looked at Mog. "I don't know. She might."

Now, I was feeling a genuine gratitude and affection for Mog and the others. We'd never had made it this far if not for Mog,

Dream, Nellie, and Wil. Dream had been watching our perimeter relentlessly and had three times appeared out of the upper branches in time to guide us to hiding before patrols stumbled across our position. At least a dozen new rivers and fens had crossed our path, bodies of water that hadn't been there before, which Nellie and Wil had guided us carefully through. The Faerie forest that had displaced so much English city and farmland was a shifting dangerous place, but a dangerous place the Faerie crew seemed familiar with.

Faith, Avonstoke, Sands and I kept our weapons ready, but they hadn't been needed so far.

Ironically, the largest obstacles we encountered were Father's railroad tracks. They were long tunnels of open space through the woods, with the tracks running through them, enclosed by a thicket, as if the forest had tried to cross the tracks and been forced to flow over instead. This formed rough wooden bridges, like falling trees, over each of them. Father's idea to impede Faerie movement had been only an inconvenience to go over.

"The stink of it," Nellie moaned as we crossed one. "Like a metallic corpse, ain't it? Not natural."

We slept fitfully and briefly under the shelter of a fallen tree and started again the next morning.

It was nearly noon, over thirty hours or so after departing the *Specter*, when we crested a small hill covered with a rust-colored thorny thicket. Mr. Sands stopped and pointed up.

"Stormholt," he said with a catch in his voice.

"No," I said. "This isn't right."

The house, a shadowy monstrosity with that familiar haphazard sawtooth roof of mismatched gables, dormers, ridges, and valleys, loomed up at the very top of a hill, presiding over the surrounding land. The nearby forest had encroached, now surrounding the place with blackened and gnarled trees swimming in a sea of pearly fog. The forest had grown so close, in fact, that branches and gnarled roots pierced the walls of the house in several places, as if the forest had had several centuries to overrun the place. A light trickle came down, which should have driven some of the fog away, but the place looked more miserable and forbidding.

Where the protective iron fence had once stood, sat a ragged trench filled with muddy water. The stone and iron should have endured for hundreds of years, but the Faerie had torn it down in a matter of days. The lawn was an overgrown thicket with trees and brush grown overnight. The house was in a state of extreme decay, as if it had stood unattended for decades.

"The iron fence is gone," Faith said. "And where are all the cats?"

"This can't be the right place," I said, which was ridiculous and I knew it. There couldn't have been two houses like that and the shape of the hill looked right. It was everything else that had changed. Could the Faerie have somehow moved the house?

Sands' face was completely ashen. "Where is . . . What could . . . I don't understand."

"You don't understand?" I said, turning on him. I could feel all the rage and frustration welling up and my next words came out dripping with scorn. We were standing on a small hillock populated with a single, gnarled, and stubborn black tree so stunted that it might have been better referred to as a bush. A half-stifled, guttural scream of pure rage burst out.

"You said the fence would keep the Faerie out, remember?" I screamed. "That's what you told us!"

"Justice," Faith said. She had that careful note you hear when someone is talking to a crazy person. Avonstoke was looking at both of us, obviously concerned.

"What about Étienne and Percy and Emily and all the other Ghost Boys?" I snarled "What about *them*?"

"Justice," Faith said again, this time more loudly. Avonstoke had gone from concern to anxious alarm. I could see Dream, Nellie, Wil and even Mog staring at me, shocked.

"What about them?" I snarled at Sands.

Sands looked very small and defeated. He lifted his hands and dropped them. "I don't know. We had troops stationed here, too, after we left. The Hussars are used to fighting the Faerie. They're very good at it. I'm at a complete loss."

Faith grabbed my arm. "Justice!"

I threw her grip off. I knew what she was going to say, and I knew she was right. Whatever had happened here, it had *already happened*. Losing my patience, temper, or just possibly my sanity wasn't going to change that. I was a leader now, her expression said. I needed to act like it.

"All right," I said, taking a deep breath. I turned away from them, from Sands damnable confusion, and kept trying not to hyperventilate.

I was a leader now. I needed to concentrate on that. Choking down my scream of frustration was the hardest thing I'd ever done, but I did it.

"All right." I had regained control over my voice and I turned to face them. "The Faerie have somehow torn down Stormholt's defenses and broke in. We need to find out if any of our people are still there, and we need to find out how the Faerie did it. We've come all this way. I'm not leaving without learning all I can."

Nellie, Wil, Mog, and Dream all nodded, their concerns and fears easily assuaged.

I felt a pang of envy for that. Avonstoke put a hand on my shoulder.

"I'm fine," I said. "Just needed a minute." He looked absurdly relieved.

Faith nodded at me approvingly. Sands still looked miserable. Probably a better commander or even a better person would have tried to assuage him, too, but I wasn't there yet.

"Come on," I said. "Let's go in."

"Christ," Faith said, making me think of Henry. She pointed to where one particularly large oak had grown through the roof.

"A lot of changes in a few short months," I said. The rain, which had been trickling, now became much more than a trickle and it became very cold. I pulled down my hat tighter and shivered into my coat as lightning forked across the sky.

"It's not all like this, you know," Avonstoke said suddenly. He had to speak louder to be heard over the rain.

I turned to look at him. "What?"

"Faerie," Avonstoke said seriously. "It's not just gloomy forests filled with fog and monsters. There are great monuments, with magical pillars of stone carved so that it's like a forest of pale trees. There's actual forests of pale trees, too, for that matter. Great fields of open grass and castles and art and theater and a beautiful waterfall called the Sylriswa that could drown all of this Stormholt place in crystalline glory."

"Why in the world are you telling me this *now*?" I said. "Are you daft?"

"I just didn't want you to think that the place I grew up in looked," he gestured at the dark shadowy house. "You know . . . like this."

I nodded. "Um . . . all right. Thanks for that."

"Mog like this," Mog said. "Dank, dreary, very much like 'ome."

"You're *not* helping," Avonstoke said.

Mog grinned and shrugged.

I saw something move out of the corner of my eye and yanked my pistol out. Avonstoke's hand suddenly twitched, and his sword appeared in nearly the same instant.

"Don't shoot, Miss Justice!"

I recognized the small figure at once and relief sliced through me. There was a shimmering glow about him that would have told me, even if I hadn't recognized the yellow hair and checkered hat. "Étienne?" I waved Avonstoke and the others down. Mog looked ready to charge anyway, but Avonstoke put a hand on his shoulder.

Étienne looked about as bedraggled and miserable as any little boy, dead or alive, could possibly look. Percy came up behind him, and also Emily, the red-haired girl from the fish cart. There were even more sad children behind them. About thirty in all. It was terribly clear in their miserable little faces that they'd had a horrid time of things lately.

"That's Étienne?" Faith said. "I can see him now! How can I see him?"

I realized that Étienne and the others, who shouldn't be part of our physical world, were wet in the rain. The rain shouldn't have touched them.

Sands saw the direction of my gaze. "They're of the next world, which borders on Faerie. This place is more Faerie now than England, and they're part of it."

"Oh, Mr. Sands!" Étienne cried, looking past Faith and I. "Where 'ave you been? Now you're finally 'ere and it's too late!" He fell to his knees in front of us and Sands mutely crouched next to him, wrapping his arms around him. It wasn't all rain making Sands' face wet.

"I'm sorry," Sands said. "You were supposed to be safe. This wasn't supposed to happen. None of this was supposed to happen. We thought Stormholt would be safe."

"Safe?" Étienne wailed. "*Safe?* The Faerie came and took Stormholt the day after you left!" The other children, including fastidious little Percy and red-haired Emily, were crowding closer now. A few of them were looking up at the formidable Avonstoke and Mog, in particular. Avonstoke sheepishly made his sword go away. Mog gave a toothy grin, but that didn't help much.

"The day after . . ." Sands said to Étienne. "What about the Hussars?"

"Dead," Étienne sniffed. "All dead."

"All of them?" Sands said.

"Yes," Étienne sobbed. He leaned into Sands, crying in the rain. It made my heart break. He'd been so street tough before, as well as being impervious to harm, being a ghost and already dead, that I'd come to forget that dead or not, he was still just a twelve-year-old boy.

I moved forward, kneeling next to him and Sands, putting my hand on Étienne's shoulder.

"Étienne," I said, "We're going to get all of you out of here. I promise. But how did all this happen? Who did this? Was it the Black Shuck?"

He shook his head miserably, trying to cough up an answer, but it was Percy who said, "It's your mum, Miss Justice."

"My *what*?" I said, feeling my stomach drop.

"Your mum," Percy said again.

"And your brother," Emily put in.

Étienne nodded. "The big one, Joshua. They were bringin' Faerie over into England with 'er magic even before they came here to Stormholt. I don't know 'ow. We ain't seen no sign of the Black Shuck," Percy added.

"Mother is here?" Faith said. I could see a terrible light of hope go up in her face, which just made me feel worse. She'd always been closer to Mother than I had. Close as mother and daughter ever were, the past few years, before the Faerie tore everything apart. If my first thoughts went to Father as a child, hers always went to Mother, and that hadn't changed for either of us. Probably neither of our hopes made much sense, but there it was.

If Mother and Joshua were here, I knew some part of Faith would hold out hope that we could try and talk to her, talk her out of this madness.

It was a hope I couldn't share. I still remembered Mother's mad, inhuman face too clearly when she abandoned us the last time, as well as the butchery that she'd done on her way out. That had been when Joshua assaulted us and I'd gotten Faerie absinthe burned into my eye. My finger went up to my face of its own accord. I could almost smell the bitter licorice and oranges of the absinthe, feel the burning in my eye again.

"How?" Sands said. "How could Martine and Joshua do this?"

"Martine Scarsdon's a powerful magician, ain't she?" Étienne said bitterly, using Mother's maiden name. Seems she'd abandoned the Kasric name. "Joshua's a 'igh-rankin' general in the Faerie army, too. 'As been for years. Even the Faerie are terrified o' him. Don't expect no mercy just on account o' you bein' family, either. They got Benedict up there and they got no problem givin' 'im up. Keepin' 'im on the roof so's the Wild 'Unt can get 'im."

Faith gasped, her eyes shot wide. My relief on hearing that Benedict was nearby, and alive, was fervent, but also short-lived as the rest of Étienne's words sunk in.

"Wait," I said. "For *years*? They only left Stormholt a month ago."

"It hasn't been just a month for them," Étienne said. "They been in some part of Faerie where time moves differently. Almost a decade, I reckon."

"A decade?" I said, trying to grasp all of this. "Is that possible?"

Sands nodded his head. "I've heard stories, but didn't think . . ." He sighed and sagged, waving his hand at everything around us. I understood his meaning at once. So little of this should have been possible, yet here it was.

A crack of lightning licked across the sky, followed several seconds later by the disconnected roll of thunder, distant but ominous.

"Oh," Faith said, her eyes growing wide. She squinted up through the slanting rain.

"What?" I asked.

"The Wild Hunt," Faith said. "Can't you feel them?"

"No."

"It's like an aching tooth," Faith said, still not looking at any of us. "Only in my chest."

"We shouldn't have come here," Mr. Sands said. "Stormholt isn't the shelter we thought it was and now the Wild Hunt shows up the same minute we do? It feels all wrong."

"I don't think so," Faith said slowly. "The Wild Hunt isn't after us."

"Benedict!" I said, remembering the awful pull he'd described to us, how the Wild Hunt called to him so irresistibly that he'd been afraid to even leave the protection of Stormholt. Protection that had been torn down. Now the Hunt were coming for him.

"You're right," I said. "It's all wrong. But we're going in anyway."

"Sometimes," Faith said, still looking up, "the hardest thing to do is also the right thing to do."

"You realize," Avonstoke said with a grin, "that using that same logic, you could justify sticking your face in a volcano?"

"Shut up," I said.

"Aye-aye, my Captain." He even bowed slightly with slow ceremony and that grin still on his face. With his hair all bundled, he didn't seem to mind the rain.

"What are you two doing?" one of the boys I didn't know said. He had a scar on his cheek and now he touched it as if it pained him. "We're supposed to be raising the alarm. We shouldn't be telling them all this, either! Joshua will know! He'll punish us!"

"Shut up, Alfie!" Percy bawled. He looked at me and shrugged by way of apology. "We're supposed to be guards."

"Joshua made us," Étienne said with shame on his face. The jaw on his little face tightened. "But we're not going to do that for him anymore!"

"We shouldn't have done it at all," Percy said.

"It's not your fault," I said. "You just did what you had to."

I took a deep breath. It was cold enough now that it came out as fog. "Now," I said, "we're going to get you to safety. Dream, you, Mog, Nellie and Wil are going to lead them out of here. Head for the rendezvous with the ship."

Sometimes it still amazed me that anyone would listen to a young scrap of a girl not even an adult, but my voice came out amazingly calm and controlled, and Dream, Mog and the rest, all of them more competent in many ways than I, just nodded and accepted my orders as easily as if I'd been in command of a ship's crew, a fleet, a war, all my life.

"Take care of them like they were me own pods," Dream promised.

"Aye," Mog growled.

I looked at Faith, Avonstoke, and Sands. They all looked back at me steadily. In for a penny, in for a pound.

"And you, Captain?" Dream asked.

I nodded up at the dark and broken-down mansion. "We're going up there."

CHAPTER 12

A Mother's Love

We approached from the rear of the place, moving quickly and quietly, on the lookout for any other sentries. If there were any, the rain hid us from them just as well as it hid them from us. We saw no one. Perhaps the Faerie didn't have the discipline for more than a smattering of precautions, or perhaps they just didn't feel there was anything to fear.

The rain had beaded down my southwester coat, but it had beaten my hat into a black shapeless slug on top of my head and soaked my boots through before I found the loose bricks on the side of the mansion that revealed the crawlspace that would lead us back into Stormholt. This was, of course, the same route that Étienne and Percy had taken when they'd led Faith, Henry and me out only a few short months ago. I led the way, and while it had been open before, now it was so jammed full of dark roots that I was barely able to squeeze through. Avonstoke, working by feel in the dark, had to cut some of them clean through before he was able to pass.

The wine cellar, too, was no longer the same. The wine barrels that had lined the walls were gone, presumably consumed, with only a pair of rusty hoops to mark their passing. Here, too, the roots had invaded, dangling down from the stone ceiling like a hundred tapered and dirty white fingers.

We emerged in a silent and empty kitchen and froze when we heard voices. The kitchen was empty now, but it hadn't been abandoned. A mound of something bloody sat in the center of the table as if someone had just gutted an oversized deer and wasn't sure which parts to serve. A foul-smelling soup lay cold in a great cauldron in the corner. I'm pretty sure I saw a finger in there, but didn't dare look any closer.

Voices and the clinking of cutlery came from the dining room.

Some of those voices sounded familiar. Too familiar. I crept to the doors that let out to the dining room and listened.

"I wouldn't mind a little of the shiver and shake, either, mum, if it's not too much trouble? I ain't done a tightener proper all day, practically ready to work the shallows, I was." That had to be the Soho Shark or I'd eat my hat.

"Of course," Mother's voice answered.

I turned to share a significant look with my sister, to find her gone. Only Avonstoke and Mr. Sands crouched next to me.

"Where's Faith?" I hissed.

"She's right . . ." Avonstoke started, looking behind him. "Blood and bone! She was right behind me!"

Sands turned, too, to see the place where Faith should have been. But when he looked back at us, his face was twisted in wry understanding.

"Where?" I hissed. Was she running from Mother? Or the Soho Shark? That didn't make any sense. Would she try and find her way up to the roof to save Benedict without us?

"The Wild Hunt," Sands whispered. "She's gone to them."

Bloody hell. I knew he was right. I'd seen her face when the Wild Hunt came—there was some kind of connection beyond what anyone, even Faith, could explain.

"She must think she can do something with the Wild Hunt," Sands said. "Drive them off, perhaps?"

"Whatever she's up to," I said, "it's too bloody late to stop her now."

But I had things to tend to here. I needed to try and help Benedict my way, and, just as importantly, I needed to get a better sense of what kind of enemies Mother and Joshua had become after years in Faerie. Besides, if Mother was here, she might have Benedict or Henry with her. I hoped Faith thought of that and came back.

I took a deep breath, slid along the kitchen floor, and nudged open the swinging door that led to the dining room. Just a tiny bit, so I could peer through the slit.

It was a dark paneled room, lit by hanging candles, but not very well. A cloud of green smoke hung around the room, partly occluding a long table and the people around it. It clung to the walls and lay in pools around their feet and occasionally billowed up in clouds behind their chairs, casting the entire place in an eerie green light. The stench of it was familiar and hateful to me, licorice and oranges, but acidic. It made the skin on the back of my neck crawl with gooseflesh and the gorge rise in my throat. Faerie absinthe. The quiet clinking of plates on silverware trickled through the room to our ears, muffled slightly by the thick curtain of smoke.

The closest person, with her back to the door, was Mother. There was no mistaking that burning copper swath of hair, or her voice. She gestured with a long cigarette burning in an ivory holder and launched a throaty laugh at one of the men next to her. I remembered a time before all this happened, before I'd seen much of the Faerie world and what it would mean for me and my family, before Mother had gotten sick, a time when there were parties at their Soho residence and Mother laughed constantly. Her laugh was a soft velvet chuckle dripping with warmth.

The beneficiary of all that warmth was a London gentleman that I didn't recognize. But something was very wrong with his slackened face. He sat with his chair as close to Mother's as the table would allow, vacantly watching her every move. When she said something, he nodded submissively at her every word. This wasn't adoration, but something else, something far more sinister. Behind that man were other men, all looking like the upper crust—government officials, important bankers, rich nobility. Two dozen or so, all of them sitting at the table as if compelled by some force.

Mother said something else and then leaned forward. I could just make out the movement past the back of her chair. She blew more of that green smoke into the man's face. Whatever magic Mother was working on him, it was working. And not just him. The entire table was populated with Mother's slaves.

On the other side of the table, the absolute monstrosity of the Soho Shark shifted his great bulk on the creaking chair.

Whatever Faerie glamour had hid his true form before, even from my ghost eye, it was lifted now. He was massive, twice the size he'd appeared under glamour, and nothing human about him at all except for his wet and torn gray suit. His skin was a moist and mottled gray-greenish color, like a sickly lizard. He had no neck, only a barrel chest that merged into a huge, dinosaurian skull.

Curved talons made a parody of holding his teacup, and he sipped at it with an enormous, toothed maw underneath a short, impossibly wide snout filled with all manner of irregular, dangerous-looking teeth. The bowler sat perched on an enormous, flat, earless skull. Huge, clawed feet tore at the carpet. He should have called himself the Soho Crocodile, only I guess it didn't have the same ring to it.

But the worst was his eye. One of his eyes, his natural eye, if it could be called that, had a long, horizontal pupil like a goat's. That was hideous enough, but the other side of his face had an empty eye socket, black and horrible, more than just the absence of the eye he'd been born with. He'd traded his good eye for darkest Faerie magic. I could see it, feel it in the ravenous cold emanating from that black pit, and it terrified me.

"Fomori," Mr. Sands whispered. "I'd thought them all dead." I remembered the tree hung with bodies on our way in. Here was another lizard creature just like them.

"No such luck," Avonstoke hissed back, with a malevolent glare at the Soho Shark.

I looked back, surprised to hear Avonstoke's normally whimsical manner suddenly dropped.

"Demonic rulers of the underworld," he hissed through clenched teeth. "They've ruled here, too, briefly, and Faerie, and both places ran with blood until they were driven out."

I shook my head, partly to try and shake off the fear and partly to get my thoughts back on target. Avonstoke's moods weren't important right now; all that mattered was finding Benedict. And he wasn't in the dining room.

I let the door fall closed silently and gestured for us to go back.

We left the kitchen through the other door, out into a series of halls that led us to the main hall intersection. Partway through, we passed a series of family portraits. Recognizing the frames I'd known all my life and assuming them to be the same as I remembered, I almost passed them by without a glance. They'd been moved downstairs, which hardly merited astonishment, but when I noticed there were more of them than I remembered, I looked more closely.

Mother's was first now. She was older, gaunter, smoking as she had been in the parlor, wreathed all in the emerald smoke. The name on the plaque beneath said Martine Scarsdon.

I'd half expected Father's to be missing, but it was there, right after hers. The plaque said Rachek Kasric and there was the handsome, lean face I'd known all my life.

The next was a shock, showing the shaggy, wooden mask-faced Faerie King I'd seen in the forest so many years ago, with the crown of thorns and the wide antlers. Father's true shape. Which made the previous picture not Father at all, but the man Father had sent to Faerie in his stead. Joshua's father, but not ours. Prudence, Faith and all the rest of us had come from this monstrous person. The plaque said Lord Lessard du Thorns.

The following one was the Lady Dierwyn du Thorns.

Not my mother, but the mother to my half-sisters, Hope and Charity. This woman, clearly not human, had skin like polished obsidian, almond-colored eyes, and pale, ivory hair, wild and untamed. She probably hated Father now, and us. I couldn't blame her.

I didn't recognize the next one, either.

"Who is that?" Avonstoke whispered with utmost gravity.

The woman in this portrait was a stranger to me, but Father had wanted seven daughters named after the seven Cardinal Virtues and the plaque said Temperance du Thorns. I pointed at the plaque and Avonstoke made a noise that he'd seen the plaque, thank you very much, but curious about more than just her name.

I didn't know much more than the portrait and plaque told me.

She was probably my sister. Or half-sister? Her hair was a liquid midnight tumble of curls, her face beautiful, but somehow empty. She wore an iron collar, and a dark stain that might have been blood was smeared across her cheek. The implications were disturbing. Did that mean she was held prisoner somewhere? Here? Either way, it seemed to indicate that Mother, the Black Shuck, and Widdershins knew a great deal more about her than we did.

Hope, the girl from Faerie was next. The dark-haired, pale Faerie girl looked as sullen and feral as she'd been when I'd seen her with her mother, the Lady of Sorrows.

The next portrait depicted another stranger, even more perplexing than the one with Temperance. The name was Love du Thorns, which didn't exactly fit into the motif. Someone really should have coached the Lord of Thorns on the Cardinal Virtues. This girl was small, slim, but athletic looking, and dark-skinned, with short, black hair that fell just past her ears. Her eyes were dark, darker than Mother's and very hostile. She held a long knife and looked like she knew how to use it.

Then came Charity, Hope's sister from Faerie, which caused me to wonder about the order. Were they arranged by birthday or age? With time moving differently in Faerie than it did in our world, it was hard to know how that might work. That might mean that all these people were born before Joshua and all the rest of us, including this childlike one. She couldn't have been more than six or seven, with bright blue eyes and golden curls, just as she had when I'd seen her. But Sands had told us that she'd been in that form for a hundred years.

Joshua Kasric was next, my only sibling to be born fully human. The one who would turn out to be the only sibling that had a right to the Kasric name. The rest of us were du Thorns of one breed or another. He wore a helmet with ram's horns on them. He might not have been Faerie at birth, but clearly the Faerie had touched his life. His dark eyes, like Mother's, looked scornful and hostile. His hair looked long underneath the helmet, and gray, though that must have been the light the artist had used.

Prudence, our lost sister, was next. Prudence, Faith, and I were full-blooded sisters, all born of the Lord of Thorns and Martine Kasric. Some part of me breathed a sigh of relief, as if seeing her face on a portrait carried more weight than what Prudence and Father had both told me. The artist of the portrait, a master, had caught both her ordinary, gray, almost kind appearance perfectly, as well as the gleam of mischief and unnatural knowledge in her blue eyes. Her hand was barely in the picture, held off to one side, and the shape of it suggested a hawk's talon, all the while still looking like a woman's hand.

Benedict and Faith followed, both looked unchanged.

I knew Benedict was a prisoner here, but nothing in the portrait reflected that the way Temperance's did.

I was next. They had my ghost eye down perfectly, and my hat, as if I'd just posed for it a few minutes ago. Mother had to know, then, the damage she and Joshua had done, even if they hadn't seen it for themselves.

Finally there was sandy-haired, cheerful Henry. I hoped he was still in the same healthy and positive state when we got him out of here.

We left the kitchen through the other door, out into a series of halls that led us to the main intersection, the enormous area with the grand staircase, front door, foyer, and the great stained-glass tree overshadowing everything.

The chandelier above us was dark. The marble floor was scarred, chipped, and broken as if horses had been raced through here. Perhaps they had. The gas didn't work anymore, so there wasn't any light except for the flickering of a few candles jammed into some of the glass lamps on the wall. The stained glass was dormant, as dark as it was outside, but you could still make out the tree. There were hours left to daylight still, but you couldn't tell with the storm. It might have been midnight. Occasionally, lightning lit the world outside, bringing the stained-glass tree to brilliant and terrifying life for an instant before everything went dark again.

The World Tree. I hadn't known what it was before, but I did now.

More laughter trickled out from the dining room. More lightning lit up the stained glass. Now I could hear other noises over the storm, howling and baying. The Wild Hunt weren't just near—they were here.

There was a flash of movement on the other side of the front doors, visible through the brown kaleidoscope of the door, long glass slivers and triangles the color of night and wood, the bottom of the tree trunk. The bottom two inches of the door were long strips of seafoam and deep blue, the colors of the sea.

More movement on the other side, muddled and fragmented, and then the door burst open.

An armored figure wearing a ram's horn helmet stepped into the foyer out of the storm, slamming the door behind him hard enough to rattle the glass. He held a wide heavy-bladed axe. Something about the set of the feet and a sudden pause said that he was surprised to see us there.

I looked again at the broad shoulders and strong, lean build and it all looked very familiar. So did the hard, green eyes. Just like Mother's. The lean, angry jaw, too. I would have known him, despite the changes, even if I hadn't just seen his aged portrait.

Joshua.

He was standing in the foyer, about three steps down and a dozen feet away from us. He'd just lifted his hands, one of them still holding the axe, to the helmet of brushed steel, putting his hands on either side of the huge, curled, dried-blood colored ram's horns, but now let them drop as he saw us.

I yanked out my pistol and aimed it at his eyes. Avonstoke and Mr. Sands both had their swords out.

"Don't be an idiot," he said flatly. "Guns don't work here." I knew that voice; it was Joshua all right.

I cocked the gun, then held it, very briefly, so that he could get a good look at it from the side while the Faerie glyphs fired up like hot embers in a stoked forge, then I gave him the barrel-first view again.

"Think again," I said.

He jerked to a stop, looking surprised. "Justice?"

Even with most of his face covered by the helmet, Joshua looked years older. Trampled by time. Gray shot through the lanky tendrils of his hair which peeked out from underneath the helmet. His face was sun-weathered and hard, so hard that any hope I'd had of talking sense to my older brother died the instant I laid eyes on him. It wasn't the kind of face that had any capitulation or forgiveness in it.

He looked like he'd filled out some, about a dozen years' worth, since we'd last seen him. His arms were strong, heavy. The axe was a beast of a weapon, double-bladed, absurdly large and heavy, the edges pitted and notched, as if he'd just used it chop down the stone columns of the parliament building, column by column. His arm was a solid mass of corded muscle, and it was still a wonder that he could even lift it, let alone hold it one-handed.

"Justice," he said again, this time sounding shocked. The axe in his hand clattered to the marble floor. Bits of marble flew up when it hit. I cringed a little at the huge clang. So much for moving through the mansion undiscovered.

Joshua's gaze flickered to my ghost eye and he clenched his jaw. He had to have seen my portrait, just as I'd seen his, and been prepared for the sight of it. But not enough. It was different in person. This was the mark he himself had left on me. Right here in this very foyer.

I'd been angry for a long time about that, but now I had to wonder. Maybe I was wrong about him, despite his hard demeanor. Joshua could be ruthless, I knew that well enough, but he wasn't stupid and he knew me well enough to know that I could puzzle the pieces of his photographs together, so did that mean he'd had a change of heart? His expression was still hard, unreadable. No help there.

"You came," he said. "through the mist and the aspects of Faerie the Black Shuck and his Wealdarin have laid over England. I wasn't sure you would."

"You knew I would," I said. "Otherwise why leave a trail of breadcrumbs? The question is, did you mean to help us or to trap us?"

"Honestly?" he said. A flash of self-disdain and regret passed over his face. "What I want seems to wax and wane like the moon. I think it might have been a little bit of both." He put a hand over his face, as if in pain, and took an unsteady step forward, battling something inside of himself. "Either way, it was foolish of you to come. There's nothing here for you, not worth risking your life over, let alone your entire rebellion."

"Rebellion?" I said. "You and the Faerie are the invasion force, not the incumbent government."

"We *were* an invasion." He lifted his face from his hands and I gasped.

His eyes, moments ago green, were now yellow, demonic goatish slits. Like the Soho Shark's. Fomori, Sands had called him, and their mention was the first time I'd ever seen hate boil in Avonstoke's golden eyes.

"Now," Joshua said, "now, *we* rule England and you're never getting it back." He lifted his hands to take off the helmet again, yanking it off with sudden gravity. He let the helmet fall on the marble with a heavy clang.

But the horns hadn't been part of the helmet at all. They were part of my brother's *head*. With the eyes and horns, he looked as much demon as man. I tried squinting through my ghost eye, but nothing changed.

"Oh, Joshua," I sighed, "what have they *done* to you?"

Mr. Sands looked behind us and gave a sharp exhalation of breath that told me that my frantic, desperate hope that the noise might have gone unobserved from the other room had been torn to tatters.

"Well now," a hateful voice said from behind us. "What 'ave we 'ere?"

The Soho Shark wore a magnificent and toothy smile. He fixed me with his one good yellow eye. His clawed feet ground and scraped the marble floor as he moved forward with a shuffling, uneven gait.

"You killed me Rose, girl," he said.

"She attacked Father, Shark," I said, forcing my voice not to waver. "She tried to kill him."

We were in the center of the main hallway, like being in the center of a spoke, with foyer, main hall, two sets of stairs and both branches of the main hall all branching away from us in different directions. In short, the worst possible tactical position imaginable.

A muffled thump came from the stairway, too, and the dark whiskered face of a huge cat with flaming eyes peered around from the landing halfway up.

"Oh good," Avonstoke said brightly. "The cavalry has come. You have a way with cats, right, Sands? Have it gobble up this Shark fellow, would you?" His words were light, but he brought his sword in line with the huge monster.

"That's no *cat*," Sands said, his voice dripping with revulsion.

"See?" Avonstoke sighed. "It's like I said. Never trust a cat."

It looked like a cat, but only if you didn't look too closely. It had all the markings of a Siamese, cream-colored body and dark face, paws, and tail-tip, only writ large. It wore an evil leering smile that no mere cat could duplicate underneath those flaming eyes. The flames trailed up and out to either side, leaving a pair of ghostly image trails as it moved. Those eyes dispelled any brief idea that it could have anything to do with the actual feline species. It licked its white whiskers hungrily as it slunk down the stairs. I kept my gun covering Joshua while Avonstoke turned to face the cat. Sands had his silver rapier pointed at the Soho Shark. None of these weapons seemed near strong enough. A few broadsides from the *Specter* seemed more like the scale we needed.

Mother stepped into hall behind him. The Soho Shark grinned and moved slowly to our left to give her center stage. Joshua crouched heavily and got one meaty hand around the handle of that evil axe, also not in any hurry. The cat sat, licking one paw idly, though its burning eyes never left us for a second. I moved to the side as much as I could so that I could keep an eye on both Joshua behind me and Mother in front of me, but there wasn't enough space in the foyer for the job, so I had to keep flicking my gaze from one to the other.

Mother, like Joshua, wore a weight of years on her, and they didn't look like they'd been gentle ones. Her hair was still ember fire, but now I could see streaks of white in it, too. She wore a long white dress, shamelessly thin and revealing, so that you could see her gaunt ribs through the fabric. The Faerie absinthe might have kept her brain fever from killing her, but it clearly hadn't made her any healthier. She coughed once, wetly, then took a long pull on her cigarette. The smoke, green and acrid, stung my eyes even from this distance. I could taste the licorice and oranges even more strongly. Her eyes were no longer the same warm brown I remembered, but now flashed a bright green, like lit up emeralds. I suddenly realized that her eyes matched the strange luminous quality of Mr. Sands' eyes, which were the same shade as Faerie absinthe. Mr. Sands had said that her powers had come from the caustic Faerie drug but had neglected to mention that his had too. A point I was determined to bring up if both of us managed to live out the next few minutes.

Mother's smile was a cold, dead thing. I thought of Faith's hope, unspoken but clear, that she might somehow talk Mother out of her assault on Father and England. Now Mother was right in front of me and Faith wasn't even here. It was, to my mind, a wildly impossible task. God knows I'd never managed to talk Mother out of anything, even before Father's betrayal had driven her to such lengths. What hope had I of doing so now? Would Faith blame me when I failed?

"How lovely," Mother said, "a family reunion. Shark, why haven't you killed them yet?" Even knowing everything I knew, a part of me, deep inside, still thrilled to the sound of her voice.

"I was just about to murder them right and proper," the Soho Shark rumbled, flexing his huge talons. "For what they done to me Rose." His hate was a palpable thing.

"Mother," I said, trying to keep my voice even, but failing miserably. "It doesn't have to be this way. You always said there was nothing more important than family." Had she said that? I couldn't remember. But I had to try. "Faith is here. And . . ." I swallowed, not wanting to say the next part out loud.

"Father's gone," I went on. "Gone to Faerie and I don't think he's coming back. He can't hurt you anymore. Benedict's here, too, right? And Henry's not far away. You, me, Joshua, Faith, Benedict, Henry. We could be a family again, couldn't we?" A desperate, wheedling, needy tone crept unbidden into my voice, but I couldn't stop it.

"Mother," Mother spat. "I haven't answered to *Mother* from any of you half-breed abominations for such a long time. I abandoned the Kasric name. Flensed it out during my years training in Faerie and became the Lady Scarsdon, like I should have remained. I have no connection left to you Kasrics anymore. There is no part any longer where we connect or meet. Joshua is the only child left to me. So you can find some other victim to call *Mother*." She pulled a vial from the voluminous sleeve of her dress, and the eerie green of the glowing absinthe precisely matched her eyes.

"Why?" she said, idly swinging the vial from two pinched fingers. "Why are you here? Did you really think that this would still be a bastion against the invasion? Protected, with a mobile force of your Hussars still here, waiting to do your bidding? You can't be that naïve. And how did you get through the forest?"

I watched that vial and tried not to flinch every time she shook it. I remembered the giant craters she'd made in Stormholt's front lawn with vials just like that.

"The Hussars are dead," she said. "My archers shot them down on the lawn outside after Joshua tore down your ineffectual little black iron gate."

Mr. Sands made a sound of anguish at this news, and Mother's eyes lit up even more.

"Oh yes," she said. Then she frowned. "We captured your spy network, all the little ghostlings, and put them to work, but the fact that you are here unannounced tells me I'm going to have to order them all killed after all."

My hand was shaking with rage, and I was having a hard time keeping the pistol steady on Joshua. We were trapped and I couldn't see a way out of it. I thought about trying to shoot Mother's nasty little vial of explosive green absinthe, but that would just as likely kill all of us. Joshua was guarding the nearest door out, but I didn't want to turn and run with both the Soho Shark and that damned huge cat behind us. I hadn't even gotten twenty feet into the place before we'd gotten caught and I still had no idea where in all this rambling mansion Benedict might be. And I'd lost Faith, too.

"Your brothers," Mother said, as if she could pick the thought out of my expression. "You came for them, didn't you? You didn't expect to find us here."

"Time run out for both of them boys, ain't it?" the Soho Shark chuckled.

Looking back and forth from Mother to Joshua, trying to keep an eye on them, I thought I caught a twisted grimace, very brief, from Joshua. He wasn't happy about my brothers' fates. That might be something.

"Would you really order your own *children* killed?" I asked. My voice was raising pitch. Why wasn't Faith here? She wouldn't be losing her temper this quick, would she?

"No children of *mine*," Mother snarled. "They're your Father's now. He took them. Let him save them, if he can."

Mr. Sands and I exchanged glances. Father couldn't even save himself and we both knew it.

I tried to get my temper under control for one last gambit.

"There's someone else," I said to Mother. "Family you didn't even know about! Prudence, your daughter! She's alive. Alive and well!" Prudence had been born before even Joshua. Maybe the name of the daughter she'd thought lost could reach her.

"A lie!" she said.

"It's not a lie! I've met her! She's entirely human. The real Rachek Kasric's daughter. And yours! She's with the Outcasts! Call a truce and come out to the fleet with me. You can meet her!"

"Oh," Mother sneered, "how like your father you are. Always ready with a lie, like all the damned Faerie. I lost my daughter when that monster came back from the Crimea instead of my husband. Joshua is the only offspring I have left. Whatever thing is walking around with Prudence's name, it's dead to me. Just as all you Faerie spawn are."

Her words hit me like a blow. I guess one tiny, deeply buried part of me had still hoped that things could go back to the way things were, somehow.

"You are all *his,*" Mother went on. "Through and through. You share nothing with me. We do not touch, at any point." She looked at the Soho Shark and the giant cat and the three of us trapped and sighed. "This is all very exhausting. Shark, kill them if you must. I don't care. As long as they don't interfere with what's going on outside. We want the Wild Hunt to receive our gift, don't we? I have dinner guests to attend to."

She turned her back and her pale form, her white dress flickering in a myriad of colors from the light of the storm, mostly the emerald coming through the stained-glass door. Her heels made echoing and crunching sounds on the broken marble tile. She swayed slowly out of view, passing back into the darkness of the house until the black had consumed her whole.

CHAPTER 13

Henry—The Trial

Henry woke bleary-eyed after another restless night. He still had no idea how long he'd been in Newgate, but it had been at least a week that he'd been mixed in with the other inmates.

Two guards came for him again. They escorted him out and down the hall, the new routine already feeling dreary and stale. Henry had decided to act the docile and terrified boy, which wasn't so far from the truth. But maybe if they didn't know he was strong enough to break free of their grip, they'd unwittingly give him a chance to escape. But no amount of magical muscle was going to dig him through sixty feet of stone and brick.

"Don't get too comfy," one of the guards said to Henry when they approached the men's ward. "We'll be back for you later."

"What for?" Henry asked, dreading the answer.

"Your trial," the guard said with a nasty laugh.

Ah, so Mother's promise was finally starting to come to fruition. He'd had a few extra weeks or months, and didn't know why, but now it was coming to an end. He had no doubt whatsoever how this trial was going to go.

"Bad night," Daffyd said when he saw him. It wasn't a question.

"Probably one of your last," Jenkens said from the other table with a sneer.

Daffyd flinched but didn't try to contradict the bigger man or tell Henry that there wasn't anything to worry about. "Here now," he said instead in a low voice. "Can't change what's coming. Best you can do is take your mind of it. Go on and show me what you remember from yesterday's lesson."

Henry did. It was far more than he'd expected to remember. The notes came slowly, but smooth and clear. He kept at it all morning.

It was just after lunch when Jenkens came over to the two of them and demanded a song out of Henry.

"Come now," he said with a nasty smile. "We've been listening to all the practicing, haven't we? It's time for a performance. After all, we'd better hear it quick, while there's still time. Trial's later today, and then it's the rope." He laughed and the other men all joined in. Henry's face burned, but he didn't move.

"Here now," Jenkens said, hauling Henry up to a standing position. "I'm talking to you."

"Don't," Daffyd said, "I'll play. You don't have to bother the boy."

"I wasn't talking to you, old man." Jenkens pushed Daffyd aside.

It wasn't that hard of a push, really, and it was a fluke that the stool right behind Daffyd's feet tangled them up. Henry cried out as the old man tripped and fell towards the large bench and table. The sound of Daffyd's head hitting the bench was the soft thunk an axe makes burying itself into a log.

"Shouldn't bother yourself with the boy," Jenkens said, laughing, to the fallen man. "You can't even take care of yourself!"

A white-hot fury burned behind Henry's eyes, in the pit of his stomach. He'd driven his fist with all the force of a wrecking bar into Jenkens' stomach before he'd even realized it. The big man folded with a satisfying gasp, falling to his knees.

One of the other inmates was shouting for the guard as Henry knelt by Daffyd's side. The loud jangling of keys came from the entrance.

"Hit my temple," Daffyd said weakly. "Hurts."

"The guards are coming," Henry said, cradling the old man's head. "They'll take you to the infirmary. Don't try and get up."

"Here," Daffyd said, pushing the copper flute into Henry' hands. "They're all thieves in the infirmary. You keep this safe for me."

"I promise," Henry said. Footsteps were coming up behind him now. His hand on the back of Daffyd's head was wet with blood.

The trial was a blur.

Henry slumped in the dock, trying to see the large crowd in the courtroom clearly, but the fuzziness in his head wouldn't let him. He'd hoped to see Father here, or Mr. Sands, or somebody.

The only face he could make out was at the barrister's bench, a face dominated by two silvered discs.

Henry was not at all surprised to hear the verdict pronounced in a hollow, contemptuous voice. Unredeemable. Guilty.

Henry did not struggle as they pulled him out of the dock and marched him back to his cell. A large turnkey took either elbow, two others followed behind. A testament to his new status as a dangerous criminal.

"Wait," he finally said as they opened the gate to put him back into his cell. "Daffyd Wyn. How is he? Did they take him to the infirmary? Is he all right?"

"Oh him?" the man on his right said. "Yes, they took him, but it didn't do much good. He's dead."

"Naw," the man on Henry's other elbow said. "It was the wardsman that died. That Jenkens fellow. Internal bleeding."

"Both dead," the first one said matter-of-factly. "Now, in you go." They pushed Henry through the gate.

"Dead?" Henry said. "Both dead?"

They left without answering.

Numb, Henry moved to the bunk. He was about to sit, when he stopped, looking down. The copper flute lay there, gleaming slightly in the half light.

How it came to be there, Henry could not possibly imagine. Certainly, the guards would not have brought it from the men's ward, would they? Some final wish of Daffyd's, or possibly a sign of Widdershins' twisted humor? It didn't make any sense, but there it was. Henry picked it up with shaking hands.

He only knew the one song, but Daffyd had made him practice it over and over, and his fingers knew the way. He found all his frustration and sorrow and the cruelties and injustice of the past few days came out as he played. He played Daffyd's death, and Jenkens', and his own coming tomorrow. His Mother's departing figure and the evil gleam on Widdershins' spectacles. Henry played his fears of what might be happening to Benedict, Justice and Faith, and even Joshua. The hollow notes poured out, heavy and heartbreakingly beautiful, so that it seemed as if the loneliest parts of the sea had come to haunt all the corridors and cells of Newgate, a place built expressly for the purpose of allowing men in and never allowing them out again.

Finally, a place inside Henry broke, torn open by his own music, and he wept.

CHAPTER 14

Benedict—Escape

Benedict crouched just inside, watching the open doorway and the rain outside. The storm raged all around. This called for another pull on the brandy bottle. He knew the Kellas Cat was out there somewhere in the angular maze of black rooftop. Benedict tipped the bottle he was carrying back, finishing the last of the brandy, then hefted the bottle. Heavy glass with a strip of lead around the bottom.

He stood up and stepped briefly. Nothing. He picked a likely gable some distance from his doorway and hurled the bottle. It exploded on the peak. Benedict waited.

A shadow larger than a draft horse detached itself from a pocket of darkness and padded silently over to investigate the place where the glass had broken. Benedict could only just make out a tawny flank, the gleam of dirty-yellow eyes and a flash of bone-white fang, but that was enough to make him shiver. Then the Kellas shifted position, briefly, and he saw eyes like two burning torches, flames trailing up and out to either side.

Benedict froze. The cat didn't see him, and turned back to the shattered glass. Benedict slipped out of the doorway and headed in the opposite direction, climbing as carefully as he could to keep from making noise. Turning his back on that thing was enough to make his skin crawl, but he knew that looking wouldn't help. Either he'd move quietly enough for the rain to mask him, or the Kellas Cat would hear, and Benedict would be dead. He climbed up a peak and slithered over as quietly as he could. Now that he'd gained a little distance, he couldn't help himself and he twisted to peer back over the peak. The tan hulk of the Kellas Cat was facing the other direction, still sniffing around the broken bottle. That was just about as much luck as Benedict could dare to hope for.

Of course, with what he was running *to*, there might come a time when he would wish for the Kellas Cat.

Benedict had decided that his choices amounted to the Wild Hunt, Mother, or the Cat. He didn't want to be torn apart and he felt the same about helping Mother conquer the world, so he'd picked the Hunt. It might end up being an eternity of servitude, but somehow it still felt like the right place for him. He could still hear the horn. In fact, his choice felt less like a choice and more like a bow to the inevitable. Even the wait of his imprisonment didn't matter. Just a short pause before the undying Wild Hunt came to collect him. Meaningless in the long run. Unless the Kellas Cat got him.

The long, peaked ridge he was hiding behind ran the length of the building, so he started crawling along the angular trench, keeping the peaked part as cover. Crawling wasn't easy in the uncertain footing, with the ridge on his right and a series of perpendicular gables and peaks on his left, but he went as quietly and as quickly as he could.

He was so busy looking back that he nearly missed the snarl and rapid muffled percussion of heavy cat paws ahead of him. Oh bloody hell. Two cats! Benedict realized his mistake too late.

Flaming eyes reared up from behind one of the furrows on his left. How could anything in this world have such hateful eyes? The cat rushed forward, and he turned to run. But he slipped and fell, and the cat was nearly on him.

The wail of a horn . . .

An enormous crash rent the air and a long spear of ash wood transfixed the Kellas Cat's body with a sudden flash of light. Spear and animal lit up together, and the hidden shadow of the huge cat's skeleton flashed as it was lit from within. The charred slab of flesh that fell heavily to the roof was unrecognizable as a living thing.

Benedict twisted around, knowing already what he would see.

The Hunt was all around him, dark shapes circling above through a swirl of black thunderclouds only a dozen feet above. The rider closest to him rode down a black tendril of storm cloud to yank his broad-headed spear out of the cat's body. Flakes of black came out with it.

The rider was tall and broad-shouldered, with a wild brown and gray beard shaped like a shovel. He wore a crown of gold and a black eye-patch and looked down at Benedict with a frightening and haunted gaze like a long-lost king. Not a peacetime king, either, but a king that had seen war and thunder and darkness once and knew that more war and thunder and darkness waited for him. He hefted his spear with the blade sticking up high over his right shoulder, then he rode back up the storm cloud path to the two others that waited.

One of the waiting riders looked like another king, wearing a similar crown to the first. He held a sword covered with runes that danced in the flickering storm light. His beard was neater, shorter than the other, but he was equally grim, equally noble.

The figure in the middle was more than a man.

He was all elements of the Hunt, man and deer and hunting dog all together. Benedict could see the similarity to the Lord of Thorns: the arcing, tined horns of a stag branching out from the head, but this wasn't him. He had a young man's torso, head and arms, though a shaggy brown mane ran down his shoulders and back. His arms ended in dangerously clawed hands and his lower half was something Benedict should have expected, but didn't: a heavy stag's body, with all four hooves standing in the black clouds. His face was draped in darkened shadow. It would always be draped in shadow under those dark curls. But his eyes shone through anyway, black pools filled with stars and the light of both predator and prey shining inside. Benedict would have known him anywhere. Cernunnos, Heart of the Wild Hunt.

He looked down at Benedict, and then the God of the Wild Hunt reached out his hand.

CHAPTER 15

The Battle in Stormholt

Say this for our homecoming, it wasn't boring.

We stood in a partial circle, back-to-back, Avonstoke, Sands and I, facing off against the Soho Shark, the strangely transformed Joshua, and a Siamese cat the size of a draft horse. I was covering Joshua with my pistol, hoping that he wasn't going to make me shoot him, while Avonstoke was facing the cat and Sands had his silver rapier pointed at the Soho Shark's head. Mismatches all the way around and not in our favor. Even so, I might have had the least terrifying of the lot, but not by much.

"I don't think you'll shoot me in the face," Joshua said. "We're family, remember?"

"Family," I agreed, and shot him in the leg.

I think I kept it off my face, how much that hurt to do, even now.

The bullet took out a hunk of flesh of Joshua's leg as big around as a halfpenny, and blood sprayed onto the marble and the stained glass behind him. He gasped and fell on the tile, clutching his maimed leg. I hoped that it would keep him busy, but also that it wouldn't kill him outright. If I'd hit a major artery, he could easily bleed out. Or stand despite it and put that axe into one of our backs. I also didn't know what magic he might have now. It was clear with those horns that he wasn't entirely human anymore. I hoped to high hell I wasn't making a fatal error when I turned my back on him.

I spun around to see the battle behind me.

Avonstoke must have rushed the cat, which seemed a colossally stupid idea, but now he was on the other side of it, lunging and slashing at it desperately. He didn't have the range to land any kind of serious blow, but all that dancing around was drawing the cat away from the rest of us.

Sands and the Shark were circling each other a little further down the hall. Sands swiped with the silver rapier at the Shark's face, but the Shark easily blocked it with his huge claws. Still, he seemed wary of Sands' silver weapon, which was something. The Shark lunged forward suddenly with a massive bite, his teeth snapping shut with a clang like rocks colliding, but Sands slid back and away.

I wasn't sure which to shoot, or if I could even get a shot, but I had six bullets left in my revolver and planned to make them count. I took a few steps into the space between the two separate battles, angling for a shot on one or the other.

The Soho Shark was advancing slowly.

Sands struck again and again, weaving back and forth so that I didn't dare shoot at the Shark for fear of shooting Sands in the back. The cat wasn't even looking at me, but trying to pounce on Avonstoke and pin him to the floor like a rodent. Avonstoke was backing up towards the bottom of the staircase. He was slashing defensively with the black sword, but the cat had enough speed and reach to threaten Avonstoke while easily staying out of reach.

I took aim and fired on the cat just as it sprang, savagely fast, at Avonstoke, who had just slid back another half-step to the point where the back of his heel thumped softly against the bottom step.

My shot ricocheted off the far wall with a spark and a small shower of marble dust. The cat landed on the far step, teeth gnashing on the bottom step, because Avonstoke had leapt suddenly backward and up four or five of the steps. He finally scored a hit, a slash across the muzzle that, instead of bleeding, dripped flame in a long, thin line, like a gas lamp gone suddenly amok.

"Pretty," Avonstoke crooned.

"I'll drag your guts through the dirt for this!" the cat snarled. It should have been a shock just to hear the cat speak, but it was the voice itself that was shocking, like a pickaxe dragged across a metal sheet, high-pitched and dripping silvery scorn in a way that was painful to hear. The edges of its wound were peeling like burned paper, but it still wasn't very large compared to the entire beast and didn't seem to bother the creature in any way. It swiped again at Avonstoke with its foot-long claws, forcing him up the stairs. Avonstoke already had a bloody slash across his shoulder. I fired, but missed. The cat, too quick, had slipped forward, leaving bloody paw prints three feet wide on the stairs. Avonstoke's blood.

I shot at the cat again, twice, but both the cat and Avonstoke hopped so that my shots put more holes in the marble but little else. The cat was half-blocked by the railing and Avonstoke was entirely out of view. Before I could try a third, the cat pounced again and landed on the turn of the staircase, and was blocked entirely from my view by the staircase itself.

I started towards the bottom of the stairs but spun around when the Soho Shark roared. Just in time to see him rush and swipe at Mr. Sands, catching the smaller man before Sands had time to retreat. Sands blocked the blow, but the power was enough to send Sands sailing across the hall to crash into the opposite wall.

Well, Sands wasn't blocking my shot anymore. I shot the Shark from a space of twelve feet away, putting my last two rounds into his chest.

Two red blotches appeared on the Shark's grimy suitcoat, about the size of a sovereign, but that was all. The Shark roared again, angry rather than injured, and started in my direction.

Although he had a limp, the huge creature moved remarkably quickly. Why couldn't something in Faerie be less dangerous than it looked? Just for once? Either they were cute, elegant, or devastatingly beautiful, and shockingly deadly, or they were hideous and even more deadly. There didn't seem to be any middle ground.

With dizzying speed, the Shark swung those huge claws at me, three times the size of a grizzly bear's. I sprang backward, terror and some hidden instinct forcing my legs into action while the rest of me was still panicking.

The blow missed and I found myself teetering awkwardly on the metal railing of the staircase. The Shark's next blow tore the railing out from underneath me and I dropped and rolled a few feet away, panting already from the effort as if a grenade had gone off in my chest. Upstairs, on the balcony, the cat was hissing and spitting, the noises drifting around the huge vaulted ceiling. I had no idea how that battle up on the balcony might be going and desperately wished that I did.

The Shark moved to follow me, but our little dancing game had given Sands a chance to get his feet underneath him. He lunged from behind the Shark, and the thin silver blade of his sword slid all the way through, sliding out neatly from the Shark's front lapel like a strange boutonniere.

The Shark's furious roar of pain shook the pillars and echoed off the tile.

Mr. Sands shifted his feet, ready to pull the blade out and deliver another killing stroke. Or at least what should have been a killing stroke, only the Shark didn't seem to know that. Sands jerked once, twice, but the blade didn't budge. It was stuck in the Shark's mammoth chest.

The Shark grinned a sickly, toothy grin, and jerked his torso to one side, snapping the thin silver blade like a dry matchstick. I fumbled frantically in my pocket, fishing for more bullets.

The Shark spun, catching the astonished Sands with a backhanded blow that sent the little man into the far wall with a horrifying, wet impact. Sands slid slowly to the tiled floor, leaving a bloody mark on the wall, and lay still.

A cry rang out above through the entire place. A bird of prey, but something huge, the size of Devonshire. Did Mother have giant birds as well as giant cats? Had the cat gotten Avonstoke?

The Shark spun again and started towards me. I fished a small handful of bullets out of my pocket while I scrambled backward on my bottom. I glanced down, seeing that I only had three bullets, and then gave a soft cry when I dropped two in my haste. The Shark was walking over with slow, solid, careful steps, like a man that's had too much to drink.

The tip of Sands' silver sword still protruded, gleaming, from the Shark's chest.

The Shark loomed over me and raised one clawed foot the size of a knight's shield, ready to stamp the life out of me. His slitted yellow eye was full of hate, but it was the empty eye socket that made my stomach clench as if filled with cold water. He grinned that vile, toothy grin. I was still fumbling the cylinder on my gun open, but I'd run out of time.

"This," The Shark said, "is for me Rose."

There was a heavy 'chock' sound and Shark's body shook. His eye clouded over with disbelief and he stumbled. I managed to squirm out of the way as his foot came down, not to stomp the life out of me like he'd intended, but to catch his balance.

He'd turned enough for me to see the long handle that jutted out of his back.

The handle of Joshua's axe.

For a few seconds Joshua was frozen in the act of having hurled that axe into the Shark's back. He looked washed out and half-dead and his leg was dripping blood all over the tile.

"Gah," the Soho Shark said. Even now, with Sand's silver sword and Joshua's axe both buried in him, he wasn't dead. Not by a long shot.

"Kill you," the Shark gurgled. "Kill you both." He was still dazed and his eye was trying to focus as he lifted his clawed foot again.

I jammed a single bullet into the revolver's cylinder and snapped it shut.

I lifted the gun and fired. God knows I didn't expect to hit anything firing off that way, but there wasn't time to aim. But I didn't blink and I didn't flinch and the bullet went directly into the Soho Shark's eye socket.

He jerked in place, then a soft, wet sound escaped from deep within his chest, as if he'd eaten too much and might suddenly be sick. Then blood geysered out of the wound. The other eye rolled up into the back of his head and his heavy shape collapsed into a heap at my feet. I stared, horrified that I'd killed again. But the idea of the Soho Shark still being alive was just as horrifying. Faint gurgling sounds came out of his mouth.

I clawed my way to my feet. I hurriedly fumbled more bullets out of my pocket and into the gun, but when I snapped the full cylinder shut, I was relieved to see that the Soho Shark's body had gone still. He was finally dead.

I glanced at Joshua, who had collapsed against the wall. He was bleeding a great deal, but he'd tied a strip of cloth tight around the leg. His face was tight with pain. When he nodded at me, I nodded back. There was so much more to say, but Avonstoke might be still fighting for his life upstairs. I hoped he was, and not bleeding out on the dirty floor somewhere.

I crouched and checked Mr. Sands' pulse. He was alive, thank God. But how much longer did any of us have before Mother wondered about the Shark's absence and sent something nastier to do the job? Then there was the giant cat and giant bird up on the balcony. *Be alive, Raythe Avonstoke. Just for a few more minutes. I'm coming!*

I dashed for the stairway, gun in hand, hoping against hope that I wasn't too late. There was movement at the top of the stars and the beating of wings, making me duck. A black explosion of feathers flew overhead and glided down into the front hall, trailing the scents of musty books and spilled ink. A crow? Raven? It was too big to be either. It banked and disappeared down one of the darkened halls.

There was another sound from the balcony at the top of the stairs and Avonstoke limped into view. He looked exhausted but very much alive, which made my heart leap.

I sprang up the last few steps, pushing past him and leveling my pistol at each corner of the entire balcony until I realized there wasn't anything up there but us. Or, at least, no giant cat, or any bodies.

A black spot a dozen feet away smoldered suspiciously, about the right size as the cat.

"It's dead," Avonstoke said, seeing me look around. He sounded almost drunk with exhaustion. "With our thanks to Drecovian. The magician with the dragon. You remember the dragon? Lovely things, dragons."

I realized with a shock that the tattoo was gone from around his face. The black wings. The bird that had just flown away had been another piece of tattoo magic. I reached up and touched his bare cheek where the bottom of the black wings had been.

"Each tattoo a magic trick," he said. "Not many left."

I sucked in a breath. There was a gash, too, just under his other eye. Not more than an inch, but only a finger's width from the eye.

He stumbled on the first step, and I caught him about the waist before he pitched down the stairs. He put his arm around my shoulder, which felt good, but he was heavier than I expected, and we nearly tumbled down the steps.

"You're not making sense," I said. "Did you hit your head?"

"No," he said. "Well, yes . . . but I don't think that's it. I think I just need to sit down a minute."

"Does it hurt?" I said.

"No," he said. "Just a scratch. Help me down the stairs, my captain, if you could?"

"Of course," I said, feeling a weight of guilt on me. It was because of me that he was here, that he'd been injured at all.

When we got to the bottom hall, Sands was sitting with his back against the wall, holding his side. The expression on his ashen face told me what just sitting up was costing him.

"I'll live," he said. "Just . . . need a minute before I try standing. Broken ribs, I think."

"You have to get out of here," Joshua said. "Before they come back and catch you." He'd dragged himself with his back against one of the pillars. A trickle of his blood was spreading from underneath him over the tile, mixing with a much larger pool coming from the Shark's body. Behind him, slow thunder and flashing light rolled in through the stained glass door. It seemed ridiculous that the fragile panes of colored glass could possibly be intact after the pitched battle that had just happened here. Mother had blown that door apart at one time, hadn't she? Who had fixed it then? I had no idea.

I moved over to Joshua. "I'm not going to leave you like this!"

"I'm stronger . . . than I look . . . now," Joshua said. "I'll be fine in a few days. Just go."

I knelt next to him. "You meant to tell me about the shipyard," I said. "Didn't you? You knew the pictures would help me find it."

He nodded. "Just because I'm at Mother's side doesn't mean I want everything she wants. The Faerie already have England. I'm not giving them the rest of the world, too."

"The Black Shuck. You can tell me how he does it, can't you?"

Joshua understood at once. I could see it in his eyes. "You'd understand most of it if you'd ever met him. He's terrifying, but it's more than that. A magical aura of darkness and fear."

"He's scary?" I said. "That's it?"

He laughed softly, then grimaced in pain and clutched his stomach. "That's it," Joshua said.

That hardly made sense. I'd already met tons of people and things that made me want to run and scream, but they weren't accomplishing all the things that the Black Shuck was.

"You'd understand if you'd met him," Joshua said again. "Widdershins is part of it. They're both avatars of the Arawn, Dark God of the Underworld. Faerie forces marshaled against mankind. Widdershins tears your mind apart, then you're helpless before the Shuck's fear. There are creatures in Faerie that could resist one, but not both of them."

I'd experienced Widdershins' attack, briefly, before Faith had stopped it. That had just been a taste, but it made sense now that he'd told me.

Joshua gripped my arm. "They got to Mother, too. She . . . hates Father and she's ruthlessly ambitious and the absinthe had affected her too, before Widdershins and the Black Shuck took her. Now . . . well, don't judge her too harshly."

I wasn't sure if I could forgive her, after what I'd seen her do, but there wasn't any time to think on that now.

"Come with us," I said. "I can get you out of this. You and Benedict both."

He looked at me. His expression was filled with pity and sadness.

"No," he said. "I can't leave her any more than you can leave Father. I'm trapped. Benedict, too, I think. You'll see when you get out there. But . . . I wish . . ."

He nodded slowly, then reached out to pick up the ram's horn helmet. He held it with heavy solemnity, as if it held all the burdens of his past years in Faerie and all the years of war to come.

Pushing his fingers through the hair behind his horns in a habitual movement, he settled the helmet on his head. The metal masked his face except for the eyes. He had Mother's eyes, warm, brown, determined. Except when he didn't, I thought, thinking of the goat's eyes, Fomori eyes, I'd seen before.

He reached out and gripped my arm. "I wish that things could be different. But you can't save everyone."

I gripped it back. "I wish things could be different, too."

He just nodded, exhausted beyond words.

I stood up. Avonstoke seemed to have tapped some inner core of strength and was helping Sands, who was panting heavily with the pain, to his feet. Avonstoke looked odd to me without the black tattoo around his eyes.

Avonstoke and I pushed open the enormous sixteen- or seventeen-foot-high doors, which were heavy as anything, with all that wood and glass. They were a lot thicker than I thought they'd be. I realized I didn't remember ever passing through these doors before. I'd been half out of my mind when we'd first come into Stormholt and everything was a blur. We'd had to sneak out another way last time. I just couldn't imagine the Soho Shark or most of the other Faerie taking care with such a thing. It had to be far more durable than I'd ever guessed. Protected by Goblin sorcery or some cunning, diamond glass of the Dwarves, maybe. Even now, I had to admit it was beautiful, for all that I hated the thing.

When I turned to help Sands, the wind ripped the stained-glass door out of my hand and smashed it against the wall, knocking out several pieces of bottle green and chocolate brown glass. So much for Dwarven glass. Avonstoke touched the door softly and sadly on our way out, as if it were an injured butterfly. I would have kicked it if I could have spared the strength.

We took Sands down the limestone steps and out onto what had once been a well-manicured lawn and now looked like the beginnings of a virulent and somewhat angry jungle. Lightning struck something above us and I realized that the flickering light just starting around us was coming from the roof.

The roof of Stormholt, which was on fire.

It was because of the fire that I could see the figures so well. The horned rider that had chased us and made Father crash our carriage. The dark and devilish riders of his horde.

And the slender blonde woman that was flying (flying!) . . . rising slowly in the air.

"I think," Avonstoke said with awe and wonder in his voice, "that I've found your sister."

CHAPTER 16

Benedict—Joining the Wild Hunt

Benedict threw his head back and let the power of the Wild Hunt wash over him. The wind whipped the smoke and the baying of the hounds and the cawing of the storm crows all around him. It was like being in a burning zoo without the fire.

Cernunnos reached out for Benedict's hand.

What else could Benedict do when a God called, but answer?

Benedict's formal studies at the seminary had done nothing to prepare him for this moment. There, he had studied scripture that talked of God, but nothing in the thin, onionskin paper and cramped type had prepared him for the presence of *Gods*. Multiple. The very notion could not exist in the world of modern England, at least not in the world as seen by the church. Cernunnos' presence did not refute that so much as crack the world of modern England right open. The Faerie had broken into England in not just a physical sense, but in a real, tangible, and spiritual way as well. Benedict could feel the whole *possibility* of it rising in him like an orchestra's crescendo, or like the rising sound of a horn made of copper and bone. The presence of Cernunnos and the other Gods didn't just change the world, they changed the very idea of what was possible in it. What the world could *be*. Now, Cernunnos and his Wild Hunt were part of the human world, but also part of the realm of Faerie and even part of the Land of the Dead, and a connecting thread between all of these. Benedict understood now that Faerie, too, even the Seelie and Unseelie Courts, feared the Wild Hunt.

The God's hand on Benedict's skin was like love and fire, like hunger and cool, meadow breezes and sweet, red wine and sex and sorrow, like everything Benedict had ever loved or hated. He could now hear the names in the storm crows' calls: Cernunnos, yes, but also Herne, Wotan, the Henniquin, Helkin, King Herod and King Soloman. All of them imperfect reflections of who and what the God was. But Cernunnos had been one of the first names that man had chosen for him when they first viewed the Wild Hunt . . .

The Wild Hunt was also the Furious Army, the Flying Hunt, Oliferne Hunt, Wild Jagd, Nachtschar, Totenzug . . . the Wild Hunt had many names in many languages and they fell around Benedict, whispers and autumn leaves.

All of them, Cernunnos, the Kings around him, his Hunt, and even Benedict were standing or riding in a smoky land that sat in the sky and Benedict hadn't even known when he'd left behind the roof and the concerns of the Earth below.

He knew this: he wasn't returning any time soon.

Cernunnos lifted the horn to his lips, and the long note, high and clear, thrummed through Benedict's center, cutting right to the heart of his desire. Benedict laughed.

The King with the eye patch stamped his spear and the sky rang with the clang of iron on stone. A neigh of response, and a riderless, smoldering horse peeled away from the host of circling riders and approached to where Benedict could put his hands on the warm, glossy flank. He mounted up. There was no question of not doing it. Benedict's leg moved easily and free, with no pain. Benedict would never feel Earthly pain again.

He wanted this. He was nothing but a burning desire to ride. Lightning from the dark, smoldering cloud they rode on struck at the jagged, geometric haze of the roof below, tearing and setting afire the shapes of humankind. Benedict laughed as the roof of Stormholt burned. At the same time, he wept, not with sorrow but with the joy of release.

Then, suddenly, there was *more* music.

Another voice in the song.

Or was it a trio of voices? Benedict couldn't be sure. A woman's voice, familiar. Or, at least, familiar to the person that Benedict had been just a few moments before.

The new part of the song was wild, as it would have to be, to weave itself seamlessly into the music of slow thunder and lunatic howls and the calling of a brass horn. Another melody, but one that fit so perfectly with the call of the Wild Hunt that Cernunnos' horn now seemed incomplete without it.

Benedict was shocked to realize that there was a woman floating in the center of the whirling storm, lit from the burning below. Not just any woman. One he knew.

Faith.

The still-human part of him, small and getting smaller, almost didn't recognize her, with her strange clothes, her head shaven clean, and bearing a glowing staff. But the supernatural part of him knew her at once. His *sister*, Faith. That was important in some way that Benedict couldn't remember.

While the Hunt rode on a plane of smoke and thunder, a merry-go-round of destruction, it was *one* terrain, a terrain that even Cernunnos had to use. Cernunnos could twist the road to his own design, but he could no more discard it than a human hunter could take to wing.

But the woman did. (Faith, Benedict had to remind himself again, but it was getting so hard to think with all this music in his head.) The wind was a living thing, lifting her. That was no small feat, Cernunnos' storm obeying her direction. Cernunnos, the god, might summon and ride the storm, but even he did not take a place at his center. That was reserved for this woman.

A dim understanding surfaced in Benedict's head, that Faith's song was a very old response to the music of Cernunnos, one that had not been heard in countless ages. He twisted in his saddle to look at her and saw the other hunters slow to a walk and then stop. The hounds grew silent and the birds flew without calling out, quieted to soft whispers of the flight. The Two Kings waited. The air was filled with the scent of lathered horse and hound, mingled with the musty scent of the birds and the wet, electric smell of the storm itself. Even the thunder and lightning waited, expectant, and there was only the soft rustle of the falling rain.

Cernunnos regarded her, his face pensive. He, too, did not speak.

Faith sang triumphantly for another full minute, her eyes closed, her head thrown back so that the hood fell off her shaven skull, her throat working as the trio of voices flowed out. Each voice sounded like her, but they differed subtly from each other as if Faiths of different ages were all joined together. Her staff, held in front of her, flashed brilliantly in time with each lightning strike around her.

She rose up to their level and the storm grew distant so that they all stood in muted silence. Finally, she stopped singing and her eyes opened.

"You know the old songs," the King with the sword said. "The songs they sang in our temples when your kind still worshipped us."

"Yes," Faith said, and a new knowledge sat in her dark eyes. Benedict could see it as truly as he felt his own change upon him. This was an old power, linked, that reawakened in them both.

"Will you sing our song in the world of men," the King with the eye patch said, "and bring back our worship?"

"Yes."

"Then we will honor the old ways," the Kings said together. "What would you have of us?"

"My brother," Faith said. "You cannot keep him. The Faerie have enough of our family as it is."

There was a flicker of anger in Cernunnos' eyes, but he said nothing, letting his subservient kings speak for him instead. An unsettled feeling, dark, deep, but unimaginably powerful, stirred Benedict, seeing that anger and knowing it to be a savage thing and undeniable once released. Another, more personal shock ran through him as a more human part of his thoughts realized that Faith was talking about him. He struggled, but could not speak. He was caught in the grip of an ancient pact, held fast. Him and all the Hunt.

Even Cernunnos. Benedict's heart wailed, even if he could not move. No! Do not keep me, his heart wailed. Don't keep me from the Hunt!

"Child," the King with the sword said, "you know this cannot be. He takes the place Lord Lessard du Thorns, your father, has left abandoned. Not even the old pact absolves that debt."

"But that's what I want!" Faith said. Her voice, so confident and filled with power, suddenly sounded like a young girl's again. Panicked, human. "Free Benedict. You cannot have him!"

Benedict felt his mouth move, not under his command. He saw, too, the mouths of all the hunters around him move in unison. Even the demonic horses, eyes blazing, and the bone white hounds and the black crows, all moved their mouths with him. The voice of Cernunnos rolled out of all these mouths together, ringing across the sky fit to shake mountains.

"CHILD," it said, "YOU CANNOT COMPEL THE HUNT IN THIS." The God looked angry still, but also gleeful. "THUNDER MUST FOLLOW LIGHTNING. IT IS THE WAY OF THINGS."

"But," Faith said, so soft that Benedict could barely hear her. "I have to save him. I *need* to save him." Benedict felt a stirring within him at her grief, but it was a faraway thing. He still longed to ride, more than anything.

"We cannot give you this brother," the King with the eye patch said. "But . . ." He looked at the other King and then they both glanced at the implacable God. Was there the briefest of exchanged looks? Benedict thought there was.

"We can," said the King with the sword, "give you *a* brother to honor the old songs. Henry Kasric is meant to die this morning. You cannot save him. *We* can."

Benedict heard some shouting from the ground and became aware for the first time that other people were down there. But they were not a part of this and he could not make out the words.

There were tears rolling down Faith's face. She looked at Benedict then nodded in defeat. "Yes. If we cannot save them both . . ."

"You cannot," the King with the Sword said.

"Then," Faith stared across at Benedict, her lip quivering. Benedict could feel that his face was wild, imperious, haughty and dangerous. There was no room for regret there, even for this. But something deep inside of him still felt a connection to Faith. She'd always understood him better than anyone else. Let her understand *this,* Benedict's heart pleaded. He did not want to be saved. He wanted to ride with the Wild Hunt.

"Yes," Faith said finally. She nodded at him as if she finally understood. Her voice was choked and tears ran down her face, apparent even in the rain. "Yes. If I can only save one of my brothers, then . . . yes."

CHAPTER 17

Faith's Bargain with the Wild Hunt

I stared up at my sister, flying in the sky, *flying,* and the majestic sight of the Wild Hunt, which had stopped, facing her.

All around, chaos reigned. The roof of Stormholt blazed, despite the rain. Chunks of the roof had fallen and crushed one of the scraggly black trees which had sprouted magically in the front lawn, and was still burning. Screams and cries were coming from inside the mansion, probably on account of that same fire, or possibly someone had discovered the Soho Shark's body. Mother would even now be seeking us out.

From the front of the house, I could see now that the front lawn, the slope beyond it, and the valley below, were all covered with Faerie troops. The rain washed many of the details away, making the fires and tents into an impressionistic painting, but there was no doubt it was a military encampment. Mother and Joshua had far more than giant cats at their disposal.

"Is she trying to negotiate with a god?" Avonstoke said, looking up.

"She is," I said, pulling my attention back up to the astonishing tableau above us. Did anyone ever get used to this kind of thing?

"Are they really gods, I wonder?" Sands murmured. Avonstoke and I had him slung in between us, half-dragging him. Which really meant that Avonstoke was almost carrying him, taking all the weight, while I was just trying to make sure, on my side, that Sands didn't fall. Sands was half delirious with the pain, I think, but not so delirious that he couldn't see or didn't understand what was happening above us.

The rain had stopped, or rather, continued all around us, but become merely a faint drizzle where we stood, in the center. The sight twisted in my gut like a blade. The words they spoke rang out through the rain and over the drenched, ragged, little jungle that the front lawn of Stormholt had become.

"We cannot give you this brother," a voice boomed from above. "But," there was a pause. "We can," another equally commanding and terrifying voice continued, "give you *a* brother. Henry Kasric is meant to die this morning. You cannot save him. *We* can."

"Benedict is lost," Sands said. He wasn't staring up, but down, whispering feverishly to himself. "Benedict's been lost ever since that first night. But with the pact honored, Cernunnos is no longer our enemy! Perhaps he might, in time, become something else! If someone dares to ride. We must have someone ride!"

"We *have* to save Benedict!" I said. "And Henry! We have to save them both."

Sands looked up suddenly catching my eye. His look was mad, feverish, his eyes so emerald bright they glowed. "You can't!" he said flatly. "You can't save them both."

He seized me by the shoulders. "But you *can* save Henry. Pavor Nocturnus! This is why you have her! Summon her! Summon her now!"

I hesitated. Looking up again.

"Trust me," Sands pleaded. "I may not be a magician any longer, but I still understand more than I can possibly explain and there are threads woven here that are only becoming clear to me, even now. Please, Justice, as you value your brother's life. Summon Pavor Nocturnus!"

I nodded and let go of Sands, letting Avonstoke take his full weight. (He was already taking most of it anyway.) I raked through my pockets and found the chess piece.

Avonstoke nodded at the conveniently still burning chunk of roof a dozen feet of away.

I rushed over and held the knight over the smoking, angular, hunk of tar and wood.

"Pavor Nocturnus," I said huskily. "Pavor Nocturnus, Pavor Nocturnus!"

The smoke coagulated, took shape.

Again, there was that hideous, horned, *something*, that revealed itself, with burning yellow eyes, before the smoke churned and fell into the horse shape that I'd been waiting for.

Nocturnus stamped the wet, muddy ground, whickered softly, and danced in place.

She shoved herself against me, gently, but there was that hint of raw power behind it. She pushed her soft, warm muzzle into my hand.

"Hello, my beauty," I said. A tenderness washed through me, completely at odds with the madness raging around and above.

"Is there someone," the voice from above boomed, "that dares to ride with the Wild Hunt?"

"Yes," Sands cackled softly. "Yes, yes! Normal horses can't ride with the Hunt, but yours can. Mount up and tell them you will go!"

Tell who? Shout my name out to the storm above? Sands glared at me and gestured up. His eyes blazed with contained anger, as if I were a child watching someone drown while I held the life preserver, but was too stupid to throw it. I looked at Avonstoke, but he was even more thunderstruck than I felt and was too busy holding up Sands and staring up into the storm. When he finally noticed my questioning expression, he just shrugged. Some bloody damn help. His face still looked odd and incomplete to me without the raven tattoo around his eyes. Younger, more vulnerable.

"Go!" Sands said.

"Can Faith fly there?" I said, pointing up.

Sands shook his head. "Not fast enough. *She* can't do this. You *can.*"

"What about you two?" I said.

"Faith will help us get back to the ship," Sands said at once, with a quirky smile. "She is, after all, a magician."

"We'll be fine," Avonstoke assured me promptly.

I swallowed audibly and mounted up on Pavor Nocturnus. She pranced eagerly, clearly wanting to run and happy to have me, and not much worried about the burning building or the storm.

Feeling both terrified and ridiculous, I raised my voice. "I will go." The words came out squeaky and dry, so I cleared my throat and shouted up at a God again, this time much louder.

"I will go!"

There was a moment of drawn-out silence, broken only by the rain. The moon was out now, and the rain trickled to a stop. Behind us in Stormholt came distant shouts. Whatever forces Mother was mustering, they wouldn't be long now.

A long, flat, smoky tendril curled down from the black cloud above, reaching all the way down to the ground.

"Then come," the booming voice said. It sounded amused, as if it didn't expect me to answer. That just made me angry, so I started to urge Nocturnus up the insubstantial ramp.

Then I paused.

I yanked the reins and made Nocturnus spin around and charge back to where Avonstoke and Sands were standing, dripping, watching. I reached down and grabbed at Avonstoke's coat. With his height, it wasn't that far down. I leaned the rest of the way, bringing my face close to his. His eyes were shining, liquid gold and very wide, younger looking without the tattoo. His hair had come loose in a radiant wash in the moonlight.

"Come back to us," he whispered. "I don't know what I'll do if you don't."

"I will," I said and pressed my mouth to his. He gave a wordless gasp of surprise. His mouth was warm and soft and tasted like cardamom or cinnamon or something I couldn't name. After a moment's hesitation, his hands buried themselves in my hair and returned the kiss with feverish passion.

I pushed him away after a few seconds, sure that if I allowed myself to pause, I'd never have the strength to leave.

"Don't let Starling break my ship," I said, not able to help myself.

He snorted in laughter. "I'll do my utmost best," he promised.

I kicked my heels and Nocturnus surged around and back to the smoky bridge. I might have been terrified, but my horse was game for anything. She surged up the ramp, which was a great deal like trying to guide a horse up a spiral staircase without any walls or guiderails. Fortunately, Nocturnus didn't need a lot of guidance from me, as usual, and we rose to a dizzying height, past the second floor, and the third, and others besides, past the roof, leaving the ground far, far below, and up to where Faith, Cernunnos and the rest of the Wild Hunt were waiting. The God's eyes were dark, sunken caves, inscrutable. His horse legs stirred restlessly in the black clouds, as if part of Cernunnos was too wild to allow the God to be still.

Benedict was pale and spectral as the rest of the Hunt. He was back in the dove and gun-metal gray suit I'd seen before, complete with top hat, like a gentleman come back from the dead and gone very bad. Just looking at him filled my gut with a chill from the grave.

They watched without sound or motion, only a thousand pairs of eyes. It was a contained silence. Thin black wisps trailed out from the horse's nostrils, as they panted. The hounds, ivory and motionless, might have been polished statues if not for the noiselessly lolling black tongues. Black birds beat the air far above.

Faith was the biggest shock to me of it all.

She floated, held by some power separate from the magic that allowed the Wild Hunt to ride the skies. Her arms were spread wide, in flight, in command, I wasn't sure. The air around us was still, but charged, expectant. Unseen and unfelt winds tugged at her hood and clothes as if she were underwater. Her eyes blazed with a sudden and dangerous power and her words boomed like thunder and even the God listened. Faith was still Faith, however, not possessed by another power, merely powerful herself.

"Benedict!" I called out, but while he stared at me, ghostly eyes wide, mouth open and panting, it was like watching some ferocious, caged beast. He saw, but he did not seem to recognize me in any way, nor did he answer.

I looked at the tall men standing on either side of Cernunnos, seeing their crowns now. Kings. One held a wide-bladed spear and wore an eye patch. The other carried a sword covered with runes. Both kings had dark eyes and expressions of the deepest sadness.

"I'll come for you," I said to Benedict. "After this is done."

Cernunnos' mouth opened but it was the Wild Hunt all around him that laughed, all of them speaking with his voice.

"Will you ride with the Wild Hunt?" Cernunnos and the Wild Hunt intoned with the weight of ritual.

I nodded. I might have failed Benedict, and Mother, and Joshua, but I still had a chance for Henry.

"I'll ride," I said.

"Will you ride into sky and fire and death?" Cernunnos chanted. It had the weight and cadence of ritual.

"I will ride," I shouted.

"Will you ride to make war with us?"

"I will ride!" I shouted again, this time so loud that the breath rasped in my throat.

Cernunnos blew on his horn, a sound wild and beautiful.

We surged forward.

I kicked Nocturnus to make her keep pace, but there was no need. She leapt into an immediate gallop with a will. The sound of hooves, rolling thunder, cascaded all around us and sooty clouds burst out with every step. They billowed all around us, filled with the scent of rain, rolling out a few steps ahead as we moved, but trailing behind us for miles.

A heavy electric feeling clung all around, making my hands and scalp tingle. Benedict was near to me, riding, like all the hunters, a mount that was as much demon as horse. Lean and rangy, with black, clawed, three-toed feet, overlong necks and heavy, armored heads with burning eyes and long fangs. Benedict's mount, with a sudden lunge, tried to sink its long fangs into Nocturnus' neck and I cried out. But the Wild Hunt horse's fangs only sent up sparks where they hit on the neck. Nocturnus' skin was like an armored shell.

But it didn't matter. Nocturnus went berserk with rage, screaming like locomotive coming off the rails. She surged forward even faster.

"No, Nocturnus!" I shouted, trying to bring her back under my control, but she wasn't having any of it. I might as well have been yanking on a bell pull and yelling at the clouds.

Nocturnus reared underneath me and lashed out, striking into Benedict's mount's side with her shoulder, knocking the Wild Hunt horse off its stride. Benedict's mount screamed back, every bit as angry, not cowed in the least.

Benedict laughed, a spectral, hollow noise. I think I realized then how profoundly we had lost my brother, and fear hit me like a fall in an arctic pool. Whatever Benedict had become, it wasn't my brother anymore. He gloried in the fight for its own sake and battle fires shone in his eyes.

We rode up into the clouds and it happened so fast that I never noticed the ascent, only realized minutes later how high we had come. I looked back and saw Avonstoke, Faith and Sands already tiny, distant figures far below us. In seconds, we were high above the English countryside and the storm that followed us, barking on our heels, obscured them completely.

When we had piloted the *Specter* through the Thames Estuary and seen the changes there, it had been more than a shock. It had been even worse fighting our way through the jungle that had overtaken the land in between Graveshead to Stormholt, and so I thought that I had gotten some idea of what kind of changes the Faerie had wrought on England.

But now I rode through the sky, feeling a dark, chill wind on my face, and I looked down and saw for myself the entirety of the changes that had been wrought on England and gasped out loud.

The countryside was a chaotic wilderness. Overgrowth, either jungle like I'd already seen or dark marshland. Behind us, there were the campfires belonging to what had to be a battalion around Stormholt. (My heart ached for Faith, Avonstoke, and Sands already, hoping against hope that Faith really could get them out of there safely, the way she'd promised.) The rest below us was all dark. No electric lights, no gas lights, no nothing. I struggled inside, thinking of all the people that might be still floundering around in the dark, if the Faerie had left anyone to flounder. Just dwelling on it made my tears well up again.

Ahead, was London, and nothing like I expected.

The skyline, much to my surprise and relief, was still undoubtedly a city skyline, with the tall outline of Big Ben in towering prominence. But as we drew closer, I could see large, Swiss cheese holes through the clock tower showing patches of the dark night behind. Thick, black branches spiderwebbed across the unlit clockface, making it seem as if it might be eight, nine, ten o'clock, or perhaps no o'clock at all. As we flew closer, dark, squat figures could be seen scampering in the torn-out bits. Goblins in the gears.

Westminster Palace, the houses of Parliament, which had been connected to Big Ben, was a ruin filled with rubble, just as

Joshua's photographs had shown us. It hurt even more to see it in person.

The White Tower was still intact, making me wonder if there was some powerful, sorcerous resistance that made their home there, repelling the Faerie influences, still. Or perhaps there was something about the place that the Faerie liked. Maybe members of the Court dined there? The rest of the city was surprisingly intact. It seemed that while Faerie magic, and the Faerie themselves, had transformed some of it, they'd been content merely to conquer and occupy many of the sections of London. They'd liked the city enough to let at least *some* of it remain standing.

That was also when I saw the bulk of the Faerie Army, and my heart sank.

They were camped out in Battersea Park. Or at least, they were centered there. Campfires and colored tents had overrun the entire area, with sections inside the main body like many villages all crammed together, making it impossible to tell exactly where the army ended and the dark buildings of London began.

In the center, there was a bustle of military activity, a great even square filling half the park with neat lines of Dwarven artillery, large cannon, and other less intelligible devices, all lined up in precise formation. Next to it, another dark, uneven patch of writhing black hordes of Goblins, many of them spilling off the banks of the rivers like ants off a table. Other, smaller groups, ponderous Trolls and a glittering line of Court cavalry, were forming up in the streets to one side.

There was a perimeter of moving shapes, loping figures that had to be the Hanged Dogs and more of those bloody ginger cats and more mismatched creatures that I couldn't make out from this distance.

Most of them, Court Faerie, Goblin, Dwarf, Troll, cats, dogs, were all looking up as the Wild Hunt tore overhead and I saw with my own eyes that what the others had said was true: Seelie Court, Unseelie Court, and even the Solitary Faerie, all of them were fearful of the Wild Hunt.

One of the Dwarven artillery even shot in their direction, a woefully inadequately ranged shower of violet sparks. God only knew what that might do at closer quarters, but neither Cernunnos nor the rest of the Wild Hunt even noticed.

We swept past in a long arc, bringing lightning and thunder to those unlucky enough to be underneath us. Rain fell in torrents beneath us, and I could see the figures scurrying for what shelter they could find. I rode, literally, at the head of the storm.

The Thames was a black stretch of black glass underneath us now. Usually, this stretch of the Thames was bristling with the conglomerate of docks, wharves, and porcupine display of masts from the many ships, but now, the docks stood empty and silent. If I'd ever had any doubt that the England and London that I'd grown up with was no longer, this was it. Even so, I saw many traces that showed me that several Londoners themselves were still alive and present, if displaced. A flicker of candles in a tenement window, a huddle of human shapes around a trash fire, a lone hansom carefully picking its way over a half-forested and half-cobbled street. London might have been conquered, but it was not dead.

As we passed over the Thames, I could see that this side of the London Bridge had fallen to chunks of rubble in the water. The huge vines I'd seen wrapped around the stone before had finished their work. On the other side of the river, another shape grew out of the darkness.

The tree. An avatar of the World Tree itself, it had to be.

I knew from Mr. Sands that Faerie magic was wild, capricious. But it also had rules, even if they were hidden. But once you knew them, which he said came from knowing and understanding the *source* of the magic, then you could rely on them to be consistent.

Faith's sudden powers and her connection to the Wild Hunt was like that, only I'd been whisked away before I had the chance to plumb the exact nature of that connection. Which was assuming that even Faith or Sands knew, and I wasn't confident of that at all. It struck me that a cunning leader, like I was supposed to be, might be able to dig up some of those details from the other end of the equation, from the Wild Hunt itself. The only problem was, how was I supposed to do that while hanging on for my life as we thundered across horizon a dozen miles above London. I didn't think Cernunnos was going to pull the entire Hunt over so I could exchange clever riddles or wrestle the best two out of three to get my answers.

In this part of the town, the buildings, amazingly, were mostly intact. But a carpet of thorned ivy lay over all of them as if a Rose Red manner of curse had fallen over everything, not destroying the town of London, only putting it into an enchanted slumber. There was less movement here than I'd seen in the other parts of town. No trash fires, no nomadic human shapes. If there were any Londoners left here, they might indeed be slumbering.

Then we turned again and started to descend, following Cernunnos' thundering hooves down a nearly forty-five-degree incline of billowing black stormcloud. Our destination became suddenly clear to me: Newgate Prison.

This building was still intact, and none of the creeping ivy that had overgrown so many of the buildings around it. The bulky, square building still looked very much like the medieval structure it had grown from, as much castle as anything else. Old and solid, like one massive brick with only narrow tunnels burrowed into it. Other buildings clung to it, presenting one long building face to the street. Three rows of windows with iron bars rose on either tower.

With another wild call of his copper horn, Cernunnos led the Wild Hunt directly at it.

CHAPTER 18

Wild Hunt at Newgate

I only got a brief look at the scene at the corner of Newgate Street and Old Bailey before the Wild Hunt turned it into a war zone, but even that was unbelievable.

I'd expected the usually busy street to be deserted and empty, what with the occupation, but I was surprised to find it as busy as ever. Only the *nature* of the street's occupants had changed.

A small series of silver-branched and yellow-leaved willows ran in a gently curving line near the prison walls. But this wasn't an unkempt and unruly overgrowth the way so much of the newly-sprung foliage in London was. This was a protective canopy, clearly planned, stretching sixty or seventy feet in a graceful arc, providing nominal shelter for the people that were milling around.

These weren't guards or invasion troops or even, as far as I could tell, any part of the Faerie vanguard.

These were party-goers.

They were Court Faerie, the tall, regal, elfish people that seemed to be at the top of both courts, Seelie and Unseelie. Which court these belonged to, I couldn't tell. A small group of musicians were softly playing music under the boisterous patter of lively conversation. Hansoms and larger carriages, looking incredibly just like they did before the invasion, were arriving and departing, bringing and taking more court members. The horses looked surprisingly normal, the drivers human. So did the musicians, as well as servants and attendants.

My brother was trapped in Newgate Prison, within hours of execution, and the Faerie in this part of town were throwing a soiree.

What astonished me weren't the Faerie, but the regular people. They weren't in chains, or under any sorcerous compulsion that I could see. Their faces were not rictuses of fear, only the carefully empty or mildly agreeable expressions they might have worn months ago. It seemed that for many working-class Londoners, being invaded had changed their lives far less than I might have expected. Did they still have husbands, wives, daughters, or sons left here in London? They served different masters now, clearly, but on the surface, incredibly, their lives appeared not to be all that different.

We rode the black cloud down to the ground and the storm's darkness draped the street in thick, black tendrils. While running with the Wild Hunt through the sky, Nocturnus' hooves had thudded on the clouds below us, as if on soft earth. Now, they made the unmistakable sharp clip-clop of hooves on cobblestones.

The Wild Hunt fell on everyone in the street, party-goer and servant, human and Faerie, man and woman, with the same howling, screaming fury. The screams of Faerie and humans alike joined the screaming of Cernunnos' hunters, and the bloodlust baying of his hounds.

Several people, some Faerie, some human, had been crowding around a low table made of a cross-section of an enormous and ancient tree. Some crazed, compulsive part of my mind wanted to count the rings, at least a few thousand. The table had been covered with ornate, tiny glasses. Expensive and rare refreshments, perhaps, which were now scattered to the four winds as a half dozen of the riders rode down table and persons, spears and hooves, leaving a bloody path of destruction. One of the hunters, a pale, wild-faced woman, managed to pluck one of the drinks out of a stunned Faerie's hand, drain the tiny draught down, then cast the glass aside before guiding her vicious mount around for another pass in which she and three other riders ran the hapless Faerie down. One of those riders was Benedict, laughing maniacally as he rode.

"Benedict!" I shouted. "No!"

A flicker of his eyes suggested that he might have heard me, but he paid no more attention to me than he would have to one of the screaming crows.

I might now be grounded, but the Wild Hunt riders were still swooping up and around with reckless abandon. One of them swept down and, leaning down from his mount, seized the collar of a fleeing Faerie courtier woman just a dozen feet in front of me, lifting her from the ground like an errant child. They both flew past me, and I had to spin to see when he dropped the woman a few seconds later. Her scream was brutally short.

Did Faith's bargain cause this? She'd helped choose the target, at least. I'd wanted the Faerie punished and driven out. I'd been firing at, sinking or burning their ships to accomplish just that, and I'd have taken any opportunities to fire on coastal targets, too. But I'd wanted military targets, not this. This ruthless and inhuman savagery inflicted on civilians was too much to bear.

I spun Nocturnus around and saw that another trio of hunters were bearing down on one of the hansoms, a single human driver and horse. The hunters were grinning like skulls, lowering their spears as they closed, ready to strike them, or anything else foolish enough to get in their way, down. The lead rider was lean, cadaverous woman, dark skinned, naked to the waist with tattoos all over like an Islander. She screamed and brandished her spear.

One quick look at the roan was enough to make me realize I knew the hansom driver and horse. A glance at the whiskered driver confirmed it. Mr. Divers and Hercules!

I was kicking my heels and driving Nocturnus to intercede before I even realized it.

Nocturnus, for her part, was more than game. We thundered past one of the pavilions and I was able to lean down and snatch a cane off one of the tables. Nocturnus had harder skin than any normal horse, but I didn't want to test it against one of those spears.

Mr. Divers' hansom was facing the charging trio, so Hercules was the closest, though the charging trio looked intent on trampling horse, driver, and hansom with equal abandon. Hercules, despite his legendary name, wasn't particularly large or any kind of fighter, and his eyes were already rolling with panic as he was resisting the reins so that even if Mr. Divers had gotten over his own fright and tried to flee, there wouldn't have been any time. They just stood there, terrified.

I charged between them, knocking the leading woman's spear to one side as Nocturnus muscled her mount to one side. The two following riders had been so close behind that turning the leader effectively turned them all and they all thundered harmlessly by. Mr. Divers and Hercules, both elderly, looked close to experiencing their own epileptic fit.

The leader, and the two behind her, wheeled their horses around. She screamed her rage at us. I glared at her, refusing to back down or drop my gaze. What I did do was slowly draw my pistol and wave her off with it. Nocturnus screamed back, still ready to have a go at one or any of the Wild Hunt horses. Finally, the woman screamed again, frustrated beyond reason, but turned and went to find easier prey.

I spun and shouted back at Mr. Divers. "Go! Get out of here! Now!"

There was no recognition and no wonder. With my black hat and billowing black coat and pistol, not to mention the oil-slick haunted black eye, and mounted on a literal nightmare, it was evident that he didn't even begin to recognize me. He was, in fact, just as terrified of me as he was of the Wild Hunt. Hercules, too, despite the fact that I'd fed him so many lumps of sugar over the years. That realization broke my heart. What had I become that gentle old Mr. Divers feared me so?

But, better to use that fear now, if it saved their lives.

"Go!" I shouted again, pointing the pistol directly at him.

Mr. Divers finally got his faculties together enough to turn Hercules around and urge him away from the holy hell and chaos all around us. Last I saw of either of them, the London fog had swallowed them. What were they riding *to* in this Faerie-damned city? I had no idea.

Even worse, dropping holy hell on a party held on the street in front of Newgate Prison was doing a damn thing to rescue Henry. None of this was even scratching the stonework on the Newgate Prison walls. I peered through the ragged war zone we'd made of this street, looking for Cernunnos, or even one his minion Kings. They weren't hard to find.

The God of the Wild Hunt was standing on a shelf of smoke, facing the front of Newgate Prison as if from a raised stage. The two Kings were on a similar shelf, a few feet below, stationed to keep any of the madness from interfering with Cernunnos. Two of the storm crows, larger, nobler and somehow more terrifying than the rest, had landed on the King with the eyepatch's shoulder. They whispered in his ear, and he nodded and sent them off again. The other King had his rune-covered sword out and ready. Both were turned, facing each other but some distance apart, so they could watch both the God and the savagery in the street. I maneuvered Nocturnus around to bring me closer.

Cernunnos raised his copper horn.

The note rang out, high and clear, and a blue-white tongue of lightning flickered down from the clouds, impacting on the top corner of the prison walls, spraying shards of burning mortar and brick in a deadly hail. When the smoke cleared, I could see a smoking hole in the stone large enough to drive a hansom through. The horn sounded again, and more lightning came.

The massive door leading into the prison burst open and a swarm of shaggy, loping shapes in torn constabulary outfits rushed out onto the street. They howled and snarled, staring up at the God and his Kings. In the shadowy doorway, I saw a hated and terrifying figure. A man with glasses like two silver coins shining in the dark, wearing a gentleman's cape, with white gloves and a black top hat. Widdershins. My chest fluttered just looking at him and my eyes ached just remembering the pain he'd inflicted on me last time.

I'd managed to get around near the Kings, or at least underneath them, since the magic of the Wild Hunt that had allowed us to ride across the sky had abandoned us once we touched ground.

This was what the Kings had been waiting for.

The King with the eyepatch, that could talk to crows, hurled his wide-bladed spear and another flicker of lightning burned the nearest three Hanged Dogs to smoking, misshapen skeletons.

"My turn," the King with the sword said, in a hollow, spectral voice, and he dismounted and stepped down to do battle with the dozen or so Hanged Dogs that remained. I'd seen an equal number of Hanged Dogs swarm effortlessly over the Soho Shark and Victoria Rose as if they'd been helpless children and those were two terrifying Faerie in their own right. At least, the Soho Shark was. I'd killed the Rose, a thought that still made me feel squeamish and more than a little sick.

I held the cane still, and drew the pistol in my other hand. That didn't leave any hand for the reins, but Nocturnus seemed to know my mind and I was finding that just a slight lean or kick of my legs told her what I needed, and she'd respond accordingly.

But I never fired or so much as lifted that cane.

The King with the sword walked toward them with the deliberate step of a man determined. He wasn't frightened, or excited, merely unshakably grim. When the nearest Hanged Dog lunged at him, the man swept the rune-covered sword in a backhanded, angled stroke that took off most of his attacker's arm at the shoulder. The return stroke, efficient and effortless, took the head. The King wasn't an elegant fighter, and he didn't seem nimble or quick, but he was just fast enough to kill every enemy the second it was within reach. Even though the Hanged Dogs were part of the unliving and shrugged off wounds that would have crippled normal men, the King whittled them down to helpless, wriggling parts littered all over the street in less than a minute of solemn effort. It was as if he fought by sheer, indomitable will alone, and it was a terrifying thing to behold.

The other King's spear had appeared back in his hand the second after his first thunderbolt stoke had hit, so that he could use it again. But there was no need.

The cloaked figure in the doorway, Widdershins, gave one last look with those shining spectacles and disappeared back inside the building, leaving the door hanging open.

The God, Cernunnos, hadn't even bothered to pay any attention to any of this, knowing, it seemed, that his Kings would handle the tiny details of murder and death. He blew the horn again, and the dismantling of Newgate Prison continued at a lively pace. Already, a good thirty feet or so of wall on each of the nearest walls, and the corner in between, had been blown to smoking piles of broken gray brick and blackened rubble.

One of the riders of the Hunt had descended and lit behind me before I even knew it, and I jumped when the heavy panting of his horse and a flash of heat from the demon steed's breath came from close behind.

I turned and stared. It was Benedict.

"Follow me," he said, his voice ringing hollow over the fog-drenched cobblestones. He led his mount deeper into the fighting and madness and I followed.

The next stroke of lightning broke apart the nearest wall, revealing a smoking hold that led into one of the open courtyards.

Benedict urged his mount up the slope of blackened rubble that led up to the hole, the black smoke trail of the Wild Hunt leading the way.

We went up and came down into the courtyard crowded with screaming men and women. The storm howled above us, whipping around ferocious, bitterly cold winds and smoke. My face was wet and cold with rain. This was the criminal class of London, apparently still held despite the Faerie having taken the place over. I'd half expected to see the faces of hardened felons, but if the men and woman (and I hadn't expected nearly so many women) inmates of Newgate Prison had anything in common, it was the look of the run-down and worn-out. The poor.

A familiar figure cried out and broke away from the crowd.

It was Henry.

He was still wearing the same ragged pants and dark shirt he'd worn when I'd last seen him, though very much worse for the wear. He'd gotten a knife from somewhere, a long, black, curved, wicked-looking thing. His sandy hair was longer and unkempt and his face, once characterized by its cheerful roundness, was thinner and covered in soot. The once friendly, hazel eyes were now wide-open and bloodshot. He wore an expression of terror that slackened only slightly when he saw me.

"Justice," he shouted. "What are you doing here?"

"We're here for you," I shouted back. "Come on!"

He shook his head, as if he couldn't quite believe this was happening, but he tucked the curved knife into his shirt and ran over. I leaned down and reached out my hand to pull him up and he took it and sprang easily onto Nocturnus' back behind me. He squeezed me so tight that red flashed in my eyes and I thought I'd pass out.

"Easy!" I snapped. "Don't kill me now that we've come this far."

"I knew you'd come for me," he said. "Where's Faith?"

"Waiting for us," I said. I turned Nocturnus towards the hole in the wall and urged her forward.

"Lor!" Henry said when he saw Benedict, who was waiting, mounted still on his supernatural demon steed at the top of the slope of rubble where the hole was. His spectral suit, the dove-gray one he'd worn back before that terrible carriage ride when I'd first seen the Wild Hunt, was resplendent in the moonlight and his eyes shone with a baleful green corpse light so that he couldn't possibly be mistaken for one of the living. His teeth were enormous fangs nearly as terrible as the smoking fangs of the horse beneath him.

"Is that . . ." Henry started.

"Yes," I said shortly. "I'll explain later."

But then I pulled up on Nocturnus' reins, bringing her to a halt. I looked back at the huddled figures behind us. There had to be at least a hundred of them.

"You have to promise they'll be safe!" I shouted at Benedict. "Don't let the Wild Hunt hurt the prisoners. Haven't they suffered enough at the hands of the Faerie?"

"Promise?" the ghost of Benedict said softly. "You cannot compel the Wild Hunt." Despite the softness, his voice drifted down to us clearly, as if the storm wasn't crashing and banging all around. Benedict tilted his head, as if perplexed at my request. Then he shrugged. "However, the hunt's thirst has been slaked with the sport out in the street. They will not be harmed."

"But where will they go?" I shouted. I couldn't imagine a way to get them out of England, but I couldn't imagine just leaving them here in the hands of the Faerie, no matter what they'd done.

"There are places to evade the Faerie in the city, still," Benedict intoned. "London is not so enslaved yet as you or the Faerie have imagined. But it will be, in time."

I stared. It was almost like he was saying that we had his sympathies. But was that Benedict or Cernunnos? Where did that knowledge come from? How did he know? There was no time to ask.

Another lightning bolt touched down on the top of the building, spilling chunks of rubble down into the courtyard.

"Come," Benedict said, and I heard Cernunnos' horn yet again.

"We shall return you to your ship," Benedict said.

"Your ship?" Henry said, looking at me.

I ground my teeth to keep from blushing. "Yes. A lot has changed while you were in Newgate."

He shivered against me. "You have to tell me!"

"Come," Benedict said again in that ghostly voice that might belong to him or Cernunnos.

"We ride!"

CHAPTER 19

Leaving the Wild Hunt

The black smoke was before us again, rolling across the sky like squid ink underwater, and the Wild Hunt rode along it.

Us too.

The great tree, the smaller buildings with their covering of ivy and bramble, and even the silver thread of the Thames fell far behind us, then the Dover Cliffs passed by underneath and Cernunnos led the Hunt in a wide arc as we followed the English Channel east towards where the *Specter* was supposed to be making its rendezvous. Of course, I hadn't told Cernunnos that, but he seemed to know that already. Being a God apparently had its privileges.

Nocturnus was surging along the smoky path as if she'd been born for it. Maybe she had. She was working her way forward, and

I was happy to let her. Several of the hunters glared at us as we passed them. Already the buildings beneath us had dwindled to matchboxes, and still Nocturnus ran all out. The fury of the Wild Hunt had infected her somehow, and she seemed determined to outrun everything in the Wild Hunt, even Cernunnos himself. Henry's grip from his perch behind me was firm, but he didn't seem to be in any kind of panic, despite our flight across the sky. I'd only seen him for a few minutes, and I couldn't really get a good look at him now, but he seemed to have matured a very good deal in just one month and I wondered what kinds of things he'd seen in a prison run by the Faerie.

Had he met the Black Shuck?

I might have expected someone going through an ordeal like that to come out fragile and terrified, but Henry seemed stronger somehow, sturdier. I couldn't wait to ask him, but there wasn't time for either of us to tell our stories.

Pavor Nocturnus was nearing the front of the pack now. I reined her in some, but she didn't like it and rolled her eyes and glared back at me. She slowed, but only a little.

The Two Kings and Cernunnos himself were directly ahead of us now, with most of the rest of the Hunt strewn out in a long path behind us.

"Look!" Henry hollered, pointing off to the left.

A pale horse the color of moonlit cream was running beside the Kings, riderless. It was glorious, shining under the starlit sky with the rippling ocean below. Even in this fantastic and august company, she looked exceptional. There was only one horse I'd ever seen that looked like that. She looked whiter than ever next to all the black horses around us.

"Actawhatshisface!" Henry shouted. "Right?"

"Yes!" I shouted back. Acta Santorum. Sands' magical horse, only it wasn't his horse anymore because he'd broken his source of magical power, his precious violin, in order to pass some kind of torch to Faith. Sands had been Father's magician and now Faith was supposed to be mine. I couldn't imagine what that must have cost Sands. I'd only had Pavor Nocturnus for a short time, and already the idea of losing her gave me icicles in my belly.

Nocturnus snorted underneath us. Clearly, she'd seen Acta Santorum and screamed at him. It's a terrifying thing to hear a horse scream and Nocturnus' scream was blood-curdling. Her pounding hooves, already moving at a blur, sped up even more and we tore across the sky. But Acta Santorum had disappeared when Sands had broken the violin. Banished, I assumed, back to wherever she'd come from. So what she was doing here, among the Wild Hunt?

Then the strangely compelling idea came to me: What if we could somehow retrieve Acta Santorum for Sands? As soon as it occurred to me, the idea began to shine in my mind. Intuition had served me well so far when dealing with Faerie magic, if intuition it was, and I was inclined to trust it now. What if Sands' magical powers could be restored? It was something we desperately needed with Father gone. Besides, my heart still cried out at the horrible scream that Acta Santorum had given when the bond between him and Sands had been broken. It had been my fault—the need for me and Faith to take Father and Sands' place at its core. If there was something I could do to heal that wound, even a little, I wanted to see it done.

Acta Santorum screamed when he saw Nocturnus. Not a scream of pain, but one of challenge. Then he sped up. Even so, we were drawing very close. Acta still wore his golden harness and bridle. Something told me that if I could just get my hands on that bridle, Acta Santorum would be mine and there would be no rule of Cernunnos' or the Wild Hunts' that would deny me.

Both magical horses, demonic and angelic, perhaps, had outstripped the main body of the Wild Hunt. Now only the Kings and Cernunnos himself were ahead of us. I leaned forward and urged Nocturnus on. She whinnied happily and pushed forward even more. Her legs moved like machine pistons underneath us.

Henry was thumping me on the shoulder, trying to get my attention. I turned and saw that someone was riding close behind us.

Benedict.

He was two lengths behind, lashing his fanged horse mercilessly. "What are you doing?" he shouted. Despite his luminescent pallor and spectral eyes, he looked deeply concerned. So there *was* something of our Benedict underneath Cernunnos' spell! That was something to know.

I shook my head at him. No time to explain.

Nocturnus was still running full out. Acta Santorum was just in front of us, so close his snowy mane flicked in Nocturnus' nostrils, making her snort. Running near the edge of the pack like this, the smoke cloud beneath us didn't extend more than a few feet to our left. I made the mistake of looking down past that smoky edge, down, down, down to the grim gray shimmer of water below. The sky ahead was a lighter shade of gray. Dawn was coming.

"Nocturnus!" I shouted, hauling on the reins. "Slow down!" But Nocturnus was chuffing and still running flat out. Shouldn't she be getting tired? Normal horses don't run flat-out for this long without getting tired, do they? Nocturnus didn't flag at all. If anything, she might be going faster. Of course, normal horses didn't run through the clouds, either.

We were starting to come abreast with the Two Kings, just behind the lead figure of Cernunnos. The cloud we ran on streamed out behind Cernunnos' hooves, spreading just wide enough a few paces back for the two Kings to ride abreast. Acta Santorum ran just behind and to the left of the left King and now Nocturnus was trying to run on the finger-wide breadth of smoke left on Acta's left side. We were gaining, too, pulling even with Acta despite running on the narrow ribbon of space we had.

"Justice!" Henry bawled into my ear. "We're running out of smoke! That's bad isn't it? Isn't that what's keeping us . . . you know . . . up here?"

"Yeah!" I shouted back. "That's bad! Really bad! Bloody well terrible, really! But she won't slow down!"

"DO NOT," a voice intoned, "STRAY FROM THE PATH."

It was Cernunnos himself, and the two Kings. The words echoed all the way back, flowing out of the mouths of the hunters, horses, and hounds. Even the crows screamed it.

Everything and everyone, all common sense and the wellspring of terror spouting inside of me, wanted me to slow down and stay on the path. A God, two ancient heroes or semi-gods or something, and the whole bloody Wild Hunt, a supernatural force I didn't entirely understand, was telling me not to do something *I didn't even want to do*. I didn't just *not* want to do it, my gut churned, and my stomach ran with ice at the thought of it.

Problem was, I couldn't get Nocturnus to slow down.

We were neck and neck with Acta Santorum now, his golden bridle and reins within reach. Maybe I could grab the other horse's reins and slow him down, and whatever madness that had taken over Nocturnus would pass once we'd caught him.

"Hold these!" I shouted, handing the reins back to Henry.

"Are you bloody mad?" Henry said. He fumbled at the leather straps, trying to get a hold. Finally, he grabbed them and held on.

He wasn't wrong. It was crazier than crazy. Crazy on wheels. But what other choice did I have?

"DO NOT," Cernunnos boomed again, "STRAY FROM THE PATH."

"Yeah, yeah," I murmured. I could see that we'd moved lower in the sky, at least, so I could see the rollers of the ocean moving underneath. So we'd only be amazingly dead if we fell, as opposed to well and truly and amazingly dead.

I grabbed the pommel with my left hand, clamped on as hard as I could with my legs and leaned, way, way out. I snatched at the golden reins on Acta Santorum's bridle . . .

. . . and missed.

Bloody stupid horses. Stupid demonic and angelic and flying-through-the-sky horses that followed stupid horsey gods . . . why couldn't I still be out at sea, where the sails and ship did what you told them to?

I swung out and lunged for the reins again. And missed.

Again.

Then Nocturnus slipped.

A black hoof must have hit dead air and she lurched beneath us.

As we fell, and the seconds crawled by with intractable, ponderous slowness, I got a sudden glimpse of Cernunnos.

Slowly, the God's head turned. His face registered surprise, which was something I never expected from a God. But quickly the expression passed, and he gave a mighty and divine shrug.

"SO BE IT," the voice of Cernunnos rang out through many mouths, like the tolling of a huge iron bell.

Henry screamed into my ear. I screamed as we tumbled over. Nocturnus screamed and even Acta Santorum screamed, as if he'd very much wanted to be caught and now gave out a keening note of despair. Then our view of the Wild Hunt was from below, and rapidly dwindling. I caught a last glimpse of Acta Santorum shining like a star in all that somber inky glory and then I was twisting in the air to get a look at the rushing wall of gray flying up at us. Nocturnus was twisting in air herself, or trying to, helplessly churning her legs as she fell upside down, also screaming, a high ear-splitting shriek. Henry, who hadn't stopped screaming, now doubled his volume.

Just before we hit the water and everything went black, my mind, which is never helpful when it was knee-deep in ice-bowel-clenching panic, remembered something I'd been told. In fact, I could hear Sands' voice: *"Above all, do not take Pavor Nocturnus into the sea."*

Would the fall kill us outright, or would we have time to drown before the demon was set loose on us? There was only the rush of air and Henry's long scream for the stretched-out string of seconds as we fell the last few feet.

Then the gray wall hit us.

CHAPTER 20

Nocturnus in the Sea

Water hit me like a runaway train. The blow drove all of my breath out as I plunged in deep, and then the muffled cold of the ocean gripped me. White foam and bubbles exploded in all directions in a whispery gust. The air rushed out of my lungs and shockingly cold, numbing water rushed in.

I must have blacked out, just for seconds, because I came to suddenly, thrashing about in the water.

The cold was everywhere, burning. It was in my lungs and I couldn't breathe and everything I knew was cold. Which way was up? The numbness settled deeper into my muscles, my bones, my gut. I noticed the bubbles and tried to follow them up. But the grip of the sea was irresistible, titanic.

I struggled my arms free of my coat.

As I pushed the coat away, it floated a moment in the deep blue water.

Then a thin black whipcord quested out of the depths. I remembered, with a rush colder than the sea, what Pavor Nocturnus *really* looked like in the infernal depths that I'd summoned her from. This was her curse. I knew, too, that I couldn't count on her feelings for me. Not in this form. You are the shape that you take, Sands had said once when talking about Father, but I knew it was the same here. Here, now, Pavor Nocturnus was a demon, and would act like one.

The tentacle came closer.

It was only as wide as my thumb for most of the length that I could see, narrowing to an almost razor thinness at the tip. But the speed and ease with which it moved through the water implied a great deal of power and strength. What the other end might have been attached to I had no idea. Part of me wasn't sure I wanted to know.

We hung a moment in the deep blue, facing each other over the wrinkled, sodden mess of my coat, which started sinking slowly. The black tentacle bumped into the coat from underneath, then twisted in a frighteningly violent maneuver, gripping the heavy cloth in a sudden stranglehold. A whoosh of bubbles escaped as the tentacle squeezed and then, shockingly quickly, the tentacle retreated, dragging the coat down with it.

I wanted to scream but didn't have the breath. At least now I'd gotten my bearings enough to see which way was up. I didn't want to turn my back on the area down below from which the tentacle had come, but I had no choice. I swam upwards, breast-stroking and frog-kicking my way to the light above. My lungs felt ready to burst or collapse or fail entirely and suck down a huge quantity of ocean cold. I kept waiting for something to grab my ankle and drag me down and that I was going to die down in the unspeakable ocean depths. My vision was blacking out, the darkness, filled with little flashes of red, closing in until I wasn't even sure I was swimming in the right direction anymore.

I kicked, stroked, kicked . . .

Then I broke the surface with a gasp.

I paddled in the ocean, lifting and falling with the ocean rollers, gulping air and water together. I couldn't see anyone. No Henry, no Nocturnus. Only the glowing mist. The roll of the water pulled me under for a few seconds, and I had to thrash and sputter my way back up. Starling and others had remarked on my strange affinity for sailing and boats and all things of the sea, but none of the seemed to make me any better of a swimmer. I kicked off my water-logged boots, but even so, it was all I could do to keep my head afloat and try and let the black and red spots fade from my vision so that I could look for Henry or Nocturnus.

A minute, maybe two passed, then I tried to turn and get a decent look around me.

The sea was too rough to see much and what I did see was bad.

I was alone.

No Wild Hunt above. No Henry. No Nocturnus. No ships and no sign of land.

"Henry!" I shouted. No answer but the sound of my feeble strokes and the sloshing of the waves around me.

I kept paddling and turning, looking. Henry couldn't be dead, could he? Probably he was and probably I was going to be in a very short time. Nocturnus, too. Damn the Wild Hunt and damn me, for being a headstrong idiot. Sobs tore their way out of my burning chest, and there were probably tears on my face, but who could tell with all the water of the ocean around me?

Then I looked at a spot off to my left, about a dozen yards away, where the water churned. I couldn't be sure at first, because the rising and falling of the waves around, and my own rising and falling, made it difficult to see over the waves. But I thought that something swam down there, agitating the water, something big moving down there.

Something very big.

I wanted to swim away, but still hadn't seen any sign of Henry or Nocturnus and was afraid that something had gotten them, so I started floundering my way over.

A black filament snapped out of the ocean in front of me. The thin tentacle probed the open air, then withdrew.

Suddenly, to my left, Henry broke the surface . . .

He gasped and sucked at the air. The churning water was a white froth behind him. A half dozen more filaments broke the water all around him, jutting up, questing. Then something yanked him back under the surface.

"Henry!" I shouted, but he was gone.

I sucked in a deep breath and dove.

The water was churned up with white foam in front of me, making it difficult to see anything, but I made out a large black shape ahead of me. It was still too far away in the half-lit water to be sure about anything, but I could tell it was big, about the size of the *Specter*. I thought I discerned a fish or shark shape, except this fish or shark had all those tendrils coming out of it.

And it had Henry.

He was struggling with half a dozen tendrils. Bubbles from their motion and from his obviously struggling lungs flew all about. He looked at his life's end, having been fighting underwater for too long. He couldn't have much more life left in him. I made for him as fast as I could kick.

My lungs were already burning, but I couldn't let Henry drown out here for the stupid thing I'd done. Henry's motions were jerky, half-frantic, and half-sleepy, as if his strength was nearly gone.

The tentacles were everywhere around me now, dozens of them, like long black ropes twining in the dark blue sea. I ducked under one as I swam.

The mass of blackness behind the filaments still wasn't clear. Something serpentine and awful with a large mouth. All the tentacles came from there. I could just make out a huge, sucking mouth at the nearest end of the beast, which made me shudder. Was this the monster that Pavor Nocturnus was when she wasn't a horse? The idea made me shudder in fear, but also filled me with pity for her. Nocturnus was clearly smart enough to have desires and wants above and beyond your ordinary horse and I had a hunch, born of watching the nuances of Father's transformation, that Nocturnus *wanted* to be a horse, to put her monstrous shape and urges behind her.

Henry's eyes went wide at the sight of me, still a dozen feet distant, and he thrashed with a last burst of energy. Two of the tentacles had his arms, but he had his curved knife out, and was struggling madly. I could see the power of the tentacles in their movement and wasn't sure how Henry could possibly manage to do as well as he was with them, but wherever his desperate strength was coming from, it wasn't enough.

He couldn't bring the knife to bear and I saw his final burst of energy dissipate and Henry sag in place, lifeless, his eyes staring blankly at nothing.

My lungs burned. I swam desperately. Finally, I slipped under yet another tentacle and got to Henry's side.

I tried yanking at the tentacle around Henry's knife hand, but it was like hauling on a taunt steel cable. My fingers couldn't budge it. No, no, no, no! A thousand times no! I wasn't going to fight my way through miles of Faerie forest, lose one brother to a Faerie God, then wrangle that same Faerie God into busting my *other* brother out of Newgate Prison, only to let him drown at sea!

The filaments dragged Henry and me closer to the creature's sucking mouth. More filaments ringed the mouth's edge, but these were edged like sawtooth blades, and waved hungrily. I could imagine those sawtooth weapons ripping the flesh of Henry's bones, or my bones, with stark clarity. I only had seconds before the longer tentacles dragged Henry into the mouth.

My only advantage was that the tentacles didn't seem to know I was there yet. I yanked the knife from Henry's hand and sliced at the closest filament in one quick swipe. The flesh parted easily, and the tentacle writhed as if in pain. The beast cried out, a long bellow that carried underwater and hammered my ears, like a saw scraping against rock. I cut the filaments off Henry's legs and then the last one off his arm and the rest of the tentacles in the water around us withdrew with shocking rapidity, churning the water as they left.

Henry was free! If only I'd been in time to save him! Was there a last flicker of life in those eyes?

I hooked an arm over Henry's neck and kicked upwards, dragging him to the surface. My lungs were bursting, and the cold sank teeth into my bones so that I could barely swim. Henry wasn't moving in my grasp, wasn't helping in any way, only dragged behind me, a sodden weight.

We broke the surface and I sucked gratefully at the air. Henry didn't move at first and I cried out and shook him, sure that I'd lost another brother. The water rolled all around us, dark and unforgiving. More mist lay on everything. There wasn't any sign of ship or land that I could see.

"No," I gasped, lungs still burning. "Breathe, Henry! Fight!" Was I too late?

Suddenly, Henry stirred and gasped, and my heart lifted. He sucked in a long, ragged breath and I sobbed in relief. Alive! Henry was alive! I gasped and sobbed, treading water.

Like a magic ray of hope, the mist parted and I spotted a length of white beach. Land! The thin, white strip appeared, disappeared and reappeared again off to my left as we bobbed in the waves.

I struck out for it, towing Henry behind me. The lightest touch brushed my ankle. Another tentacle.

I kicked away, fear renewing my flagging strength. Stroke, kick, stroke, kick. I couldn't get a decent breath with the waves in my face and already I was fighting just to keep my head above water, but I had to get away from the monster, had to get to land before my strength gave way and Henry and I drowned out here.

An agonizing length of time of stroke and kick stretched by. The whole time I waited for another touch or sudden grab of my ankle. Another bellow rang out behind us, and I redoubled my efforts. I was dragging Henry with my arm around his neck, keeping him face up as I stroked with one arm and kicked with my legs. I wasn't very graceful about it, either, and wasn't setting any speed records. Already my arm was tired, but I didn't dare switch arms. Henry gasped and started to move a little bit more.

"Come on, Henry!" I gasped as I swam. "I really need you to start swimming now!"

Then I heard possibly the most wonderful sound in the whole wide world. The crash of cannon. I craned my neck to see, and staring out far, far behind us, glimpsed in snatches as we rose and fell, I thought I could make out the white of sails.

Were they shooting at something, or was it a signal? I couldn't be sure, but I thought the sails looked like the *Specter*, which was a welcome sight. The Wild Hunt *had* been taking us to my ship, and probably would have honored their promise to deliver us there if not for my foolish bravado.

Then sea between us and the ship exploded upwards behind us as the tentacled behemoth broke the surface.

The beast roared. An odd sound like an overwrought pipe organ. It was a good distance away now, but surged through the sea towards us with powerful surges of its long body. It breached the water a number of times, revealing a long, bulbous body, like an enormous leach with a mouthful of teeth and the swarm of tentacles on its back. The tentacles thrashed the air. The creature had a sort of tail that propelled it through water with alarming speed.

"Do you have my knife?" Henry gasped.

"No," I snapped. "I dropped it." I couldn't even remember when that had happened. Sometime after using on the creature and before I'd hauled Henry up to the surface.

"Shame," Henry whispered. "I liked that knife. Took it off a big Goblin that tried to gut me with it when the place started coming apart."

I stared. It was hard to imagine Henry taking anything off anyone, let alone the way he described it. But people change under extreme circumstances, and I couldn't imagine anything more extreme than a Faerie prison. This new Henry was going to take some getting used to.

"I can swim now," Henry gasped, "I think."

"Are you sure?"

He splashed his arms down and craned his neck to get a good look at the thing chasing us. "I can bloody well swim away from that!" A tentacle splashed in the water next to us, grasping and groping in the water. Henry shrugged himself free of my grip and started splashing energetically towards the beach. It was maddening, twice as terrifying as being pursued by anything on land, since most of the time the moving waves made it impossible to tell if the beast was closing on us or not.

The beach didn't look any closer and the fog was thin, but moving enough to make it impossible to be certain we were even swimming in the right direction and twice I had to call out to Henry to shift to our left to keep on track. The cannon of the *Specter* (God, how I hoped it was the *Specter*!) thundered out again.

"Dive!" I gasped and followed my own advice. I had no idea where the cannonball went or if they were even close, but I didn't want to risk getting killed by shots from our own ship if they were now shooting at the monster fish.

After a minute of frog-kicking underwater, I broke the surface again. Henry did the same to my right. The beach looked a little closer. My arms were lead and my legs numb, but I kept struggling to crawl just a little bit closer. Just a little bit . . .

I felt soft sand beneath my bare feet! Henry squealed with laughter.

After a few dozen more strokes we could stand up, kind of, with the water about at our shoulders.

I turned and could feel all the blood drain from my face when I saw the creature was much closer behind us than I'd hoped. It roared again and tentacles reached out towards us.

This time, Henry was ready. Another tendril wrapped itself around his arm, but he dug in his heels and tore himself free from the pulverizing grip of the monster's tentacle as easily as I might slip free from a child's grip. I'd forgotten about him swinging a giant chunk of wood at the Hanged Dogs back in London. Whatever powers Faith and I had gotten, we clearly weren't the only ones. But hadn't Father intended for only us girls to be part of fighting the Faerie? That's what he had said, but intended or not, Henry, at least, was also something far more than human.

Another tentacle reached for my head and I ducked, which gave me a face full of seawater. Even so, the monster got a clump of my hair and yanked me backwards. I thrashed in the water and finally managed to tear free, though it cost me a painful tuft of my locks. I labored towards shore, bouncing as much as swimming.

We slogged on and now the sand under my feet sloped up sharply and we climbed up until the water was down to cold waves breaking over our ankles. A glittering white beach lay all around us. I wasn't at all sure where this might be. Somewhere in what had once been Wales, maybe? White sand, with black-flecked rocks in a ragged line all a bit further in and past that, tall witch grass and a few stunted trees. I dropped to my knees, gasping and choking, as if I'd swallowed half of the sea. Still on my knees, I turned to see if the monster was still coming.

It was, but it jackknifed awkwardly through the wet sand with most of the shark-like body above the water. It didn't look very dangerous now, more like a beached slug the size of a railway car, if railway cars came with thrashing tentacles. The tentacles were directionless, aimless. One of them still clutched my dripping coat. The beast that had been Nocturnus thrashed about on the beach, helpless but no less determined, as if it would rather die on land than give us up. Its gills sucked at nothing while soft moans escaped with every breath it took.

Clearly it was dying out of the water.

It thrashed twice more and then all the strength seemed to run out of it until it lay feebly in the wet sand, its grayish, slick sides heaving. A cold wind ran through me.

"I've got something for you, you bloody monster," Henry said. He took two steps over, bending down to seize up a white and black chunk of rock the size of a large watermelon. The rock must have weighed a hundred pounds, easy, but he hefted it over his head as easily as I might have lifted a basket of clothes. The behemoth groaned and rolled its eyes up at us. I was up on my feet. Henry didn't know this was Nocturnus, or even know who Nocturnus *was*. I was trying to get the words out as Henry stepped closer.

"No," I gasped. "Wait!" But the words came out too softly and were whipped away by the wind and anyway Henry didn't look too ready to listen.

I forced my numb feet to get me there. Henry's eyes were hot, flashing with rage, but I stumbled in between him and the creature anyway. I hoped desperately that the creature's tentacles were out of commission because I was now standing with my back to it and didn't want to get throttled trying to save it.

I hoped Henry wasn't going to hurl that rock and crush both of us anyway.

Then a soft whuff of imploding air came from behind me.

I looked back to see the creature collapse in on itself, like a burning building falling in, only without the fire. After the smoke collapsed and settled, there was only my horse standing there on the beach in a cloud of brimstone. The cloud was torn to tatters by the wind like smoke from a cannon, and my horse nickered softly. She quivered uncertainly, then stamped. Her eyes were terrified, but they were the same soft brown eyes that I knew.

"I'm not falling for that," Henry said heavily. He stood, his arms straining, only a few feet in front of me. "I've seen what that thing turns into. We have to kill it now, while we can." He took another heavy step forward.

"No!" I said, flinging myself at Henry and grabbing at his arms. "No! Don't hurt her!" It was a ridiculous motion. If he could lift and fling that thing, he could just as easily fling it with my interference.

"Don't hurt her?" he said, incredulous. "Did you see that thing?" But, he stepped back and lowered the rock hesitantly. "You did see it, right? Right?"

I spun and faced Nocturnus. "It's all right, sweetheart," I murmured to her, holding out my hand uncertainly. I approached as slowly as I could. Now that it had come down to it, I didn't have any rational reason to believe that Nocturnus wouldn't change back to the horrible thing she'd just been. But I *felt* that she wouldn't. I felt that she didn't *want* to. Her legs were quivering, her eyes rolling with panic and fear. She'd been just as terrified by what happened as we had. Maybe more. She had a soggy mess of cloth in her mouth. My coat the tentacle had grabbed back in the water.

She danced and shied away like she was going to bolt. I was exhausted enough from the swim. I sure as anything couldn't chase her.

"Don't run," I whispered. "I won't hurt you." I reached up to stroke the side of her face. She quivered and blew out a warm breath through her nostrils into my hand, but still wouldn't give up the coat.

"It wasn't your fault," I whispered to her. "It was mine. I was told what would happen if you went into the water."

"Someone told you," Henry said incredulously, "that your horse was going to turn into a monster and try and *eat* you, and you rode it anyway?"

"It's complicated," I snapped, then to Nocturnus, in a much softer voice, I said, "you couldn't help it, baby, could you?"

Nocturnus whickered once and stepped closer. She pressed her face against my hand again. My face was wet, and it wasn't just from the ocean. I stroked her neck and mane, then buried my face around her warm neck. Then I stepped back far enough to look her over, check her mane and neck and all the rest. We'd cut a lot of tentacles off the monster in the sea, and I had the sudden, horrid concern that Nocturnus had returned to me with missing pieces. But she was unharmed.

I guess her magic didn't work like that.

Far behind her, I saw the sails of the ship that had been following and firing. It sure *looked* like the *Specter*, gold with black trim. I breathed a deep sigh of relief.

"This is crazy, Justice," Henry said. "You're supposed to be the smart one."

"She can't help what she is," I said. "It's like us, Henry. She thought she was a horse just the way we thought we were human."

"What are you talking about?" Henry snapped. "Of course we're human!" But his voice trailed off at the last few words. He looked down at the rock he carried, easily sixty or seventy pounds or so, the way someone else would hold a cricket ball. He rubbed his jaw thoughtfully and let the rock fall into the sand with a wet *whump*.

"What are we Justice?" he whispered.

"We're Faerie," I said, "but we're part human, too. We just need to learn to reconcile those parts of us. Control them. Nocturnus is the same. She just needs control."

"So what is she?" Henry said. "A Faerie horse?"

I kept my hands on Nocturnus' head, but turned to face Henry. His eyes were deadly serious. He wasn't just going to follow me on faith unless I explained myself. The Henry that had gone into Newgate would have, but not this boy. He'd seen too much.

"She's a demon," I admitted.

"Oh, well," he said, laughing bitterly. "That's much better than Faerie, isn't it now?"

"She doesn't *want* to be a demon anymore!" I insisted. "I can tell!" It sounded crazy, even as I said it, but looking at Nocturnus, I could just feel that what I said was true. "If we let her stay as a horse, she'll become a horse, through and through, just the way Father isn't really Faerie anymore. Not entirely."

Henry blew out his breath and made a wry face. He hadn't been there for Father's story, or Sands' explanation or any of the discoveries or events in the past month. "Lor . . . I think there's a whole lot you're going to have to tell me."

"There is," I agreed.

I turned back to Nocturnus. "Come on, girl." I tugged gently at the lump of wet cloth in her mouth. She held onto my coat a moment longer, then finally relaxed and let it go. I shook it out. It was outrageously slimy, but otherwise unharmed.

Henry was still giving Nocturnus the evil eye, keeping his distance. Then his gaze lifted to the horizon. "What are we going to do about that ship?"

I grinned at him. "That's another one of those things I need to tell you."

I waved my coat in the breeze to flag the *Specter* down, but they were already launching a boat to pick us up.

Not wanting to make the same outrageous mistake twice, and with nasty visions of how things would go if I were to take a supernaturally heavy nightmare onto a glorified rowboat without getting her wet, I unsummoned Nocturnus before the launch arrived.

"We'll bring you back soon," I whispered to her just before, and she responded with an affectionate nudge of her long, horsey head, then I said the words and she disappeared in a brimstone puff that drifted darkly on the beach, looking for all the world like the smoke from a cannon shot, before the wind tore it to dark rags and carried it away.

"Soooo," Henry said slowly, "they made you an admiral and then gave you a magic horse that can't get wet? Whose brilliant idea was that?" I'd only had time to give him the briefest of explanations while the launch drew closer. It was still a good distance away, advancing slowly.

"No one's idea, exactly," I admitted. "Nocturnus wasn't part of Father or Sands' plan. I stole her." It didn't make much more sense out loud, even to me, so I tried again. "Well, I stole a chess piece out of Father's office, but only because he'd given it to me many years before as part of a bargain to keep quiet about what I'd seen in the woods."

Henry's brow was furrowed. "So it *was* part of Father's plan? I mean, he gave it to you, right?"

"Well, sort of," I admitted. "I don't think he meant for me to take it back."

"You don't know where he is now?" he asked.

"No," I'd explained how Father would be waiting for the match, somewhere in Faerie, and that had been one of the most painful parts. The match I dreaded was drawing closer, too.

"And he's supposed to be, the best tactician the Faerie have?" Henry frowned. "Doesn't sound like much of a planner. I mean, that's not how I remember him growing up, exactly. But then, he wasn't around much."

"He's not really the tactician he was, I guess," I said. "He's not a powerful Faerie lord at all anymore. He's become human." The painful memory of Father being moved over to the Faerie ship, too ill to walk by himself, scratched my brain.

"So does that mean, that someone else *is*?" Henry asked. "The real Rachek Kasric, who's now . . ."

"Acting as the Lord of Thorns," I said.

"And we've never even met him?" he said. "What does he look like?"

"I saw him once," I said. "Briefly. Though I didn't know who he was back then. He's huge, with a cloak of grass, antlers, a face like a wooden mask, and one hand larger than the other."

Henry shuddered. "Sounds hideous, poor sod."

"I called him the Faerie King," I said. "Not to his face. We never spoke. But in my head. But he wasn't a king at all, he was a prisoner."

"Wasn't he a king, though," Henry asked. "He was standing in for the Lord of Thorns, wasn't he? He must have been."

"I guess you're right," I said. "I've been thinking about him as a prisoner, but I guess he'd still be king. At least at first. But I know they eventually found out who he was."

"So he's a prisoner now?"

"I would guess so," I said. I really didn't know where he was now nor how he'd fared.

I realized, looking at Henry in the sun, that he needed a shave, something I'd never seen on my little brother before. As good a reminder as any that Henry wasn't fourteen anymore. He'd turned fifteen in prison. Practically a man by some reckoning, though that felt like a foreign term applied my little brother.

Soon, after Father lost the game, the real Rachek Kasric would get to return to England. Come home after almost twenty years away, to find his wife gone, his country overrun by the Faerie, his children scattered.

No, wait. He didn't have children, did he? Just Joshua. Would Rachek Kasric join the invasion forces? The Outcasts? Would he want any part of the Faerie war?

Somehow, I thought not.

Father and the Faerie had destroyed Rachek Kasric's life. What would he do when he gained his freedom? What could he do? I couldn't possibly imagine. Probably he would hate us beyond all possible comprehension. I'm pretty sure I would.

"Ho land!" someone called from the approaching launch, the words echoing slightly over the surf. Not just anyone, but Faith! I could make out her shaven head and serious expression from here, despite the distance. Behind her sat Avonstoke, an even more welcome sight, his face still looking startlingly different and younger without the raven tattoo around his eyes.

The boat was still five or six hundred yards away, but sailors were coming out of the surf only a few yards away, cutlasses out, Nellie and Wil near the front, looking for trouble. They'd been sent ahead to help us, except there wasn't any danger now.

"It's alright!" I shouted at them. "The danger's gone."

"Just our loyal steed," Henry said under his breath, but he was smiling. "You know, steadfast and true except when he tries to *eat* us."

"Firstly," I said, "Shut up. Secondly, Nocturnus is a *she*. Thirdly, she's on our side, she just has this curse . . ."

"Hell of a curse," Henry said.

"Fourthly," I said. "Shut up!"

Henry giggled and I couldn't help but giggle back and then we both burst into uncontrollable laughter. We bent over, my hand on Henry's shoulder, both of us gasping for breath.

The launch was crashing through the surf and Henry and I ran towards it. Faith and Avonstoke were in the prow, but Mog and the other Goblins, were all grinning with joy and amusement behind them. That was a happy sight—if you didn't count the disconcerting number of fangs. Nellie and Wil both nodded to me, a brief smile even flashing across Wil's surly face before his usual sour expression reasserted itself. Nellie, for her part, was grinning ear to ear.

Faith was helping Avonstoke out of the launch. Something was wrong with him. His eyes were usually blank technically, pupilless and yellow, like all the Court Faerie, but his constantly changing expression kept them from looking featureless. Now, they *looked* blank. Avonstoke misplaced his foot and Faith had to hold him up. I'd never seen Avonstoke uncertain of his footing before. Suddenly the meaning of his blank look, obvious to anyone not addled by falling a quarter mile into the sea, was plain. He couldn't see! I rushed across the sand.

Faith said something to Avonstoke, who straightened, turned slightly to face me better and called out, "Well, reports of your imminent death and destruction appear to have been greatly exaggerated."

"Not really," Henry said. There was still a trace of laughter in his voice from before, but then, he didn't know anything was wrong.

Faith hugged Henry with ferocity. "Oh, thank God you're out of that terrible place."

"Yes," Henry said, the last of his laughter falling away. "Thank Justice and the Wild Hunt, I guess. They broke me out."

"Because of her," I said, nodding at Faith. "She bargained with the Wild Hunt to set you free. I just came to get you out when it was done."

I embraced Faith quickly, then stepped around her to reach Avonstoke, who had hung slightly back.

I took two quick steps and gripped him fiercely by the arms. I hesitated, then grabbed a handful of his golden hair, dragging his face down so that I could press my mouth to his warm lips. Captain's decorum be damned. He seemed startled, then slightly awkward, then he was kissing me back fiercely, enough to take my breath away.

"Well," Faith said tartly, rolling her eyes. It was such an unconscious imitation of the disgust I'd shown over her flinging herself at Mr. Sands so long ago that a laugh burst out of me.

"Oh my Captain," Avonstoke murmured, "I am very glad that you are not dead." His golden eyes were very close. But they still gazed out at nothing, blankly, blindly.

There could be no mistake.

"Your eyes!" I said. "What happened?"

"That tiny cut I told you was nothing," Avonstoke said, touching a spot nearly under his eye. "It seems I was a bit hasty in making that judgment. The Kellas Cats aren't just large cats, of course, but witches that have changed their shape, and their vile magic includes a dangerous poison. It got too close to my eyes and . . . well . . . you see the result."

"His vision started to go," Faith said, "about twenty hours after you left us."

"Oh God," I breathed. "How did you get him out of England that way? It must have been horrible with the Faerie on your trail!" I'd expected Avonstoke to be instrumental in getting Faith and the others out, but Faith hadn't needed the help, Avonstoke had.

"She has quite come into her own," Avonstoke said, "as a magician, I believe."

I half expected Faith to deny it, or to add further to Avonstoke's claim on her behalf, if she could. But instead, she glanced once at him, then me, then nodded in brief agreement. That reaction alone from my usually flamboyant sister was enough to confirm Avonstoke's claim, as much as anything.

"She summoned a typhoon to drive the Faerie to the ground," Avonstoke said dryly, "while simultaneously bringing the *Specter* the wind it needed to pick us up. She's acquired significant control over the weather."

Henry whistled low. "Lor! Calling the winds. Handy thing for a ship at sea!"

"I'll say," I said.

"It's not that handy," Faith said bitterly. "It only works when the Wild Hunt is nearby. But they were then, as you know, and that gave me the chance."

"What about Sands?" I asked. "What does he know about this Kellas Cat poison? Have you gotten word to the fleet? Maybe Prudence or Drecovian . . ."

"We don't have to get word to the fleet," Faith said. "Prudence is on board the *Specter*. She says there's no known cure."

"Oh God," I said again. The full weight of what that meant hit home to me and I stared at Avonstoke in horror. "But there has to be a cure!"

"It's not so bad," Avonstoke said. "I can still make out rough shapes. If the light's bright and they have the decency to hold still for a moment."

"It's not fair," I said, a hitch coming to my voice. I kissed him once more, then reluctantly let go before I lost control and started weeping. "Your face looks funny now," I blurted out. It wasn't his eyes, despite the blindness. The raven-shaped tattoo *around* his eyes was gone, as a result of the spell that he'd cast at the Kellas Cat, yet he was still breathtakingly handsome, with his long, angular face and wry, sardonic smile.

"My face," he said, "has always looked peculiar, I'm sure, without camouflage."

I just grabbed his arm again in comfort and admonishment. I couldn't seem to stop touching him.

Mog was there, too, his fanged face grinning. Four more Goblins were manning the oars and their faces were all smiles, too. Nellie and Wil were nearby, swords still out because they had no actual sheaths to put them into. Everyone that had gone to Stormholt with us. Or almost everyone.

"Did you get Étienne and the others safely back to the ship?" I asked Faith.

"Yes," Faith said. "They're fitting in nicely. Seem to think that we named the ship after them."

"That's a relief, at least," I said.

Faith looked at me sadly and shook her head. "Not everyone made it back," she said. "I'm sorry."

Mog, Nellie, and Wil bowed their heads, too.

"Dream?" I said, dreading the answer. Everyone else that had come with us was right here, but I didn't see the Leaf Rider anywhere.

"She didn't make it," Faith said. "Avonstoke makes our escape sound simpler than it really was. We still had to fight more Hanged Dogs and those little fanged Faerie, the Pix. Dream led a bunch of the Pix out into the typhoon and never came back. It was because of her that we got out."

I felt a dark depression swell inside of me. Dream. Benedict. Avonstoke's eyes, and God knew what else, lost to this damned Faerie war. Then I felt that darkness harden inside of me. Any chance we had of turning this war around, no matter the risk, I wanted to grab it.

"How did you get Henry out?" Faith asked.

"The Wild Hunt did most of it," I said. "Then they brought us back here."

"They didn't exactly drop us off," Henry said. He looked back past the softly roaring surf, out at the sky we'd fallen from, down to the rolling part of sea that we'd fallen into, where we'd nearly drowned fighting Nocturnus' demon.

"Yeah," I said, laughing softly. "I could have planned that part better."

He snorted with dark laughter, then tilted his head as something occurred to him. "Wait, what about Benedict?" I hadn't yet had a chance to tell him.

"No," Faith said. "We couldn't save him. The Wild Hunt took him."

CHAPTER 21

Ambush in Faerie

"You're sure you can do this?" I asked Faith. Navigating through the mist was one thing, but this was something else.

"I can do it," Faith said.

"You're sure?"

She turned to look at me. "You want to get to Faerie, don't you?" The mist rolled lazily all around us. The water was unnaturally flat and calm. There was no sound around us and no scent came on the wind. In fact, there was no wind, either. The compass in our binnacle drew slow, lazy circles. This was a thoroughly unsettling place.

"Yes." She and I had discussed this already, the burning knowledge that Father's contest, in Faerie, was the center of everything now. England's fate, the invasion, our family's role in it, all of that was bound up in the contest between the Lord of Thorns and the real Rachek Kasric, and we had to be there.

"Then stop asking questions you know how to answer," Faith said tartly.

"You sure you can't help with this?" I asked Prudence, who shrugged.

"I've never been able to do it," she said. "Both Lessard and Drecovian did try to teach me. Brocara and Drecovian are the only ones that can. Oh, and Lessard, of course." She shrugged apologetically, not coming out and saying that Lessard, Father, didn't count because he was gone.

Henry was there with us, too, still pale but otherwise looking much recovered from his time in Newgate Prison. I could see him taking everything in and wondering how so much change had come about. We'd all been just children running around London when the Faerie had captured him; now he'd come out and found Faerie everywhere and his two sisters commanding a ship, to say nothing of the Outcast Fleet, in a war against the Faerie army that had taken over the whole country. He'd been very quiet since coming aboard and had occasionally gone off by himself to noodle on a copper flute I'd never seen before. Now, his eyes were very wide watching us. His sandy hair needed a cut, badly.

Faith looked pale and worn-out, too. Probably I didn't look so fantastic myself. None of us had been getting much sleep lately. Before leaving the channel, Faith had been spending her nights aboard *Seahome*. With Prudence, Drecovian, and Brocara, the other magicians in the Outcast Fleet.

Sleeping under the wing of a dragon couldn't make for good dreams and hers already sounded more disturbing than most.

Faith caught me looking at her.

"What do the other magicians think of you doing this?" I shot a glance at Prudence, but she just shook her head and walked back to the quarterdeck stairs, descending out of view. She didn't want to watch.

"Conflicted," Faith said crisply. "They all agree that I need something to come into my power, but they don't agree as to what that is. Consensus is that I'm just as likely to fail doing this, in which case we could all get lost. But, if I succeed, it could push me past whatever's holding me back."

"Get lost?"

"Lost in the mist is the same as getting lost in Faerie," Faith said. "Which is the same as getting lost in time. Do you want to turn back?"

"No," I said. "I believe in you."

"That's lovely," she said. "Now shut up and let me concentrate."

With her hood back and her shaven scalp gleaming in the uncertain light, she stretched her arms wide.

The mist, Faith had reminded me earlier, hadn't originally been a force to hide England from the rest of the world. That had been the Black Shuck's doing, twisting the mist somehow to his own purposes. Sooner or later, I was going to have to take the Black Shuck, a monster I'd never even seen, head on. The idea made my blood run cold, but that was for a later time.

Now, Faith was trying walk the Faerie mists, using them the way magicians had for centuries, to get to Faerie so that we could be there for Father's contest.

The crew idled behind us on the main deck. With no wind, no current, and no destination discernable through normal means, there wasn't a lot for them to do. They looked at ease, though. Starling and Swayle hunched together near one of the cannon, discussing a flaw the dwarves were fixing in the carriage. Several of the Prowlers were splicing rope while some of the ship's carpenters were working on a splintered railing. Catching up on small tasks while things were slow. Others were below, catching up on sleep. Several of the Goblins in the sail crew hadn't even bothered going below but had put up hammocks in the rigging and were now snoozing together in fuzzy bundles of three or four. None of the crew seemed worried.

They didn't understand what Faith was doing any more than I did but seemed to trust us both implicitly. I wished I could do the same.

In the end, Faith made it seem easy. We spent less than three hours, according to the hourglass, in the Faerie mist before *The Specter in the Mist* slid its way free of the ghostly embrace and into open air.

It was brilliant. Yellow light shone off a sea far, far bluer than the gray waters we were used to. An impossible, lemon-yellow sky hung above us, giving everything a sharp, unreal feel to it, as if the whitecaps in the water, and the water itself, were somehow more potent, more real, than the water in our world.

I immediately shaded my eyes, looking in all directions for threats. But I didn't need to shade them. Bright light usually hurt my ghost eye, but it wasn't like that here. It seemed my Faerie eye was only sensitive to normal light and didn't mind the Faerie sun at all.

Then I forgot all about that as I saw what lay off the port bow.

"We should be close to . . ." Faith murmured. "Ah . . ." She pointed. "There."

The rest of the crew, following the direction of Faith's hand, turned as well. The Goblins started chattering up in the rigging while someone else, I didn't see who, screamed and dropped something heavy on the deck.

"Mother of Gods," Swayle said from nearby. I'd never heard her surprised at anything before.

At first, I thought it was a mountain range, enormous, like the Himalayas, except more lushly wooded and wreathed all over in tendrils of white mist. Green. Like Ireland in spring. But something itched at the back of my brain as I stared and some of the things weren't resolving in my understanding the way they should. There was a flatness to it, seven or eight verdant plateaus seemingly suspended in overlapping patterns, like emerald plates the size of London.

It had to be some kind of Faerie glamor but checking it with either eye didn't change anything.

For starters, there wasn't any snow on the peaks, which looked more and more impossible as I stared at it. There was something wrong about the bottom of it, too.

"Lor!" Henry breathed. "It's a great bloody tree! The whole thing!" He reached absently into his jacket, an ornate broadcloth coat one of the Dwarves had found for him, and pulled out a long copper flute.

The vision in front of me finally snapped into place, like a visual puzzle I hadn't been able to make sense of at first. The deep furrows that were branches coming out from the core, the great leafy canopies that dipped, but didn't quite reach the white beaches below. A multitude of elevated forests, all of them one tree, gleaming in the impossible light streaming down from an unnatural, Faerie sun.

"That . . ." Faith couldn't get the rest out. "That can't . . ." I knew how she felt. I could feel my mouth trying to get something out, but it just wasn't coming.

"The World Tree," Mr. Sands said. He and Prudence had come up onto the quarterdeck unnoticed. He wore bandages across his shoulder and side from his injury in London.

"The tree," Faith suddenly intoned, "that looms over London is just a reflection, an avatar, of this one here in Faerie. Everything is, from the Faerie point of view."

I turned, looking at Faith, who looked a little surprised at having spoken.

"You read that in one of Sands' books?" I asked.

She shook her head. "No. I dreamed it. Brocara. She gives me dreams."

"Ach," Prudence said, throwing up her hands with the same frustration someone else might show at a child throwing their biscuit at the table.

"Is that what you do when you go to *Seahome* at night?" I said. "You sleep and dream?"

"I do," she said in a soft whisper. "But it's not sleeping next to the dragon that gives me the dreams. Before I sleep, I drink of Brocara's blood. Again. Even when I come back here, I have dreams of the Faerie. Their history, their passions, their magic. The blood is inside of me. I doesn't matter where I sleep anymore. There's no escaping the dreams." She hugged her own shoulders and shuddered.

Prudence snorted.

Faith rounded on her. "Is it a secret? Carefully preserved dark ritual we're not supposed to talk about to preserve the mystery of magicians?"

"It's not a secret," Prudence said tartly. "It's just gauche to talk about." She leaned forward and whispered. "It's like talking about *sex*. It just isn't *done*, girl."

Sands and Henry both blushed. The crewmen at the guns and tiller were all very busy doing something else that took their complete attention and very much not looking at any of us.

A sharp, sudden laugh burst out of Faith, then she stopped and got control of herself. She took a deep breath and put on a brittle smile. "We're here then. In Faerie. It worked. Yes?"

"Quite," Prudence agreed. "Well done. I've never had the knack of it myself. This and baking. Two skills that always eluded me." She sighed.

My gaze was dragged unwillingly back to the World Tree. The sky didn't seem big enough to hold it. That tree wasn't anything anyone should have to see or try and understand. It was all too much.

I dragged my attention back to Faith. "Do you feel different, as a magician? Did this push you past whatever was holding you back?"

"No idea," she said at once. "I don't feel any different. I can see patterns in the mist now, though, things I couldn't see before. Does that mean I'm finally a real magician?" She looked at Prudence, who shrugged elaborately.

"You've been a magician," Prudence said. "Now we're just figuring out what kind of magic you can actually *do*." She gestured back the way we'd come. "You can now move between your world and the Faerie world. That's no small thing. Many a magician would be content with that."

"I just wish," Faith said, "that I'd figured this out sooner. If I'd been able to do this a few weeks ago, we could have been the ones to bring Father here. We wouldn't have needed to give him to Lady Rue after all."

I finally managed to get my mouth working. I hadn't thought of that. "Better that we're here now than not at all."

"Is it?" she said. "What exactly can we do here? Sands, you said Father's curse is unbreakable. We can't change anything."

"It's true, I'm afraid," Sands said sadly.

I shook my head. "I don't believe that. There must be something we can do."

"Well," Prudence said. "Let's see who's waiting for us on that island."

She lifted her arms, then suddenly collapsed inward on herself, like she was crushed by an invisible hand. It was horrible to look at, unreal and sickening.

I shrieked. So did Faith and Henry. A lot of people did. One of the gunners fainted dead away.

The gray shapeless small thing that had been Prudence a second ago stretched out two wings and gradually settled into the shape of a large bird. We'd seen that bird, long ago, back at Stormholt, before we even knew who Prudence was.

"I'll be back as soon as I can," the bird said in Prudence's voice. It beat its two heavy wings against the air, cleared the railing and dropped. A few seconds later, it lifted again, already climbing steadily.

"Lor!" Henry burst out. "If that's magic, count me out. That . . . that was *disgusting.*" He looked at Faith. "Is all magic like that?"

"Most," Faith said with a tight voice.

"Well," I said. "I'm not going to stand here and wait for her." I licked my finger and held it up, trying to get a sense of the wind.

That wasn't usually necessary, but the wind was apparently a fickle beast here in Faerie. I could already feel it twitching from one direction to the next and gallivanting around in all directions. It was going to take all the seamanship I could muster to keep the *Specter* moving in a straight line in this mess.

"I don't suppose," I asked Faith, "that you can do anything about the wind here?"

She shook her head. "Only when the Wild Hunt is near."

"Just when it would have been handy," I said. I lifted my voice. "Mr. Starling! Bring us around on the starboard tack. We're going in."

"Aye, Captain," Starling called back. He didn't sound very happy about it, though.

Starling started bellowing at the crew and the Faerie pipes trilled while more shouting rang out on the deck and down below and the *Specter* exploded into a disciplined fury.

I kept half an ear on the sequence, just to make sure he timed things right, but I needn't have bothered. He was starting to get a real feel for the pressure that moved a ship, the bite of the prow in the water against the pressure the wind put on the sail. Sails moved and then Starling called for the helm to come over. The Prowler helmsman put the helm over deftly and I could feel the movement of the ship change as we came around.

Whatever we were about to sail into, I felt we were ready. The crew had developed remarkably. The Dwarven gunners and the Court Faerie marines were working together marvelously and all of them had learned, on their own, how to jump into the various tasks required of the Prowler deck crew that required all hands. All the tedious and unseemly tasks on board the ship, like reefing and turning the sails or bailing and working the pumps, were tackled with a fierce will.

A sudden cacophony in the rigging broke loose. The Goblins were hooting at the Ghost Boys, who hooted back. I didn't get what they were excited about until Faith, standing next to me, said, "Well, will you look at *that*."

She was pointing at Étienne and one of the Goblins, hooting back and forth and mimicking each other.

Mimicking . . . each . . . other. It seemed that here, in the mist, in Faerie, the rest of the crew could see and hear the Ghost Boys.

I'd put the Ghost Boys, Étienne, Percy, Emily and the rest, up into the foremast sail crew, with Étienne in charge of the lot. That left the Goblin foremast and mizzenmast sail crews with far more personnel. Sands had said that being dead, the Ghost Boys, even in Faerie, were proof against normal dangers like falling. This hadn't protected them from Joshua, of course, but that was something else again. The regular dangers of the topmast were nothing to them. Between them and the nimble Goblins, prancing and swinging easily like monkeys, I had what had to be the only accident-free sail crew in nautical history. In the Royal Navy, ships reported deaths as often as every ten days. We'd never lost a crewman out of combat. But after that, everything went more smoothly than I could have hoped. Goblins and ghostly children worked together when needed easily and without reservation, none of them seeming to think it odd at all, even though half of them couldn't see the other half. Apparently, most of the Ghost Boys (and Emily) had adapted their ability to interact with inanimate objects enough to tug on clothing and this was enough communication between them. The children, for their part, also adopted the Goblin hoot. Emily was particularly good at it.

In fact, most of the crew seemed to have developed a genuine respect for each other that was new for the Faerie.

I'd been startled last week to see Swayle, Starling, Mog, Nellie, or Wil down in the mess together more and more often, mugs in their hands, laughing and carrying on. Starling and Mog, in particular, spent a fair amount of their duty time there. Rumor had it that Mog's mug was the one holding Dwarven Ale now, while Starling's held the sweet honey wine that Goblins favored.

Even the Troll, Wargan, had made improvement. He was a strangely shy creature, so I wasn't going to be sending him on any boarding parties any time soon, but he'd become a real asset to the repair crews. He'd been taken under wing by the Dwarven women, to help with moving cannon or spars. He was still frightened of the sun, but they were working on it.

I was startled out of my reverie when Étienne, Percy, and then Emily flung themselves, shrieking, off the topmast yard. Étienne clutched his hat on the way down and Emily's long hair flew all over. Percy had his eyes closed.

They landed, completely unharmed, on the main deck. There was no impact, as if they'd floated down. They laughed and bowed, and the Goblins hooted and applauded. The deck crew were all grinning.

"Avast there!" I bellowed. The cheering, clapping and grinning all vanished instantly.

"It's all right, Capin'," Étienne said. He knuckled his forehead underneath the checkered hat his always wore. "It don't hurt none." His blonde hair was bright in the sun.

"What happens when you miss?" I snarled. "Can you swim? Can all of your boys?"

"We didn't mean nothin'," he said, but his face went white.

"Well, we can't drown neither," Emily said. "Least I don't *think* we can." Her hair, slightly red before, was somehow burnished a deeper red by the sun, despite her being a ghost. That was going to hurt my head if I thought about that too much.

"I'll tell you what happens when you miss," I went on relentlessly. "If you're lucky enough for me to be on deck, assuming we're not here in the mist, I might be able to get the ship around in time to find you. *Might.* Any bit of weather or current and I'll have as much finding your man as finding one drop among the oceans."

Étienne's face had gone white. Percy broke out in tears. He was the youngest of the Ghost Boys and somehow still fastidious despite being part of a ship's company. Emily pulled a pocket handkerchief out of Percy's little suit coat, handing it over to him. He took it gratefully.

"We didn't mean nothin'," Étienne said again, horrified at his own actions now.

"*That's* if he can swim and we can see you," I went on. "If he or she can't swim, or if no one sees them fall, then your *boy,*" I jabbed one finger at Percy, "or *girl,*" I jabbed the other at Emily, all the while keeping Étienne's eye, "is drifting along with the current until he, or she," again I pointed at each, "somehow gets to shore. For all we know that could take years!"

"Years!" Percy burst out, hit with another fresh rush of tears.

I hunkered down in front of Étienne. I could afford to soften my tone now. I'd made my point and gotten him properly scared. That had been my intention, and necessary, but I still hated myself for bellowing at children that shouldn't even be engaged in the brutal, unforgiving art of war.

"It's dangerous out here," I said, "doing what we're doing. You're the crew leader. I need your help keeping them safe."

Étienne had tears in his eyes now, too. They all did.

"It won't 'appen again, Justice," he said, gulping.

"I know it won't," I said.

They all knuckled their foreheads like proper British crewmen and took off back to their work. The rest of the crew, ostensibly busy while I'd been chewing out the children, all got suddenly very much busier.

We were coming closer to the tree island. I took my spyglass out. Most of the island was dark, the sun kept out by that enormous tree, but I saw now that the nearest part of the land thrust out in our direction, displaying white sand beaches. They were empty, unguarded. Or at least appeared that way. What lay behind them in the darkness was anybody's guess.

I conned higher, up in the crooked maze of branches and dark, leafy covering. You could probably hide a legion up in there and we wouldn't know it from here. With a human force, you could at least count on not having to deal with mounted cavalry up in the trees, but with the Faerie, you couldn't count anything out.

"Lor . . ." Henry said, still looking at the enormous tree island. The closer we got, the more overwhelming it was. He was leaning on the forecastle rail, fingering the copper flute, though he hadn't been playing.

Faith reached over and tousled his sandy hair and he grinned at her. We were finally back together, the three of us. It felt bizarre and glorious at once.

Avonstoke was next to Henry on the railing, able to sit rather than lean because of his much longer legs, balancing easily despite the motion of the ship. He was facing the island, but squinting, clearly not able to make anything out.

"Describe it to me," Avonstoke said softly, and Henry began quietly explaining as best he could. Avonstoke was still remarkably competent at getting around, considering his lost vision, but still needed help and the kind-hearted Henry, having few duties himself, had attached himself to Avonstoke's side to assist.

The sight pained me. Avonstoke had gotten his injury in my service. It should have been me helping him around now, repaying that debt, but my duties as captain prevented me. If I was honest, I wasn't sure I had the temperament required, either, and that realization wracked me with guilt.

Avonstoke, Henry, Benedict—I owed them all a debt I could never repay.

A warm, windward breeze swept in from behind us, as if even the unnatural Faerie winds had designs on rushing us towards the religious mecca and center of the Faerie world. Maybe it did.

If Father lost—when Father lost—the Seelie Court would almost certainly imprison or execute him. An enormous loss to any hope of resistance.

We were here to stop that. The only problem was—*how*?

A cry from the crow's nest broke into my concentration. "Sail ho! Ship on the port side!"

I spun with the spyglass.

At first, I didn't see anything. Then, sliding out from around the island, just the edge visible to those of us down here on deck, came a boat pulled by a trio of swimming horses. Seahorses, my brain automatically labelled them, though they looked more like charging land horses than the gentle marine creature of that name. These moved forward in great leaps and bounds, long ears flattened back on their heads, their nostrils flaring. They were marvelously colored, pink and blue, like coral, with tall sailfins running down their backs and large fins instead of forelegs and a long, fluked tail that churned the water. They pulled the boat at incredible speed, far faster than the *Specter*.

Then I took a better look at the boat. It was a launch, the largest of rowboats, crammed to the brim with all sorts of armed and hostile Faerie. There had to be at least a couple hundred in there. A swarm of beefy and dangerous-looking Goblins, most of them larger than all of our Goblins, even Mog. Behind them were a dozen of the Hanged Dogs, the cadaverous minions of the Black Shuck. I shuddered. Two Trolls sat aft, both of them waving huge spears and not looking at all like our timid and peaceful Wargan. Just our luck to get the only pacifistic Troll in the war.

I conned the Goblins again, something Avonstoke had told me tickling the back of my brain. The largest of them was standing with one foot on the gunwale, wearing a bear-skull helmet over his face and a heavy-looking morningstar. More than heavy. The spiked weight at the end of the chain had to be fifty pounds and the Goblin hefted like it was a toy. The head smoldered red and trailed black, oily smoke.

A skull mask, Avonstoke had said, days ago, describing the Faerie that had killed his Father. The Goblin Knight. Killing this Goblin had been the motivation behind Avonstoke joining this war in the first place.

I shot a glance behind me. Henry was describing things to him as they occurred, but he hadn't been specific enough for Avonstoke to know about the Goblin Knight yet. There was no telling what Avonstoke might do when he found out, blind or not.

"Clear the ship for action!" I hollered at Starling. "Call all hands! Man the braces and run out the guns!" The Faerie pipes wailed their ghostly trill, alerting everyone below decks.

"Henry!" I said. "Man the cannon."

"Yes!" Henry said. With the addition of the Ghost Boys up in the sail crew, and assisting in other duties, it freed up just enough crew to muster a gunnery crew for both sides of the ship. But it was a little thin and Henry, with his freakish strength, had proved an enormous asset the past few days during drills, so I'd assigned him to the gunnery crew for the bowchasers.

"Permission to join him, my Captain," Avonstoke said. Henry had stopped with his arm on Avonstoke's elbow, waiting for me to make up my mind.

I hesitated. Faith gave me a look, though what she was thinking I couldn't tell.

Avonstoke gave a thin smile. "I've been assisting during drills. I can help, despite my . . ." He waved his fingers over his blank eyes. "Impairment."

What I wanted was Avonstoke to be safe. Damn. I wanted everyone safe, but that wasn't going to happen.

Avonstoke had been oddly quiet, introspective, since his injury, which was deeply unnerving. His handsome face, still so odd to me without the black raven domino mask tattoo, wore a wry expression. Did he blame me for what had happened? How could he not. I couldn't meet his golden gaze.

"Go," I said.

He nodded gracefully and Henry led him off.

Shouts and thudding feet were already sounding underneath us as the officers below deck rousted the rest of the crew. It wasn't like I'd had any choice. We were clearly heading for action, but I felt a pang of guilt at how the timing kept Avonstoke in the dark.

"That," Faith murmured next to me, "was the right decision. I just hope we don't regret it."

"Me too," I said.

"For what it's worth," Faith said, "it was like dying a hundred deaths waiting down in that hold while the clamor of battle went on above. Better to be up here and have some impact on what happens."

"Let's hope so," I said. "What in the world?" Six smaller boats followed the boarding launch. I put the spyglass back to my eye. They were half the size of the lead boat, almost rowboats. These had cannon mounted in the bow and a team of enemy Goblins to man them.

Damn! The Faerie must have worked out, like Father, a way to make their cannon and cannonballs out of bronze and copper to avoid the destructive effect that iron had on the Faerie handling it. More swimming horses pulled these floating cannon boats, six gunships in all to support the boarding launch. I shuddered to think what the Hanged Dogs, Goblins, and Trolls could do to our crew, who were more sailors than warriors. We had Swayle's marines, about two dozen, but they'd be outnumbered in the extreme.

Then it got worse.

Behind the attacking fleet, just now coming in sight around the curve of the island, was the prow of a larger ship. A *much* larger ship, a triple-decker about twice the size of the *Specter.*

I saw a familiar figure on the prow, large, with heavy shoulders and gray hair peeking out from underneath a horned ram's helmet.

Damn and bloody damn.

Joshua Kasric, my brother and general to the invasion.

"Ah," Faith said. That was all.

I shot a look at her. Her face was controlled and the hood shaded her eyes enough to make them hard to read. She'd changed these past few days, and it wasn't just the magic. Something about learning the magic must have altered her perspective, altered her probably in more ways than she herself knew. That iron control, however, somehow reminded me of the times when she hadn't been speaking to me and that worried me, which was a ridiculous thing to think about when heading into battle.

"Time to join them on the quarterdeck," I said.

"Yes," Faith said.

We made our way down onto the main deck and then climbed the stairs to the quarterdeck where Starling and the helmsman waited for us. Henry, Avonstoke, and the rest of the bowchaser gunnery crew were a bit further back near the two long nines. Smaller cannon here, but more accurate and with a longer range.

"Justice?" Henry said, as we passed him. "Is that . . ."

"Yes," Faith said tightly.

"Joshua," I said. Our brother. Technically, only our half-brother, I knew now. He'd helped us before, back at Stormholt, but hadn't been willing to leave Mother or her cause. I didn't think we could count on him giving us any quarter now.

Henry squinted at Joshua's distant figure. I held out the spyglass and he took it. We'd told him about our older brother's extra years in Faerie, but he needed to see for himself. He'd been a lot closer to Joshua than Faith or I. Henry had worshipped him before this Faerie business had started and Joshua had been a young, lean man. While Henry had been in Newgate for a few weeks, Joshua had somehow spent years in Faerie.

"He's here to stop us," Faith said.

"Yes," I said.

"How did they know we'd be here?" she asked.

"I don't know," I said. "We didn't even know we were going to be here. We're not even sure we can do anything here, either, so why put forth so much effort to stop us?"

"Must mean they think we *can* do something," Faith said.

Surprisingly, I felt my spirits lift at the thought. Maybe this wasn't such a fool's errand after all.

Henry looked back at us, his eyes wide. He solemnly handed back the spyglass and looked back at the quarterdeck. I put a hand on his shoulder and squeezed.

I took another look through the spyglass at Joshua's ship. It was big and dangerous, but clumsy. They looked to be using the same wind we were, so they didn't have the weather magic that the magicians of *Seahome* had. The *Specter in the Mist* would be more maneuverable. Joshua's ship would be slower, too.

The sea horses on the gun boats and the boarding launch were clearly fast and powerful, but were all hauling a lot of boat, heavily loaded. They were moving faster than we could now, but perhaps they couldn't keep up that speed for very long.

"Prepare to wear . . . I mean . . . flugelstan the ship!" I shouted and Starling started bellowing orders. We'd turned into the wind a few minutes ago to bring us on the starboard tack. Now, we'd continue that turn in the same direction and run with the wind, coming back the way we came, which should provide us with the fastest speed we could muster. Also, we wouldn't have to turn into the wind this way, which made things easier.

I ordered Starling into the turn, which he did at once, and very neatly. The *Specter* started to gather speed as soon as we completed the turn, running full with the wind and away from the enemy boats. They'd catch us, but it was going to take them a lot more effort. This meant the battle would take us away from Father and the World Tree. Win or lose, Joshua had accomplished part of his goal. For now.

I looked at the range. We weren't in danger yet, but that was coming. Nor could we attack.

Even our long nines wouldn't have much of a chance at this distance.

As if prompted by that thought, the first of the enemy's cannon went off. Several more followed so that the rolling crash of it echoed across the water. It was a ridiculous attempt. Those twenty-four pounders, rigged as they were in the unsteady boats, were meant to work at close range, angling their shots up into the hull and through the main deck from below. But it wasn't any good at this range. Unless they'd found some way of steadying cannon that we didn't know about?

Wanting to coax every little bit of speed I could, I ordered the topsails out and, after watching how the ship handled, the uppermost gallants. While the crew worked and the water slapped the hull, rolling boom after boom came from the cannon behind us.

I was terrified to my very core. We'd never faced this much firepower from such a determined adversary and those damned seahorses could follow us in whichever direction they chose and pay no attention to the wind. I'd managed every encounter before this with superior seamanship so that the other ship always took the worst of it. This time, I sensed things might be different. At least Joshua didn't seem to have any magical way to target the cannon. The shots had all missed so far.

Of course, they could always get a lucky shot.

"Fire the bowchasers," I said to the gunnery captain. The words came out tight and clipped. "I think they're in range now."

"Aye, aye, Captain!" Render, the gunnery captain said. The bowchasers were the two cannon in the rear, so we couldn't fire any kind of broadside with them, but we should have better accuracy than the gunboats chasing us, as we'd be shooting from a steadier platform.

Render had finished aiming the first bowchaser and nodded at the Dwarf holding the torch, who touched it to the fuse.

The cannon crashed, splitting ears and shaking the deck. The cannon rolled sharply back on the carriage. Two of Render's assistants immediately sponged and started reloading. Render went to the other cannon to aim and fire that one. By the time he was done, the gunners on the first cannon shouted ready and Henry and Avonstoke hauled it back into firing position. Render fired it again, watched the result carefully with a short telescope, grunted, then started adjusting for the next shot.

Meanwhile more cannon fire came from behind us, at least ten times the firepower we could bring to bear. I just hoped they continued to miss. I found myself gripping the railing until my fingers went white with each bang.

I saw a splash erupt about fifty yards ahead of us and off to one side, but that was all. Or so I thought, until I heard a splintering crash and screams from below decks.

The shot, moving with terrifying speed, had skipped off the water and hit our hull.

A thin wail followed immediately. They'd hit someone.

Everyone on the quarterdeck, on the entire ship, stopped, eyes wide, listening for the screams from below to try and see who it was. Henry's eyes were as wide as I'd ever seen them. Then something passed over his face, an anger and determination that I'd never seen in him before, and he took a firmer grip on his rope, ready to haul the cannon again on command. Faith's mouth was a hard, tight line.

"Mr. Starling," I said stiffly.

"Aye, captain," Starling said, and sent two crewmen down to assess the damaged, injured, and killed.

"Keep firing!" I snarled at the gunnery crew, and they jumped back into action, twice as urgent as before.

It was madness to stand here while enemy fired cannon at us again and again. But there it was. War was a special madness and we'd committed ourselves to it. Besides, it wasn't like there was any safe place to go.

I checked the enemy ships for the hundredth time. About a quarter of a mile off. They were still gaining, but I thought more slowly than before.

One of the Prowlers that Starling had sent down came back up to report to him.

"Two dead," Starling relayed to me. "That we know of. Talnorgin and Bogfir, we think. Two carpenter's mates. The hole in the hull is bad. We're drawing water into the hold."

"Order the hole plugged," I said evenly. "Get someone on the pumps."

"Aye, captain."

Damn their luck! The distance was still long range for the *Specter's* long nines, let alone the setup they had. We were outnumbered eight to one and outgunned to boot. Another lucky shot might cripple us in one fell blow.

A second series of shots rolled like thunder, but this time nothing came near us. I felt my gut clenching and my teeth grinding. Did Joshua have some way of increasing his cannon accuracy or had it been a lucky shot? Our lives might depend on the answer.

"Furl the topgallants, Mr. Starling," I said.

Now it was time to play a distance game, slow us down a little bit to let the little boats into decent firing range for our long nines, while still staying out of range of Joshua's huge triple-decker ship of the line. I just needed to make sure I didn't let the gunboats get too close. They'd be a lot more dangerous there, where they could fire up into the hull without any chance of missing. Nor did I want to let the boarding launch too close. Even if we *could* fight them off, that would give Joshua's ship the time it needed to close and it would all be over.

The sharp bang of one of the bowchasers went off again and the side of the nearest gun boat exploded, sending bits of wood up.

A ragged cheer went up from my crew and I felt a cold, tight smile come across my face.

It had been a glancing blow to the gunwale, and hadn't injured any of the enemy crew, but that was enough. Water was shipping in over the side. That was all it took. The great weight of the cannon in the bow sent the boat down as if yanked from below, leaving the crew treading water. I was slightly relieved to see that the seahorses hadn't been hit. Freed from the traces, they dove at once and were gone. Another of the gun boats had to veer and pick up the stranded crew.

The other boats were still gaining ground.

"Deploy boarding nets, captain?" Starling asked me.

"Aye," I said.

Starling bellowed and several Prowlers started stringing nets across the rigging. It wouldn't keep boarders out for long, but it might slow them down enough for us to get a shot in.

Swayle's had three archers up in the crow's next, shooting slowly and carefully. It was long, long range for bows, but they managed to wound several gun boat rowers before the enemy crew produced shields. Still, it slowed them down enough for what I wanted to do next.

"Starling!" I said. "Bring us around on the starboard tack," I yelled. "Let's see how they like a broadside." One wrong move and those gunboats would be on us like hounds on a stag, but if I timed things right, we could let loose with a broadside and really make them feel it and then turn back to running with the wind before they caught up with us. Starling was already getting the sail crew ready with his consistent bellow. It had been hard to teach most of the Faerie the nuances of sailing a warship, but Starling had extremely competent, despite his hesitation. More than competent, really, and I realized how thoroughly I'd come to rely on him. I couldn't imagine running the ship without him now.

A team of Prowlers, confident and swift, had grabbed hold of the braces on the foresail on Starling's command, ready for the next command to haul and tilt the sail as we came about.

"Henry," I said. "Help them." Unassuming Henry was proving to be the strongest crewman we had, not counting Wargan the Troll, and I wanted the braces and sail to come around as quickly as possible to make our turn as sharp as we could.

"Aye, Justice!" Henry said, and dashed across the deck to comply.

More enemy cannon shots boomed from behind us, but I couldn't take the time to watch them now. If they got another lucky shot, there wasn't anything I could do about it.

Only four of our main cannon, two to a side, were on this deck, with the rest down below on the gun deck, so Render had opened the hatch down to the gun deck and scrambled down below. This left one of his lieutenants in charge of the two starboard cannon up here, a youngish looking Dwarf with a blonde beard and a permanently startled expression.

I put a foot on the edge of the hatch and leaned over. "Render!" I shouted down at the gunnery captain. "Are your teams on the starboard side ready?"

His face appeared below, grinning hard enough to show white teeth through his red beard. "Just give the command, captain!"

I looked at the young Dwarf up here on this deck, the one in charge of the two main deck guns, a blonde, fuzzy Dwarf, smaller than most. Bartlebottom, I suddenly remembered. His name was Bartlebottom. He looked very young.

"Go," I said.

"Helm a lee!" Starling bellowed. "Bring the ship around!" The helmsman, a stern looking older Prowler, obeyed promptly. The ship turned and Starling timed the call to pull on the braces perfectly. We completed the turn, pretty as you please. We didn't have the number of cannon Joshua's three-decker boasted, but ten cannon were nothing to sneeze at.

I clambered back up the quarterdeck stairs. "See how they like a full broadside. Another few seconds now."

Starling nodded. "Aye captain!" Then he smiled at me. I just about dropped my spyglass it surprised me so badly.

"I might," Starling said, "be startin' to understand 'ow the sea might call to man. Or woman, pardon, captain."

"We'll make a captain of you yet, Mr. Starling," I said, returning his smile. If we were extremely lucky and somehow captured Joshua's behemoth of a ship, we might just need another captain.

Cannon fired from several of the gunboats. An instant later, one of the main topsail spars fifty feet above me exploded with a heavy crunch of splintered wood. A short cry from one of the sail crew followed, ending abruptly with a sudden splash over the side. Damn their luck! But the range for the long nines was ideal now. It was our turn.

"Fire!" I shouted. The commands echoed down the chain. The guns on deck roared. An instant later, in the gundeck below, I heard Render barking at his crew and the rest went off below. The deck shook and smoke belched all around. The bang was deafening, making my ears ring and my eyes water. Cannon smoke and the stink of gunpowder was everywhere.

I held my breath, waiting for the wind to shred the smoke so that I could see what damage we'd wrought, hoping and dreading what I'd see at the same time.

When the smoke cleared, a cheer went up again from the crew. Two of the gunboats were gone. Sunk so quickly it was like they'd never been.

"Flugelstan the ship back around!" I shouted. "Smartly now! Fire the bowchasers as soon as they bear." We had to get back to our position running with the wind or lose too much speed and I didn't want to get caught. The topsail was partly fallen now because of the damage, but even as I watched, Mog's crew was getting it back up again.

Starling called out the orders and the crew moved, swift and sure, and we were back on our previous course in under a minute. We were running with the wind again, dashing up one smooth roller and down another. Both bowchasers started up, putting out great puffs of smoke that caught in the wind and blew forward towards the front of the ship, before dissipating in the breeze.

"Well done," Faith murmured. She'd been watching quietly with an approving expression on her face.

"It's not enough," I said. "If we keep fighting a running battle, it'll take us days. Even if we win, we still won't be in time to help Father." I put the spyglass back to my eye, grateful for the extra clarity that my ghost eye gave me here in Faerie. I could even make out the name on Joshua's ship. *The Emerald Demise.* Cute. No H.M.S., of course. I carefully counted what I could see and extrapolated the number of guns, expecting bowchasers and the like. Probably a hundred and twenty guns, at least.

"Not as many crew in evidence as I'd expect," I mused.

"Let me ask you this," Faith said. "He had to sail here the way we did, right?"

"Sure," I said. "So he's got someone that can navigate the mists. We knew that."

"Sure," Faith agreed. "But I couldn't have pulled all those little boats along with me. This boat was hard enough."

"Ship," I said absently. "They could have loaded all the boats on board Joshua's ship."

"Ship then," Faith said. "The important part is that there's got to be close to two hundred Faerie on all those little boats," Faith said. She was getting excited, working something out as she spoke, and I thought I knew where this was going.

"Closer to three hundred," I said.

Almost a dozen on each of the gun boats, times six boats. At least two hundred on that launch. At least. Plus the boats themselves and the cannon.

"How many people could he bring," she asked, "just on that ship? And still have room for all the little boats."

"Not that many," I said. "Besides, we've seen no evidence of any real sailors from the invasion force so far. What he could bring wouldn't be that experienced." I started talking quickly, seeing how it all fit together in my head. "Even if he cobbled together a rough crew, he probably couldn't count on that lumbering behemoth to keep us out. We're faster, more maneuverable. It would be too easy for us to double back. So he comes up with these seahorses and the gun boats. Now he's got an attack maneuverable enough to catch us, or at least chase us away for good. But the launch full of troops was overplaying his hand. He hasn't left enough to properly crew or defend his ship."

"So," Faith said, "we get past those little boats and charge the big ship?"

I grinned. "Yes. We charge Joshua's ship."

"We're going to what?" Starling said, mouth open.

Footsteps came up the quarterdeck stairs and Swayle came up, her green and white uniform stained with gunpowder.

"A moment, captain?" She'd taken her helmet off, freeing her short hair, which made her less of a faceless officer, more like a person.

"Yes?"

"Some of my sharpest-eyed archers have been looking over the enemy vessel," she said. She pointed at Joshua's ship. "The large one. We think it is only lightly crewed and guarded. If we . . ."

"Joshua's ship is barely defended," I said. "Yes. We were just thinking the same thing."

She blinked. "Ah. You have?"

"Oh yes," I said. "Mr. Starling, prepare to turn and give another broadside."

Starling looked at the gun boats and launch behind us.

He was right to look concerned. We'd lost a lot of distance and speed with our last maneuver. Doing it again so soon would let the pursuers close with us. "That will cut it awful close," he said carefully.

"It will," I said. "Which is why we're going right at them after we shoot. We turn, give them one broadside, then complete the turn and plow right through the launch and gun boats. Hopefully we'll surprise them."

"Surprising the 'ell out of me!" Starling muttered.

"If we deal with them quickly," I went on, "it might force Joshua to retreat. If we get by them, we can engage Joshua's ship and board them while the smaller boats are still far behind us."

Swayle, nodded with satisfaction.

There were flaws to the plan, to be sure. But anything else would involve more time than we had. If we were going to do Father any good, we had to get to that island today. There was no time for us to play a game of cat and mouse with Joshua's ship. He wanted to keep us from Father, clearly, but he also couldn't let that enormous ship of the line fall into our hands.

I looked at Swayle. "I'll be relying on your people for a good deal of the fighting."

"Aye, Captain," Swayle said and her face split into a happy smile. I hadn't actually expected any reaction from the stoic commander at the news of impending close-quarters combat, but if I had, this wasn't it. She spun and called out to her three lieutenants to confer. I didn't understand the language, but it was clear they were all happy and excited at the prospect.

Starling said something, but one of the bowchasers went off and I shook my head at him.

"A chance to redeem themselves," Starling said again, shouting to be heard, though we were in between cannon shots and there was only the ringing in our ears to overcome.

"What's that?" I said.

"The Crow Whisper Brigade," Starling said, using the formal name for Swayle's marines. "They're also known as the Unforgiven. Ever since they arrived late at the Battle of Silver Falls and their lords were slain. They were leaderless for over two 'undred years before the Lord o' Thorns accepted their fealty." A ghost of a smile crossed his face. "I almost feel sorry for Joshua's crew." He shook his head. "But even Swayle's people aren't goin' to be able to fight the entire crew of a ship like that by themselves. There's only two dozen of 'em."

"They won't be by themselves," I said. "After we close, we'll have the chance to fire at point-blank range . . ."

"So will Joshua," Faith said quietly.

"He will," I said, "and we'll do what we can to minimize his opportunities for that. When we close, we'll pull as many crewman as we can for boarding. All the gunnery crew and as many deck and sail crew as we can possibly spare. Starling, open up the armory and make sure everyone has a weapon."

"Aye, captain."

"Also," I said, "we'll need a fire."

It worked more beautifully than I could have possibly expected.

We took two more cannon shots to the hull from the gun boats, who were getting nearer every minute. One shot shattered the bowsprit and tore away part of the jib sail, which was going to make steering more difficult, while the other put another hole in the hull. But the boats had bunched themselves up in their eagerness to finally do damage now that they were in their proper range, and I managed to time our turn well enough to present an entire broadside to all three remaining gun boats.

I'd ordered Render to the gun deck to prepare for the broadside and the bowchasers had fallen silent as we readied for the turn.

"You know what we should do?" Henry said next to me.

"Hold on," I said. "Starling, flugelstan the ship." It still chafed me to use Avonstoke's stupid terminology, but I had to admit it worked better.

"Aye."

"You know what we should do?" Henry said again, talking faster. "Instead of running, we finish this turn and drive right at them! Surprise that big ship. I don't think it turns very well."

"Yes," I said, sighing and rubbing the bridge of my nose. "Good idea."

"Isn't it though?" Henry said brightly. "Why don't you look happy about it? This could work!"

"Yes," I said. "Go help the gunnery crew."

"Really?" he said. "You're going to do it?"

"Yes, yes already. Go help the gunnery crew."

"Outstanding!" Henry said, scurrying off.

"I'm looking at Joshua's boat," Avonstoke said, putting his hand theatrically to his shield his blank, sightless eyes. "You know what I think we should . . ."

"Shut up!" I said automatically.

Avonstoke laughed, his quiet spell momentarily gone. He was blind because of me and here he was making jokes about it. But then I saw his pantomiming of scanning the horizon—in the wrong direction—and felt a helpless laugh burst out of me.

We were just completing the turn now, and a panicked clamor rose up from the enemy boat crews as they saw our cannon coming to bear. I felt my smile turn to a merciless grin as we brought our guns to bear.

"Fire!" I shouted.

The deck shook and smoke and flame belched out our starboard side and two of the gun boats went down amid burbling screams.

I felt that small pang of guilt, particularly for the sea horses, that came every time I ordered cannon fired, but it was a small thing now, more easily dismissed during the moment. The night after would bring it back, the fear and guilt all ambushing me in my dreams. There's a price to pay for everything.

The third boat had been hit as well, but not badly enough to sink it. The ensuing confusion made the gun boat's crew lower their wooden shields, however, and Swayle's archers put them down.

We hadn't been so lucky with the boarding launch. They'd managed to brave cannon and arrow fire and were closing. We weren't going to be able to avoid them. My only hope was that if we dealt with them decisively, we could force Joshua into a retreat.

"Everyone to the defense of the ship," I growled, then nearly choked as our Prowler helmsman let the tiller go and ran off. The tiller spun, unattended.

"Are you daft?" I shouted. "Not you!" But another of our cannon went off, drowning me out.

I leapt for the spinning tiller. Starling and Avonstoke did the same and we all grabbed it together.

"Blast him!" Starling, glaring after the departed helmsman. "Followin' orders is one thin', but 'ow stupid do you 'ave to be to . . ."

"I can hold this," Avonstoke said. "You need every fighter you can get!"

"You can't steer!" I said. "You can't even see!"

"How hard can it be?" Avonstoke said. "I can feel the wind. I'll keep it as straight as I can while the fighting lasts. You and Starling call all the directions anyway." He closed his eyes, sagging ever so slightly as if shouldering a weight. "I can't help with the fighting, much as it pierces my heart to admit. This I can do. Go! Just be careful!"

I started to turn, then paused.

"Listen," I said, talking quickly. "I don't want you to go flying off, but I think that Goblin, the one that killed your father, is part of the boarding party coming in. He's wearing a skull mask, anyway. A bear's skull."

Avonstoke's golden face went white and he staggered, very slightly, but then stood up straight. "Now? When I'm . . ." He closed his eyes again and hand lifted up to briefly touch his closed eyelids. "Very well, if you aren't too busy, and it isn't too much of a bother, could one of you do me the kindness of ending his life for me? I hate to impose."

"Consider it done," Starling growled, then looked away, as if Avonstoke's pain was too much to look on.

"Yes," I said quietly. "We'll see it done."

"I thank you," Avonstoke said. "I shall keep your tiller well. Don't forget to send someone back if we're about to run into anything, yes?"

"Yes," I said again. It felt like I was agreeing to something larger than I could wrap my mind around now.

"They're nearly here, captain!" Starling said.

I followed him down.

On the main deck, a smaller Goblin named Itch was holding a makeshift tether we'd made for Nocturnus. He looked at me inquisitively.

"Yes," I said. "It's time."

This was the last place I wanted to summon Nocturnus and the last place and time I wanted to introduce fire, the bane of ships everywhere, into an already chaotic situation, but nonetheless, I'd ordered these preparations. Itch had a brazier ready and lit it with quick, practiced motions. The Faerie didn't have the sailors' nearly instinctual fear of fire, so I was probably the only one that flinched when he did it. As soon as it was blazing, I went quickly through the ritual.

In less than a minute, Pavor Nocturnus was with us on the deck. She was a little uneasy, being a horse on the deck of a ship, but her ears perked up and she chuffed a greeting when she saw me. Having an enormous supernatural horse on the deck of a ship seemed like madness, especially when that same horse turned into an indiscriminate force of destruction in the water. We'd just have to keep her *out* of the water. We needed her overpowering brute force for us to survive the boarding action.

"Hey girl," I said. "You ready?"

She whickered happily and pushed her nose into my hand. Her hooves shifted on the deck, making Itch nervous.

"It's all right," I told the Goblin. "I have her now."

The crew was ready. We'd passed out cutlasses from the ship's armory and gathered in force on the main deck. Swayle's marines were still taking advantage of their elevated positions on the forecastle and quarterdeck to rain down arrows on the enemy, but it wasn't enough. Swayle herself was standing next to us, loosing arrow after arrow straight down.

"For the love of God," Henry shouted at me from the other side of the ship, pointing at Nocturnus, "don't let her fall into the water!" He was, in fact, as far as he could get from Nocturnus and still be in the fighting. He had a point. If Nocturnus got into the water and turned, she could sink the entire ship.

Starling, hefting his axe next to us, suddenly looked alarmed. "Wait! It's not goin' to turn into that sea beastie *again*, is it?"

"Not as long as we don't get her wet," I said.

"Beggin' your pardon, captain," Starling said, "but we're at bloody *sea*!"

"Here they come!" Swayle shouted, discarding her bow and lifting her spear.

Goblins and Hanged Dogs swarmed up the *Specter's* hull without even the need of grappling hooks and line. One of the Trolls, bristling with several dozen arrows, fell back into the water, but the other leapt from the boat, passing its fellow Faerie in its eagerness to get to our deck and start tearing us limb from limb. The Troll reached our gunwale before the rest.

But it never cleared it.

Nocturnus reared, screaming like an enraged steam-engine, then coming down with both forefeet in the Troll's face. Two heavy thuds hit like falling boulders and the Troll fell back into the water, roaring in pain and fear. I don't think Trolls can swim. This one didn't.

The enemy swarmed over the rail then in a wave, and we met them head-on. I was in the thick of it, shooting from Nocturnus' back until my gun clicked empty. Swayle's marines, spears flashing in the sun, took the brunt of it, driving Goblins back as fast as they climbed up.

The crew was fighting, too, and Henry, and Faith. Sands, still so injured it was all he could do walk, stood next to the tiller and Avonstoke, his sword out, but unsteady.

Then Henry, rushing headlong into battle, did something that surprised me.

Dropping the cutlass he'd been given, he seized up a heavy spar ten feet long and big around as my fist and rushed to the scuppers where a half dozen of the cadaverous Hanged Dogs were clawing their way up. Henry, my little brother who was still a head shorter than me, held the spar even with the deck and rushed them, screaming fit to burst. He shoved the spar so hard that Hanged

Dogs and spar all went flying twenty feet back and fell into the passing sea.

Henry's face, always so amiable and cheerful, was now a furious mask. Whether it was some nature of the Faerie rising up inside of him, or some ripple of the torment he must have suffered in Newgate Prison, I didn't know, but watching his expression of hate and rage, was terrifying.

He seized an enemy Goblin and bashed his head mercilessly against the mast, then discarded the limp body like a wet, broken cord. I was suddenly very glad he was on our side and deeply ashamed and terrified of what all us Kasrics were becoming in this horrific war.

On the forecastle, a tight knot of battle swarmed around. I caught sight of both Starling and Mog, along with a few of Swayle's marines, fighting a group of enemy Goblins with terrifying ferocity. Among them was the Goblin with the skull mask. Starling and Mog were moving right towards him.

The Goblin Knight, seeing two of his comrades next to him fall, stepped suddenly back, out of battle.

He held his smoking morningstar high and screamed six words of power in a high-pitched, terrible voice. Then he thudded the handle down on the deck with all the authority of a judge hammering a gavel down on a death sentence. Smoke billowed suddenly from the morningstar, covering the entire forecastle.

"Gods preserves us," Swayle said next to me. Her voice was as shaken as I'd ever heard it, which sent a pang of fear through me.

Screams bubbled out of the smoke.

"Faith!" I screamed, turning Nocturnus, and hoping against hope that she could counter this sudden plague.

But she was already on it.

Facing the elevated forecastle, across the main deck, from the equally elevated quarterdeck, she lifted both of her arms and sang.

I shoved my empty pistol back into my coat pocket and drew the short cutlass that Starling had pulled out of the armory for me. Nocturnus was pushing her way through the battle on the main deck, but slowly. I lashed out to both sides with the cutlass, urging her again for speed.

Faith's triple voice rose up. The same voice that had called storms and spoken to a God.

The smoke thinned and slowly, so slowly, blew away.

The Goblin Knight was standing, his morningstar dripping blood, with no one living standing to oppose him. I couldn't see Starling or Mog or anyone else for that matter.

An enemy Goblin came at me from the left, but I jabbed at him with the cutlass and it slowed him down long enough for Nocturnus to ram her chest into him, sending the hapless Goblin screaming over the rail.

With my elevated position on Nocturnus' back, I was just high enough to see onto the forecastle and meet the Goblin Knight's gaze. He grinned a foul, toothy smile, his own teeth equally as yellow and lethal as the fangs on his bear-skull helmet.

Nocturnus took the forecastle stairs in two powerful strides. I saw both Starling and Mog's bodies, covered with blood, at the Goblin Knight's taloned feet. To one side, several the marines' bodies lay, mashed to a pulp.

"You'll pay for that!" I snarled.

Probably, my words were drowned out by the din, but they must have been clear enough. The Goblin Knight's grin grew wider, more feral as he met my gaze. He raised the handle of his morningstar again.

He brought it down on the deck again.

Nothing happened.

Faith, behind me, was still singing. She'd used her own magic to snuff it the same way she'd suppressed the magical properties of the mist.

Nocturnus moved forward and I hefted the cutlass, but the Goblin Knight shouted one last shrill and unintelligible Goblin deprecation at me before he turned and dove over the side.

I wasn't sure if he could swim. When I led Nocturnus to the other side of the quarterdeck and leaned out as far as I dared, I could see no sign of him.

After our quick disposal of his gun boats and our decisive battle with the troop launch, Joshua confirmed our suspicion about the skeletal nature of his ship's crew, because he immediately turned the Emerald Demise's prow west, fleeing out to open sea. That was one success, at least.

The plan wasn't to follow Joshua, but I desperately wanted to. It burned me to the core to watch him fly away free and clear when his ship was ripe for the taking. If not for our mission, I had every confidence that we could have followed and, with our superior maneuverability and his lack of crew, harried the bulky ship to a helpless wreck.

But we couldn't afford the delay if we were going to do anything to save Father, and England, and the rest of the Outcast Fleet. Joshua and the *Emerald Demise* would be matters for another day. After we dealt with the aftermath or our battle, the worst of which being the butcher's bill, it was time to count the wounded and the dead.

I made my way past where Swayle was kneeling, getting ready to set a broken bone in one of her marines' leg.

“Ready?” Swayle said quietly. The marine nodded, his eyes wide. Swayle pulled and the man whimpered like a beaten dog.

“There,” Swayle said. “That’s done. Now we brace it.”

I put my hand on her shoulder. “Your marines were brave today, Colonel Swayle. I heard the story about how you were given the name of Unforgiven for being late to battle. No more, I say. You’ve earned your honor back today, all of you.”

“No,” Swayle said. She looked up at me, weariness on her face. The pure white piping on her uniform was smeared with blood. “But it’s a start.”

I squeezed her shoulder and moved on. More wounded were on the aft part of the main deck. And the dead.

Mog was there. The Goblin Knight had broken Mog’s arm and collarbone, but our gruff, toothy leader of the sail crew had still been alive when we pulled him out of the pile of bodies our enemy had left. He sat now with several bandages and his long floppy ears droopier than ever. His large, clawed hand resting inconsolably on the body next to him. The deck was bustling with activity, repairs and people assisting the injured and preparing the dead for burial, but Mog didn’t seem to see or hear any of it, only the body next to him.

Mr. Starling’s body.

The Goblin Knight had caved in my brave first mate’s head so much that it was hardly recognizable as a person’s head anymore and someone had draped a sailcloth over the mess. Starling’s body looked too small under the cloth and patches of red had bled through. I couldn’t bear to look at it and I couldn’t tear my gaze away.

Avonstoke was with nearby, playing Henry’s copper flute very softly, tears glistening silently on his cheeks. I still wasn’t used to the tattoo being gone from his face. Maybe I never would be. He took the flute from his mouth. "A fair prince of a man," he said softly. "Gruff, but true. Never was there a truer man, Dwarf or otherwise."

Mog seemed surprised to hear his voice, then he nodded. "Never 'ad . . ." Mog said, then his gravel voice choked and he had to start over. "Never 'ad *not*-Goblin friend before. Showed Mog 'ow to drink beer." He sighed. "Mog like beer. Now, no Starlin' to drink 'oney wine while Mog drink beer."

"I would be honored," Avonstoke said softly, "to share a tankard with you, Mog."

"Avonstoke is 'nother not-Goblin friend," Mog said. "But is not Starlin'." The whiskers on his hooked snout quivered.

"No," Avonstoke said sadly.

I crouched down to speak to Mog on an even level. Faith and Henry were with me, and Mog gradually became aware of the small knot of people standing in front of him.

"Captain," Mog said. "Mog sorry. Should 'ave killed Goblin Knight before . . ." He waved a clawed hand at the blood-stained sheet. "Mog know 'im, the Goblin Knight. Very bad. Mog's clan always at war with Saltblood clan, but Goblin Knight more than just enemy. More than war. 'E likes blood, death. Very bad."

"It's not your fault," I said. "You did what you could." If Starling's death was on anyone, it was on me.

"It's war," Henry said in a haunted voice. "People die." I shuddered inwardly, remembering how battle had twisted Henry's normally innocent-looking face. The rage he'd shown frightened me, for all that I was trying hard not to show it.

"It's not your fault," I said again. "Listen Mog, if this battle is going to mean anything, I need to get to the center of the World

Tree." The new spokesman for the Leaf Riders, a yellow-headed little mushroom-cap of a Faerie named Golden, had reported nothing more sinister than an empty beach on the island. We had no reason to delay.

"I need . . ." My eyes slid to the bloody sheet again, then I yanked my gaze back to Mog's rough, earnest face. "I need a new second mate to take Mr. Starling's place. You're head of the sail crew and understand how to deploy them. You've proved yourself again and again these past few weeks. I know the rest of the crew will listen to you."

"Who would dare disobey him?" Faith murmured.

I ignored her. "Will you keep the ship safe for me until I return?" I asked Mog.

Mog looked at the body a moment longer, then patted it twice and started to stand up. It was an awkward thing with one of his arms out of commission and I made the mistake of trying to help. Mog's one burly arm nearly slammed me accidentally to the deck. Finally Henry stepped in and helped, keeping both Mog and I from falling.

"Yes, captain Justice," Mog said. "Mog keep ship safe for you."

CHAPTER 22

On the Island

I stood in the captain's quarters, watching the crew lower one of the boats into the water. They were lowering it from the stern of the ship and the gallery window in my quarters made for a perfect place to view everything without getting in the way. Avonstoke had just been relieved at the tiller and I barely heard his soft tread cross the quarterdeck above me.

His were the hardest steps to make out, but I always knew them at once. I realized that was because I was always listening for them.

His steps travelled down the stairs, not sounding careful or hesitant at all. I thought, I *hoped,* he might be coming into my quarters—I'd left the door open—and so knew when to turn to see him put his hand on the upper part of the door frame and duck slightly as he came into the room.

Even blind, he moved easily, gracefully. The small, mostly enclosed world of the ship was as ideal a place for a blind man as you could ask for, and Avonstoke seemed to have learned its stairs, railings, ladders, and holds well in a remarkably short time. He touched the walls briefly, and once the chair, so casually that you could hardly tell he was checking their position if you didn't know to look for it. He flopped with exaggerated insouciance onto my bed and gazed up at me. I hadn't made any sound, but he looked unerringly in my direction.

I still couldn't get used to his face without the black raven tattoo across it. It felt like a good omen, somehow, him looking closer to my age, or perhaps I was reading into that.

"I wish, oh my Captain," he said, "that I were coming with you."

"Me too," I said fervently.

"I know," he said. "I'd only be a hindrance to you now." He waved his hands at his eyes.

"That's not true!" I said immediately. "I'm just worried you'd get . . ."

He took my hand. "I know," he said. His hands were rough, but gentle as he rubbed my palm with his thumb. I squeezed it, hard.

"Get hurt," he finished for me. "I know."

I bit my lip, wanting to say something to deny it, but knowing that I couldn't lie to him, either.

"That's how I feel about you, too," he said. "I want to be there to make sure nothing happens to you. Now I can't be. That's the hardest part." For the first time I heard true sorrow in his voice when he thought of it.

"I'll be careful," I said. "I'll have Faith and Henry with me."

"You Kasrics are damnably hard to injure," he said with a rueful smile. "You've proven that. I'm beginning to think that your father is on to something. This magical prophecy he's manipulated and encouraged, the favor of the Gods, I don't know, something. It almost makes me feel a bit sorry for the forces of Faerie trying to deal with you." He flashed that rueful smile at me again and I leaned down and kissed him.

We were starting to make a habit of this. I liked it.

His mouth responded to mine, warm and tasting of him. The blood pounded in my chest and ears, and lower, and a warm flush crept over me. His hand was in my hair, nearly knocking over my hat.

"Ahem!" a gentle voice said from the doorway.

Avonstoke and I broke apart.

"It's time," Faith said. She wore a comic, fabricated, and completely overdone look of prim disapproval.

"Still no sign of Prudence?" I asked.

Faith's expression turned serious, and she shook her head. "No."

That wasn't good. There hadn't been any sign of the Faerie magician since she'd gone to the island. She should have been back by now.

"I'll see you on deck," Faith said, and withdrew with a slight smile.

"I think she suspects us of something dire," Avonstoke said with a broad wink. "Possibly frivolity." His golden eyes smoldered, and a sly smile played about his lips.

I socked him in the chest. Of course, he didn't see it coming.

"Gods preserve me," he gasped, "what under the moon was *that* for?"

"You looked entirely too pleased with yourself," I said, which made him give a throaty laugh.

Then I kissed him one last time before I made for the door.

When I looked back and saw Avonstoke's worried face, it smote me all over again, I knew that I was hopelessly, profoundly, and irreversibly in love with Raythe Avonstoke of the Faerie.

"Come back to me," he said.

"I will," I promised.

Henry, Faith, and I pulled the launch up onto a long stretch of white sand, dappled in alternating sun and shade from the mountainous canopy branches overhead.

The water was ultrablue in a way our seas aren't, churning into purest white foam onto the beach. It was almost hard to believe that our naval battle had happened only a couple of miles off this coast.

We were all quiet, introspective. The solemnity of the place didn't invite idle chatter. I crouched and picked up a handful of dry sand, feeling the smooth flow as it poured out in ivory, silk streams. Father had first met the original Rachek Kasric on a beach, hadn't he? Our family was tangled into the very roots of this war, and it felt right that Faith and Henry and I were together here. It also made the absence of Benedict feel like an open wound. I missed Joshua, too, and even Mother, which made their betrayals all the more painful.

What about Prudence? Or Hope and Charity? Or even the strangers, Temperance and was it... Love? Could you miss strangers you'd never even met? I wasn't sure, but I felt certain that their fate was connected to this time and place, too, same as ours.

The sands turned a few hundred feet inland, with no transition at all, to a thick, strangely-formed green forest.

The strangeness of it came from the branches, some of them as big around as ships, that all slanted down above or simply ran back into darkness.

You had to look close to see it, but while some of them rested on the ground, none of them actually rooted there. The forest floor was moss, but no other plants. This was a forest made of one tree, and one tree only.

"Somewhere in there," Faith said, leaning on her staff. "Think we'll have any trouble finding it?"

It wouldn't take us much longer than a full day to cross the island, but there were a lot of hiding places in a forest like this, to say nothing of going up. We couldn't even be certain the site would be at ground level.

"How long do we have?" Henry said.

"Sometime tomorrow," Faith said. "They always meet the day after Christmas."

"Today is Christmas day?" Henry said, surprised. I was too, to be honest. The day of the contest had loomed so large that I'd nearly forgotten the other days involved.

"That means tomorrow's your birthday," Henry said to me. "Doesn't it?"

"Yes," I said. "I guess it does." I turned sixteen tomorrow.

"I have to ask something," Henry said, quietly. "I should have asked before we came here, to this island. Well, before we left England, I guess."

He turned, looking at Faith and I standing in the green light together. His brown eyes were very serious.

"Why are you doing all this?" he asked.

"Haven't you been paying attention?" Faith said. "Saving Father, which could help us save all of England."

"No, I get that part," Henry said. "I mean, why are *you* doing this? We hardly know the Faerie . . ."

"We are Faerie," I said.

He waved that off. "We didn't know anything about them a year ago. We still don't. Avonstoke said there's a whole fleet of Faerie with magicians and generals and nobles and even a *dragon*, so why you? Just because Father made you two promise? What if we're better off letting one of those people deal with . . . all of this? There must be other people that can fight for England. Christ, the whole world is going to rise up once they realize what's happening there."

"This is our family's fight," I said automatically. "We're at the heart of this."

Henry shook his head. "Not enough." I was struck, yet again, at how different he was from the boy I'd known, changed by his time in Newgate. More certain, but with an impossible well of sadness inside of him, as if he'd finally figured out the world and didn't like the answer.

He sucked at his teeth, putting his hands in his coat and looking at the forest around us. "It would be one thing if we were all on the same side, but we're not, are we? Father and Mother . . . there's nothing we can do about that. It's not like we can restore the two of them and then we'll all be back in London celebrating Christmas like other families. That's all gone now. How do we know that this . . ." He pointed inland, into the green darkness. "Is it even the right thing to do?" He looked questioningly at us.

When we didn't answer, he went on. "I haven't had a chance to talk about what Mother was like when she visited me in Newgate."

I could feel my eyebrows shoot up. They were going to fly right off someday. "You didn't tell me she came to visit."

"Been trying to," he said. "It's a little hard to think about, if I'm honest. It hurts too much. My point is this. She's not family anymore. She's not Mother. We're not getting her back." I couldn't argue with that. She certainly hadn't seemed like family when she'd ordered the Soho Shark to kill us, had she?

"My gut tells me," Henry went on, "that we're not getting Father back either. Joshua's gone. Benedict, too, you said. Maybe . . ." He looked down at his shoes. "Maybe we're better off hiding somewhere and let someone else, I don't know, one of those generals, handle this? Maybe it's too much for us?"

"I would have trusted Father to help," I said. "Before all of this happened. Not sure I would have trusted anyone else with anything this important."

"I would have trusted Mother, too," Faith said. "Before the Faerie got to her." Her dark gaze met mine. It was clear that, unlike me, she'd never really trusted Father. He'd been gone most of the time while we were children, and now we knew that Father hadn't even been human, among his many other secrets. *Why did you trust him?* that look asked. *Why do you trust him still?* It was a fair question, and one I didn't have a logical answer for.

"So Mother, Father," Henry said, "they can't help us anymore." His tone was quietly relentless.

"That's why we have to try and do something," I said.

"Yes," Faith agreed. She met my gaze and nodded. "They can't do it. So it falls to us. We have to try."

Henry sighed. "I guess so." He grinned weakly. "Do you think, if we find Father, that he'll have any food? I'm starved."

"We brought food," Faith said.

"Ship's biscuit and dried beef," I said. "Starling . . ." I stopped. Starling would have been the person to take care of it before, but now, with him gone, it would have been someone else. Mog hadn't really started yet. "Someone was supposed to give it to you," I finished lamely.

"They did," Henry admitted. "I ate it in the boat."

"What? *All* of it?"

"It wasn't *that* much," he said.

"Boys," Faith said fondly, and ruffled Henry's sandy hair. "Of course, if we starve here, I'm going to turn you into a frog before I die."

"You can do that?" he said, and a flash of the young boy he'd been just a few months ago came through.

"Come on," I said. "We need to keep moving."

My first instinct had been to summon Pavor Nocturnus, but one look at the forest changed my mind about that. Discounting the odd open spaces, it was just too congested to think of riding through. Nocturnus would slow us down more than anything. It was thick and warm and green here, while England was in the middle of winter.

We all agreed that inward was the way to go and several paths through the upside-down forest led in that direction. This close, the leaves, about the size of my hand, were gathered in great, bushy clusters. Green with red dots. I rubbed one between my fingers without pulling it off the thin branch. They had a familiar look. It took me a second to place it. Dream's leaf. The leaves of all the other Leaf Riders, too, had come from a plant like this. Did they grow all over in Faerie, or were they rare? I didn't know. The leaves seemed normal enough now, but Dream's had been a living thing, as lively as any spirited stallion. Did the Leaf Riders give the leaves life, or was it just a trick, an extension of the Leaf Riders' magic? There was still so much I didn't know about the Faerie. If Dream's leaf had had life without her, what had become of it? Had it been killed with Dream, or was it running wild somewhere, mourning? I didn't know that, either, and I wasn't sure I wanted to.

The unique nature of the forest left many open spaces, some dappled, some sunlight from far, far above, some in murky green darkness. The branches themselves, enormous and grotesque above us, provided a guide to the center of the tree like roads to a capitol city.

"It's like we're being guided," Henry said.

"Or led," Faith murmured.

"You have some kind of connection to the Wild Hunt," Henry said. "Right? Could you call on them if this thing turns out to be some kind of trap?"

"I didn't ask for that connection," Faith said. "I don't want it. But it does have the advantage of giving me a feel for them, for what they want, and reminding me that they can't be trusted."

"But Cernunnos is a relative of sorts, ain't he?" Henry said carefully. Clearly this was something he'd been trying to work out on his own, but hadn't gotten anyway.

"We are part of their lineage," Faith admitted, "but that's not a point in their favor. I wouldn't trust any Faerie and that goes double for a relative. You two are the only ones I'd trust."

I thought of Avonstoke, then Mog and Starling, before he'd passed. Even Nellie and Wil, who had hated us weeks ago. I *did* trust them. If that was a weakness, then so be it. But I could see from Faith's face that getting drawn into an argument with her on this matter wasn't going to get me anywhere.

"Lor!" Henry said as we broke through a cluster of down-thrust branches and came into an open space.

"We're definitely being led," Faith said grimly.

I nodded. "I just wish I knew if that was a good or a bad thing."

"You and me both."

A branch the size of the Specter trust down at us from the canopy, wide and flat and dry. It had branches and leaves on either side, but was completely bare on top, a clear road and tunnel up into the canopy for us to follow.

On either side, walls of thick bramble made it near impossible to go in any other direction. Short of conjuring a trio of machetes and hacking our way through, it was a choice of taking the offered path or turning back.

"We go up?" Henry said.

"We go up," I said.

"Yes," Faith agreed.

But the discussion was the merest formality. We had paused briefly just to take it all in, but our feet started us in the direction before we'd even finished speaking.

The tip of the branch flattened and widened so that it came flush with the mossy floor. Mounting the path was as easy as taking the steps from the garden to the house.

"Can't say the Faerie don't have a flair for the dramatic," Henry said.

More branches came down towards the path, forming more walls and a ceiling of sorts, making our path into a tunnel.

The thicket of branches on our sides rustled occasionally, and I tried not to think about what could be hiding in there ready to slither out at us or drop on our heads. Virtually anything. Some light trickled down, but not nearly enough, and we walked for long minutes through a twisting path without getting a direct look at the sun.

We continued going up.

Then a glimmer of bright light ahead grew brighter, and I became aware that someone was waiting for us in a pool of yellow and gold at the top of the rise.

I knew him at once.

The large antlers, the shaggy bulk of him, were unmistakable. As was the wooden mask of a face, now twisted into a rueful expression. The wooden face was framed by a ragged mane that nearly hid the crown of thorns. An equally ragged beard flowed from his chin. One hand was vastly larger than the other and he wore the same tarnished armor and bushy cloak of loam and grass that I remembered from my childhood. He looked exactly the same as I remembered him. He rested his hands on the pommel of an enormous stone sword which stuck point first in the ground.

The acting Lord of Thorns shifted his grip on the pommel and cleared his throat, a noise like coal being shoveled. Rachek Kasric, the man who wasn't our father, but might have been. The man who'd taken the Lord of Thorns' shape and place in Faerie while Father was passing himself off as Mother's husband and living the man's life.

"Ah," he said in a voice like the whispering of trees, "the Kasric children. I've been waiting a long time to meet you."

CHAPTER 23

Rachek Kasric

"Let me look at you," said the Lord of Thorns.

The Lord of Thorns. It was odd and difficult to use that title—one I'd always associated with Father—for another man, but while Father had used the name to drive and motivate the Outcasts, he hadn't been the man living the Lord of Thorns' life. He'd thrust that duty on someone else.

This man, who'd been born Rachek Kasric.

He was magnificent, shaggy, and regal with barbaric splendor, the antlers—echoes of Cernunnos' own—towering above.

This and the wooden mask of a face, the mane, the tarnished armor and cloak of brambles and the enormous stone sword were all just as I remembered them.

He cocked his head to one side, making his antlers sway, looking at us. The mouth of his wooden face twisted in a rueful smile and the black eyeholes squinted, little lines forming around them.

"You," he said to Henry, "look a great deal like my brother Victor did at your age. Spitting image. I see my wife's eyes in you, Faith, and both of you girls have my have my mother's hair. How is that possible, conceived as you were by another man?" He snorted, a noise filled with black humor and derision. "The answer, of course, is that Rachek Kasric fathered you, but he wasn't me." He sighed deeply, his great shoulders heaving. "Your father has a great deal to answer for. Now, step into the light. I've imagined you all so many ways, but seeing you still comes as a bit of a shock."

"You're Rachek Kasric," I said. "The real one, I mean." I'd put my hand into my pocket, seized my pistol, and thumbed back the hammer when I'd first seen him, but I didn't pull it out. It was hard to know.

Was this man our enemy?

Were we his?

He didn't seem hostile or angry, though he had a right to both. His hands were still resting easily on the pommel of his sword which stood before him, point stuck in the ground. His hands were gnarled, leathery things and not at all the same size.

The left was twice the size of a large man's, but the right, which he had on top, was an oversized giant's hand, easily five or six times his left.

"You were born with the Kasric eyes," he said to me. "Same as mine used to be. Same as my grandfather's." Then he tapped the left darkened hole of his wooden mask. "But that other eye, that comes from the Faerie, doesn't it?"

"Mother gave it to me," I said, which wasn't exactly an answer.

"Did she?" he said.

"You're Rachek Kasric," I said again.

"No," the Lord of Thorns said, "but I used to be. I will be again, very soon, I think. You two," he waggled a huge brown finger at Faith and I, "are two of the virtues, as well, aren't you? He used his own daughters for that, didn't he? You'd have names to match, wouldn't you?"

"Justice," I said. "That's Faith, and Henry." I nodded at each. I still didn't want to reveal or let go of the pistol.

"I still say we're lucky not to be Etiquette and Proper Table Manners," Faith murmured.

The Lord of Thorns nodded gravely, taking Faith's joke at face value in a way that was slightly disconcerting. Years of living with the Faerie, in a land of the strange and miraculous, lay behind that grave nod. "Come. I wanted to meet you before the others knew you were here, but things are happening very fast now. It would be better if we walked as we spoke."

I looked at Faith and Henry, who both shrugged. What other choice did we have? We didn't come all this way to wait in the forest.

The woodland tunnel leveled off and widened until it felt like walking through a half-lit stadium, and we were all able to walk abreast.

The Lord of Thorns had to adjust his shambling gait so as to not leave us quickly behind. He also had to dip his head ponderously to bring the widespread antlers out of the way of the occasional straggling branch coming down from the thicket ceiling.

He poked idly at the wooden path as he walked, handling the mammoth sword with his oversized right hand the way a London gentleman might a walking stick, then he seemed to think better of it and put it away, threading it through a loop behind his shoulder.

"We meet every year, you know," he said while working the sword into place. "My enemy and I. In different forests around the world, but these places are also under the World Tree."

"The day after Christmas," I said.

"Yes," the Lord of Thorns said. He looked up at the slanting light. "But I'd be careful about that word here. The Faerie have a natural distrust and loathing for our religious holidays. They see it as part of the changes in the world that pushed them out."

"Is it?" Henry said.

I looked curious at my brother, sure that the answer was obvious. The antipathy between Christianity and Faerie magic was clear enough.

"No," the acting Lord of Thorns said, surprising me. "Probably not. They loathe black iron, and churches, which represent man's turning away from the old ways, but the combustion engine probably helped drive them out of England more than those other things. Modern technology leads men away from the Faerie more than Christianity ever did."

"Hmm," Faith said.

The Lord of Thorns gave us a sideways glance, looking down from his great height as he walked beside us. "Is it true? Has the Black Shuck really landed troops in England?"

"It's true," I said. "They've taken over England, Ireland, Wales, and Scotland. They'll jump to France and the rest of the world, too, if we can't stop them."

The Lord of Thorns shook his shaggy head in disbelief and his antlers swayed. "I was so sure the rumors were just lies from the

Courts. How did he get past the Outcast Army at the Bridge of Sorrows?"

"Mother," Henry said. "She helped him get troops across and into England without using the bridge. When the defenses in England fell, it threw the Outcasts on the bridge into confusion. Everything went to pieces."

"Martine did that?" the Lord of Thorns said. "Hmm. I should not be surprised. She is an amazing woman." His voice was filled with sorrow and more than a little pride. Martine Scarsdon was the woman he'd married and, thanks in no small part to Father, she wasn't going to be waiting for him when he returned home. "Even so, I had not expected the Faerie invasion to hold onto England for this long. Why haven't the Outcasts made a counter attack?" He sounded hurt, as if Father might have sabotaged his military strategies just to enrage *him*.

"We've been trying," I said. "The Faerie Army was so much larger than anyone expected. We didn't expect it to hold together this long, either. Father, everyone, expected the army to fall apart in disarray. Most factions within the court squabble among themselves. No one imagined that forces belonging to both the Seelie and Unseelie Court would stay united this long."

"The Black Shuck and Widdershins," the Lord of Thorns said bitterly. "They are a potent combination. Widdershins' presence muddles the minds of those around them. Between him and the Black Shuck's dark powers of dominion, they held great sway in the Unseelie Court before invading England. That must be it."

"Just the two of them?" It was hard to believe. Henry had described the Black Shuck's fearsome presence and I'd felt Widdershins' power myself. But still . . . "They can control an entire invasion force?"

"I can't be sure," the Lord of Thorns said. "But in Faerie, they'd gotten control of a dozen or so of the *right* people, important people, and managed to terrorize hundreds in both courts with threats of the same. You'd be surprised how far that goes. It's given them control over generals, kings, magicians, dragons, the Wealdarin. No one can resist it. Your mother has come the closest and she has been ever at Widdershins' side for years."

"Ah," Faith said. "The years they spent in Faerie. They haven't actually been gone that long from our point of view."

"I'm never going to wrap my mind around that," Henry said morosely.

"Time," the Lord of Thorns said, "does not behave properly in Faerie."

We strode on, the path leveling off. We were about four stories or so above the ground and now the thicket on either side was bare in patches, leaving great openings any of us could have toppled into, should we misstep. The path was wide, and we kept far away from the edge, but it was still unnerving.

Henry sidled a little closer to the edge and looked down. He whistled and quickly stepped away from the edge.

"This controlling effect of the Black Shuck's," Faith asked. "Could that be the answer we've been looking for? If it is, does knowing how they do it help us any?"

"None can resist it," the Lord of Thorns said sadly.

"I did, I think," Henry said quietly.

The Lord of Thorns stopped walking. "Did you now?"

"They came to me at Newgate," Henry said. "Widdershins . . ." He shuddered and pushed his sandy hair out of his face. It had grown longer in prison. He'd have to do something about that, assuming we lived long enough for something as mundane as haircuts to matter. "It's hard to talk about," he murmured. "White hands." He started walking again and the rest of us, including the Lord of Thorns, followed suit.

I wasn't sure what to make of Henry's statement and I could tell the Faith and the Lord of Thorns didn't either.

"People fear the Black Shuck and Widdershins so greatly," the Lord of Thorns mused, "because they feel no one person can stand against them. If Henry can resist them, publicly, it may mean a great deal. Something like that could help us drive them out of England, properly leveraged."

"Us?" Faith said.

The Lord of Thorns' wooden face smiled. "England was my home long before the Lord of Thorns came, long before any of you were born. My years in Faerie have not changed that. I'll not stand with Lessard, but I'll defend England, if I can."

It was a splash of cold water to be reminded, again, that Lessard was Father's original name. I hadn't even known it a few months ago and still had a hard time remembering that. The Lord Lessard du Thorns.

The sun, far above us, was starting to wane, and the shambling hulk of the Lord of Thorns, massive and shadowed, stopped.

"Bide a moment," he said. He pulled up the corner of his cloak, bunching the folds of it in one massive fist. From this close, I could see that outside of the cloak wasn't just thick grass and brambles, but also included tiny wildflowers, like an expensive lawn gone wild. But the interior was dark, a rich, brown loam. He poked a small hole in the loam and then blew on it slowly and carefully, like someone starting a fire.

A light shone out of the hole he'd made. First it was weak, as if shining from a distance away, but then it grew stronger. Finally, a burst of shining moths flew out, a cascade of golden shapes dancing above us that cast glittering light everywhere.

"Oh!" Faith said with delight. "That's marvelous!"

"Lor!" Henry said, grinning as the cloud of glowing moths lit our way.

"That's better," the Lord of Thorns said. "There is, of course, a question. *Do* I get to return to England?" He looked pointedly at the three of us. "I was hoping you'd have the decency to tell me. It's not the Faerie way to ask directly, but then, you haven't been raised as Faerie, have you?" There was a tightness in his voice and sudden tension in his massive shoulders that told me what it cost him to ask that question. He was walking on our left, so that it was his right hand, so much larger than his left, that was nearest to us. It was clenched tight, hard enough to powder stone, the brown, barklike skin of his hand turning white.

Faith and I looked at each other, confusion and the thin wisp of a black idea starting to rear up inside of me.

"How should we know?" I said.

The Lord of Thorns shrugged his massive shoulders. "I know the cunning mind of my opponent better than anyone. He had scores of contingency plans in motion, even if he doesn't remember them all in his decline. I've defeated many of them. Others fell by the wayside when the invasion disrupted things. I'd assumed you were the last contingency."

"We came," Faith said slowly, "to try and prevent Father from going back to Faerie. It's true."

"I'm sorry if that makes us enemies," I said suddenly, my voice near breaking. "He's . . ."

"The key to stopping the Faerie invasion," Faith said when I couldn't continue.

"Our father," I finished instead.

Henry was looking back and forth from Faith and me.

"It's true, then," The Lord of Thorns said. "I'll not stay here in Faerie. I've waited too long to return home to England!" He turned to face us, then drew the giant stone sword in one smooth motion. The glowing butterflies swirled overhead, making his shadow sway and wobble around him crazily.

Somehow the pistol was out and pointing at him, though I hadn't remembered pulling it out.

"Don't be ridiculous," the Lord of Thorns barked. "Guns don't work in Faerie. Nothing with gunpowder does. The technology is an anathema to this entire place."

I jerked the pistol to the right and squeezed the trigger.

The gun went off with a sharp crack and a branch in the ceiling that had to be at least three inches thick exploded, sending woodchips in all directions.

The Lord of Thorns' face was a picture of shock and dismay that would have been comical under other circumstances.

"How?" he said. "How did he do it?"

Of course, he was right. We were Father's contingency plan after all.

The pistol was a rare and special thing, a weapon capable of injuring a Faerie, but also protected so that it still operated here. There couldn't have been another like it and hardly any other weapon in the world that would allow me to kill such a formidable person as the one that stood in front of me.

Father had hired Avonstoke, probably given him the weapon, and somehow made certain that it came into my hands. Avonstoke had been open enough about who had given it to him, but didn't want it, not having any experience with arms of that sort. It was possible that Avonstoke was even in on the scheme, but somehow I couldn't believe that.

But for him, giving this weapon to the Lord of Thorns' daughter was a perfect solution. As Father had certainly planned. All the pieces moved into place so that I'd have this weapon, here, at this time. The wood path beneath me seemed uneven, tilting. I thought I might pass out, or barring that, vomit all over myself.

The Lord of Thorns struggled visibly, then let his hand open. The sword thudded to the wood path below us, heavy enough that we all felt it through our feet. "Ah," he said softly. "It seems that I didn't anticipate him as well as I thought I had." His voice broke with the last word.

Faith and Henry were looking at me, their eyes enormous.

The Lord of Thorns took in a deep breath, coming to terms with how things were now. "I can't blame you," he said quietly. "This would be the worst possible time for the original Lord of Thorns to be back in Faerie. The Seelie Court tried to compel me to join the invasion, but I would not obey. I'd never actually sworn any fealty to them. But your Father has, long ago. Such things matter more to the Faerie than they do even to us. When the court gets him back, he won't be able to resist. They'll send him right to London, as a general for the Faerie army."

"Oh God," Faith said.

"You see?" The Lord of Thorns said. "I'll go back to being plain Rachek Kasric, and he comes back into his full Faerie powers as the Lord of Thorns. He'll be more powerful than you have ever known him, the most ruthless and cunning general the Faerie have ever known, and he won't be fighting for England anymore. He'll be leading the invasion. He won't have any choice. The Seelie Court will see to that. That needs to be prevented, at any cost."

Father's last gambit, and I was the one that held it.

I suddenly knew, as sure as I'd known anything, that Father had moved all the pieces in place, me, this man, the gun specifically for murdering Faerie, and who knew how much more, into place so that I would have the opportunity to kill this man.

Faith pushed back her hood, revealing her shaven skull. Her dark eyes were sober.

"I really did want to return," the Lord of Thorns said. "But when I consider it, I'm forced to wonder what would be left for me to return *to*? Martine is lost to the Faerie. And so is my son, Joshua. I've seen that now for myself. My life, my home? What part of that is left? All I can look forward to is England itself. Except that if I return, it will be as England's death knell."

He stood up straight. "You can't allow that. I see that now." The black holes of his mask held a depth of sadness and tragedy.

"Justice?" Faith said. She was looking hard at me, her face carefully empty of judgment, just waiting to see what I was going to do. Henry's expression had turned to horror.

I could feel the magical logic to it. If this man died, it would be a way for Father to sidestep his doom. The link between him and this man would be destroyed, and any magical compulsions or prices to be paid would die with him. Father wouldn't be compelled by his own magic to return to a Faerie shape. Without the compulsion weakening him, he could recover from his illness. England would have a real fighting chance. Better him than me or the Lady Rue leading the resistance.

My breath caught. I could even sail with Father! Just like I'd always dreamed. Father, Faith, Henry, and I, sailing in a glorious campaign to save England. Together. Maybe Father could rescue Benedict, too, and Mother and Joshua. Anything was possible!

All I had to do was shoot an innocent man.

The moments ticked slowly by. A green-scented wind rustled through the ticket all around us and the wood branch underneath creaked, ever so slightly. Water was dripping somewhere close by. The pistol was very steady in my hand. That surprised me.

Everything about this surprised me.

This wouldn't even be the first person I'd shot. Victoria Rose. The Soho Shark. I'd proven surprisingly adept at killing people. Had Father expected that, too?

"You have to shoot," the Lord of Thorns said, his voice hollow. "I was a casualty of this war over a decade ago. The Crimea should have had me, and we cheated it. Now, my death will finally find me. Better one man die, than an entire country of people."

"Justice?" Henry said again.

"You have to shoot," the acting Lord of Thorns said again. The wooden mask looked sad, but calm, resigned.

What kind of person would I be if I did this? What would other people think of me if I did? Would Faith and Henry accept it? I couldn't tell by looking at their faces. What would Avonstoke think? I wished I could see his face now, too.

Slowly, so slowly, I let the gun fall.

"It doesn't matter how much we need Father," I said. "I can't shoot you. I don't have the right to take what little you have left. Whatever you can gather back of your old life, you deserve the chance to look for it. We . . . the Kasrics, the House of Thorns, whoever we are, we owe you that much."

The Lord of Thorns stared at me for a long time. "Yes. Yes, I suppose you do."

"Sometimes," Faith said, "the hardest thing to do is also the right thing to do."

CHAPTER 24

Under the World Tree

We left the long, briar-encircled tunnel of the tree branch bridge we'd been walking on for all this time, Faith, Henry, the Lord of Thorns and I, and came down onto a moss-covered floor. The ground sloped downwards now. Descending was a welcome change after the long climb. The silence grew heavier and deeper and came with the sharp, pleasant scent of tomato vines. The thickets, growing taller and farther away as the space opened up, were covered in white blossoms.

It opened, then, into an even more vast and open space, a great hollow underneath the canopy of the World Tree filled with thick shafts of moonlight. The Lord of Thorns' glowing butterflies flew up towards the ceiling sixty or seventy feet above us, shining in the half-light like stars returning home. They flew into the branches above us and became lost to sight, but thick shafts of moonlight slanted down through silvered air into emerald shadows, allowing us to see everything below.

It reminded me forcefully of the hollow where I'd seen Father play as a child, which made sense, considering what the Lord of Thorns had told us.

Several people waited for us down in the center.

Father was there, of course, seated under a corner of the pavilion, waiting. He looked small and fragile, especially compared to the hulking presence of the Lord of Thorns next to us. Prudence was there, too, with Father, looking even more colorless and gray than usual. Next to her, the Lady of Sorrows was a stark contrast with her black skin and cascade of ivory hair. She was expected, but what was entirely *unexpected* was the presence of several more people.

The nearest of them turned. It was Hope, her face etched with hatred, looking wild and feral with her short, dark hair and pale skin. Charity, looking as young and innocent as ever with the golden ringlets, stood just behind her. They'd both stayed with Lady Rue after the Lady of Sorrows had sailed away, so it was a surprise to see them here.

That went double for the Lady of Rue herself, who looked just as surprised to see us. She turned her thin silver mask our way and her golden eyes blazed and her red mouth opened in shock and surprise.

"What is it with Faerie and the eyes?" Faith murmured. "Can't they ever just have . . . I don't know . . . normal ey—"

I turned and cocked an eyebrow at her. The eyebrow over my ghost eye, in fact. Henry laughed.

Surprisingly, Faith blushed. "Sorry," she murmured, gripping my shoulder.

I touched her arm back to show I wasn't angry. If we sisters didn't stick together, who would?

"You are safe from your enemies here," the Lord of Thorns said, "The Faerie Gods enforce a truce in this place, the hollow below the World Tree. This was where Cernunnos, the Morrigna, Arawn, Llyr, Taranis, Ogma, Brigit, Lughus, and even Arawn all came into being. No Faerie will perform violence here."

"Enemies," I murmured. I hadn't thought of these people as enemies the same as I'd thought of the Black Shuck and Widdershins. Perhaps that was a mistake. I could see from Faith and Henry's faces that they were thinking the same thing.

As if to turn the Lord of Thorns' words to a lie the very instant he uttered them, Hope shrieked in anger when she caught sight of us. She melted out of existence, the same trick we'd seen her do at sea, so I wasn't surprised when she coalesced only a few feet in front of us.

But she didn't stay Hope-shaped very long, she swelled into a huge black shadow of a wolf. Hope had tried to kill me the last time we met, so I wasn't taking chances. I whipped my pistol out. Henry growled and stepped in front of us, nearly as feral an expression on his face as Hope had on her own. Faith put a hand on his shoulder to try and calm him.

"Hope!" the Lord of Thorns barked. "Stop at once!"

The wolf slid to a halt, clearly stopping because of the Lord of Thorns' command, not at all intimidated by my pistol.

The wolf shimmered and changed back to Hope again. She rushed over and embraced the Lord of Thorns with feverish concern.

"Father!" she said. "Did she hurt you? They just told me she means to kill you! But she can't do that, can she?" She glared at me with unbridled hatred, insinuating herself into the narrow space between the Lord of Thorns and the rest of us.

She was the same height as Henry and I, her snarling face was very close to ours. Henry looked less certain now, looking at Faith and I for guidance.

Hope had called the Lord of Thorns Father. Why? Sands had told us that Hope and Charity were Father's children, not this man's.

"Yes, my dear, Justice Kasric *could* have killed me," the Lord of Thorns said evenly. He put an enormous hand on Hope's shoulder and gently coaxed her into taking a step back. "She chose not to. At great personal cost. At great cost to everything she loves, in fact."

My confusion likely obvious on my face, the Lord of Thorns said, "Hope and Charity are your father's children, but he's had little to do with them other than their conception and naming, all so he could embroil them in his Seven Prophecy scheme . . ."

Hope spat on the ground and glared at me at the mention of Father's prophecy, clearly demonstrating her feelings on *that*. And on Father in general, I suppose.

"But," the Lord of Thorns continued, "I did not find the task of raising them to be too onerous. Most of the time." Here, he gently prodded Hope on the shoulder, and she flashed her teeth at him in a shy smile. The smile disappeared when she looked back at us, though.

"Who told you I was in danger?" the Lord of Thorns asked her. "Surely not . . ." He looked curiously at Father down at the bottom of the hollow.

Hope shook her head. "The Lady Rue," she said. "She's a nasty and vile woman. I don't like her."

"Very curious," the Lord of Thorns said, "considering that I wasn't certain I'd be in danger, and I certainly didn't tell anyone. How could she know?"

Hope shook her head, uncertain. She was still standing protectively close to the Lord of Thorns.

"This will be strange for us," the Lord of Thorns said gently to her. "I'll be restored to my true shape soon."

"You'll be very ugly," Hope said to him seriously. "But we'll still love you."

The Lord of Thorns smiled. "That is good. I may not be able to come to Faerie after. You'll have to come visit me."

"I will, Father," Hope said. She put emphasis on the last word. The Lord of Thorns might have been her biological father, but clearly, the human Rachek Kasric, trapped in a Faerie shape, fulfilled that role in her mind just fine. I wondered about the time difference between my world and the Faerie.

How long had this man acted as Lord, husband, father, to the people of Father's land?

"You'll explain it to Charity?" he said.

Hope nodded. "Yes, yes, of course."

"Good." The Lord of Thorns patted her gently with his huge giant's hand. "That is good."

A gray hawk landed on the sand a few feet from us. Prudence joining the party. She began her own transformation, starting to swell, to burst, white shapes thrusting out of its beak and eyes and wings until the entire nauseating process, mercifully swift, was complete and Prudence stood on the beach with us, her gray hair blowing idly in the breeze.

"That," said Henry with a green face, "was disgusting. I'm going to throw up if you make me watch that again," All his anger was gone now. "I thought it was bad when you turned into the bird but turning back is *far* worse."

"Then don't watch," Prudence said primly. "Now, if you all would care to join us?"

We had to descend a short distance before I could see the center of the space under the pavilion, where two great stone chairs were placed on either side of a stone table. The chess board was already laid out, waiting.

Father saw us coming and seemed to come back to himself. He sat a short distance away from the board, wrapped in blankets although it wasn't that cool here. His face was gaunt, with his cheekbones jutting harshly out. Clearly, their trip here in the launch had been an ordeal in his weakened condition. His hollow eyes tracked the acting Lord of Thorns, then they came back to us as Faith, Henry, and I approached.

I had a difficult time meeting his gaze, knowing that I'd failed him and knowing the price he'd have to pay for my failure. I'd ruined all his plans. Possibly doomed all of England. But he didn't look angry, only thoughtful.

"You didn't do it," he said. "Why not? Didn't the plan work? Did I miss something?"

"No, Father, you didn't miss anything," I said, crouching down in front of him. "But . . . I couldn't do it. It just wasn't right."

"She did the right thing, Father," Faith said. Henry, next to her, nodded emphatically.

Father sighed and closed his eyes. "Ah . . . that." He took a deep and shuddering breath, as if acclimating himself to this knowledge. "All right," he said softly. "All right."

He opened his eyes and gazed at me with his clear blue gaze as if seeing me for the first time. "I guess I did miss something. That part of it didn't seem important back then. I kept with the plan because I thought . . . I thought my earlier self had thought things through better than I could. Now I see now that he, that I, didn't understand anything at all. Not any of the important things."

"I'm sorry, Father." I was crying now and angry that everyone could see it. My heart felt like it was going to burst in sorrow. I still couldn't look him up at him, couldn't look him in the face.

"Justice," he said. He leaned forward and put his hand on my chin, tipping it up. "Don't be sad. You've shown me something today. Perhaps I would never have understood how things should be, how *we* should be, as people, if you had done what I asked. It's better this way. I'm prouder this way."

"Really?" I sobbed. I clutched his hand, dropping tears onto it.

"This is one last thing you've taught me," he said. "It really is better this way."

"Is it?"

"It is," he said, "though it will be even harder. But you've made me proud to be a Kasric, all of you." He reached out his hands, pulling Henry and Faith closer around the two of us.

Faith and Henry were sobbing now, too. We all were.

"Is this," Prudence said in a distant, but infinitely sad voice, "what it means to be human?"

Father laughed very softly. "I suppose it is. Come, help me up. I've delayed this enough."

We helped him to his feet, and he turned to face the game board sitting in the center of the pavilion.

The Lord of Thorns, with the Lady of Thorns, Hope, and Charity standing nearby, were arrayed on the other side of the board from us.

We helped Father stagger towards the board slowly.

Partway there, he stopped.

"I have one last contingency plan," he whispered softly. "It will be very difficult." His clear blue gaze met mine. Faith and Henry, on either side of me, looked confused, but I suddenly knew, with creeping horror, what that plan had to be.

"It's more than I have a right to ask?" he asked more than stated.

I nodded. "I'll do it."

"Justice?" Henry said.

"You can't let the enemy get the real Lord of Thorns back," Father said. "I don't want to be part of bringing London and the rest of the world under Faerie rule."

"I understand," I said.

Faith's eyes were wet and wide. I couldn't tell for certain that she understood what Father was asking. I didn't think Henry did. Not truly.

"There will be repercussions for you, doing something like that under the World Tree."

"I don't care," I said.

"Good," he said. "Be strong, all of you." He raised his hand to touch my face, briefly, and then gave us all a ghost of a smile. "Three moves. You have to let me make three moves first."

I nodded.

"Good," he said again.

CHAPTER 25

The Game

We finished helping Father into her chair and he thanked us with a thin smile.

Stepping back, I was looking across the board at the Lady Rue. She favored me with her hateful, mocking smile.

"Why are you here?" I said.

"Representative of the Unseelie Court," she said.

"Does that mean," Faith said, "that the Seelie Court has also sent a representative?"

"It does," the Lady of Sorrows said. She looked at us and inclined her head, indicating that we follow her a short distance away. She turned without waiting to see if we were following or not, her hooves making soft thuds on the mossy ground. Her tall and gangly frame, combined with the strange, backwards-bending legs, made me expect a gait like a bird's but she had a gentle sway more like a gracefully swaying tree than anything else.

I looked at Faith and she shrugged. Henry too. There appeared to be a minute before the game was going to get underway. We followed.

"It has been pointed out to me," the Lady of Sorrows said without preamble, "that you are victims in all of this as much as we are." Her eyes, gold as they were, blazed with intense emotion.

"Who said that?" Faith asked.

The Lady of Sorrows ignored her. "Being born into the Kasric household is not your fault, I suppose. But I am here to tell you that *I truly don't care*. You are both Kasric and human, and I find neither worthwhile or trustworthy."

"Yeah," Henry said with quiet bravado. "We get a lot of that."

"Make no mistake," she went on, "you are not welcome at Gloaming Hall. When he returns home, your father is *mine*. I won't let the courts take him and I won't let you. I received all the instruction on human courtesy when my father and sisters perished on the Bridge of Tears, when your people first drove us out. I need no more." She leaned far over in order to better rain down her words on us. Her eyes were pulsing with hot, yellow light. "My lord and husband is dead to you. Lost to you as he was to me all these long years. On first sight of any of you, I will set the rock hounds on you, and I assure you, for beasts that normally dine on volcanoes and thunderstorms, you will be a most welcome treat. Soft, succulent, if *very* brief."

"Is this," Prudence's voice broke in, "what passes for Faerie courtesy in this place, blessed of the Gods, under the World Tree?"

The Lady of Sorrows straightened and favored Prudence with a mild look. "Simply gentle instruction. Gentler than we have ever received at human hands."

"Not counting, of course," Prudence said, "how dutifully the *human* Rachek Kasric tended to his lordly duties when he was forced into the role? Wars won against the Giants of Ulroth. Peace brokered with the Iron Mountain Gargoyles. Prosperity to its people. Of course, he did not visit your bed, believing it wrong to love another man's wife."

I stared at Prudence, my mouth open. At my side, I could see Faith doing the same. How could Prudence possibly know *that*?

Prudence continued. "Can you say as much for the Faerie Lord that lived out Kasric's life? I think Martine Kasric would tell a different story about Faerie courtesy." The casual comment about Mother made me flinch.

"My Lord will pay for his sins soon enough," the Lady of Sorrows said firmly. "But he will do it in Gloaming Hall, where he belongs."

"It's been good to talk again, Mother," Prudence said tartly. "I look forward to our next opportunity."

"As to my Lord's by-blows," the Lady of Sorrows said with a significant look in our direction, "I believe events will soon account for that. Wars are such dangerous things, are they not?" With that, she stalked gracefully back over to the game board.

"Great," Faith said dryly. "More enemies. It was feeling like a slow day." Her words were brave, but I could tell from the shiver in her voice that she was just as shaken as I was from this new development.

"Ah," Prudence said, "the blessings of family. Come, I believe they're starting."

They were. We hurried back over.

The board was heavy, dark wood, with squares of inlaid silver and obsidian. The pieces were the same and I thought, perversely, that the silver pieces at least, could make traditional Faerie weapons, if the players couldn't decide things the usual way. The silver pieces had emerald eyes and accents on the major pieces. The black pieces had glittering rubies.

We helped Father settle into his chair, an open-backed, black lacquered wood affair. The Lord of Thorns settled into the chair opposite, making it creak heavily. A rising current of tension ran through the entire place. It became even stronger, as if the entire place pulsed with an encompassing heartbeat that became the heartbeat of all of us here.

There were no places for the rest of us to sit, leaving Faith, Henry and I hovering to either side of Father while the Lady of Sorrows, Hope, and Charity hovered around the other side.

The Lord of Thorns, playing the silver, advanced his queen's pawn. He had to use his left hand, just as he had years ago when I'd seen him. A light wind rustled, but nothing else made any sound except for the quiet click of the piece on the board.

Father reached out unsteadily. It took him several tries to fumble with his own queen's pawn into the right place to match the opening move.

I put my hand in the pocket, finding the pistol waiting there, like a serpent.

The Lord of Thorns advanced his queen's bishop pawn. Father hesitated, then took the piece with his pawn. The acting Lord of Thorn's response was immediate, advancing his knight.

I took a slow, small step backwards, looking around at the other people. They were all watching the players and board.

Father took his third move, developing his rook. Three moves.

I took another step and cocked the pistol.

Then stopped.

Charity was watching me with an oddly guileless expression in her blue, blue eyes. Kasric eyes, I thought. I felt certain that Charity knew about the pistol, the special nature of it, what I planned to do, everything, but she didn't make a sound. She merely contented herself with watching.

I tried to pull the pistol out, wanting to hurry before Charity changed her mind or someone else caught on . . .

Only to find that Henry had gripped my arm near the elbow. His fingers were like iron, unyielding. Despite being three inches shorter than me, my younger brother might as well have been three hundred pounds of muscle. That's what his grip felt like.

You can't, he mouthed silently. *It's not right.*

I nearly panicked and tried to fight him, which would have been useless and might have attracted attention. Finally I forced myself to take a deep breath.

Trust me, I mouthed back.

He squinted, regarding me carefully. Finally, he nodded and let my hand go.

I pulled my pistol and pointed it with one easy, sure motion. Then I fired, point blank, into Father's back.

The crack was shockingly loud in the quiet of the hollow.

Father jerked, twisting as his back recoiled, his hands clawing at the air in sudden pain. He dropped them onto the board, which was now splattered with his blood. Father and the board both toppled over, spilling red-stained glittering pieces all over the moss.

The Lord of Thorns jumped to his feet. "What have you done?" he bellowed.

The gun's barrel smoked, a thin wisp of gray. The gun was a hot and sinful weight in my hand.

"Treachery!" the Lady of Sorrows hissed as she bent to Father's side. Hope stared at me, her expression astonished. That was Henry's expression, too. Faith's eyes were closed, her face turned away. Charity's expression, underneath her golden curls, hadn't changed at all.

"You'll pay for this," the Lady of Sorrows said. "The Gods' curse will be on you!"

"What have you done?" the Lord of Thorns said again.

"What Father wanted," I said hoarsely. "What Father wanted."

CHAPTER 26

After

With the Lady of Sorrows bent over him, I didn't have a clear view of Father any more, but I'd gotten him in the back, near the heart, with enchanted, specially made bullets to kill Faerie, even here, under the World Tree.

The throbbing feeling that had started near the beginning of the game grew stronger. The heartbeat built to a crescendo. The space between the circle of people around Father and the acting Lord of Thorns, flashed, and the tipped-over table burst apart in a flash of light.

"At last!" the Lord of Thorns screamed, feeling the change come over him, his arms outstretched. "At long last!" A shimmering glow seeped over him like the dawning of day. The same light lit up Father and the Lady of Sorrows, who backed in sudden surprise and fear. A crackle of electricity swelled around the two players. I could feel it making the hairs on my arm and neck stand up, even from several steps away.

Another flash drove us all a few steps back. I heard Faith cry out next to me and Henry fell. The light from the two linked forms swelled and grew, as if twin suns poured from within.

The acting Lord of Thorns twisted and swelled, and his flesh, crawled, bubbled, and sloughed away, falling onto the mossy ground, where it became a blackened writhing shadow.

The crawling silhouette snaked across the space between the two men, a rushing beast of shadow. The blackness encompassed Father, and antlers burst savagely out of his skull, forming a majestic sweep of tines.

The blackness flowed down, leaving bulky shoulders and the two mismatched arms and hands behind it. One by one, the monstrous shaggy features melted off the Lord of Thorns and grew on Father's frame.

The wind, the light, the noise all fell away, leaving only the absolute stillness underneath the World Tree.

Father lay still, larger now, but immobile. The wound on his back was more visible now, through a hole in his newly-grown cloak of loam and brambles.

He gave a long, ragged breath.

"He lives!" the Lady of Sorrows hissed. "If we take him back to Gloaming Hall immediately, there may be a chance."

My heart leapt, and then fell again as I realized the full implications.

The Lady of Sorrows gestured at her daughters.

"Hope. Charity."

The two Faerie stepped closer to their mother's side, Charity already brandishing a long, curved knife that she'd pulled from her little girl frock.

"Where did *that* come from?" Henry said, climbing to his feet, as if the knife were the shocking part.

Charity, with no expression whatsoever on her young face, cut a long slash in her own hand.

The blood flowed freely. More than it should have. It was a torrent, as if from a broken dam. In seconds, the pool of blood beneath her had grown to also encompass the feet of Hope, as well as surrounding the Lady of Sorrows and Father.

The Lady of Sorrows spoke a word then, a word I couldn't make out clearly and probably didn't know. Not a human word.

The pool of blood shimmered, then faded. When it faded, the four people inside faded with it, until Charity, Hope, The Lady of Sorrows and the newly-restored Lord of Thorns, Father to me, had all disappeared.

Father was gone, returning to Gloaming Hall, a place that I'd never even seen. Back with his original family.

The Lady Rue was standing in front of us. "Oh, magnificent treachery," she said, sounding impressed. "To betray your own heart, your own desires. To incur the wrath of the Gods to craft your own misery. Marvelous! Even if he lives, which is unlikely, the Court will not be able to compel him to join the invasion now."

I pointed the gun at the Lady Rue's face and though my vision was blurry with tears, my hand was completely steady.

Her eyes grew wider, and then more thoughtful. "You've already incurred the wrath of the Gods to save your precious England. Would you make enemies of the Outcast Fleet, your allies, as well?"

"Lady," I said. "I just shot my father, and I love him. I don't even *like* you."

Her face grew supernaturally grave as she thought this through. Finally, she bowed and withdrew.

The Lady Rue moved off into the trees. The others were gone.

That left only Rachek Kasric.

He looked like Father now, of course, his same face, same hair, same eyes, build and features. Only, he somehow wore them differently. He was tall, and should have been handsome, but there was a haunted look to those glacier-blue eyes in direct contrast to the manic energy that had always characterized Father. He looked around slowly, literally seeing everything with different eyes. He moved slowly in our direction as if it might all be just a dream.

"Mr. Kasric," I said awkwardly. "We should leave this place. It occurs to me that you might possibly need a lift back to English waters?" He looked so unsteady that I slowly reached out a hand to help him.

"Yes," he said, reaching his own hand out to take mine. "Please."

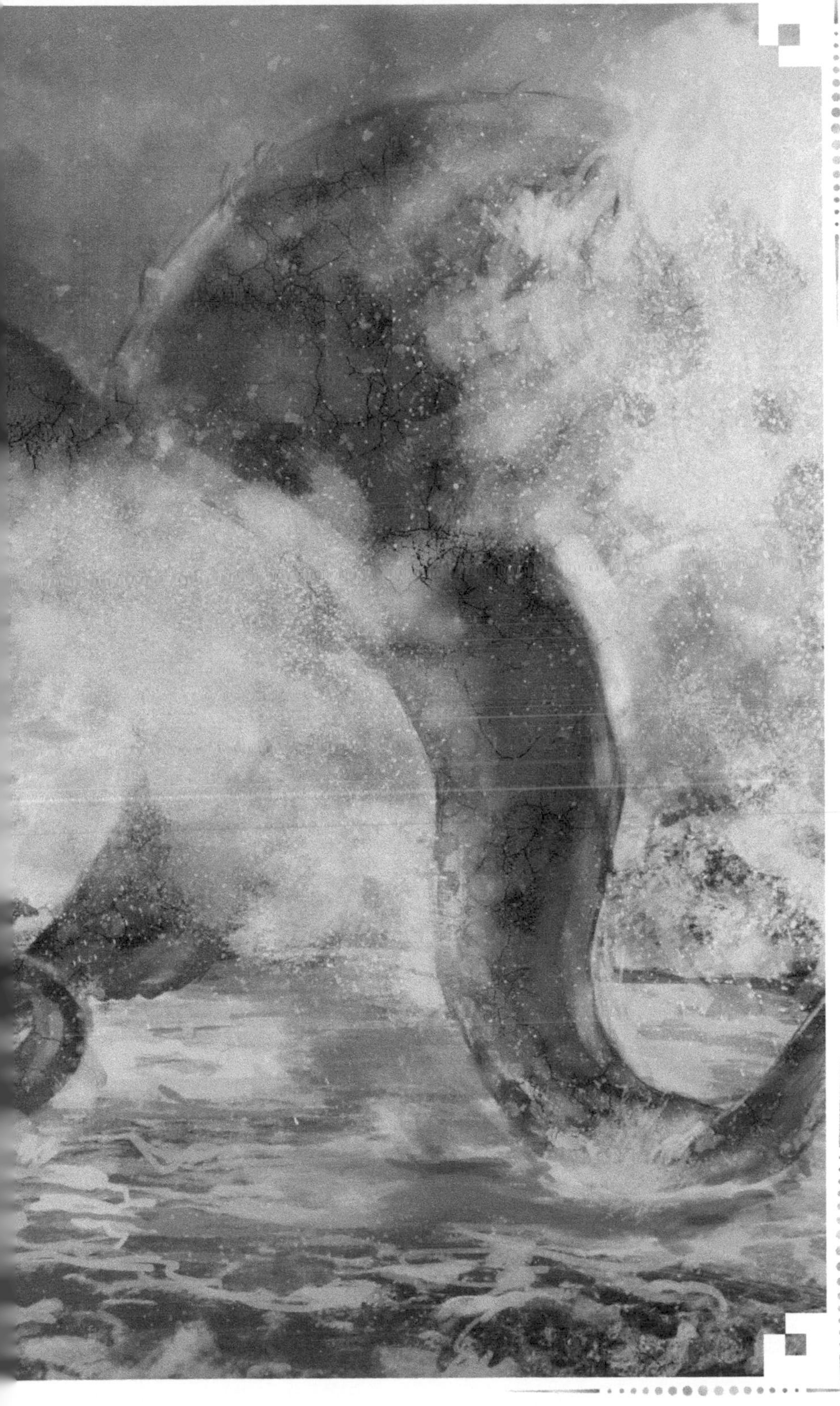

Acknowledgments

Heartfelt thanks again to the Untitled Writers Group: Cindy Spencer Pape, David Erik Nelson, Diana Rivis, Mary Beth Johnson, Cristine Pellar-Kosbar, Jonathan Jarrard, Erica Shipper, Steven Piziks and Sarah Zettel for the countless revisions. Ink is love at revision time and I deeply appreciate yours. To my many friends and family, especially my dad, Craig Klaver, who always provided support and encouragement.

Also to my agent, Lucienne Diver and editors, Helga Schier and Elana Gibson, who continue to put so much time and effort into a pristine finished product.

And, as always, to Kim, my wife, and Katie, my daughter, who both keep doing everything right.

About the Author

Christian Klaver has been writing for over thirty years, with a number of magazine publications, including *Escape Pod, Dark Wisdom Anthology,* and *Anti-Matter*. He's the author of The Empire of the House of Thorns series and the Classified Dossier—Sherlock Holmes and Count Dracula.

He has worked as a bookseller, bartender and a martial-arts instructor before settling into a career in internet security. He lives just outside the sprawling decay of Detroit, Michigan, with his wife Kimberly, his daughter Kathryn, and a group of animals he refers to as The Menagerie.

If you've enjoyed

Christian Klaver's *Justice at Sea,*

you'll enjoy

Jordan H. Bartlett's *Contest of Queens.*

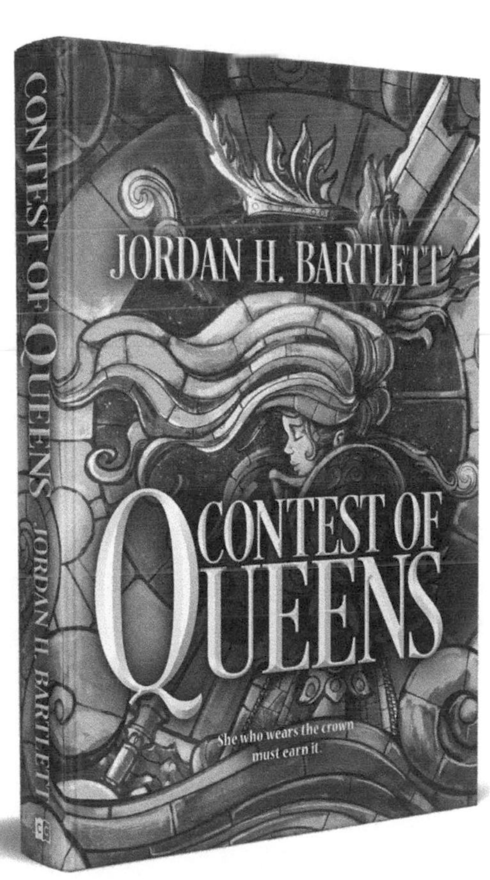

CHAPTER 1

The First Voyage

"There's too many of them!" Iliana roared, her long black hair streaming behind her like a war banner. Connor's keen eyes studied the battlefield and he cursed, sweeping his hair from his face, the wind whipping the acrid stench of battle around him. Their eyes locked for a moment.

Adrenaline still coursing through her veins, she grasped his waist and drew him in for a deep, passionate kiss. When she let him go, he took a moment to catch his breath. Eyes wild, smile flashing, she drew her sword. "But with you here, we just might have a chance." He stood up straighter. Her words burned in his mind, and the ghost of her lips lingered on his. He drew his sword and brandished it high.

"Let's finish this," he bellowed. Iliana's battle cry rang in his ears and they leaped forward as one. A light flashed across his field of vision, blinding him. He staggered back, his sword dropping to his side. Iliana looked at him, confused. The light flashed again, and he felt the world around him begin to fade.

Rolling over, he groaned. The weight of leather armor dissolved to the weight of featherdown.

The first fingers of sunlight crept their way through the crack in the heavy velvet curtains. Gentle rays inched along the cold stone floor, up a mahogany bedpost, and dusted the sleep from the Prince's eyes. His brow wrinkled as he fought to stay with Iliana a little longer behind his closed lids. Reluctantly, Connor blinked his blue eyes open. Once. Twice. Then he sat upright.

It's Sunday, he thought. *Finally. Every good adventure starts on a Sunday.*

Stretching, he threw back the covers and cast his gaze around the room. Already, his mind whirled with preparations. He would need light clothes—nothing to weigh him down—and his compass. A list of items ran through his head, and he started moving about the room to retrieve them all. Although he tried his best to pack quietly, his excitement inspired slamming drawers and heavy footfalls.

He rummaged through pairs of leather boots. Buckles clinked together, and fabric murmured softly as he sifted through blacks, browns, and tans. He picked up a tall pair, frowned, then exchanged them for shorter ones, the leather well worn. He couldn't risk blisters today, and the tall ones rubbed his ankles.

Next, he dragged his knapsack from under his desk. The canvas was worn on a corner, a leather strap needed mending, and it had the faint aroma of wet dog; this was not something a prince would own. He had traded one of the serving boys for it, as all of his bags were much too fancy for expeditions.

He tightened one of the straps and his mind floated to the leather hilt of the sword in his dream. His sword. The sword of a knight. He paused and sighed as the thought struck him. To be a knight. Now that was the dream, but that was ridiculous. His mother had explained to him once that only women could become guards, and of them, only certain guards could become knights. The Knights of the Queendom carried the responsibility of taking another's life. Only those who could create life could be trusted with the burden of extinguishing it. Besides, at fourteen he wanted the glory, not the burden.

Indulging for a moment in the fantasy, he saw himself in the light armor of a knight, sword aloft, cape unfurling behind him, the wind blowing through his brown hair, commanding a battalion of strong and beautiful guards, all secretly in love with him, of course. He, the first male knight. Much more exciting than being one of a long line of princes. All princes got to do was learn how to be good advisors. Shaking the fantasy from his head, he turned back to his task.

He sighed. He couldn't be a knight, but he could be an explorer. He could be a conqueror of realms.

When he was younger, he used to pretend he was a bold adventurer: Connor the Conqueror. A man who bravely explored the herb gardens and discovered new tracks through the manicured hedge mazes. He chuckled at the memory. Since then, he had never felt quite comfortable as Cornelius; Connor was a better fit. Less stuffy, and most important, it was his. Something private. A rare possession for a prince. His eyes scanned the bookshelf for his telescope. Not spying it there, he opened the large, studded trunk at the end of his bed. The hinges on the lid groaned weakly. He sifted through its contents, his fingertips brushing across an assortment of forgotten items at the bottom, until he located the desired object. A small brass spyglass. He tucked it in his belt in the same fashion as Amelia the Daring on the cover of *To The World's End*. He was almost ready.

Wincing at the thought of the commotion he had most definitely caused, Connor stepped back lightly to where his project of many evenings lay finished and gleaming on his desk by the window. In the new daylight, the hull shone a warm, rich red. It was a wooden boat and his ticket to adventure. The hull was about half the length of his forearm and was topped with a canvas sail. He picked it up carefully from where it had been propped up to dry and surveyed his handiwork. Not a splinter in sight (they had tended to prefer ending up in his thumbs).

He gently opened a small hidden compartment in the center of the ship's deck to reveal a rectangular recess. Then, placing the boat back on the desk, he opened the top drawer, withdrew the letter he had written the night before while the paint was drying, and rolled it up into a tight tube.

He slid his signet ring off his pinkie finger and held it up to the morning sunlight. Tilting it between his fingers, he admired as the light danced off the engraved Griffin. It pranced with wings unfurled and talons flaring as if to grasp the clouds it rose above. A design of his own request. It marked his first attempt at his own coat of arms.

Every fourteen-year-old should have their own coat of arms, even boys. He had debated what creature to choose for days. His mother had the lion on hers, his father had the eagle, but he had wanted something entirely his own. He had seen their likeness in paintings and tapestries throughout the palace, and twice in person when the Griffins had overseen an important audience in the throne room. They were magnificent. He had never been more in awe of another living creature in his life. When he one day became the Queen's advisor, he wanted to inspire that same awe. So, the Griffin he chose.

Master Aestos, the court goldsmith, had been delighted when Connor described the desired ring. Master Aestos, who insisted that Connor call him Heph (even though any person who was a master of their craft must be referred to as Master), would be far less delighted to find out where his intricate work was headed. Connor shook his head and pushed that thought out of his mind.

Placing the scroll inside the ring, he fished a small glass vial out of the top drawer and slotted the bundle into the vial. He stoppered it with a cork and took some time to seal the top with melted wax. That done, he delicately placed the sealed vial into the hull, slid the lid shut, and grinned.

Now, he was ready.

Connor glanced out the window. The sun shone brightly on the horizon and sent tiny rainbows through the crystalline pattern around the edges of his large bay windows. It was shaping up to be a fine day. He wrapped the boat in a kerchief and placed it carefully in his knapsack. Swinging the pack onto his back, he shrugged his shoulders, letting it settle. With one last sweeping glance around his room, he crossed to the door.

Listening for any noise out on the landing, hand hovering over the pommel of a sword that was not there, Connor eased the door open a crack, an inch, then all the way. He looked up and down the empty carpeted hallway. Surely, not all adventures began so casually. He was almost disappointed not to be intercepted.

It wasn't until he descended the servants' stairwell that he encountered his first challenge. The decadent smells from the kitchen wafted up the stairwell and caressed his nose, making his mouth water. He had forgotten to pack food, and, as his days as Connor the Conqueror had taught him, he would need to maintain his strength for the long journey ahead.

Quietly, he snuck into the kitchen and ducked behind a large barrel of potatoes. The kitchen was alive with smells and sounds. Master Marmalade—no, Master Marmaduke, the head cook, was firing off instructions to her minions and sending them scuttling to and fro. Flour flew, pans clanged, and spoons were held out on demand for a taste.

The Prince could see the morning's breakfast coming together like a well-choreographed dance. He watched them for a minute before his stomach growled in protest and forced him into action. Crouching and hiding his face, he sidled casually along a sturdy counter until he reached the spot where an assortment of muffins and scones were laid out on cooling racks.

Using sleight of hand he and his friend Hector had practiced together, he swiped three muffins into the knapsack he had nonchalantly placed open on the floor. Careful not to draw any attention, he forced himself to slow his actions. He took a moment to lick his fingers clean of the crumbs and berry juice from where he had squashed a raspberry.

With that same practiced calm, he picked up his knapsack and sidled toward the door.

He was almost free when Master Marmaduke's loud, booming voice silenced the clatter of the kitchen.

"Wait!" Her voice cut cleaner than the knife she was using to slice a still-steaming loaf of bread.

CC
CamCat
Books

CPSIA information can be obtained
at www.ICGtesting.com
Printed in the USA
LVHW091733091221
705745LV00013B/762/J